PRAISE FOR
KELSEY'S CROSSING

"A deftly crafted, emotionally engaging novel that is all the more impressive when considering that *Kelsey's Crossing* is author David Randal's debut as a novelist. Its theme is that of the past not irrevocably repeating in the future and the value and necessity of second chances. Original and inherently fascinating, *Kelsey's Crossing* is a compelling story of corruption, struggle, and redemption. Of special note is how David Randal's distinctive and narrative-driven storytelling skills have raised his novel to an impressive level of literary excellence—making it especially and unreservedly recommended for personal reading lists, as well as both community and college/university library contemporary American literary fiction collections."

—MIDWEST BOOK REVIEW

"David Randal's *Kelsey's Crossing* is a whirlwind of political scandal, personal redemption, and the messy gray areas of morality. It follows Greg Smith, a high-powered Washington insider whose world comes crashing down when the FBI raids his home, exposing a plot to rig an election. The book takes us through his fall from grace, prison years, and eventual reentry into society, one that forces him to confront not just his past sins but the kind of man he wants to become. What starts as a political thriller morphs into something deeper, more introspective, and surprisingly heartfelt.

"*Kelsey's Crossing* is for readers who enjoy political dramas with substance, but also for anyone who likes a redemption story with some real grit. It's for those who want a character study as much as a thriller. If you love stories about second chances, messy, imperfect, but honest ones, this book is worth your time. Greg isn't easy to like, but by the end, you'll find yourself rooting for him, flaws and all. Randal doesn't give him an easy out, and that's what makes the journey feel real."

—LITERARY TITAN (5 STARS)

"David Randal's debut novel shows us that redemption comes in many forms, from the genuine sense of remorse for things done poorly to the selflessness of those in even the humblest circumstances. And within this panoply is the subtle recognition that all of us might require a restart from time to time. With prose that is clear, precise and often lyrical, Randal takes us to the heart of what it means to be human—flawed, anguished, but ultimately drawn to one another in compassion, dignity, and community. This is a book to be read, savored, considered, and reread, one that introduces us to a new literary light."

—GREG FIELDS, *The Bright Freight of Memory*, 2025 American Writing Award for Literary Fiction

"An inspiring exploration of the enduring power of forgiveness, the potential for redemption, and the unwavering human spirit. This skillfully crafted debut novel from David Randal is a must-read for anyone who believes in the inherent goodness of humanity and the possibility of positive change."

—EMILY H. KEEFER, author of *The Stars on Vita Felice Court*

"With *Kelsey's Crossing*, David Randal has rendered one man's halting journey toward redemption as a story that is at once specific and universal. Humbled by his fall from grace, protagonist Greg Smith finds himself adrift, knowing only that he wants to start life anew, a life of modest ambition. It is a life in stark contrast to the one he led, full of flash, power, and perks but lacking in fulfillment. Working at a soup kitchen becomes the catalyst for Smith's evolution. Randal's prose is restrained: He lets his characters and the situations he has adeptly crafted pull the reader along. Like the character of Smith himself, Randal has chosen elegant simplicity and clarity to mirror the interior life of his protagonist. The novel is innovative in its form: part character study, part political thriller. There is an optimism to Randal's worldview, a sense that acting for the good without the expectation of a reward is in itself a reward of the highest order. And yes, a man may fall in love and rediscover his soul in the process. Randal's story reflects a bygone optimism, a belief in second chances that is sincere and openhearted."

—**ALFREDO BOTELLO**, Author of *Spin Cycle: Notes from a Reluctant Caregiver*

"This political thriller has it all—an engaging but flawed protagonist, insider portrayals of the corridors of the White House and Congress, and action-packed scenes that keep you glued to the page. It's the kind of book that seamlessly entertains while offering valuable insights, making every page both engaging and enlightening. David Randal tells an eloquent tale of redemption, romance, and second chances, delivering a gripping story with timely, real-world parallels."

—**JESSICA BARROWS BEEBE**, award-winning author of *Muddy the Water*

"Such a deeply meaningful story of redemption at a moment when our society is deeply in need of redemption . . . and hope. *Kelsey's Crossing* is the perfect story for this moment."

—**ANDREW WELCH**, author of *Field Blends*

"*Kelsey's Crossing*, David Randal's debut novel is a testament to Randal's rich background as a storyteller. Randal vividly portrays complex social issues with an ability to distill intricate topics into engaging narratives. Greg Smith's journey from 'hard ass political deal maker' to serving meals at the Kelsey Rescue Mission underscores the transformative power of community and the belief that one's past does not always dictate the future. A must-read for anyone seeking a story that inspires and challenges societal norms."

—**LACY FEWER**, author of *Yankeeland*

KELSEY'S CROSSING

Kelsey's Crossing

by David Randal

© Copyright 2025 David Randal

ISBN 979-8-88824-721-1

All rights reserved. No part of this publication may be reproduced, stored in a retrieval system, or transmitted in any form or by any means—electronic, mechanical, photocopy, recording, or any other—except for brief quotations in printed reviews, without the prior written permission of the author.

This is a work of fiction. All the characters in this book are fictitious, and any resemblance to actual persons, living or dead, is purely coincidental. The names, incidents, dialogue, and opinions expressed are products of the author's imagination and are not to be construed as real.

Cover art and design by Lauren Sheldon

Published by

3705 Shore Drive
Virginia Beach, VA 23455
800-435-4811
www.koehlerbooks.com

KELSEY'S CROSSING

DAVID RANDAL

VIRGINIA BEACH
CAPE CHARLES

To Debbie, who never gave up on my dream to write,
And who never gave up on me.

To those without a home.

To those who seek and grant second chances.

CHAPTER ONE

The beginning of the end of life as I knew it was loud and sudden. As a prelude to events unfolding, I watched the small caravan of unmarked black SUVs on my home security monitor navigate my long driveway and park close to the garage. I was impressed by the precise movements of eight uniformed FBI agents gathering in a semicircle on my front porch. Two of them held a giant battering ram pointed at the door. It was clear they had done this before.

I had come home early from work to await the calvary. My inside informant, whom I had paid to keep this from happening, could only muster a heads-up regarding their scheduled arrival. He was just one of my many poor investments lately.

In the brief time before their final approach, I texted my daughter to tell her I would be a no-show at her soccer match and then left a short voice message with my wife, warning her that we were about to have visitors. "Please come home. I need you." Explaining my criminal behavior to my family would be pure anguish.

"Mr. Smith, it's the FBI. Open the door now. We have a court order to search your home," shouted the lead agent through a handheld megaphone. "Please know that we can forcefully enter if you don't open immediately." Other agents banged on the door, their knocks resonating through the house like exploding bombs.

When the banging became unbearable, I abandoned my watch over the monitor and slowly approached the foyer and the seldom-used front entrance.

"What the hell is going on?" I yelled through the door with all the fake indignation I could muster. But I knew. My blatant lawbreaking was about to be exposed, and with it my membership in Washington's political elite, where big money and inside operatives like me had joined forces to become an unofficial equal branch of government.

The agent repeated his demand to open the door, shoving the warrant up to the peephole for me to view. When he commanded the battering ram duo to take the door down by force, I finally opened it. There was no need for unnecessary property damage, I decided.

"Please stand aside," instructed the lead agent. Without hesitating, he handed me the search warrant. His fellow agents burst inside like locusts, spreading in all directions. I was ordered to sit in the nearest chair while another agent hovered over me.

I watched helplessly as my computers, electronic devices, and several boxes of paper files were carried outside to waiting vehicles. The agents' methodical search included every room, closet, drawer, and cupboard in the house. Nothing was left unexamined.

They seemed to love their work. I saw the glee on their faces. Later, they would tell their spouses what a great day they had at the office. They lived for assignments like this one.

The confiscation of my files would reveal contracts, correspondence, overseas bank deposits, and relationships with some of the most loathsome dictators, oligarchs, and business giants in the world. Men who paid me hundreds of millions of dollars to use my relationship with the administration to influence US policy and direct US aid in their favor, much of it deposited into super PACs that I controlled so I could decide which candidates won or lost. The rest went into one of my many accounts.

But it was when I saw them carry my iron safe—pried from its bolts in the basement—that I knew I was fucked. The safe contained a computer drive with my plan to overturn the election in three pivotal states and make a mockery of American democracy. It promised to be the most sophisticated and calculated voter fraud scheme in history.

Attempting to steal an election might not seem like a serious crime, especially if it's your guy or gal doing the thievery. Night after night, TV viewers are exposed to one side accusing the other of so many abuses that we become numb, willing all too often to accept bad behavior as normal. But as a student of government and politics, I knew better. Except for offenses against children, rape, or murder, there are few crimes more serious than undermining the democratic threads that knit our nation together.

I had done a bad thing, fully expecting to get away with it. The plan was brilliant, designed to go undetected. Simply altering the results in twenty-three counties spread across three states predicted to be razor-close would change the election results in those states.

"Am I under arrest?" I finally asked.

"Not at this time," the lead agent responded. "But you should know another team is searching your office as we speak."

That would explain why my iPhone was bursting with messages from my assistant, who begged me to return her calls. "Do you mind if I call my office?"

"Go ahead. Again, you're not under arrest. Yet." He chuckled under his breath. *What a prick*, I thought.

When I reached Angie at the office, she described a scene similar to what was happening at home. Through sobs she informed me that the only office being searched was mine, but they did demand access to the office's central computer.

"What's going on, Greg? What have you done?"

I instructed her and the others to comply with everything the agents wanted. Fighting the federal government only works when it's not fighting back.

"Mr. Smith, we are done here," the lead agent said with his official cop voice. They had been there for three hours. "I need you to review the list of items we secured from the house and sign it," he continued, handing me the form on a clipboard. "I am also requesting that you provide passwords for the devices. You are not required to do this, but refusing to provide your passwords won't prevent us from entering your accounts."

No more than a minute after the last SUV left, I spotted Liz cruising slowly up the 300-yard driveway. Sydney was with her, making me think Liz had attended the soccer match. Sydney must have called her. We had long ago agreed that at least one parent must attend all of Sydney's events.

The two of them burst through the door from the garage just as the six o'clock news came on the kitchen television.

"Capitol Hill was rocked today by a Department of Justice report alleging the most massive election fraud scheme in the history of our nation, one that may have affected the results in three pivotal states. Earlier today, FBI agents searched the Virginia home and Washington office of Greg Smith, a Washington lawyer and political adviser to dozens of Republican elected officials, including the president. According to the DOJ document, FBI officials believe Smith coordinated the elaborate plan. It will be interesting to see whether Smith, known in Washington circles as the ultimate dealmaker, has a deal to get himself out of this one. More on this story as it unfolds."

Liz reached for the remote and switched off the report as Sydney, still in her soccer uniform, reached for a slice of pizza from the box in the center of the table. I just put my head in my hands, knowing I was in deep shit. Liz immediately took control of the situation, not even pausing to ask if the charges were accurate.

"I'm calling Marty," she announced, not giving me time to say, "Please don't do that."

Within the hour, Martin O'Rourke, arguably the most high-profile criminal attorney in Washington—and inarguably the most expensive—was sitting in our living room. It was convenient that he lived next door. After listening for an hour to my version of the story, he summarized my situation and laid out an initial plan.

"In addition to election fraud and vote rigging, the government will pursue money laundering, tax fraud, and illegal foreign lobbying charges. If these charges can be proven, you're looking at a couple of decades in jail."

I looked at Liz and Sydney, who were both fighting back tears. I thought of sending my daughter upstairs, but it was our practice not to exclude her from essential family discussions. At eighteen, on the verge of graduating high school, she was an astute and savvy thinker. But how would she feel about having a father who had tried to change the results of a national election by using artificial intelligence to alter vote shares for a particular candidate and manipulating electronic voting machines?

"You have very few chips to play," Martin said flatly. "However, you do have a play. My guess is the feds want the names of the coconspirators, and you are the only one who can provide them." I had already informed him that the names were the one item the feds did not get today. "I think your best play is to give them the names in exchange for a lighter sentence."

When I began to object, Liz interrupted. "Damn it, Greg, listen to the man. You will go to the FBI and do what you do best, and that's make a deal. I don't care who you have to name."

CHAPTER TWO

THREE YEARS LATER

For those of us who were once wealthy and powerful, prison is especially punishing. In our past lives, my fellow prisoners and I were commanders of our domains and princes of the universe. But inside those walls, where the only color is gray and the only speed is slow, we were faceless captives, each left to ponder our crimes and deal with our shame.

It could have been worse. Instead of being assigned to a minimum-security facility like the one in Morgantown, West Virginia—one of the so-called "Club Feds"—I could have been sitting in a high-security prison alongside rapists and murderers. Federal Correctional Institution, Morgantown, housed 900 mostly White middle-aged male inmates who were not likely to hurt anyone or try to escape. We were cheaters, schemers, and liars; I would guess that most had never held a firearm.

My little group of friends was a who's who of headline criminals: a former congressperson, an Army colonel, a federal judge, a Wall Street securities company CEO, and a Catholic priest. As a group, we debated the affairs of the day, whether cultural, economic, or political. We read and shared books or other research material and discussed its contents. It was the niftiest think tank one could imagine, fueled by some of the greatest minds I had ever known. It was too bad that very few people would have trusted what we had to say.

Over numerous late-night discussions, we decided the worst

part of being convicted of a serious crime wasn't the loss of prestige or incarceration. It was the shame we brought to our families. How many lectures had Sydney gotten from me on always doing the right thing? "In the end, Syd, all you have is your self-respect. Did you act morally, with others in mind, or did you think of yourself?" And then there were my parents, now in their seventies and retired, still living in the same modest home they bought before I was born. I could not read one more letter from my mother on how I broke my father's heart.

There was little denial about why we were there. We were guilty, and we knew it. We burned with remorse for betraying the trust others had given us. "I handed down judgments to people in my community for three decades," Judge Worley said during one of our chats. "I was known for my decency. People had faith in me. That is, until a guy paid me a million dollars to let his son off easy from a manslaughter charge."

We listened intently as this seventy-year-old intellectual giant fought off tears and poured out how he had thrown away his life.

"After my arrest and conviction, I was a pariah. My daughter, who is also a lawyer, won't talk to me. I can't say that I blame her."

We also decided we had very few "real" friends, if any. What we had were people who wanted something from us. Far removed from our past provisional relationships, back when we'd gather at golf clubs or fancy parties where men made deals and lied to one another about their conquests, we were now in our own tiny world with little incentive to embellish. Prison does that to a person. It fades you to your colorless core.

"You must be in deep shit, Mr. Greg," Officer Kesler greeted me, interrupting my thoughts. "The warden wants to see you in thirty minutes." He had appeared from nowhere and was peeking through the slightly ajar door of my room, his vast, pearly-white grin shining against his jet-black skin. His presence was a welcome diversion.

"Hilarious, Kesler. When I'm out of here, I will use all the muscle I have left in Washington to get you demoted." Our familiar relationship had convinced me of the validity of Stockholm syndrome. We needed one another.

"Oh, pa-lease spare me, Mr. Greg. I promise to be a good boy. I'll start by letting you win at chess tonight. But first, I have to deliver you to the front office. The warden said it's important."

The drive from cell block D, located in the back of the prison, to the front of the facility where the administrative office was located took about five minutes. Outside, we were greeted by a pleasant March day that would warm to an unseasonable seventy-five degrees. The brilliant sun against the cloudless blue sky was a welcome change from the plain cinder block interior of the prison.

Although the facility had originally been a youth detention center, the immaculately landscaped grounds, complete with a creek and a walking bridge, created a picturesque appearance. Boasting several basketball and volleyball courts, an oval running track, and a well-groomed softball field, it reminded me of summer camp as a kid, a pleasurable, if not fading, memory.

"Any idea what the warden wants with me?" I asked Kesler as we approached the front building.

"I have no idea why you're getting called to the principal's office," he replied, again with his wide grin. "That is way above my pay grade."

Roger Cannon had been the warden at Morgantown for twenty-five years. During that time, he built a national reputation for fostering respectful treatment of inmates. He often sought my insight on political and policy issues, as he did other inmates on other subjects, according to their expertise. "He probably wants my take on his March Madness brackets," I told Kesler, who laughed. I assumed he knew I was only half joking.

Kesler escorted me to the reception area, where the warden's assistant walked us into his office. To my surprise, Roger wasn't alone.

"Greg, please come in. It's nice to see you." The warden warmly extended his hand, a gesture I returned in kind. "Greg, please meet Raymond Presley and Luan Jagger, prison liaison for federal prisons."

I knew Presley as the deputy attorney general from watching his regular media interviews.

"Nice to meet you. Sorry I didn't dress up for the occasion," I said, referring to my tan onesie and white canvas sneakers, the assigned garb for all inmates. Thankfully they laughed.

At the warden's invitation, we took seats around the small conference table. Cannon's office was impressively large, with four "ego walls" displaying framed pictures of himself with several presidents and governors, various college degrees and award plaques, and framed newspaper articles. In the middle stood an enormous mahogany desk with a high-backed judge's chair for him and two comfortable cushioned armchairs on the opposite side for visitors. Behind him stretched a beautiful aerial photograph of FCI Morgantown. It was his realm, which he ruled with absolute authority. Fine by me. Benevolent rulers, of which I considered him to be one, are always the best form of government. But they were hard to find.

"It's your meeting, Raymond," said the warden, turning to the deputy AG.

"Thank you, Roger. Greg, let me get right to the point. The president has issued you a full pardon. By this time tomorrow, you will be a free man. The paperwork is being prepared. Your wife is being briefed on your release later today."

A frozen moment passed where nothing moved and no one spoke. I couldn't blink or take a breath.

Finally, I stared directly into Presley's face. "I didn't expect this," I uttered, barely above a whisper. "Please tell the president I am grateful."

"You should know the attorney general's office privately opposed your pardon. You should have served at least half of your sentence, which would have been four years."

"I'm happy your opinion doesn't count," I responded with a snarky smile.

"It's good to have friends in high places," he said, returning my smile.

"I never thought of myself as a personal friend of the president. It was more of a business relationship."

Presley ignored my comment. "Greg, we are concerned that your life on the outside could be in danger."

"You have my attention," I replied earnestly.

The deputy AG opened a file from the box beside him on the table. "When you gave up the list of those who were paid to carry out your plan, you made some serious enemies, chiefly Lamar Goodman, who, like the ten others you named, are doing time in a much tougher prison than this one."

"I'm sure every one of them would boil me in oil if they had the chance. What's your point, Mr. Presley?"

Goodman was the Illinois secretary of state to whom I'd delivered gobs of cash to conduct my vote-fixing scheme. He had close ties to the largest crime syndicate in Chicago, which had been grooming him for governor. But there was no way the mob bosses would come after me; they were satisfied with not having been implicated in our scheme.

"Goodman's attorney has convinced a judge in Chicago to do a retrial based on a technical glitch in the evidence submitted by the prosecution. The FBI believes the judge was paid off, but that doesn't matter now. What does matter is that Goodman is being released next week while awaiting a new trial."

I glanced at the warden, who remained silent. He seemed worried, as though sending one of his own out to face a firing squad.

"We will provide as much protection for you and your family as possible, but there's only so much we can do."

I quietly gazed out the large window for a few moments. "I appreciate the agency's efforts to keep me safe, but I'm a big boy. I can take care of myself."

After the meeting ended, I asked the warden if I could walk back to cell block D alone, explaining that I needed time to think. He reached into his desk drawer and handed me a pass. "You might need this if one of the guards asks why you're roaming around. Take your time, Greg. I'll see you tomorrow morning when you leave."

My fifteen-minute walk turned into a two-hour soul search. I wouldn't miss this place for a second, but I would never forget it. There is a certainty to prison life. A daily pattern that you can count on. Now everything seemed uncomfortably uncertain. I was about to restart my life at forty-eight and had little idea where to begin. I looked forward to having a cell phone and a passport someday. The normal things. Beyond that, I only knew what I didn't want—no more law, lobbying, or politics. Perhaps I would become a sommelier or barista to keep me close to my favorite things: good wine and rich coffee. I wanted to live a quiet life where no one knew my name or background. To be left alone. But would it be enough to satisfy the conquering warrior within me?

It was almost ten when I finally crawled into my metal-framed single bed that night. It felt like Christmas Eve; I would wake up with what I wanted most: freedom. Most people take it for granted until it's abruptly taken from them.

Kesler and the warden walked with me the following day to the visitor parking area to await Sydney. The building I had called home for thirty months loomed behind me. Halfway up the sidewalk, Sydney tackled me with an embrace that nearly knocked me over. I had called her from the warden's office, and in a role reversal, she was now rescuing me. I thought of all the times I'd had to pick her up at the principal's office for one school violation or another.

We headed directly to her Audi SUV and climbed in.

"Where to, Daddy-o?" she asked.

CHAPTER THREE

"Mom asked me to give you this package. She got it into FedEx when she heard you were getting out today."

Sydney and I were having lunch at her favorite restaurant in Morgantown, Oliverio's Ristorante on the Wharf. She had reserved a table for two on the covered outdoor porch with a view of the Monongahela River. After lunch, I would rent a car and head nine hours south to Kelsey, Tennessee, to spend a few days with my lifelong friend Tom Garrity and his wife, Jane.

For now, I was content to get caught up with my daughter. Sydney had grown into an impressive young lady—witty and intelligent, with a fresh and bountiful spirit, and poised and beautiful like her mother. Sydney was a senior at West Virginia University, having transferred from Maryland to be closer to my prison. She'd visited me at least twice a week, sometimes more. God knew I didn't deserve such unconditional love.

Following a briefing on every class she was taking for her final semester, I perused the contents of the mailing package. "What a lovely note from your mother," I told Sydney. "Maybe there's a chance for us after all." My comment was entirely facetious.

"I'm, like, not feeling it, Dad. You are better off as ex-spouse best friends." Her mother and I were still technically married but legally separated. "Read me her note. I want to know what she said."

Hey There,

I am so happy for you. Let freedom reign, right? I'm also excited that you and our daughter are spending a little time with one another. She is more like you than I care to admit. Meanwhile, here is an American Express card, a debit card for your checking account with an initial deposit of $200,000, and a printout of all our accounts, numbers, and passwords. Give me a call when you land somewhere. (The enclosed iPhone is on me.) I'm off to a conference in Brussels. Much love always, Liz.

PS It looks like you're not the only dealmaker in the family.

"Aww, isn't she a sweetheart? She's always so good at writing love letters," Sydney teased.

"How is your mom? Is she happy, or at least content?"

"To be honest, Mom is tired. Or she's bored with the whole Congress thing. She's talked about not running for reelection. Her fighting spirit is fading a bit, and she wants to get it back by doing what she says has a 'purpose.'"

"I can't believe she's been in Congress for eighteen years. And I'm sure that last election pushed her over the edge," I offered. All because of me, of course. Guilty by association with a jailbird husband. But, like Sydney, Liz had found the "forgiveness button" on her life's dashboard and absolved me of my many wrongs. They were members of a small group. Most people either wanted me dead or to have nothing to do with me. I had decided not to share with them the potential danger posed by Lamar Goodman.

"It wore her down for sure. I was proud of you for helping her campaign on her record, not yours. She didn't want to crap on you, so I'm glad you encouraged her to distance herself from you publicly."

The line Liz used in the televised debate with her opponent was classic: "Mr. Jennings, may I remind you that you're running against Congresswoman Liz Smith and not inmate Greg Smith, although if you wish to discuss the need for prison reform, I am happy to do so."

"Well, we were legally separated for three years before this happened. You would think people might acknowledge that small detail," I opined to my daughter.

Granted, despite the separation, we were often out together in public—certainly enough to be seen by the Washington elite, including the gossip media. We had decided to stay married until there was a reason not to be, such as a second marriage. Our childhood, daughter, and finances linked us and our extended family. In addition to being my wife, Liz was Tom Garrity's sister, and we had grown up on the same street.

I thought back to her first campaign when, at the age of twenty-eight and only a year into her position as director of the Buffalo Planned Parenthood clinic, she decided to run against the longtime incumbent, Charles Tomes, who was trying to cut federal funding for reproductive health services. Her campaign began as a protest, with few experts on either side of the aisle giving her a chance to win. I had emerged as a sought-after political strategist and lobbyist on the national scene, so, naturally, my wife turned to me as her unpaid adviser.

I tried to talk her out of it. We had a young daughter and a modest home in suburban Buffalo, plus a small but costly apartment in Washington, DC, two student-loan payments, and what I thought was zero chance of her winning. However, working to defeat a Republican member of Congress could hurt my standing with the leaders of my party.

Of course, this made it all about me, something that Liz hated.

"This campaign is about me, Greg, and I'm running whether or not you help me," she said in one of our discussions leading up to her announcement.

So I told my party leaders to go fuck themselves and ran Liz's campaign anyway. We targeted female voters, focusing on expanding access to affordable health care, protecting the environment with green energy policies, and improving working families' lives while embracing job training for veterans, displaced workers, and at-risk youth. By then, we had socked some bucks away, so we bought TV and radio time and created some ads. Overnight, Liz was a known entity and a viable threat to the incumbent, who, in his arrogance, refused to see her as such. She opened a campaign headquarters filled with volunteers eighteen hours a day. Women—often with children in tow—walked neighborhoods handing out fliers. She held rallies in the parking lots of grocery stores and shopping malls. Her slogan, one borrowed from Dr. Martin Luther King—"This is our time"—became a rallying cry throughout the district.

District voters weren't the only ones who noticed Liz Smith. The nation was paying attention as well. In early October, a month before the election, a *New York Times* poll showed her only five points behind the Republican incumbent, who had held the seat for over two decades and had given me my first job on Capitol Hill. This new perception of her momentum turned on the money faucet; smelling blood, labor unions and dozens of other progressive organizations sent contributions by the truckload for us to buy additional ad time and mobilize voters. By the time Tomes knew he had a close race, the Liz Smith train had left the station and was zooming at a hundred miles an hour. The distinguished chairman of the influential Ways and Means Committee never saw it coming.

On Election Day, Elizabeth Garrity Smith became a congresswoman-elect with a slim victory of 51 percent. For a minute or two, I was the scourge of the national Republican elite for being a traitor, some even calling for me to be blackballed from the party for daring to manage a Democratic campaign. So much for conservative family values. As I said when Liz and I were guests of Oprah on national television, "She's my wife, for God's sake. For some, not even marriage is more important than party politics."

The *Oprah* interview sealed our future. And it was true. As Liz's fame rose, so did mine. The media loved the drama of a conservative consultant running his progressive wife's campaign. We were dubbed the "odd couple"—a moniker more valid than any of them knew, but that was between us, like secret boxes in the closet.

The waiter at Oliverio's came by and refilled the water glasses. Through the opening to the bar area, Sydney and I watched the wall-mounted television, which was showing a news clip of me leaving the prison with her earlier.

"Geez, Dad, I almost knocked you over," she laughed. "My entire sorority is in front of the TV right now so they can see my dad and me at the prison."

"Is that supposed to make me feel good?" I asked. "Why would they want to see that?"

"Because they love drama, and what could be more dramatic than a sorority sister getting her dad out of prison?" she laughed. "Don't worry; they're harmless."

The volume on the bar TV was loud enough to hear the local anchor's voice: "Greg Smith, onetime presidential adviser and political kingmaker, was released from the Morgantown federal prison today following a surprise White House pardon. His daughter, Sydney Smith, a student at WVU, was at the prison to joyfully greet him as he walked free for the first time in more than two years. Smith declined our invitation to comment or be interviewed."

After sharing a hot fudge sundae for dessert, we began to wrap up.

"By the way, what did your mother mean when she said I wasn't the only dealmaker in the family?"

"You, like, honestly don't know, do you?" Sydney said mockingly. She knew I hated not knowing things. "Remember the president's tax-cut bill that passed by one vote in the House last month?"

"I read that Mom voted for it against her party leadership, and she's taking a lot of heat."

Then it hit me like a hallelujah choir booming out of the sky: Liz had cut a deal for my pardon.

• • •

It was three o'clock when Sydney and I finally said our goodbyes and I climbed into my bright-red Jeep rental for my drive to Tennessee. The trip would take me through West Virginia and Kentucky and then into Nashville, forty miles from Kelsey. It was a route I had never taken, which was fitting as I embarked upon my new life. A "road less traveled" thing. I found myself oddly excited. Cruising at seventy-five miles an hour down the highway represented unvarnished freedom for a guy who had just sprung from prison. I felt like a kid going to college, away from parental supervision and rules for the first time.

Sydney had argued that I should return to our suburban home in Washington to relax and refocus. But I eventually convinced her that the "scene of the crime" was the worst place for me to go. Maybe at a later time, I told her. For now, I was all about fresh starts.

"My only plan at this point is to lay low and try living away from the hubbub," I explained. I wondered whether I would be tempted to return to my old life or if I could be satisfied with a smaller world, a more leisurely rhythm, and real friends. Would things like nature and beauty replace conquests and victories as values to be cherished? Would I discover a purpose?

I had no intention of finding answers to those big questions in Kelsey. I simply wanted a safe harbor, to hang out with my closest friend, and time to plan my next move.

As the I-79 curved south through the beautiful Cumberland Mountains, I thought back to when I was first arrested. It felt like watching myself die. One day, I'd had everything a driven person like me could aspire to. I was at the top of my field. Respected and feared, influential, even domineering. People craved my opinion. When I walked into a room, I sucked the air out of it and then divvied out the remaining oxygen to whomever I chose. I thought I was even getting away with a crime that would negate the will of an entire body of stupid, uninformed voters in three states. It was my version of high-grade cocaine, as I never did drugs.

But the next day, when I walked into the FBI office in DC and confessed my crime, it was all stripped from me, and with it the image, the persona, I had so carefully created.

Prison and the counseling that came with it helped me deal with my addiction to power and attention. But now I was lost, unidentifiable even to myself.

CHAPTER FOUR

I pulled up to Tom and Jane's at midnight. Their home was how I imagined: warm, cozy, and humble. Nestled in the middle of a long block in what appeared to be a safe, working-class, well-kept neighborhood, it reminded me of the houses Tom and I were raised in back in Buffalo.

"How was your trip?" Jane greeted me on the front steps. "We've been worried about you all day." Jane was the official worrier of the family, wanting the best for everyone. Whilst imprisoned, I received regular packages from her in the mail, always consisting of something useful like a sweater or new socks. Judging me was God's job, not hers.

"Hey, buddy," Tom roared as he wrapped his big arms around my neck. "Welcome to freedom. We waited up for you."

"Thanks, guys. I appreciate you having me."

I knew I couldn't have been anywhere else. This was the perfect halfway house between prison and the real world—a place where love was a given and acceptance guaranteed.

"Mi casa, su casa," Tom responded with the only words he knew in Spanish other than "taco" and "burrito." "Let's get you settled into the guest room. Take a shower if you like."

"I'll make some hot chocolate," Jane announced.

We stayed up for another hour, and Tom talked me into going to work with him in the morning. He claimed they could use volunteer help, especially in the kitchen.

I agreed because telling him otherwise wouldn't have done any good. Tom Garrity—or Pastor Tom, as most people know him—was the director of the Kelsey Rescue Mission, a facility that housed up to a hundred homeless men at a time.

He had made providing for people without housing his lifelong profession and passion. It was a journey that began shortly after his divinity school graduation twenty or so years before. He was as selfless a person as I knew. I appreciated Tom in part because he served as my foil. Regardless of how big a shitbag I was, I could always say that my best friend was a saint.

Tom's first mission was in Albany, New York, and the second in Gilroy, California. Coming to Tennessee was the result of a nationwide search by the Kelsey Rescue Mission Board of Directors, who were making a concerted effort to expand and improve services to their ever-growing homeless community. A modern facility managed with professional leadership had long been the dream of founder Doug Pollard, the highly respected owner of Serenity Funeral Home, who had raised over two million dollars—mostly in small donations—first to build and now to double the size of the Mission.

It was not an easy lift. Pollard's efforts to expand the Mission prior to Tom's arrival had been met with as much opposition in the community as it had support, if not more. Opponents included most of the city's upper crust, who only saw the downside of placing dozens of would-be thieves and drug addicts in the middle of an urban area carved out for renewal and regentrification. I supposed they had a point. The old me would have joined them, especially if they had hired me to twist every law and regulation on the books to my client's advantage. Getting folks to fear the homeless was like getting kids to be afraid of the troll under the bridge.

When a permit to expand the Mission came before the mayor and city council, a nine-to-zero vote defeated it. In addition to other considerations, Mayor Frank Simmons and the other members of the council were controlled by political boss Max Weber and his powerful party organization.

"Mr. Pollard," the mayor had declared following the vote, "you have fought the good fight, and while we need to offer better care for those without, we also need to balance that need with strong economic growth for the good of our city." In other words, get lost.

If nothing else, the disappointing vote by the city council taught Doug an important lesson: This was not a place for a pie-in-the-sky preacher man. Accordingly, Tom was hired by the Mission's board before he left the building following the interview for director. The Mission needed a savvy operative as its director, and Tom Garrity's proven political acumen and fearlessness made him the clear choice. One capable of mixing it up and making deals—all in the name of the Lord, of course. No one did that better than the Reverend Thomas Garrity. When I thought about it, Tom and I were a lot alike, except that he did it for Jesus. I did it for myself.

Max Weber remained a formidable opponent. His money and influence brought spoils, including the power to appoint planning commissioners and other officials in critical positions who could slow down the permit process or, in some cases, deny them altogether. In the following election, Weber's team of candidates was swept to victory with the slogan "Save Our City," which focused on stopping further expansion of the Mission. I wasn't there then but might have gone along with that campaign if not for Tom. Who wouldn't want to "save our city," especially from the vagabonds who lived for free in a group house in the middle of town?

Tom occasionally called me for advice during the campaign, prefacing every call with something like "I know this is small-potato politics for you, but I could use your insight on how to manage this situation." The question usually involved how to frame a response to a question from an aggressive reporter or Weber's latest attack ad. Since our conversations took place from a pay phone in the prison, I had to be fast. "Don't worry about it," I would tease him. "I don't have a lot on my schedule today."

Like he'd done all his life, Tom was determined to fight for the underdog and the rejected. Back in the fifth grade, he once took on the school bully in a fistfight for picking on an autistic kid. Tom got the crap beat out of him, but it didn't matter. He held his own, and no one, including the bully, dared to fight him again. Weber was just another kind of bully—albeit one with both cunning and a bottomless bank account, a formidable combination.

In addition to being the local party chairperson, Max Weber was a local developer whose company had built half the homes in the county, not to mention the lion's share of office and medical structures that dotted the urban landscape, including the William J. Weber building, the tallest structure in Kelsey—named after Max's father. He hand-selected all subcontractors and laborers, making sure each was a contributing member of his party. His detractors complained that no contracts were made without his approval.

Weber's influence extended beyond the Kelsey city limits, as statewide and federal officeholders and candidates often sought him for advice and financial support. But his current obsession was all local and had everything to do with his most crucial economic concern: his wallet. Which, of course, I could relate to, but I was working on new skills, like how to be a decent human being.

Directly across the street from the Mission, in what had become a blighted area of the city, was what remained of the old Kelsey Woven Mill Company. The mill had been closed for forty years, allowed to become a crumbling, dilapidated eyesore. Its demise reminded us of the world we once lived in, where people had secure middle-class lives manufacturing necessary products. In this case, it was socks and underwear, once making Kelsey "the skivvy capital of the world."

Although city leaders had proposed various uses for the old mill over the years, all the good ideas required massive funds to bring them to light. It was money that few private companies or government agencies were willing to commit. That is, until Max Weber announced an agreement with Rockwood Holdings, a vast out-of-state company specializing in building hotels and resorts. Although Dallas-based,

Rockwood was willing to purchase the mill and invest millions of dollars transforming it into a premier destination resort offering 500 rooms, a golf course, three pools, and four restaurants.

As the property's owner and local developer, Weber stood to make millions, not only on the transfer of the property but on commissions as well. He claimed that Rockwood Holdings had one crucial condition: Stop the expansion of the homeless population at the Kelsey Rescue Mission and either close it or relocate to another location. "Find out where Weber lives, and we'll move to his neighborhood," Tom once sarcastically told a reporter.

In one discussion with Pastor Tom, Weber got right to the point. "Tom, if Rockwood wants to build this resort—which could be great for Kelsey's economy—they will bring a team of lawyers and public relations specialists in and just make it happen. Besides, think about it from their angle. After spending five hundred for a room, two-fifty for eighteen holes of gold, and another two-fifty for dinner, is it right that their patrons should walk out on their balcony and see a drunk homeless guy pissing on the front lawn?"

"I admit that some of the Mission's residents don't always behave like scholars and gentlemen," Tom responded. "But most of them are pretty respectful."

He was right, of course. While occasional reports of loitering, fighting, and drunkenness made many fine citizens in town afraid to visit the downtown area, such incidents seldom were instigated by the residents of the Mission. But the Mission and its occupants were blamed anyway. And Tom knew it. He fought constantly to maintain a positive reputation for the Mission. He started internally by demanding each resident behave like a good neighbor and citizen. Even as a kid, Tom had a sharp, persuasive tongue. On the high school debate team, he was always our best closer.

Tom then implemented a beautification program on the Mission grounds and the surrounding streets, mostly daily litter cleanup. A new lawn and plant scheme made the front of the building at least as lovely as the row houses and local businesses. One of his more ingenious ideas was to routinely invite city leaders to the Mission for a meal and a sit-down discussion with staff and residents. He carefully selected his residents, ensuring the eight or ten in the meeting were articulate and drug-free. To prepare, they would practice, each learning to address and listen to that day's guest respectfully. Tom unofficially dubbed them the "rescue mission ambassadors" and made it an honor to be a member.

Pastor Tom's strategy was little more than Public Relations 101, but it mattered. While there would always be those in town who remained suspicious of the homeless, acceptance of the Mission had risen ever so slightly.

Though Tom's foes in Kelsey tended to be in the conservative wing of politics, a few outspoken advocates on the political left had difficulty accepting his religious policies. They accused him of being old-school, especially when it came to the Mission's insistence that residents be taught about religion, specifically the Christian religion, as a criterion to be accepted and housed at the facility. Tom was a Christian disciple and took his calling very seriously. When we were teenagers and just starting to drive our parents' cars, everyone wanted Tom to come along. Number one, he was fun and made us laugh. But most importantly, he didn't drink alcohol or smoke weed, meaning we always had a sober driver. He was Jesus at the wheel long before Carrie Underwood sang about it.

Today, three years after Tom's arrival, the Mission was only half completed. The part that had opened was basic but modern. It boasted two sections of dormitories and ten private rooms, a full-size commercial kitchen, a large central area that doubled as a cafeteria, and a chapel with a hundred seats. It also contained a social room with a large-screen television and a work area with twenty personal computers, complete with high-speed internet. The expansion would add a second floor of dormitories and bathrooms with showers.

During the week, on a regular schedule, nurses from the nearby hospital were on-site, as were job counselors and teachers. All volunteers. Whether the credit belonged to Tom or Jesus, something worthwhile happened at the Kelsey Rescue Mission. "All glory to God," Tom would say. Tom never took personal credit for anything he accomplished.

He also created a strict rule culture. According to him, "You don't put a hundred or more men of mixed ages and races under one roof and expect them always to like each other." His top lieutenant, Cooper Dornan, was often aggressive with residents who broke those rules. "All communities need a sheriff," Tom told me with his signature wryness. He certainly couldn't be the one getting tough with these men; and he warned that these guys would take every advantage possible.

"Last year, we had one who didn't pass the pee test. He had been out all evening and came back drunk as a skunk. He blew a one-point-eight on the breathalyzer and could hardly stand up. But get this. He told us that someone must have put vodka in his soup." Tom let out a belly laugh. "I can't make this stuff up."

The importance of PR to the Mission had become apparent. One slipup by any of these men that resulted in an injury—or worse—would be used as a gotcha attack by their opponents, something neither the Mission nor the men they fed and clothed could afford. On the occasion when one messed up, Tom would retrieve them. Though I'm not usually one for biblical references, the imagery of the good shepherd and his flock was fitting for Tom Garrity.

But make no mistake. This was a formidable flock. Life on the street, with its foul weather and daily skirmishes over territory or drugs, had hardened many hearts. A meal and a dry mattress didn't make their anger disappear. It merely kept emotions at a low boil beneath the surface. In my first month, I witnessed three fights, one between two homeless women who had shown up at the thrift store. The women, especially those with children, had a shelter of their own a few miles away but were always welcome at mealtime at the Mission. No one was turned away.

CHAPTER FIVE

Tom Garrity's secret plan to save me from my past took months to understand. It wasn't to convert me to religion or make me into something I would never become. No, his intention for me was far cleverer. He wanted me to grow a heart.

On day one, Tom assigned me to the kitchen breakfast shift on Tuesday and Thursday mornings. Along the way, he found other ways for me to help, but this was my main gig. As I peered out from the serving window toward the lengthy line of men dressed in old hoodies with names of colleges and sports teams from the donation bin, I chuckled at my friend's genius. He knew this was where I belonged, at least for now.

The large round clock on the cafeteria wall said it was 6:59 a.m. We would begin serving in one minute and continue for the next half hour. Anyone who missed it would have to wait until lunchtime, four long hours away.

A lucky few in line had faded secondhand jeans that fit them. But most wore pants that were either too short or too baggy, long ago donated by more fortunate men who could afford a fresh annual wardrobe. Most of them looked tired, like they had just gotten out of bed—which they had. Their uncombed hair and beard stubble gave them away, as did their drained faces and hollow eyes. Many were also battling drug or alcohol addiction.

"We thank you, Lord Jesus, for this new day and the meal we are about to share." Tom had a bellowing voice meant to inspire, but for some folks, it was way too loud for such an early hour, especially when projected over the large sound system. "We also thank you for the donors and the volunteers who support and sustain us. May we go out and be your disciples as we do our jobs and deepen our love for you. We pray in Jesus' holy name. Amen."

Tom's booming "amen" was my signal to turn on the overly bright light in the middle of the serving room, indicating we were open for business. In front of me sat three serving trays, one each for scrambled eggs and pancakes, a third tray half filled with bacon and half with sausage. Other than the size of the serving trays, it reminded me of the breakfasts my grandmother would make for Grandad and me when I visited. The quality of the food––all prepared by a crew of residents and outside volunteers like me and donated by local stores and individuals—was impressive.

"Hey, Billy, first in line, I see; you must either be hungry or in a hurry," I greeted the first "customer." Billy wore a Pittsburgh Steelers sweatshirt and a Dallas Cowboys hat.

"I begin a new job today at the Anderson distribution plant, and I start at eight."

"That's awesome, Billy. I heard they pay well. Good luck, man."

"I wouldn't have got the job without you, Mr. Brad," he said, addressing me by my middle name, Bradley, which I'd elected to go by at the Mission to hide from my past.

I had assisted Billy with his application, helping him explain several months of unemployment. His landlord had evicted him for consistently paying his rent late due to the timing of his monthly paycheck. Following his eviction, he lost his job and stayed in a local motel dive for ten days until his money ran out. He then started rolling up to the alley behind it at night, digging through dumpsters for something to eat. Billy finally gave in to his hunger and the weather and walked to the Mission one rainy night. Cooper Dornan, Tom's top assistant, greeted him by the front desk and got him a shower, clean clothing, and a warm bed. That was a year ago.

Billy was what Pastor Tom would call a success story. He came seeking a meal and a dry place to sleep, owning nothing but his backpack and the worn wool blanket he kept inside it. He was informed about the protocol, and he signed, agreeing to the rules and the education program. At the time, he did not mention that he had graduated from the University of Maryland with a degree in ancient literature. Unfortunately, his degree did not include classes on managing cash flow or keeping from drinking a fifth of rum daily.

One by one, the rest of the men appeared at the window in front of me, each hungering for a nutritious breakfast to start another hard day. The rough mileage of their lives could be seen in their wrinkled, ashen faces. Most were expressionless. The breakfast line was just another mundane task; today's scrambled eggs, pancakes, and bacon were the same as yesterday's and a prelude for tomorrow's. Like Billy, few wanted to be here, but, at least for now, they had run out of options. The Kelsey Rescue Mission was their last resort, the better choice between scooping potatoes out of a can beneath an overpass and having clean sheets, a hot shower, and three squares a day.

For some, it wasn't an easy choice. The cost was a slice of their freedom, as each man accepted the regimen of common-sense rules and expectations kindly but strictly enforced. No firearms or weapons, no fighting, no swearing, no drugs or alcohol use, and a curfew at 9 p.m. "The Program," as it was called, consisted of attending a daily Bible class and a brief chapel service in the evening. And, with the assistance of the staff volunteers, seeking employment. The lofty goal was to get each man off drugs and alcohol and back on his feet and out into society within eighteen months. However, for most, this became their longtime residence—lifers, as Tom called them. "What am I going to do," he asked, "turn a sixty-five-year-old guy with no family and no job out in the street? No way."

If I knew their name or nickname, I addressed them by it. If not, I kept up the banter and did my best to offer a friendly greeting. "How are we doing this morning?" and "Where do they have you working these days?" were among my standard questions. Or "Are we hungry today?" and "It's going to be another cold one," speaking of the day and not the meal. Just something to say that might make them feel someone cared about them. Following our brief exchange and armed with a whole tray of food, they would slowly move to one of thirty long tables, each with five place settings of coffee cups and eating utensils. I noticed they would eat at the same table with the same people for every meal.

"Sammy, how are you doing? I haven't seen you in weeks. Are you okay?" I could see that my cheerful greeting brightened his mood as he suddenly transitioned from Sleepy to Happy, a comparison I conjured due to his short stature and cartoonishly sized mouth.

"I failed the pee test for the third time, and they kicked me out," he deadpanned. "Two weeks on the streets, and they're giving me another chance. A last chance, they told me."

I didn't know if he had failed to pass an alcohol or drug test or both. He didn't say. I just knew the Mission rules against chemicals of any kind—whether drunk, snorted, or smoked—were strictly enforced.

"Where are you working these days? We miss you in the kitchen."

"They have me in the warehouse. The kitchen was too much pressure for me," he said.

Sammy had bipolar disorder. I once saw him point a knife at the kitchen manager, threatening to carve him instead of the five hams he had been assigned.

If residents didn't have an outside job, they were assigned a full-time task inside the Mission six days a week. The kitchen and warehouse were but two of the designated areas. Others included cleanup of the cafeteria and working the recycling center, laundry, thrift store, yard maintenance, building repairs, and the front desk, usually reserved for older and disabled men. No one got a free ride.

"Are you taking your meds, and I mean the prescribed ones?" I asked him quietly.

"Yep, I haven't missed in over a week, so I'm doing well. No pancakes, by the way. Just eggs and bacon. I'm trying to maintain my svelte figure," he said as he patted his ample belly.

Over lunch a few weeks before, Sammy had told me he was an experienced website designer whom three companies had fired. "It was for the same reason every time. I showed up either high as a kite or drunk on my ass."

Each man had his own story about how he landed there, although it was impossible for me to know all of them. I was only there two days a week for breakfast and lunch. Their ages ranged from eighteen to eighty, although age was often challenging to assess.

Ballard's mother had dropped him off at the Mission a month ago on his eighteenth birthday because, as he said, "She couldn't stand to look at me, and I wasn't allowed to live with her anymore." With his carrot-colored hair and buck teeth, Ballard was an odd-looking kid, but I was sure there was more to the story than his looks, just as I was sure he was a know-it-all who thought the world owed him a living. To him, the Mission wasn't so much a sad ending—at least, not yet—as a rude beginning to adulthood.

"Good morning, Mr. Stone, and how are we today?" I continued to motormouth like a Walmart door greeter.

I had a budding friendship with Mark Stone, a Black man in his fifties who had once been the chief financial officer of a publicly traded manufacturing company. We had much in common, including our criminal rap sheets, although I hadn't told him about mine yet. We had even agreed to hit the golf course when the weather warmed up. Mark was tall, handsome, always clean-shaven, well dressed, and graceful in his speech and mannerisms. If I had to sum him up in one word, it would be "corporate," a look or a vibe that he honed at the Harvard School of Business, where he earned his MBA, or Stanford as an undergraduate. "I had a good life," he once told me, "until I didn't."

Mark was busted for embezzling over $200,000 from his company. By the time he was released from prison after serving three years of a ten-year sentence, his wife had divorced him, remarried, and financially cleaned him out. He now temporarily possessed one of the twenty coveted private ten-by-twelve rooms set aside for Mission residents with longevity, special needs, or unique talents. Mark fit the latter category as Pastor Tom's in-house bookkeeper. He was one of the only residents paid a small stipend for his work. The other ones included the forklift operator, bus driver, and thrift store manager, all requiring professional licenses or specialized experience.

"The one thing you need to understand, Bradley, is that no one chooses to be homeless," Mark told me during one of our late-morning talk sessions. "That is a myth promoted by those who don't want to solve the crisis of homelessness in our nation. The second thing you should know about homeless folks is that we have dignity, despite our failures or bad choices, because we are human. And that makes us just like you or anyone out there." He pointed to the front door as he finished his point. Of course, he did not know then that he was preaching to one who had lost all sense of pride and dignity.

I grew to learn that Mark was right. Take away the mismatched articles of clothing, the sullen eyes, yellowing teeth, and untidy hair on their faces and heads, and these men were more similar than different from those I knew from any number of business, family, and social circles I had run in during my life. In a community that ranged in size from fifty to over a hundred, the range of personality types was at least as broad as the hundred-person law and lobbying firm where I had been a senior partner for government relations. Most of us would have also failed a random pee test. I could see it now: a dozen cocaine-snorting attorneys from Hart and Jones selected to line up in their K Street conference room in DC to piss into small plastic cups. I laughed just thinking about it.

When the last resident was through the line, I shut off the light and started to clean up, carrying the three serving trays back to the kitchen. I scraped the last of the eggs, pancakes, and bacon into the trash can. As much as I hated throwing away fresh donated food, these items would not be good tomorrow.

I was the only volunteer on duty this morning. The other four crew members were residents working the six-to-two shift. I finished wiping around the serving area and sweeping and mopping the floor. It was time to get ready for lunch.

"Hey, Brad, can you come here for a minute?" Mike, the kitchen manager, called from the walk-in refrigerator, a restaurant-grade gadget the size of a small bedroom. Inside, everything from fruit and vegetables to chicken and pot roast was stacked neatly on wall-to-wall shelves.

"Can you take over making the salads and the mixed fruit for lunch and dinner today while I focus on the meat and the veggies?"

"Be happy to do it, boss man," I replied cheerfully.

"Hey, I like that name. Keep it up," he laughed. Mike was about fifty, thick through the middle but not obese, and sported a spotty gray beard—more like fuzz—and a completely bald head.

As I began chopping salad and slicing carrots and cucumbers for the first of two salads I would make, I thought of the humble exercise of preparing a meal for homeless men and how it had become a regular part of my life the past six months. My world had dramatically shrunk since the days when my life was governed by the pace and prestige of our nation's capital. Or had my life expanded? Become more enriched? Of course, other than Tom, no one in this building knew where I had once been. Here, I was just Brad. I had every intention of keeping it that way.

When I walked out into the hot morning to empty the kitchen garbage bags, I encountered several small groups enjoying their last smokes before heading to Bible class.

"Hey, Mr. Brad," Billy called out as I swung the large bag over my shoulder and into the bin. "Thanks for all you do around here. We appreciate you."

"You are too kind, my friend. It's an honor to be here."

It had become my truth. I was starting to believe I was with some of the best men I had ever known.

CHAPTER SIX

"It is eight thirty. Again, it is eight thirty. Everyone who has morning class should be reporting now. Please drop off your cell phones at the front desk."

The morning announcement from "Sheriff" Cooper echoed from mounted speakers running throughout the building, inside and out. Unlike Tom, who had a loud, upbeat delivery, Cooper delivered the day's messages with a dry monotone that made me want to lie down and nap.

"If you do not have a class, you should be at your assigned job. If you do not have a job, please report to the front desk, and we will assign you one. All visitors to the Mission must now leave the premises. Lunch will be served at eleven thirty. Thank you for your cooperation."

A minute later, Cooper came into the kitchen. "Hey, Brad," he said in his friendly way. His kindness made me feel guilty about judging his speaking voice so harshly. Cooper knew nothing about my background or history with Tom. He knew what everyone else did: I volunteered in the kitchen for six hours every Tuesday and Thursday. "Do you know where I can find Mike Hart?"

"He's outside having a smoke," I said, "but he should be back any second. Is there anything I can tell him?"

"Just remind him the county health department is due today for an inspection, so we need to be ready. Please tell him to come by my office if he has any questions."

No sooner had Cooper left through the front door than Mike entered through the back.

"Ah, shucks, did I miss Cooper and his daily kitchen sermon?"

"Yeah, he wanted me to tell you that your salary has been cut in half."

"Ha ha. Half of zero is still zero."

I had grown friendly with Mike. I liked his gentle spirit and his courteous manner. He thought it particularly amusing that I played rock music on the Alexa speakers in the kitchen while I was there, something that was taboo for the residents to play. "Christian music only" was the rule.

Around midmorning, while I made two huge salads on one side of the long steel table that ran the length of the kitchen, Mike stood directly across on the other side, taking chickens apart and preparing them for baking. We both wore latex gloves, black aprons, and baseball caps, his with a St. Louis Cardinal logo and mine boasting an "NY" for the Yankees.

"I never asked where you were from, Mike."

"I'm from a little farming town named Mountain Ridge, about sixty miles out of Knoxville," he replied quietly. "Most folks work for the local chicken processing company."

"What did you do there?" I asked without pausing in my tomato-slicing assignment.

"I worked at the processing house like everyone else. For thirty years," he laughed. "Ever since I got out of high school."

"So, something must have happened to get you here."

"My mom died from cancer, and I had a tough time coping without her. I lived with her and never moved out of the house. It was just the two of us. For the last ten years, I was her only caretaker. The house sale proceeds were split equally between my older siblings and me. I asked them if I could live in it, but they wanted the money, so we sold it. Then I asked if I could live with them for a while, but they each claimed no room. So I took my part of the house money and rented an apartment, and I started drinking heavily."

"Grief and alcohol can be a lethal mixture," I offered.

"I learned that lesson the hard way. Pretty soon, I wasn't showing up for work. And then, one day, I came in thoroughly smashed and smelling like a small distillery, and that was it. I was fired. Now I had no job and hardly any of the money left. Then I lost my apartment and ended up camping down by the river when, one day, a hiker stopped. He told me about a homeless shelter in Kelsey that he had stayed in a while back."

Mike reminded me of my great-uncle Jerry, my grandfather's brother, a one-armed auto mechanic and part-time school bus driver whose highest academic achievement was the third grade. He lived on a small five-acre farm in northeastern Pennsylvania, about three hours from Buffalo. Uncle Jerry, who lost his right limb hopping freight trains when he was a teenager, was a gentle and thoughtful man with a quiet approach to life but was also eager for a bit of laughter and enjoyment. I always thought it remarkable that he could fix an engine or drive a manual shift with one arm and hand. He was also the most religious man I ever knew who never went to church or talked about God.

"How did you get here?" I asked Mike. I was interested in how he came to submit to a homeless shelter after being independent for so many years.

"I got here because I hitchhiked. But if you're asking, 'How did I get here?'"—he held up two big air quotes—"I can only explain it this way, and promise you won't laugh." Tears filled both eyes, and Mike paused, then blurted, "God led me here." *That's it for comparisons with Uncle Jerry*, I thought, *now that Mike brought God into the mix.*

"I'm not going to laugh at you, Mike. Don't ever worry about that." But I got what he was saying. A lot of us cannot express spiritual things because it makes us sound weak or plain weird. It flies in the face of how our culture tends to reward the so-called real man—the guy who marches to his own drummer and is self-made. "So, I take it this has been a positive experience. How long has it been?"

"This is my ninth month here, and I feel it's making a difference. When my mom died, I couldn't cope. When my siblings rejected me, I had nowhere to turn. I spent ninety-two days on that river sleeping in a damp tent before God sent that hiker to me. He didn't have wings and long flowing hair, but I know he was an angel.

"I'm not here forever," he continued. "I'm going to move on. But that first step was the biggest one for me. Now, enough about me. We need to get this chicken in the oven, and you need to finish those salads, or there's going to be a hundred bummed-out men here for lunch."

Just as we placed the seasoned meat into the large commercial ovens, Tom bounded into the kitchen, full of kinetic energy.

"Hey, Tom, what demons are you up against today?" I said laughingly.

"Oh my, would you believe the VA?"

"Come on. Over what?"

"Against all of my rules, that's what. I have let three addicts—all veterans—who have stayed here at the Mission for the past two months. Why? Because they've been accepted to the VA drug rehab program and these knuckleheads at the hospital made us a deal that if we can hold them for ten days while their paperwork is being done, they can enter the program for ninety days. So every day, I email or phone someone over there, and they say, 'Sorry, we don't have room right now.' But I know they have two hundred beds, and not even half are full."

"That sucks," I said. "What's their problem?"

"They're lazy. If they let more people in, someone has to take on a larger workload. Well, I fixed it this morning. I drove down and demanded to see the head guy, who had no clue I was getting stiff-armed. I told him my predicament, and he called the rehab center's director right in front of me. The long and the short of it is that my three veterans are heading to the VA tomorrow morning."

"Sounds like the problem is solved. Nicely done," I said. Of course, I once made a living knowing whom to call when something needed to get done. Then I would send a handsome invoice for my services to the one paying to grease the skids. Meanwhile, Tom was happy helping vets get off heroin.

"Say, do you have time to chat before you leave today? We have a legal situation that might heat up, and I could use a little free advice." I could tell Tom was worried about something. He had that expression I knew all too well. I told him I'd come by his office when we got everything cooked and out on the serving line.

"Hey, Brad, when you get done schmoozing with the boss, can you hold the oven doors so I can lift the trays in?" Mike asked from across the room. "Unless you want to lift them, and I'll do the doors."

"I'll get the doors. Lifting the food into the oven is too much responsibility for a lowly volunteer," I joked. I enjoyed feeling like part of a working team where honest labor and human respect had value.

It was noon when I finally broke away from the kitchen. I walked through the cafeteria full of signs emblazoned with Christian adages and Bible verses: "For I was hungry, and you gave me food; I was thirsty, and you gave me drink; I was a stranger, but you welcomed me, Matthew 25:35." It was the most conspicuous sign, appearing on the wall above a hundred homeless men enjoying a donated lunch of baked chicken, mashed potatoes, green beans, fresh salad, and fruit. In the background drifted the soft sounds of religious music. Yes, indeed, this was a church, and with no government dollars, I imagined it would stay that way. Tom's house. Tom's rules.

Tom's office looked how a clergyperson's lair should look, complete with the large mahogany desk and muted lamp, a couch, a chair—also with a lamp—and a simple, bare wooden cross hanging on one of the walls. It was an intimate room that screamed for quiet, spiritual conversation.

Tom's early religious training was the same as mine, although he was the better listener. We grew up a block apart in Buffalo's blue-collar Irish Catholic neighborhood. His dad worked on the docks, loading and unloading the boats and ships coming through the Erie Canal. My pop was a mail carrier in our neighborhood. Dad was perhaps the most known and loved man in the First Ward. When we graduated from high school, Tom and I went to separate colleges on scholarships, his for wrestling and mine because I aced the SAT and was valedictorian. "You're too smart for your own good," my grandpa used to tell me. He ended up being right.

While in college, we visited one another as often as possible, me crashing at his dormitory or he at mine. Syracuse, my hoity-toity school, was only an hour away from his even more hoity-toity school, Cornell. I went to his wrestling matches when I could, a sport he didn't like but was his ticket to free education, so he dutifully applied himself. I also hated wrestling but loved Tom.

College brought significant changes for both of us, but not as much as our religious views. Tom dropped out of the whole Catholic thing but in the process became an even more devout Christian of the nondenominational type. I quit religion altogether.

"How are things in the kitchen?" Tom asked. I waved him off.

"The kitchen is fine, but come on, Tom. You didn't ask me to come by and tell you how many carrots I peeled today. What's up?"

"In light of the council vote to deny us a permit to expand, we are going to sue the City of Kelsey in state court," he stated solemnly. "I could use your help."

Tom was no longer the gregarious pastor in front of the congregation or the back-slapping encourager of Mission residents. He had morphed into an "I mean business" superhero in the blink of an eye. All he needed was a cape.

"You know I can't officially provide legal services. I'm disbarred, Tom."

"I know your situation, Greg." He only called me by my first name when we were alone. Nobody knew my last name, but "Smith" wasn't exactly distinctive anyway. "I need you as a strategic adviser to the legal and campaign team to direct the overall public relations effort behind the scenes. Weber has declared war on this Mission, and I want to kick his butt. And you, my friend, are the man to do it."

Here goes, I thought. It looked like Gregory Bradley Smith was about to suit up for battle one more time.

This wasn't something I relished doing. I had come to enjoy my shadowy new life. But as I had learned repeatedly, no one said no to Tom Garrity.

CHAPTER SEVEN

I was now a familiar face at the Mission, especially to the longer-term residents. Showing up twice a week gave me a sense of belonging. Still, a volunteer at the Mission wasn't the same as a resident. I couldn't truly "be one of them" because I was not. I had a home—well, really, an aging houseboat I was restoring—and money. They might have had these two things at one time, but not currently.

I always wanted to ask, "Where in life did you not read the directions and make such a wrong turn?" Of course, they had no idea I had also made a few wrong turns. Part of me wanted them to know my criminal past. It would make me more relatable, I thought. "Don't do that," Tom insisted. "Most of these guys are drug addicts and alcoholics. Some have serious mental illness issues, and others are just plain unlucky. But they are patriotic and honorable. A lot of them are vets and have seen combat. The less they know about you trying to cheat the American system and subvert democracy, the better off you'll be."

My houseboat was twenty years old, and the interior needed work, such as new carpeting and paint, but mechanically it was in great shape. It was forty-eight feet long and twelve feet wide, complete with a living room, kitchen and bathroom, and two bedrooms. The vessel also has two small patios, fore and aft, and a large sundeck on top. It was essentially identical to my grandmother's mobile home in Florida, where she lived when I was a kid, except mine floated and came equipped with an engine and steering wheel. And she didn't have a sundeck on her roof.

As early as 6:30 in the morning, arriving at the Mission was like approaching a human anthill. Everyone had a task. Mack, waving from his forklift, was transporting boxes of donated clothing from the warehouse to the thrift store. Ron was loading wooden logs into the fire chimney that provided heat to all of the buildings. Four of the guys were loading an out-of-state trailer attached to a semi with crates of recycled plastic and metal, much of it discarded from the kitchen. Tom told me that 22 percent of the Mission's income was from recycling and profits from the store. The Kelsey Rescue Mission was a city within a city.

The frenetic pace continued inside as the dining room crew set places for more than a hundred residents and visitors and the kitchen staff hurried to get the serving trays into place.

"Brad, we've got you at the window this morning," Mike announced when I entered. "And then you're off the hook. Pastor Tom wants to see you in his office immediately after breakfast."

"Thanks, Mike. I appreciate you telling me."

"I don't mean to pry, but what's up with you and the pastor? He seems like he wants to talk to you all the time. You're not spying on us, are you?" he laughed.

I was always embarrassed when my closeness to Tom was observed by the residents.

"It's nothing. Tom and I were best friends growing up, but we haven't lived in the same town for twenty years, so I think we're just getting to know each other all over again." There was just enough truth to prevent my fib from being an official lie—my specialty.

By then, the other three kitchen staff members had gathered to hear our conversation.

"Where do you work, Brad?" asked Jimmy Keefer.

Jimmy, a tall, handsome Black dude whose outgoing personality made him popular with both the staff and his fellow residents, wasn't prying so much as making conversation. I was reminded of my years in DC, where a person's entire persona is defined by their job and title.

"I repair boats at the lake but have a flexible schedule." Well, it was almost true. I was repairing a boat at the river and didn't punch a clock.

"So why do you come here to volunteer?" Jimmy continued earnestly.

I paused for a few seconds, the way I used to coach politicians and CEOs to do in media interviews. The answer is more believable and carries more weight.

"I've lived a life where the only thing that mattered was my ego and bank account. I now realize there is more to life than that. I wanted to do something because it was right. Tom suggested I try helping at the Mission, so here I am."

I omitted the part about being in prison for two years. Besides, I'd learned in prison that good people can do terrible things. I got this insight from a fellow prisoner—a former Catholic bishop—who had been convicted of siphoning $385,000 from his diocese for personal gain and exotic travel. "It certainly is not what Jesus would have done," the Reverend (inmate) Peter Simpson told me. "Only humans fall into the trap of greed and self-pleasure." The prisoners and guards called him Padre Pete. He actually thanked God for his prison experience, a step I wasn't willing to take, but I nonetheless grasped his point.

Mission residents had access to the computers in the activity room in the front of the building and to their devices, meaning they could have looked me up at their will. I never again wanted to see my name or picture in a newspaper. Hopefully, the trimmed brown beard and long wavy hair that hung nearly to my shoulders would remain an adequate disguise. I wasn't a recognizable celebrity like a television personality might be; I was just "that guy." But I knew that any day, I could get a question like "Aren't you 'that guy' who worked for the president and got sent to jail?" Then again, who would ask that of a middle-aged hippie in worn jeans and open-toed sandals who drove a fifteen-year-old pickup? Tom told me I looked like Jesus, his other best friend.

When I entered the conference room adjacent to Tom's office, I saw the meeting had already begun. Tom abruptly stopped talking, taking a moment to introduce me to the others, including two well-groomed men in their thirties and a nicely dressed woman of about the same age. Doug Pollard and Mark Stone joined them at the table. Tom's inclusion of Mark clearly showed that he trusted Mark to be something more than a bean counter. This would be Mark's first awareness that I had a relationship with Tom beyond volunteering in the kitchen. Our next conversation would be interesting.

"Let me introduce everyone to our top-flight legal team," Tom began. "This is Christine Culpepper. She oversees the pro bono cases for the Williams and Williams Law Firm here in Kelsey, including all legal matters about the Mission. Her associates, also from Williams and Williams, are Ted Copper and Charles Tanner. Ted and Charles are great friends of the Mission and are also here to offer support."

The two Mormon missionary knockoffs were impeccably attired in matching navy-blue Brooks Brothers suits, white shirts, and blue ties. I once looked and dressed just like them, although I would have chosen a green tie. I noticed that Ms. Culpepper, a fair-skinned Black woman, was also conservatively clothed, from her close-toed high heels to her white satin blouse and maroon pencil skirt with a matching coat. Her straight black hair lay gently on her shoulders. The truth was that her beauty was clashing with my attention skills. Although I said hello to Mark as I sat down, I struggled unsuccessfully to take my eyes off Christine.

"Brad is one of our best volunteers here at the Mission. He is also a retired lawyer and public relations practitioner who agreed to help and offer advice. I might add that he is my best friend, which is why he had no choice when I asked him to join us."

They had no idea how true that was. I remembered our first

time on an upside-down roller coaster at the Buffalo Amusement Park. We were eleven years old, and I was too afraid to ride it. That is, until Tom bought two tickets and got in line, waiting an entire hour for me to say yes.

Tom started the meeting by methodically summarizing the facts. "Suing city hall is never easy," he began, "but it is our only alternative if we are to realize our goal of expanding the size and scope of the Mission. The hearing is in five weeks. As needed, Christine will be the lead, backed by Ted and Charles. Brad will be available to assist in a consulting capacity."

He left out that I had never been in a courtroom other than the one I was convicted in. My job had been to use my connections to make deals. I opened and closed bank accounts and ran interference for politicians, moguls, foreign emirs, and chiefs of Native American tribes. The law degree—a nicely framed piece of paper that once hung on the ego wall of my overly ornate office on K Street—was a ruse.

Christine took over from there. "Thanks, Pastor Tom, and it is very nice to meet you, Brad." *Did she lock her eyes on me?* I couldn't tell exactly, but I wondered. "Judge Ralph Swanson will hear this motion request for us to cease building the expansion. He is known as a hard-liner law-and-order type who generally caters to the establishment and the business community."

"So, what's the good news?" Mark asked, provoking quiet giggles around the table. A little wit was always welcome in a serious meeting.

Christine continued. "The good news is that Judge Swanson is up for reelection this coming November, which means he might be more aware of public opinion than, let's say, a judge in his second year of an eight-year term. Outward persuasion from people on our side might make him think twice about dumping on the poor and the homeless."

She was not only drop-dead beautiful but also intelligent. Her assessment was spot-on. Politics, not merit, often influences laws and legal decisions. Nobody understood this better than I did.

"Victory for our side is for the judge to declare the council action unlawful and allow the Mission to continue its building efforts. Remember, this is only a temporary injunction request. The full lawsuit will come later."

"Isn't his wife a bigwig of some sort?" Mark asked.

"Yes, Diane Swanson is president of Kelsey United Bank and chairs the annual United Community campaign. I am sure she is on our side, at least privately. Diane is a high-minded woman who is incredibly supportive of the Mission and all causes that help those in need," Tom replied. "The judge will not want to cross her, at home or in public."

"Is Rockwood Holdings on this motion?" I asked.

"No, they are not," Christine responded. "Max Weber and his local ownership group are highly motivated to sell the mill to the highest bidder. While that appears to be Rockwood, they have yet to establish a legal claim and therefore cannot be sued. This deal will make Weber and his associates even more fabulously wealthy than they already are, but only if they can get rid of their Rescue Mission problem first."

"Rockwood Holdings doesn't want this controversy surrounding one of their projects. They hate bad publicity and will run from this if it gets ugly," I said. Dan Johnson, Rockwood's CEO, was a former client; I wrote his "bad publicity" policy years ago. He was also a significant contributor to conservative candidates and causes, many of which I managed for him.

"And you would know this because?"

Tom was asking the same question I would have asked.

"Aw, Pastor Tom, you know I can't give away all my trade secrets," I jested. "But maybe I'll take a trip to Dallas to see my old friend Dan."

Doug, who had been silent throughout the meeting, asked, "Brad, what would you say to Mr. Johnson?"

Grinning, I said, "I would appeal to his humanity and suggest we can all be winners here. Dan will understand that."

Then I'd tell him it's time to pay up.

CHAPTER EIGHT

When the meeting broke up, the serving window had five minutes before closing. I was hungry, and the spicy chicken breasts that Mike and I had baked earlier were calling to me.

"Christine, would you and your friends like to grab lunch? It's on me," I joked.

Ted and Charles politely declined due to a luncheon appointment at a downtown restaurant. But to my surprise and delight, Christine agreed to stay without her colleagues and try out the day's cuisine. "I hope you won't think I'm bragging, but I can honestly say that I made a fresh salad and a fruit cocktail mix just for you . . . and a hundred thirty homeless men."

"I love a man who cooks," she teased. "Especially when it's a yummy salad."

"And I love a lawyer who uses words like 'yummy.'" I was out of practice when it came to bantering with humans of the opposite sex.

Ray Moore was serving up the day's fare. "Hey, Brad, who's your friend? You sure know where to take a date. Say, would you mind helping me with my résumé this week? Everyone says you're the best when it comes to writing stuff."

"Be happy to help, Ray. Do as much as you can on your own, and we can sit in the computer room after breakfast on Thursday. By the way, this is Christine Culpepper. She does all the Mission's legal work. Christine, meet First Sergeant Ray Moore, US Army, retired. Ray is a twenty-year veteran who saw combat in the Iraq War."

"Nice to meet you, Ms. Culpepper."

"And you, Ray. Thank you for your service."

With our green plastic trays full, we sat at the end of a middle table. "I see that you do more around here than scramble eggs and chop onions," Christine observed.

"Very funny," I laughed. "Yeah, Tom asked me if I would help with job applications. Now he has me counseling them on minor regulations, like how to pay their fines and get a driver's license reissued. I'm confident that he leaves the heavy lawyering to you."

Four Black men, each around thirty, took the other seats at the table, arguing over what they thought were the overly strict rules at the Mission. "It's like a fucking prison," one of them claimed. "What right do they have to tell me when to be in? I got shit to do at night."

Hmm, two bad words in a row. Perhaps I'll suggest a "swear jar" to Tom.

"And they make us work for no pay. Who do they think they are?" asked one of the other men. "I thought we abolished slavery a hundred and fifty years ago."

"Have you guys ever been in prison?" I suddenly offered without being asked—a once-central trait of mine I thought I had ditched. "If you have, you know this is nothing like a prison. Do you know why? See that door? You can walk out of it anytime you want with no repercussions. Total freedom."

The four stared at me like I was from another planet, no doubt resentful that I had interrupted their discussion with the blunt truth.

"So what do you know about prison, White boy?" the first one asked as he and his friends picked up their trays. "Did you visit your dad there?"

There was no value in poking the bears on this one. Each one of those guys could have pulverized me. I said nothing as they laughed and moved off.

"I see that you like to speak your mind." Christine smiled, then took her first bite of spiced chicken. "That was brave."

"I don't usually lash out like that, but I know how hard Tom and his staff work to maintain a decent shelter, and when the very people it helps don't appreciate it, I get a little feisty. It's like when we're serving steaks and someone tells us his meat is overcooked. I want to ask them, 'What part of free don't you understand?'"

"It can be frustrating, for sure. Just remember, the goal of the Mission isn't simply to feed them or offer a dry place to sleep at night. It's to give them the hope and confidence that they can someday care for their needs. These guys may not like the rules, but aren't we all subject to certain boundaries? On the outside, we call them laws."

I envied her clarity of purpose and her knowledge that there was more to life than self-indulgence—the same qualities I admired about Tom. I had serious doubts that my darkened soul would ever rise to their level of compassion and empathy, regardless of how many meal trays I served. But it gave me something to shoot for.

"Tell me, Greg, was prison hard? Or should I continue to call you Brad?"

Damn it. She knew everything about me.

"Tom told me your story, which is all covered by client–lawyer confidentiality. I won't tell a soul."

"It could have been worse." I wondered what she thought of working with an ex-con. "Minimum security is pretty tame compared to regular institutions, but it isn't a picnic."

"Were you guilty?" It was a gentle question, asked without judgment or attitude.

"Let's just say the judicial system we both learned about in law school usually works." I briefly considered stopping there but decided against it. "But yes, I was guilty as charged. I cut a deal for the lighter sentence and a privileged prison assignment."

"But a deal implies you had something to give them in return."

"And with that, Ms. Culpepper, this interview must end. You

know I can't get into those details." For what I gave up, I had been offered witness protection, but I wasn't going the rest of my life without seeing my parents and daughter. I also looked forward to seeing Liz, who, along with Tom, was still my best friend. Our conversation made me recall Warden Cannon's warning about my vengeful former associates.

"Well done, Counselor. I was testing you," she laughed. "However, I am interested in how you ended up in Kelsey, of all places."

"It had the two things I wanted most: one devoted friend and a community where no one knew me. My goal was to push the reset button and start a new life. You could say I am searching for the proverbial clean slate. How about you, Christine? Tell me about yourself, at least the part you want me to know." I desperately wanted to stop being the topic of our conversation.

"Well, after seven years as a Lutheran pastor with a passion for social justice, I decided I could do the Lord's bidding more effectively as a lawyer doing pro bono work. I had gone to Yale as a divinity student on a full scholarship, so I went back to the same well for law school and got another full ride."

Impressive credentials.

"Wow, using the law to help people. Sounds revolutionary."

"To you I'm sure it does." Although she had directly offended me, she pulled it off without making me feel bad, delivering her line with a fetching smile. "But if you went into law because you wanted to be rich, you wouldn't be the first one, would you?"

"So, you want to change the world and help the less fortunate; how did you choose Kelsey, Tennessee, to pursue such a worldly ambition?"

"Kelsey chose me. I was born and raised here. Doug Pollard is my father." I must have looked surprised and confused. "Mom is the Black one, in case you were wondering."

Okay, she reads minds too, I considered.

Christine explained that the Mission had been a big part of her life growing up, thanks to her father. Over twenty-five years ago, he was inspired to start a soup kitchen in the basement of their church, offering hot meals to so-called street people. Within a year, the food lines had grown so long that he organized the other churches in Kelsey into action and formed the committee that would later become the Kelsey Rescue Mission. They rented the old warehouse where we were now sitting and started offering three meals daily and later providing beds.

"That first year, when I was ten years old, I would come to the church and serve soup to the homeless. So, you can see that this place means everything to me. It launched my career, both as a pastor and a lawyer."

"Culpepper must be your married name?" I wanted to withdraw the question immediately.

"Culpepper is indeed my married name. My husband died in Afghanistan. Before he deployed, we lived in Washington, DC, where I was a pastor at St. Timothy in the Adams Morgan neighborhood. He previously served as an Army attaché and national security adviser to the Senate Foreign Relations Committee."

It hit me. "Bill Culpepper was your husband. I knew him. He was a great guy, and I am sad to hear about his passing. I did a lot of work with the chairman of that committee, Senator Simon Randolph." Influence-peddling, really, but I sensed she knew about my role with the senator. Her husband was a patriot in the purest form, totally dedicated to protecting American values—very different from those of us who saw the system as a complex apparatus to achieve personal gain while pretending we cared about esoteric concepts like "values."

"He talked about you. You were the guy who was never on the payroll but had total access to the senator. Bill could tell that you were important to Senator Randolph and other senators. How does a young guy like that without a title or rank rise to such prominence, he would ask. You were an enigma to him. After he passed, I followed you in the news right up to the end of your plea deal."

It was clear that Tom hadn't just come out and told her about me. She went to him and asked.

"Working in the shadows was a big part of my game. I made things happen, but I was always behind the scenes. I was rarely on anyone's official meeting log."

"We will keep you behind the scenes in this situation too. Max Weber would have a field day if he knew we were paying the infamous Greg Smith to run the Mission's legal and public relations program."

"Wait a minute, Christine, I do not want to run anything, and I certainly don't want to be paid."

"Fair enough. A volunteer without a portfolio. And since I am their pro bono lawyer, this is an all-volunteer team."

I still wasn't sure what I had agreed to do, but I felt my juices—my sense of purpose—rising for the first time in ages. Other juices were flowing as well, but they remained undefined. As we put trays in the dish pit window, separating eating utensils, she turned to me.

"Have you ever walked through downtown Kelsey? Do you have time for a little stroll? I'd love to show you my hometown."

"That'd be great," I answered, wondering if I sounded like an eager schoolboy. "Invitation accepted."

We strode out of the Mission's front door to face a bright late-April sun and an unseasonably warm day. A tiny breeze blew east to west, providing a comfortable fan for those of us lucky enough to be outside.

"It's only a three-block walk from the Mission to the gentrified streets," Christine said as we crossed the bridge that separated the neighborhoods surrounding the old mill from the more modern downtown area. Beneath the bridge was the Kelsey River, occupied by several homeless encampments, including some housing families with young children. I easily discerned the contrast between the refurbished row houses and newly built condos and how we moved from crumbling, dilapidated buildings to apparent signs of renewal. Rising above the rebuilt, tree-lined street, we entered the visible signs of progress framed by a mini skyline of shiny new office buildings, many of them with restaurants, taverns, and shops on the ground floor. The traffic—foot, bike, and vehicle—gave this surging city a positive, robust feeling.

"The city leaders, including the dastardly Max Weber, have done a nice job with all of this," Christine commented, "but with progress comes even more homelessness, as people are forced out of their once affordable homes. As in Los Angeles, they'd all live on the sidewalks without the Mission. I don't know why the residents don't see our efforts as helping and not hurting them. By the way, have you seen our park? Do you still have time?"

"I'm unemployed. I have all the time in the world." And I certainly had time to spend with a beautiful, intelligent, poised woman with a positive and pleasant personality. Who could say no to that? "Lead on," I said agreeably.

I couldn't remember when I'd last strolled through a city. To me, cities were a necessary inconvenience. A place where Uber drivers raced me from one meeting to another, dodging traffic and stretching yellow lights to greens because I promised them a twenty-dollar tip if they got me there on time.

After several blocks, the entrance to the park stood directly across a busy intersection. Above the entrance rose a steel archway with engraved lettering: "Welcome to Kelsey War Memorial Park." *Which war? All of them?*

There was a brilliant oasis of groomed fields, a pavilion with a stage, and dozens of picnic tables with swing sets and slides rooted in play sand for the children. Off in the distance, I saw a public swimming pool and a miniature golf course. "It's beautiful," I said to Christine.

"Hey, Mom, what are you doing here?"

Surprised, I looked over as a boy charged forth from a group of twenty or so kids, all of them climbing over one of the jungle gyms and pushing each other on the swings, under the attentive watch of a young woman.

"Cody! I forgot your class was going to the park for Nature Day.

Hi, Miss Thompson," Christine greeted the teacher. Cody, who looked about nine, ran to his mother and jumped into her arms, receiving a vast and affectionate hug. I saw instantly that he was a perfect blend of his mom and dad, with a light-chocolate complexion and curly dark-blond hair that meandered over his ears. He looked like he could star on one of those Saturday-morning Disney shows. "Cody, this is Mr. Smith. He knew your dad."

"It is nice to meet you, Mr. Smith," he said and stuck out his hand, giving me a firm handshake.

"And you as well, Cody Culpepper," I said formally, impressed with his manners.

"Mr. Smith and I work together at the Mission."

"You must know Pastor Tom and my grandfather, too."

Quite the little conversationalist. "I sure do," I replied. "Pastor Tom and I were best friends when we were your age."

"Wow, that's eons ago."

Eons. Hmm. I couldn't argue with him.

CHAPTER NINE

After six months at the Mission, I had developed a knack for identifying new residents and guests. One morning, I noticed a stranger standing near the end of the unusually long line. Yet he looked familiar. His neat grooming and fresh clothes made him stand out. As he got closer, he never took his grim stare off me. I could not place him until he arrived at the serving window, practically nose-to-nose with me.

"Hello, Greg," he said with hard, cold eyes. "We have a few things to settle. You can find me in the warehouse, where I've been assigned to work. And if I were you, I wouldn't tell your buddy Tom we're acquainted. This is between you and me."

I stood frozen in place, unable to move or speak as Lamar Goodman strolled out the back door and across the alley to the warehouse.

"Hey, Brad, can a guy get a little breakfast around here?"

"Sorry about that, Miguel. You caught me in the middle of a deep thought," I laughed nervously, pretending to be cheerful. I scooped up some scrambled eggs and sausage and added a pancake before handing Miguel his tray. Thankfully, he was the last diner, getting in just before the 7:30 deadline. I turned off the light in the serving room, signifying that the breakfast hour was over.

Lamar Goodman—the former and now disgraced Illinois secretary of state—had been the odds-on favorite to become the state's next governor. A bare-knuckled politician who learned his trade on Chicago's rough streets and back rooms, Lamar had secured the anointing of his party bosses and appeared unstoppable. All of that came tumbling down, however, when Goodman was charged and convicted, along with three other coconspirators from Wisconsin and Pennsylvania, for executing an intricate plan to change the election results in their respective states. I paid Goodman two million dollars.

Of course, the rest is well documented. It was a lead story for weeks, not including the continued on-air speculation that the president was involved. My deal to provide a list of names to the feds for a lighter sentence in a minimum-security facility had made me a target for their revenge. And now that Goodman had been temporarily released, I was faced with a situation I had hoped would disappear. So much for hiding in a men's homeless shelter.

I would have to confront him.

• • •

My morning flight out of Nashville the following day on Southwest Airlines was scheduled to leave at eight. I almost missed it, delayed by a freeway accident that slowed three lanes into a virtual parking lot. By the time I sprinted to the gate, I had been relegated to a dreaded center seat in the last row on the plane. In my days as a million-miler, I would have never settled for coach class, or, for that matter, an airline that didn't reserve specific seats. But that was then, and this was now, an aspect of my new, more humble life.

It will be fine, I kept telling myself, wondering if I was experiencing first-class withdrawal. The flight to Dallas—surrounded by ordinary people looking for bargain-basement prices—would take only ninety minutes. One thing I'd learned in prison was to just let things happen. Of course, in prison, there is no other choice.

I traveled lightly, carrying only a small backpack with a mobile phone and laptop computer. I didn't need it for my meeting with Dan Johnson, but if delayed at the airport on my return trip later in the day,

I could work on some television scripts for the Mission's PR campaign. We were shooting the spots next week and still had work to do.

As much as I resisted playing a leadership role in the effort, I was now fully engaged, thanks to Tom's insistence and the encouragement of my new friend Christine Culpepper, whom I had been talking to at least twice a day. Although our discussions were strictly professional, focused mainly on the legal case and garnering public support for the Mission, I liked and admired her personally. I also knew that a man with a prison record would not likely fetch attention from such a decent woman. But she did suggest we have dinner soon at her house, which I reciprocated with an invite to see the houseboat, for her and Cody, but only after I had it looking nice.

When it came to dating, I was in uncharted territory.

When I finally sat down, my mobile phone buzzed with a text message from an unknown number: I'm sorry you didn't come over and talk yesterday. We still have some ground to cover. Maybe when you get back from Dallas? Make sure you say hello to Dan for me. You know where to find me.

I tried to put Lamar out of my head, but it wasn't easy. The fact that he knew my schedule and the person I was meeting was especially troubling. *Is there a mole at the Mission?* I wondered.

After arriving in Dallas, I grabbed an Uber and headed downtown. I had never flown into Love Field, so the journey was unfamiliar.

The corporate office for Rockwood Holdings occupied four levels of the Bank of America Plaza, which, at seventy-two floors, was the tallest building in Dallas. Located in the Main Street District, it symbolized gleaming success. If your company resided here, you had or appeared to have made it.

Dan had instructed me to meet him in his office on the sixty-second floor at noon. He informed me he would have lunch delivered.

On the way in, I reflected on how many times I had been to his office. At least a hundred visits, I figured. Dan's penchant for doing business in person, regardless of the time and expense it took to travel, was especially true regarding his extracurricular activities, such as working quietly behind the scenes to build his political empire. When you met him for the first time, it was easy to think of the iconic television character J. R. Ewing, from the television series *Dallas* back in the eighties, who is always in charge and scheming. If someone was crushed along the way, it was only the consequence of real life. He thrived on being able to call governors, senators, and presidents—not to mention a group of monarchs and emirs—and having his call returned within the hour. Two Supreme Court justices were also on his instant-call list. With his various super PACs—each with millions of dollars and thousands of wealthy donors he brought to the table—he wielded enormous power, the kind of clout that galvanized public support and influenced elections. Not surprisingly, his candidates usually won.

Like most successful self-made tycoons in the industry, Johnson also hired well, respecting the expertise of masters in their chosen fields. His award-winning international companies, specializing in building everything from towering office buildings to luxurious resorts, required that he retain the best architectural engineers, designers, and legal minds money could buy. This also required him to have the best political operatives. His nickname for me was "the Engineer" because I was his guy for engineering political deals and drawing up winning blueprints. Dan Johnson was the principal reason for my wealth. But now he owed me a favor, and he knew I was here to collect.

"Well, if it isn't the Engineer," he greeted me as his secretary escorted me into his enormous office. Dan met me halfway between the door and his desk with an extended handshake and a giant bear hug. "I missed you, my friend."

He said nothing about my long hair or casual attire—jeans and a light-blue T-shirt covered with a plaid sport coat, Sperry boat shoes with no socks. He had never seen me in anything but a suit and tie.

"Congrats on your early release. The president is taking a load of crap, but he did the right thing. How are you doing? Getting back into the game, I see."

Dan poured two neat Johnnie Walker Blue Label glasses and handed one to me. The open bar in his office was a throwback to the belief that business with a buzz went smoother.

"It's good to see you too, Dan. It has been a while. Thank you for making the time for me." Like a rushing river, I recalled what the two of us had once created, mostly with ideas and schemes developed right here in this office. We were the perfect political duo. I implemented it, and he wrote the checks. Big checks. "Money is the mother milk of politics," he would often say, quoting the iconic Jesse Unruh, former Speaker of the House in the California State Legislature, also known as "Big Daddy." The nickname would have suited Dan as well.

"I always have time for you, Greg. We've been through many battles together. I will forever be in your debt for what you did." Dan was making this easy by acknowledging the outstanding bill for services rendered. "What can I do for you? Put you on the payroll, hire you again as a consultant? Just name it."

How to put a price on what I did for this man? Putting his name on the list I had given the feds would have sent him to prison for a decade or more, not to mention dragging his son, Congressman Andrew Johnson, down with him and ending what party leaders saw as an eventual path to the White House. Dan owed me more than a few bucks or an employment contract.

As two male servers in black suits presented our steak lunch with all the trimmings and a bottle of red wine with a label I didn't recognize, I momentarily busied myself with my napkin and moved my seat closer to the small table. We were stationed near the large window overlooking the busy Dallas metro area.

"I'm not interested in your money, Dan. Thanks to the obnoxious fees I charged you and my other clients, I have made more than I need for a good life."

Despite my crimes and the fines that came with them, I had also earned a healthy amount of clean money. Unethical, one could argue, but legal.

"You want something, don't you, Greg? A dealmaker like you doesn't just go away. It's in your DNA. So, tell me, what's the deal?"

Dan Johnson was the *only* name I left off the FBI list.

• • •

The flight back to Nashville was mercifully unlike the one earlier in the day. I arrived at Love Field in time to be the first on board with a choice of front aisle seats. After takeoff, with a vodka and soda securely in my grasp, I glanced at the middle-aged man seated by the window, an empty seat between us. He was reading a *New York Times* article about the president's falling poll numbers. PRESIDENT CONTINUES TO DEFEND PARDON OF WASHINGTON DEALMAKER, the headline read. Next to the article was a picture of me, looking clean-cut and shaven, a far cry from the image I now touted. As insurance against possible recognition, I reached into my backpack and pulled out my coveted Yankees hat. Much to my relief, the disguise worked on my row-mate, assisted by both of us taking hour-long naps as we winged toward Nashville.

I felt terrible for the president, having to suffer the wrath of so many, at least in part because he got me out of jail. Current polls indicated that only 28 percent of voters were satisfied with his presidency. "Be mad at me, not him," I wanted to scream.

While Jesus might forgive, Americans—including those who love Jesus—could be unforgiving. Were the president's poll ratings all my fault? No. Inflation and unemployment were high, suggesting a recession was approaching. The cultural wars that had dominated the nation's politics for years continued to burn, and tensions with China were at an all-time high. There was much to be angry about in today's America. My pardon was just one item on the list.

I also found myself thinking about Dan Johnson. The select few who knew the whole story had asked me why I spared him. On this topic, I was clearheaded. Dan Johnson went forward with the plan because I convinced him we wouldn't be caught. He was reluctant not because he was afraid but because it was wrong. Yes, pushing the rules to their shady edges was his custom. But crossing those lines was rare. I talked him into bankrolling our ill-begotten scheme, and while he was technically as guilty as the rest of us, he didn't plot or execute it. I asked myself a thousand times whether that was justification or rationalizing. I knew the answer.

When we touched down at precisely nine o'clock, I joined eighty or so other passengers in reaching for our mobile phones. Three urgent text messages from Christine instantly appeared on my screen: CALL ME. IT'S IMPORTANT, the first read. The second, WHERE ARE YOU? YOU MUST NOT BE HOME YET. WE NEED TO TALK. But the third text explained her heightened anxiousness: THE JUDGE REFUSED TO OVERTURN THE COUNCIL. INSTEAD, HE'S SAYING THE PEOPLE SHOULD DECIDE. HE'S ORDERING A VOTER REFERENDUM. I HOPE YOU HAD A GOOD TRIP.

I immediately responded. I'M NOT SURPRISED. THIS IS A SAFE ROAD FOR HIM. HALF THE CITY WOULD BE ANGRY WITH HIM REGARDLESS OF HOW HE RULED. LET'S MEET AT THE MISSION TOMORROW MORNING AT NINE, AFTER BREAKFAST. MAKE SURE TOM AND YOUR DAD CAN JOIN US. P.S. I MISSED YOU TODAY.

It suddenly felt like the old days. I'd flown off to Dallas in the morning for some dealmaking and returned quickly that night, only to face another crisis and a next-day emergency meeting to plan a response. And that didn't count the stress of knowing Lamar Goodman was now a resident at the Mission. Did I not leave that pressurized world behind in favor of a peaceful retreat on a houseboat and a search for inner peace? Or was I so addicted to the adrenaline of my old life that there was no antidote? Not even Jesus—whom I had casually asked to help me—seemed willing to explain it to me.

Or did my loyalty to Tom drive me? I suppose both explanations deserved a hearing, but something bigger was pushing me forward.

As I drove home from the airport, I remembered that I was due tomorrow morning at six to help prepare and serve breakfast. That's when my "awareness rush"—as I liked to call "aha" moments—hit me. I began to see them in my mind, one by one: the tired, weathered faces I would meet at the serving window tomorrow morning. Men who had turned left when they might have turned right. Guys who zigged instead of zagged. Veterans who protected our freedoms and came home with PTS or got hooked on opioids supplied by drugmakers who were happy to meet the demand. These were the men my best friend had been fighting for all his life. I wanted it to be my fight too.

My phone buzzed again with a text. I MISSED YOU TOO.

CHAPTER TEN

By the time I arrived at 6:15, Mike had already put the bacon and sausage in the oven to bake and was mixing up a massive drum of pancake batter. "Hey, Brad, can you make the eggs this morning? They were cracked last night, so you just need to pour them on the griddle."

"Got you covered, chief." I was struggling to tie my apron string behind my back when Jimmy walked out of the dish pit—the small, contained area where the dishes were washed—and completed the task for me. Through the open serving window, I saw that the cafeteria area had already begun to stir, with guys slowly making their way from the bunks into the cafeteria. "Thank you, Jimmy. You are a true gentleman."

"Nope, I didn't want to get stuck doing eggs," he chuckled. "And I know you won't do it unless you have your apron on."

Tom burst through the kitchen's back door, eager to get the lowdown. "How was your trip?"

"Not sure yet."

I wasn't being coy with my old pal. The truth was that nothing Dan and I had discussed was final, although we agreed in principle to work on a creative solution.

"Dan is very hands-on with Rockwood's efforts in Kelsey and has a personal interest in its success. He'd like to wrap up the acquisition and move forward this year." I held back from Tom the one thing I knew: Dan Johnson wanted his "Greg Smith problem" to go away, which meant settling up. I had offered my terms. The rest was up to him.

"That sounds good. I'll see you at the meeting at nine. By the way, you're doing an excellent job on those eggs. You could do this professionally."

"I am happy you finally realized how valuable I am to your Mission. Now, if you don't mind, get out of my kitchen before I have you thrown out."

He humored me by faking a jogging motion as he exited.

The breakfast window opened promptly at seven with about thirty guys in line. The first ten minutes were always the busiest. I looked for Goodman, but he had not yet appeared in the cafeteria. However, I noticed a gathering of well-dressed men and women at the front door, each personally greeted by Tom. Among them was Christine, who, after giving Tom a polite hug, walked across the busy cafeteria toward me at the window.

"Good morning, Counselor. May I scoop you up a warm breakfast? I made it myself."

"I would have loved that, but I had chocolate pancakes with happy faces this morning with my favorite little man. Rain check?"

"You can come anytime. Just make sure it's a Tuesday or Thursday."

Her wide smile was infectious, as was her friendly, energetic demeanor. She played several parts: ordained pastor, savvy lawyer, single mother, and widow of a combat hero. I was impressed by how she gracefully moved from one role to another.

"Why are all the people in fancy clothes here?"

"Tom called the Mission's board of directors for an emergency meeting to brief them on our legal situation and get their thoughts on how we proceed. After this, we'll meet with Tom and Dad to discuss legal and campaign strategy in more detail. We want the board members to stay invested. You can sit in if you want, but I'll cover the same material in our smaller meeting."

"Sounds good. I might drop by briefly and slip into the back."

When I arrived at the emergency meeting, Tom was finishing a prayer and introducing Christine. Never a huge fan of public praying, I was okay missing the first part. Christine stepped up to the small podium in front of about ten rows of seats ten across. They were half filled, and I wondered why the Mission had so many people on its board of directors. "The board is large because we depend so heavily on the generosity of others. The more generous people we have, the better," Tom explained later when I asked.

I also learned that about half of the members were ordained ministers from all faiths, including a Catholic priest and a Jewish rabbi. The other half were business owners and executives. "The bottom line is that the board's makeup is whomever Doug asks, and Mr. Pollard can be very persuasive," Tom said.

As promised, I sat in the back, undoubtedly the biggest sinner amid this holy gathering.

"Good morning, everyone," Christine began. "Thank you for coming out this morning on such short notice." The beam of light from above highlighted every strand of Christine's dark hair, giving it a glowing, angelic look. "We had quite a day in court yesterday," she continued.

Christine explained that Max Weber's attorney had asked the court to stop further expansion of the Mission at its current location. "They brought in an economist to testify that so-called homeless shelters inevitably bring property values down and deter businesses from wanting to invest," she informed the group. "Of course, I asked him if he had ever been to our mission, and he said he had not." She paused for effect. "I hope you don't mind that I invited him for lunch."

The audience loudly applauded, knowing that his acceptance was unlikely.

She led them through the process, eventually arriving at her conclusion. "In the end, the judge showed compassion for our cause and the plight of the homeless, in general. But he considers this a political matter, not a legal one, and therefore ruled that it should be decided by a vote of the people in a citywide referendum."

"Does that mean construction is now halted?" Doug asked.

"Leave it to my father to ask the pertinent questions." Christine smiled as she responded, indicating this was only a bump in the road, not a catastrophe. "Yes, for now. We will have to pause construction and turn our attention to public support, which we have already begun with our PR campaign. We will need all of your help as we directly appeal to the goodness of our city residents to support our wonderful mission."

She was the forever optimist, refusing to consider the nature of gullible voters who would be persuaded by a fear-based campaign against vagrant street people like those who populated the corner of Fourteenth and Mill Streets. I imagined the thirty-second commercials I could have created on that mandate.

"The election will be in November," Christine concluded, "so we must organize quickly and begin raising money for TV and internet advertising, campaign staff, and printed materials like signs and brochures. God bless you all. Let's get this job done."

She was met with a chorus of "amens" and applause. I suddenly felt like I had attended a revival, not a legal briefing, and that was before the hugging began. When she looked to the back of the room and spotted me with her penetrating eyes, I gave her a thumbs-up.

I quietly exited the chapel and headed down the wide hallway toward Tom's conference room. When Tom, Christine, and Doug arrived, I had already pulled up a chair to the center of the table along with Mark Stone, who had established himself as part of the core campaign team. Mark sat across from me, each of us sipping our bottled water.

"Good briefing," I said to the trio as they entered. "They seem energized."

"Thank you, my friend," Tom answered. "Christine did an excellent job, as always. Greg, do you think you have enough information on what's going on to give us direction? We could use your insight." By now, I had dropped Brad as a first name with those in Tom's inner circle. Using a different name had grown tiresome and useless, if not dishonest.

As each sat around the table, I gathered my initial thoughts.

"I think that going into this, they have a better chance to win a public referendum than we do," I began, knowing that was the thing they did not want to hear. "Kelsey is a wealthy, conservative city, so spreading voter fear won't be hard. Nor will voters think it is fair that a bunch of homeless men should have the right to prevent the mill from becoming a beautiful resort and an economic engine for improving the downtown area."

"It's funny, isn't it?" Doug added. "Everyone will say that a homeless center is good, but no one wants it in the center of town or their neighborhood. We've been fighting this battle since the beginning."

"The only play we have, as I see it," I said, "is to 'humanize' the residents. Let's introduce them and let them tell their stories. Present them as real people and not as a social or economic nuisance. If voters can see these men as we do—hardworking, diligent, patriotic, and honest—then we might have a chance to get voters to think with their hearts instead of their wallets or their biases.

"We need to appeal to the goodness that most people have inside them, regardless of their political leanings. Tom's ambassador committee, which consists of ten selected residents, can play a significant role in the campaign. We can put them through some speech training and send them out to speak in churches and service clubs. Our very capable Mark Stone would be the ideal leader of this group. They trust him."

Mark raised his eyebrow at me. My recommendation was news to him.

I paused to take the room's temperature and ensure I had their attention. Advising a group of leaders on running a compassionate campaign that could help real people was new ground for me. Other than Liz's first campaign eighteen years ago, my clients had been more like Max Weber than Tom Garrity, unapologetically conservative and pro-business, and usually helpful only to those who got tax breaks or investment incentives.

"As Christine told the board of directors, we must run a smart, well-organized campaign. We'll start with a website and go from there, but we'll also move quickly to build our social media platforms. All of this will be driven by our overall campaign theme, 'A City with a Mission.'"

Tom raised his hand. "This sounds great, Greg, but how will we pay for it? Ads are expensive."

Yes, the money question. It always seems to follow the "good idea" presentation. I thought back to the multimillion-dollar campaigns I had run in the past and funded with wealthy donors and rich super PACs, most of it taking the political world's most advanced lawyers to skirt around the edges of legality so that no one went to prison. That is, until some of us went too far and broke the law. No one would violate the law in this campaign, but the pillars of financing a successful campaign remained the same.

But this felt different. It wasn't about me or what influence or power I could gain. This was bigger. More urgent. This wealthy nation was ignoring one of its most embarrassing flaws, and here, in a small city in Tennessee—part of the old South—we would display to the nation that homelessness was a problem we all owned and had to solve. I thought of the dozens of times I had walked past a homeless person sleeping in the doorway of a building and ignored their pleas for food or money.

"I've talked to Doug, and he has agreed to head up a fundraising committee of local businesses for larger donations while going to the pews of every church in the city for smaller contributions. Meanwhile, I will approach some national groups to gauge their interest in investing in our efforts. Liz will also help activate her network. As you know, your sister is chairing the subcommittee trying to pass the American Homelessness Act and will hold hearings later this year, so her ability to reach the right people is honed. By the way, Mark has completed all the paperwork necessary to file a legal campaign with the state's secretary of state office."

No sooner had I answered Tom's funding question than Christine walked over to the window looking out on the crumbling mill property across the way.

"What is going on outside?" she asked mildly. "I'm counting three TV trucks, reporters and camera crews for each. Who sent out the press release? I thought we decided to lay low on this until we had a plan of action."

"I got a few calls from reporters early this morning and agreed to some interviews, but not until after ten," Tom confessed. "I couldn't tell them no. It would have looked like I was dodging. I apologize for not telling you."

"You did the right thing to accept, Tom," I offered.

I was interested in what he would say but knew my media-savvy friend would be fine. Tom believed correctly that this could have all been avoided with a judge courageous enough to do the right thing and disregard Weber's request. But courage is often in short supply when defending people without homes.

We watched him walk confidently out the front door, where we had gone to stand, signaling with his hands to the assembled reporters and camera crews to gather for an impromptu press conference.

"Nice to see you all here this morning," he greeted them. At six foot two and slightly over 200 pounds, barrel-chested with a head of thick graying hair, Tom looked and acted like a man in charge. "I am assuming you are all here to get the Kelsey Rescue Mission's take on yesterday's court decision that our intention to expand capacity will require a voter referendum. We welcome having a ballot measure on this issue and intend to wage an all-out campaign. We trust the people of Kelsey to make the right decision. Now I would be happy to answer any questions."

CHAPTER ELEVEN

The shovel was intended to strike my head. Had the blow landed, it would have been lights out for sure, maybe to an early grave. My assailant popped out from behind one of the metal shelving units lined up in rows along one side of the Mission's giant warehouse, giving me no time to do anything but flinch and take a half step to my left.

The half step saved me. Or, more accurately, the puddle of motor oil I stepped into saved me. By the grace of God—yes, I gave Him credit—I slipped and fell in the grease, thus avoiding the crack of cold steel against my skull. At that exact moment, I let out the loudest plea of my life.

"Help me! Help, someone! Someone is trying to kill me! Help!"

It sounded like an army thundering toward me as the warehouse workers came running en masse. Alvarez, a young Hispanic man I had just met that morning, was the first to arrive.

"Mr. Brad, are you okay? What happened?"

"Someone swung a shovel at my head, and then I slipped on the oil spot," I yelled out. "Where the hell is he?" Still lying on the concrete floor next to the shovel, dirty oil and grease splattering my sweatshirt, jeans, and sneakers, I craned my neck to look behind me. The back door that was usually closed was wide open, revealing a ray of sunshine at the otherwise dimly lit rear of the warehouse where Lamar Goodman worked stocking shelves. It had been several days since our encounter at the serving window.

I shouted to the others, "He got out the back door. Quick, someone run after him!"

Several resident workers sprinted out the door and down the alley, searching. They saw no one.

I had not seen his face to be certain, but if the assailant was Goodman, he most likely knew where I lived. *What's next, a sinking houseboat?* I needed to speak with Liz, the person I trusted most in a crisis.

Answering my call on a single ring, she was the proper antidote for my frightened state. I called her later from the interstate as I sweated in the cab of my aging pickup. The air-conditioning wasn't working.

"What's up with my favorite homelessness advocate?"

I got right to the point, bypassing pleasantries. "Someone tried to kill me this morning, and I have a strong hunch it was Lamar Goodman."

"What? He tried to kill you. How?"

"With a shovel to my head in the warehouse," I said, sounding like I was playing the board game Clue.

"Holy shit, Greg. Are you okay? Please tell me you're okay." I could tell she was choking up.

I explained the whole story about how he had shown up as a resident at the Mission two days ago, said threatening things to me, and told me he was assigned to the warehouse. I ended with his fortunate swing and miss.

"I'm not sure where I want to go with this," I confessed. "I'm worried that if I tell Tom, he'll put the Mission on lockdown, and I don't want to be the reason a hundred guys can't go in and out."

"Most people who are almost killed go to the police. Have you considered that?" she asked cuttingly.

"I hear you, but it would instantly become a news story, and I don't want the attention. This is between Lamar and me, not the world."

"The hell it's only between you and him," Liz snapped. "Go tell our daughter that a vengeful asshole from Chicago is trying to kill her father and that it's only between you and him. Or tell Tom, who loves you with all his being, that this doesn't affect him. For that matter, how about me? We might not be together anymore, but I'm not ready to lose you. How dare you, Gregory Bradley Smith, be a narcissist at a time like this? This is about all of us who love you."

I had lit her fuse, but I needed to hear her. I'd known she wouldn't sugarcoat a difficult situation like this. Elizabeth Smith, my estranged soon-to-be ex-wife, was now in her ninth term in Congress. Despite our marital complexities, she and I had been best friends for too long. The reason we opted for legal separation and not divorce was that managing our daughter's young life and our assets was smoother as a legally married twosome. That we thoroughly trusted one another was the key to our unusual arrangement, although I wasn't sure how her new "friend" would feel about our closeness.

"You are correct. This is bigger than a barroom brawl, and I appreciate you calling me out on it." I paused for a second before continuing. "But for now, at least, I am not going to the police and making this a news story. The FBI told me they would do all they could to protect me and my family if Lamar was released. At this point, I am choosing to believe them."

"I'll call the FBI director and ask him to look into it. If Lamar Goodman did this, he's an idiot. And when he slips up, he'll return to jail for a long time," Liz responded. "Hey, bud, is it my turn? I have something I wanted to bring up as well."

"Sure, what's up?" I hadn't seen Liz since her Christmas visit to the prison, although we spent a couple of minutes on the telephone every week or so to catch up. She rarely asked for my advice on congressional stuff, and I offered it even more rarely.

"Let me get right to the point. Were you meeting with Dan Johnson in Dallas yesterday?"

Her question stunned me. Tom and the working-group members at the Mission were the only ones who knew I had visited Dan, although they had no clue about the nature of our relationship.

"Did Tom tell you that?"

"No, Tom and I haven't talked in over a month. But I will take your answer as a yes, and you were indeed in Dallas yesterday. Why in the hell are you with guys that could put you right back in jail?"

"I'm trying to get him to give a billion dollars to help the homeless."

"What? Did Dan Johnson have a soul transplant? Or did you, for that matter?"

"Liz, how did you know I was there? Am I being followed?"

"No, you are not being followed. The FBI has eyes and ears on Johnson. That's how they flagged your visit. I serve on the Crime and Federal Government Surveillance subcommittee and speak to the FBI director regularly. He called me this morning to tell me."

"What are they after?"

"I do not know and couldn't tell you even if I did. Look, Greg, I don't trust Johnson. I will never understand why you protected him. Just believe me when I say Dan Johnson isn't the kind of man who likes owing people, and that alone could make you a target. He is talking to someone in Kelsey about buying a lot of land to develop. Promise me you'll be careful. No more visits."

"Okay. Message received."

"Got to go. Give Tom and Jane my love."

Our call ended as I was pulling into the parking lot adjacent to the Nashville Marina, which held, among its ten wooden docks, the two docks where ten live-aboard houseboats were tied up, no two of them alike. We were like a small neighborhood—a cul-de-sac—living only feet apart but respecting one another's privacy. I had met my neighbors in all nine of the other boats. Six housed retired married couples, including a lesbian couple; one belonged to a single middle-aged man who was a real estate lawyer; there was a young millennial couple, both high school teachers; and then there was Joey Martino, the marina's owner.

The other docks were spread downriver across the marina, with sixteen slips on each. The slips were a hundred percent filled with a wide array of vessels, primarily cruisers and runabouts owned by individual boaters, with a dozen others held by the marina as public rentals.

I looked up at the clear night sky with its quarter moon above the glistening high-rises of Nashville reflecting on the water. Although it was a beautiful picture, I hadn't decided whether to stay at the marina long-term. My initial plan was for something a little more remote, but I jumped on it when this twenty-year-old Trifecta came on the market. This happened to be its docking place. I figured it was also a blessing most days to get out of Kelsey and away from the Mission, retreating to a larger city where blending into the crowd was oddly comforting. The truth? I was on a journey with no destination. A quasi-wealthy forty-eight-year-old ex-con barred from practicing law, now living incognito, and my only plan was to lay a new floor on my floating home and hang out part-time with homeless men. Now I was dodging swinging shovels in the warehouse. It was hardly the peaceful life I had envisioned.

Entering the boat through the sliding door on the side, I headed directly to the liquor cabinet, poured a scotch over ice, opened the sliding doors out to the front patio, and found my most comfortable padded chair.

Had I walked into a dangerous situation when I arranged a meeting with Dan Johnson? The thought haunted me. It was no secret that Dan stopped at nothing to get his way and that anyone who blocked him was subject to his wrath. But was I blocking him from anything? I didn't think so. He flat-out asked me to rejoin him as his "political guy," an invitation I politely declined. Dan would have paid me any amount I asked—not because I was worth it but because he could have controlled me. The way he did all his employees and contractors and the way he tried with his son, Andrew, the only person I knew who wasn't afraid of him.

But I was finished with Dan's world. I would never again be a political gun for hire. Or a dealmaker who peddled access to the powerful for more money than a surgeon would make for saving a child's life. The only thing I wanted from Dan Johnson was for him to help the Kelsey Rescue Mission provide hope to good men with bad breaks. "Well, Greg, let me think about it. I'll get back to you on all of this" was as far as he would go. Liz was right. Johnson couldn't stand the thought of owing someone, especially when they tried to collect.

At eleven o'clock, I received a call from an unknown number. The number had a Kelsey prefix but was unfamiliar, so I let it go to my cheerful but brief message: "Hi, it's me. I can't reach the phone now, so please leave a message, and I'll call you back. Thanks."

The message was equally cheerful. "Hello, Greg—or Brad, as you go by these days. This is Carl Noland, a reporter with WKRN-TV. I saw you at the Kelsey Rescue Mission today. I wasn't sure it was you at first. But later in the day, it came to me. I met you once when you spoke at the National Press Foundation annual meeting about fifteen years ago. I'm not doing a story on you, at least not now, so don't worry. I want to connect and have coffee sometime. Thanks. My apologies if I am intruding. If you want to call or text me back, this is my cell phone."

I thought about the people who had my new number: Liz and Sydney, of course, along with Tom and Jane. Christine also had it, as did my attorney and accountant, who lived in Washington. At the dock, Joey Martino was strictly instructed not to share it. I had a landline on board—an internet line—that I used for all purposes, including callouts.

Then I remembered one more person I had given it to: Dan Johnson.

CHAPTER TWELVE

"My daughter is driving down this weekend from college with her boyfriend, and Tom and Jane, otherwise known as Sydney's uncle and aunt, are joining us for a waterfront cookout on Saturday night," I explained to Christine during our call, which had become the official start of my mornings. Days rarely went by that we did not see one another, and I now kept one of my bicycles in her garage for our rides along the Kelsey bike trail. The week before, we'd made it down to the annual county fair for most of the afternoon and evening. Cody, who was always with us or nearby, had an entry in the art contest, a watercolor painting of his late father, which won a red ribbon for second place.

"Would you and Cody like to join us? No business, I promise. Just a nice time on the houseboat."

"I would love to join you, but beware, Cody will have a million questions about the boat, including why you live on one." She didn't even hesitate, which I took as good news.

"Oh yeah, I'm sure he will," I said with a laugh.

"Is there anything I can bring—a salad, wine, or whatever?"

"Hmmm, a salad would be nice. I usually forget to make one."

"That will be no problem. A salad it is. Sydney goes to West Virginia University, right?"

"Yes. She just turned twenty-two and graduates next month with a degree in sociology. She wants to be a therapist for disadvantaged children. I would say that Syd is a typical only child, a little spoiled and much loved by us. She started at the University of Maryland but transferred to be near me while I was in prison in Morgantown," I couldn't help gushing, reminding Christine once again of my ex-con past.

"What a great role model she has had for a mother. I have a lot of respect for Elizabeth Smith and what she has done in Congress."

I could tell Christine was a true admirer and not just saying it because it might sound good. Regarding role models for Sydney, Liz was the clear parental winner. However, if we measured which parent stood in the rain for the most soccer practices, attended more school plays, and made a million pigtails, I'm sure I earned that trophy. Sydney was the only thing I had done right in my life until I started at the Mission. My staff and clients knew my calendar was built around Sydney's schedule, even when it meant chartering a private jet to get home, which I did on two occasions. I once put the president on hold to take a call from my daughter. She was in the eighth grade.

That was the agreement Liz and I made when Sydney was born. As a member of Congress, Liz rarely had the luxury of moving her schedule around to accommodate her personal life as I did.

"A girl could not have a better mom to look up to. Sydney is fortunate in that way. Regardless of who influenced her, Liz and I are immensely proud of our daughter, just as I'm sure you will be of Cody."

We agreed that she and her son would arrive at the houseboat at five o'clock on Saturday, the same time as Tom and Jane. Sydney and her boyfriend were due around noon and would want to tan on the top deck and maybe take the kayaks out, so it seemed like perfect timing for a lovely evening, including a cruise if everyone was up for it.

I had not met Sydney's boyfriend and honestly wished he weren't coming. She'd had several beaus in her high school years, and I didn't recall liking any of them. Fortunately, she didn't keep a guy for long before they ended up in "the Sydney Swamp," as Liz called the place where discarded hopefuls went when their round was complete, and the trend had apparently continued in college.

"When is your best time to get together and start mapping out this campaign?" Christine asked. "I can make it work anytime this week during the day."

"Tomorrow after my Thursday kitchen shift is best on my end. I'm planning to work on the boat today and Friday, and I'll need every bit of two days to prepare for my first guests on Saturday. I have to lay an entire floor with teak planks."

"I didn't know you were such a handyman. I pictured you with a fancy suit, a briefcase, and a large vocabulary."

"Well, my dad taught me some things, like how to measure properly and handle a saw, but truthfully, I did a lot of fixing in prison. I was on the repair crew. And as luck would have it, we once laid a new floor for the warden's office. I learned by watching and doing, I guess." *Another prison reference. I really must stop.*

• • •

I had stripped the floor of the worn carpet the week before, so today's task was to cut and place the new planks delivered near the dock entrance. Luckily the weather was set to be comfortable and dry, with a temperature of seventy-two.

My houseboat occupied the last of five boat slips on dock A, resulting in a thirty-yard walk down to my entrance. Wheelbarrowing the planks would require about twenty round trips. I made a mental note to stock up on Tylenol the next time I was out, for the backache I would inevitably own by the end of the day. I had rented a table saw that I placed on top of a makeshift worktable on the dock, from which I would cut each carefully measured plank to the appropriate size. Of course, in my former life, one which seemed to have permanently faded in my rearview mirror, all of this would have been done by workmen charging exorbitant labor fees. Yesterday, I was peeling carrots in the kitchen of a men's shelter. Today I was sawing floor planks. And I was loving every minute.

Yet last night's call from the reporter, preceded by Liz's ominous warning about Dan Johnson, had unnerved me. As much as I was focused on my flooring project, I could not shake the worry that I had walked into something contrary to my goal of a simple, autonomous life. I even said a little silent prayer—something like "Please, God, keep me out of this shit"—as I went about my measuring tasks. I was being drawn back into the daily drama of conflict and consequences, once my "drugs" of choice. "You like the game too much to give it up," Johnson had goaded me during our meeting. "Besides, you're good at it, the best I know. There's no way you can walk away."

I turned on the news that morning just in time to see Carl Noland do his report from the Mission the day before. I was familiar with his face, although I hadn't recalled his name last night. I knew him only as a handsome guy in his mid-thirties with blond hair and bright white teeth.

"Yesterday's ruling by Judge Swanson places an essential question to Kelsey voters: Can a special interest prevent, or even stop, the kind of progress and urban renewal that many consider vital for the city's future? One thing is certain. It will be exciting to see how this David versus Goliath battle develops. Reporting from the Kelsey Rescue Mission, I'm Carl Noland."

The subtle power of the media at work. It's not so much what they say but rather how the question is formed, in this case presenting the dichotomy as progress that benefited all or just a few, especially when the "few" were a bunch of faceless men without homes.

He had a point, but many men whose lives were turned around at the Mission were not losers. If they had the chance, they could be as vital to the city's future as anyone. Seeing both sides of an issue was always a strength of mine, which freed me to work for the side that either asked first or paid the most and not necessarily in that order. The difference now was that I no longer had skin in the game, except for my emotional attachment to the Mission.

My offer to Dan Johnson that this could be a win-win situation for all involved remained pending, reminding me to think again of my real annoyance: *How did Noland get my number?* Did he know of my meeting with Johnson? I decided to send him a text asking him to coffee.

By the day's end, I was exhausted, but in a positive way. The floor was solidly laid with only minor issues around the edges that would be unnoticeable to anyone but me. And to my surprise, it looked fabulous. The last time I'd experienced that kind of personal satisfaction was after building a treehouse for Sydney on her tenth birthday.

"Hey, Brad, let me check out this floor."

It was Joey, the only one who didn't bother with the familiar boating etiquette of "Permission to come aboard."

"Wow, this is great. Nicely done. When you get a day, you can come over and do mine," he laughed.

"I appreciate that. Thanks. That old carpet was as old as the boat, I'm sure. The whole place smells fresher."

No sooner had Joey stepped off the boat and onto the dock below than I felt the vibration of my phone buried deep in my left front pocket. When I pulled it out, the text message on the screen read, Look forward to meeting up. Coffee Roaster on Third Street Monday morning? Is 8 ok? I replied with a thumbs-up, congratulating myself on getting hip with text lingo.

I spent the early evening sweeping up my dust and the mess I had made on the dock, requiring another ten or so round trips up and down the dock to the trash bin. I thought about calling Christine but chose Mark Stone instead, asking him to bring the ambassadors in for a meeting tomorrow at noon. That would give Christine, Tom, Doug, Mark, and me a chance to spend an hour together. I had an idea that I wanted to share with them.

• • •

The line for breakfast the following day had already started forming by the time I arrived shortly before seven. I immediately donned one of the old aprons hanging in the food pantry and started moving the plastic serving trays filled to the brim with the usual fare from the kitchen to the window area.

"Georgie Porgy," I greeted the first customer, "did you spend the night down here just to get the first position?"

Georgie, a short, bald, and cheerful man of Greek descent, replied with his usual good humor. "No sir, Mr. Brad, I came early to make sure you remembered that we have an appointment this afternoon for a mock interview."

I had not remembered, but I wouldn't let Georgie know that.

"I do remember, my friend. What time is good for you?"

"My Greek father would always say, 'Let's do it in Kairos time,' meaning the time that offers the best opportunity. It was Plato who originally produced the concept."

"I don't know much about Plato," I confessed, "but how does three o'clock in the study room sound?"

After the serving window closed, I scooped up a plate of eggs and pancakes for myself and joined Mike at the nearest table to the kitchen in the cafeteria. "Good morning, Bradley. Nice you could join the plebeians today."

"Hey, I'm the plebe. You're management."

My retort had the others at the table in stitches, one of them being Michael Forbes, a Black man about my age but better looking and in far better shape. Like retired Marines everywhere, Michael stayed true to his regimen of physical workouts and a healthy diet. He had been a resident of the Mission for six months and had recently started a new job operating a robotic machine at Cavalier Industries, an international manufacturing plant located twenty miles out of Kelsey. Tom had visited his friends at Cavalier and lobbied for

Michael to enter their training program. "If he can drive a tank, he can certainly work any machine you have in this place," he pleaded. Tom didn't mention that he had sent Michael to rehab twice for alcohol addiction.

"Don't forget about our meeting at noon," I reminded Mike and Michael. Both were on the ambassadors committee.

"What is that all about, anyway?" Mike asked in a tone suggesting annoyance that he had been invited to a meeting that he wasn't running and didn't know the purpose of. Funny how those were the two things that had bugged me the most in my old days. I had little time and zero patience for not being in control unless it came to Sydney, where no concern or interruption was too small. "I just got a note from Mark that said we're having a meeting," Mike added. "No details were given."

"I promise it won't be a waste of time," I told him. "I need you there, so thanks in advance. It's about the campaign to expand the Mission."

Before that meeting, however, I had to go to the first meeting, which reminded me again of my old life, which was one boring meeting after another. But these were different. It was amazing how liberating it was to work as a volunteer without expecting compensation—though I did bag a dozen leftover all-beef wieners and hot dog buns to cook on my grill that weekend, along with a large box of BBQ potato chips.

Despite it being ten minutes past ten, the meeting started promptly when Tom arrived, asking us, as usual, to bow our heads in prayer.

"We thank you, dear Lord, for your blessings, especially the work you have us do here at the Mission. Please be with us as we prepare to do right by your people. Amen." Separate amens were uttered around the table from the meeting attendees—Christine, Doug, Mark, and me. My amen was quieter than the others, but I figured Jesus is good at reading lips.

"Folks, it looks like we have a campaign on our hands, and I can think of no better team to lead us than those present today," Tom began. "Each of you has a vital role, but we will only finish if we work together. Christine has briefed us well and will continue to guide the legal end. Mark will be our liaison to the ambassadors committee and the residents in general, while Doug will head up the fundraising end of the campaign. I will manage outreach to the churches and the city's community."

When Tom paused, I could tell he hadn't entirely formulated how to explain my role, one we had talked about privately since the court ruling.

"And that leaves Greg, who will be our consultant and adviser."

With all eyes turned on me, I began to explain my initial thoughts on what we were up against and the challenges we would face. "As I said during the last meeting, the key to our chances of winning is making the residents of this Mission real people and not a bunch of vagabonds and criminals. We will do this mostly by using online and local TV videos. Our guys will tell their stories to the people of Kelsey, hoping voters will agree that all people deserve a second chance."

Christine reintroduced the subject of financial concerns. "Greg, we all know that you were once a high-powered campaign consultant who created million-dollar TV ads. But surely we can't afford to hire a professional production team."

I nodded. "The good news is that we have a professional team in the building. Mark Stone has overseen advertising buys for two large corporations during his career, so he knows what programs to buy to reach the best and largest audience. We also have a top-notch camera and audio operator and a website developer who have completed rehab programs and been sober for several months. They want to be part of the campaign, especially if it gets them out of doing laundry and mopping floors."

The last line brought laughter and helped to lighten the mood. I heard myself getting excited like I had as a young, eager campaign volunteer working to pass a measure to increase funding for early childhood education in Buffalo. Later came Liz's first campaign, another memory of how democracy could work for the good of all of us.

"Will you stay and direct the campaign, especially the media part? I know nothing about that stuff," Christine asked in her familiar, straightforward manner. No wonder she admired Congresswoman Smith. They shared many of the same traits.

As Christine and I had increased our time together, not just at the Mission but also sharing lunch at nearby cafés or talking over a glass of wine after work, we had begun to turn down the volume on "Mission talk" and instead share the details of our lives. Although I worried about what she might see in a loser like me, I couldn't help but feel that she had lately been a bit flirtatious.

"I'm not going anywhere. But as you have pointed out, I need to be as much in the background as possible. None of us want my past to derail our worthy cause."

The one thing I had not shared with Christine or Tom was that at least one of the men I had sent to prison had been released and was possibly after me. The thought of bringing my past into the Mission was troubling. Yet I needed to know whether Lamar was still here.

I reached into my pocket for my phone and googled Lamar Goodman. His picture appeared. I adjusted the image to hide his name.

"Hey, guys," I said, handing my phone to Tom and Mark, "do you recognize this man?"

"I sure do," Mark replied. "He was here last week for three or four nights and then left."

"Yes, I remember him," said Tom. "He seemed like a nice guy, but he needed to get back to Chicago to care for his mother, who was leaving the hospital. His name is Lamar."

Had they read my texts, they would have seen an earlier message from my unknown caller: NEXT TIME, I WON'T MISS.

CHAPTER THIRTEEN

Mark Stone took the lead in the first campaign meeting with the ambassadors. "I think all of you have met Brad in the food line or the kitchen. He has also helped with job résumés and applications. And, of course, you know Christine, our extraordinary legal adviser."

I looked around the room and noticed that most wore a "deer in the headlights" expression.

"We invited you here today to ask you to help in our campaign for the Rescue Mission to double our space and improve our facilities. Brad, it's all yours."

"Thank you, Mark," I said as I stood. After a pause I began, "All of us here have a story about how we got here. Some of you have shared your story with me. I haven't gotten to know you all. But none of you, except for Mark, know my story."

"You have a story, boss? I just figured you were one of those religious do-gooders who took pity on all of us losers." Zeke was a second-generation Italian in his mid to late sixties who grew up in Boston. We ate lunch together most days at the Mission and developed a nice friendship, primarily over our love of baseball. He was a Red Sox fan, the sinister enemy of my New York Yankees.

"Yes, Zeke, even I have a story." I then proceeded to tell them that a felony conviction had landed me in prison for two years and that I had only recently been released. I needed a place to hang out while I figured out my life, so my old friend Pastor Tom invited me to Kelsey to volunteer at the Mission. "I'm not proud of what I did, but now I feel like the luckiest guy alive. I have family and friends who love and support me, no matter what. But a 'do-gooder,' as Zeke called me? Well, that's a joke."

I was taking a chance by sharing this with them, but the reward of being viewed as one who had also experienced adversity was worth the risk. It was one of the few times I had disagreed with Tom.

"You're that guy," Ernie Sanchez, a tall thirtyish Hispanic man at the opposite end of the table, announced. "The one that got all those presidents and senators elected. I can tell it's you. No? I watch Rachel Maddow every night. She no like you, man."

I looked to my side at Christine, who was rolling her eyes either at my newfound celebrity or because she didn't like Rachel Maddow.

Ernie was also my new camera and sound operator, and he added, "It will be a pleasure working with you, Mr. Brad."

"You busted me, Ernie." I laughed. "You have my number."

"What Brad is asking each of you to do," interrupted Mark, the ex-officio captain of the ambassadors, "is to tell voters who you are and how you landed at the Mission. He wants the people of Kelsey to see you as he sees you: real guys who are hardworking and love their families but have experienced tough times. Now you're working to turn your lives around."

"I will be there to direct and coach you, guys," I added. "You won't have to memorize a script. We want your story to come from the heart." A few heads nodded. At least they were considering it. "So, who's in?"

To my pleasant surprise, it was a hundred percent buy-in. They all wanted to be on TV.

"That's great," I said. "Thank you. There will be other things I may ask of you, like speaking to church groups. Mark will be collaborating with you to put a little speech together. Just remember the one rule:

Do not talk to reporters. If someone approaches you from the media, refer them to Christine. Only she and Pastor Tom are authorized to represent the Mission and the campaign."

Mike's hand shot up. "Brad, that reminds me of something I forgot to tell you this morning. That reporter with the big white teeth from Channel 4 asked about you yesterday. You may have seen him on the news."

"What did you tell him?"

"I told him you're only here Tuesday and Thursday. He was very polite and didn't ask any other questions."

Carl was doing his due diligence, ensuring I did indeed work at the Mission as a volunteer.

"You did the right thing, Mike. You were truthful. But next time, refer him to Christine. By the way, I'm meeting with Carl next week for an off-the-record discussion about the campaign. I'll make sure he knows that only the city health department is allowed in the kitchen for unscheduled meetings. Are there any other questions?"

"When do we start?" asked Sammy Reynolds, the bipolar former kitchen worker who was my new website designer.

"Thanks for asking, Sammy. I need you and Ernie here for a meeting next Tuesday at ten." Turning to Christine, I asked, "Can you be here too?" When she gave the affirmative, I shifted back to the group. "The rest of you should plan to be here one week from today at noon. Mark will have a schedule for you by then, listing the days we will interview you in front of the camera. Pastor Tom has told us we can convert this conference room into our campaign headquarters, so be prepared to help move furniture around when you get here."

I took a deep breath. "Look, fellas, this isn't going to be easy, but I guarantee that you will know you have accomplished something on election night. This isn't just for Kelsey. It's for the unhoused communities in every corner of our nation. When we're done, America will be watching and noticing what we do here. Have a great weekend, and I'll see you next week."

Christine tapped me on the shoulder as the room emptied. "Is 'that guy' willing to walk me home, with a slight detour to pick up Cody from school?"

Her fresh, smiling face with her hair pulled back into a short ponytail had distracted me through two meetings so far today, and now I found her invitation irresistible.

"I would love to, Ms. Culpepper. Thank you for asking."

Within minutes, we were out the front door and over the bridge into the newer and shinier part of town.

"Tell me more about your meeting with the reporter. No offense, but that doesn't sound like something you want to do," Christine said. It was a gentle remark, not nebby, as they might say in my old Buffalo neighborhood.

"He called me. But here's the thing: He knows who I am, including my real first name. The weirdest thing is that he called on my mobile phone." I explained to her the select group with that number, then about Liz's call warning me to be suspicious of Dan Johnson. "He played his hand well, meaning he won't jump to a story about me right now if he has a chance to talk. Do you know him? Can he be trusted?"

After a couple of blocks, we veered in a slightly different direction than last week, toward Cody's school.

"Carl and I went to high school together. I was captain of the cheerleading squad our senior year, and he was the star quarterback. He later played at a small college outside Tennessee, but I can't recall the school. I was his date at the prom, but we never went out after that. Between you and me, he was an arrogant dick, but an ordained pastor would never use language like that," she said with a chuckle. I laughed too.

"What about now? Is he still arrogant and a, well, whatever you wouldn't call him?"

More laughter.

"Probably. Leopards don't change spots—present company

excluded, of course." I didn't join in the laughter this time. "Oh, come on, Mr. Serious. I was only jabbing you."

We walked in silence for a few moments before Christine continued. "Carl is an honest reporter, but he's still a reporter. If he told you he'd hold his fire on doing a piece about you, he wouldn't burn you. He's also smart, meaning that if you could be an asset to him, like providing inside scoop, he might consider you an ally. He knows a gossip story like 'Ex-con now works in the Rescue Mission kitchen' would be a one-time shot, and nobody would care the next day. As he said in his news report, he's looking at the potential of covering a David and Goliath angle, with the Mission playing the David role and the bullies led by Weber, the aggressors."

An interesting observation.

"So, that's what you think of me? An ex-con who works in the kitchen?"

To my surprise, Christine took my hand briefly as we approached Cody's school, which was now in eyesight. I noticed it was a Catholic school. I would know one of those anywhere.

"I know you're kidding, but the ex-con stuff means nothing to me. It is who you are now that matters to me." Her wide smile and bright bluish-green eyes were comforting as she rose on her tiptoes to give me a tiny kiss on my cheek.

"Mr. Greg, Mr. Greg," Cody shouted as he ran toward us across the school's front lawn. It was chaos as parents lined up in their cars and two school buses slowly filled with happy boys and girls who had been released from forced captivity. Christine was the only mom in sight who was retrieving her child on foot, a luxury afforded her by the location of her townhouse, which was about 200 yards around the corner from the school.

Cody wore gray corduroy pants, a white shirt, and a navy-blue button-up sweater, the same uniform as all the other boys and pretty close to the ones Tom and I wore at St. Agnes in Buffalo.

"Hey, little buddy. How was school today?"

I was comfortable around kids thanks to Sydney and her active social life, and Cody's young spirit reminded me of my daughter's undaunted wonder about the world around us. Since she was five, Sydney and I had been great pals. We hiked in dozens of mountains, rode dirt bikes in two deserts, surfed in three oceans, and zip-lined through a half dozen jungles. We were explorers, sportsmen, movie critics, and always Yankees fans. From what I could see, Christine and Cody had a similar relationship.

"School was great today, except when Sister Nancy yelled at me for talking during the study break. I couldn't help it. Jonas made me laugh."

"What was so funny, Cody?" his mother asked.

"He drew a picture of Sister Nancy in his notebook and showed it to me. He got in trouble and got sent to the principal's office."

"Well, that's what happens when you break the rules." As an expert on behavior and consequences, I freely offered this last insight.

We strolled toward the townhouse, soon arriving at the three-story brownstone with its tiny front lawn and a step-up patio that framed the front door. "Mr. Greg, would you like to see my room? Mom painted it my favorite color since you were here last time."

"Not today, Cody. I'm afraid I have to get home and start getting ready for our cookout tomorrow night. You're still coming, aren't you?"

"Yes. I can't wait to see your boat. Is it true that you live on it?"

"I do," I replied, holding back laughter. "And guess what? My little girl will be there too. Only she's not so little anymore. She's in college."

"I'm going to college someday. And then I will be in the Army, like my dad."

I looked into his wide, innocent eyes without flinching. "Your dad was a great man, Cody. Everyone loved and respected him. You should be immensely proud." I turned toward Christine. "By the way, did you get my text with the directions to the marina?"

She nodded while mouthing "Thank you."

"Well, I will be on my way. See you tomorrow night."

On the way back to the Mission to retrieve my truck, I noticed that Sydney had sent me a text saying she and her friend would arrive by noon tomorrow. I was excited to see her but also concerned she was walking into more of my drama, which I had promised to avoid in the future. I assumed Liz had told her about my visit with Dan Johnson in Dallas and that I needed to be careful, so there would be no need to keep it from her. Having each other's backs was our tradition, even if we were no longer a traditional family.

CHAPTER FOURTEEN

I was scrubbing bird poop off the top deck of the houseboat when I glimpsed Sydney and the young man whose name I had forgotten strolling down the dock. I had been wondering why the birds excreted a purple color when letting it go over a white boat deck but pooped white when they did it on my black truck. I wrote it off as another of the world's mysteries.

"Hey, Dad," she yelled as she waved from two boats away. "You look all tan and fit. I love it. And oh my God, I have never seen you with long hair."

"Did you come all this way to embarrass me in front of the neighbors?" I stood shirtless and shoeless in light-blue swim trunks with a watering hose, perfect attire for eighty-two degrees and bright sunshine. I had forgotten that she hadn't seen my new look, aided by a better diet and a near-daily bicycle riding routine.

She scampered up the chrome ladder and wrapped her arms around my neck. "Did I ever tell you that you're the best dad ever? And I can't believe you live on a boat, just as you said you would someday."

We looked down from the upper deck at her friend, who was gazing up at us.

"Dad, this is my boyfriend, Eric Bader. Eric, this is Greg Smith, captain of the . . . what's the boat's name? It must have a name."

"Go down and look at the stern above the motors," I instructed. I'd had the name painted just two days before.

"Just a minute, Eric. I'll be right back," she called down to him.

I watched her climb back down the ladder and walk to the back deck, extending herself as far as she could over the rail to read *The Sydney*, painted in Kelly green, her favorite color. She straightened out and looked back up at me. "I have a boat named after me," she said excitedly. "What an honor."

"It's nice to meet you, Eric," I greeted. "Come on aboard. Put your stuff in the small bedroom." I wondered if Eric knew that the average shelf life of Sydney's boyfriends was approximately ninety-three days.

"It's nice to meet you too, sir. Thank you for having me."

Hmm. Respectful to the girlfriend's father. He had either been raised properly or Sydney coached him on the drive down from Morgantown. "Please call me Greg. We're both adults."

"How do you like living on a boat?" he asked earnestly. So much for original questions.

"I love it. It is amazing how little space you need to be comfortable, especially living alone. But it's constant work. There is always something to screw, sand, clean, or fix."

We both turned abruptly at the sound of the *General Jackson Showboat* dinner cruise ship's horn as it passed by. A restored 1930s vintage steam paddle vessel, it served as one of Nashville's premier floating venues for music and partying at night and as a way to drink mimosas and enjoy a lovely cruise during the day.

"Hey, Dad, I know you have cold beers stashed on this vessel. A seven-hour drive can make a girl very thirsty."

"In the cooler on the aft deck, honey. Help yourself. You too, Eric. If it gets low, I have more in the storage closet."

Within an hour of their arrival, the three of us were seated on the top deck, soaking up the sun, sipping on our beverages, and comparing notes about our lives.

"I don't know if he told you, Dad, but Eric is a second-year law student at WVU."

That is what the world needs, I thought sardonically—*more bright young lawyers.*

"Very impressive," I chirped. "Second year was my favorite. I was over the fear of failing and hadn't entered the scary job-search phase yet. I just attended classes and studied."

"I get what you're saying, Mr. Smith. I'm having a fun year. Finals are next week."

I reminded him again that it was okay for adults to call each other by their first names.

I watched closely how they interacted. Sydney was clearly no longer the girl I had left behind. She was an impressive, mature young adult who exuded confidence and beauty. It was easy to see why she would attract a bevy of young suitors. Or frighten them away.

"How's your mother?" I asked during a lull in my inquisition of her new boyfriend. "Have you seen her lately?"

"I talk to her at least once a day but haven't gotten together with her in two months. She is seeing someone, Dad. Has she told you?" She asked the question casually as if inquiring about the weather forecast.

"She mentioned she had gone on a few dates with Susan Hutton. Are they getting serious?"

Hutton was the primetime evening anchor on *Nightly Update*, a popular cable TV magazine show, and a woman I respected as an honest journalist. While I was still in Morgantown, Liz had called to ask my thoughts on her coming out publicly, something Susan was urging her to do. Susan had done the same three years ago, and it hadn't marred her public standing. I advised Liz to follow her heart and let the chips fall where they may; the voters in Buffalo would still love her.

"They flew down to Vita Felice for a week, so I think they're pretty serious. And that reminds me to ask: Would it be all right if I took a group of friends to the house to celebrate our graduation? They would pay their way." Vita Felice, Italian for "happy life," was our beach house in St. Lucia, a six-bedroom villa in the Vieux Fort region on the island's southern tip. I wondered if Hutton's journalistic curiosity extended to how Liz's congressional salary afforded such a home as she floated on a lounge chair in the infinity pool that overlooked the Caribbean Sea. I'm sure she didn't want to know about the foreign despots who paid for it in exchange for my advice on influencing American policy.

"It's okay with me, but you should clear it with your mom first."

"Dad, I've already done that," she said with a self-assured smile. "I know the rules." It was funny that Sydney remained committed to the natural rhythms of an intact family arrangement, clearing it with Mom for approval and then asking Dad for permission. I hadn't been to Vita Felice since I went to prison. Still, I knew from the accounting statements that vacationers had occupied it continuously, usually for a month at a time.

I glanced at the ship's clock hanging over the upper helm and noticed it was just shy of four o'clock. "Guys, it's time for me to take a quick shower and start getting ready for our guests. They will be here in an hour. You two are in charge of keeping the beer and wine cold. I'll also put out cheese and crackers and get the grill ready for hamburgers around six. Sound good?"

"Aye aye, Captain," Sydney declared. "I've been waiting all day to say that to you." She paused. "By the way, you haven't told me anything about Christine. Who is she, and why is she coming? Does Daddy have a girlfriend?"

"Christine Culpepper heads up the designated pro bono counsel for a Kelsey law firm. She's active with Uncle Tom at the Mission. She also happens to be a former clergywoman and is a single mom. Now, Sydney, does she sound like my type?" I asked, my sarcasm designed to get Sydney's bloodhound nose off my trail.

"So, what you are saying is that she's just a friend?"

My daughter's line of questions started to annoy me, mostly because I didn't know the answers. But there was no doubt that something was stirring between Christine and me; it was apparent in the tenderness of our conversations and the glances only we noticed.

"Here are the facts. We have spent time together during the past few months, but it is still a new thing—if it is a thing. I really don't know the answer. This is the first time we've done anything socially together with other people. She has never been to the boat." Before she could respond, I added, "Christine is also beautiful, intelligent, caring, and loads of fun. But, yes, for now, she is just a friend."

"I look forward to meeting her. She sounds like a wonderful person. And if you ask me, my father deserves a wonderful person in his life. Other than me, of course."

"He's already got a wonderful person in his life—me!" Tom and Jane had arrived.

"Hi, Uncle Tom," Sydney said as they shared a big hug. "Aunt Jane, you look great. I love your outfit." Tom and Jane were dressed in matching boating attire: white shorts, navy-blue polo shirts, and deck shoes. "I have missed you guys so much."

"You two are early, and I still need to shower before Christine and Cody arrive, so I'll be back on the deck in fifteen minutes. Syd and Eric will take care of your drink needs. Sydney, the cheese and crackers are in the refrigerator."

Tom and Jane had been Sydney's surrogate parents from the day she was born, despite the geographical distance separating them from us. Even as a child, she would fly alone to spend multiple days and sometimes weeks with them. Tom's example had strongly influenced her decision to major in social work and pursue a career in counseling.

As I climbed down the ladder to go inside, I heard her telling him that she had been accepted to several master's programs but was leaning toward either UCLA or the University of Buffalo. "Both are top twenty programs in the field," she explained. "In LA, I could learn to surf, and in Buffalo, I could live in Mom's condominium for free. Besides weekends or congressional breaks, I never lived in Buffalo, so it might be good to experience my historical family roots. And it's free. Did I mention that?"

"Take the free one," I yelled from the bottom deck.

Among the things I learned from living on a boat was how to

take a fast shower. The hot water tank was only ten gallons, so those wishing to take a leisurely rinse would soon find themselves in a freezing downpour. No lollygagging was the general rule. Get in, soap up, rinse, and get out.

It didn't give me much time to reflect on Christine, who was arriving in thirty minutes for her first visit. Sydney had never seen me in the "company" of a woman other than her mother. Not that I was officially in Christine's company. But I was eager to explore the possibility, surrounded by the safety net of my family. The truth was that I was scared.

"Permission to come aboard, Captain." It was the voice of a child.

I poked my head over the side of the upper deck, where I was preparing the grill, and saw Christine and Cody standing on the dock next to the boat's entrance. Although I had been sending occasional glances down the pier, they had slipped past my wandering eyes.

"Permission granted, mate," I answered in my best Australian accent, which wasn't very good, as I climbed down to welcome them. "And who might the lass be that follows you?"

"My overseer, of course. Allow me to present the maiden, Christine Lee."

"Well done, Cody," I complimented. "It's great to have you guys here." With my firmest grip, I shook Cody's hand and gave Christine a warm, but not intimate, hug. She was eye-poppingly beautiful, dressed in a casual white T-shirt and green shorts, with white flip-flops that showed off her manicured toes, painted to match her shorts. After taking the beach bag and setting it on the couch, I asked if they would like the house tour. Of course, Cody was eager to see everything.

"Well, this is the living room. Like any home, it has a couch, comfortable chairs, and a TV. I hope you will notice that my teak floor is brand new. Over there is a small galley kitchen with a table and chairs, and a bathroom down that hall. As you can see, the front sliding glass window opens to a covered patio. The back has a patio too—great for looking at the river and watching the boats go up and down. The city skyline isn't bad either. And this room is also the driving area, or the helm. Another helm just like this one is upstairs on the deck above us. It's called the flybridge."

Cody ventured over and turned the big steering wheel, which was taller than he was.

"Where do you sleep, Mr. Greg?"

I did not doubt that Cody was that one kid in every classroom who always had their hand up with another question, reminding me that I had mercifully abandoned my first career ambition of being a schoolteacher.

"Follow me," I replied. We proceeded down the hall, past the bathroom to the back of the boat, the aft, where two bedrooms—staterooms—were located side by side, each containing a queen-size bed, a small four-drawer dresser, and a tiny closet. I wanted to make a joke that I didn't usually show women my bedroom on the first date, but I scrapped that notion as soon as it entered my head.

"Wow, Mom, maybe we can spend the night here sometimes," Cody exclaimed.

"Cody, we do not invite ourselves to spend the night at other people's homes," Christine admonished gently.

"You are welcome anytime, Cody, but there will be chores to do to earn your keep, like swabbing the decks and cleaning up bird poop." I could tell that no amount of negativity would dampen his thirst for a boat overnight.

"Dad, are you back here?" Sydney's sudden appearance now made for a crowd at the entrance of the bedrooms. "Oh, hi, you must be Christine. It is so nice to meet you finally. Dad talks about you all the time."

Thank you, my daughter. So much for playing coy, I thought.

"I could say the same about you, Sydney. He is quite the proud papa."

"Well, what do you say we get upstairs, grab an adult beverage, and think about grilling those burgers?" I suggested, changing the subject to one I could more easily control.

"Uncle Tom and Eric have it all going, Dad. You just need to show up. By the way, where do you keep the plates and condiments?"

Although we tabled the boat cruise for another time, we enjoyed a festive evening of conversation, story swapping, and laughter. Sydney and Christine hit it off, and I begrudgingly grew to like the boyfriend. To Tom's credit, he stayed away from any talk of Mission business but did provide a hilarious stand-up act of true incidents from his previous shelters.

By the end of the evening, I was as happy and content as I recalled being in a long time. I walked Christine and Cody up the dock to her car shortly after Tom and Jane disembarked, just before ten. After giving Cody a high-five and helping him to the back seat, I hugged Christine goodbye.

"Thanks for coming. I had a blast."

"Me too. It was nice seeing where you live and meeting Sydney."

With our arms still locked, I reached down and kissed her bright-red lips. To my delighted surprise, she returned the gesture, her tongue gently entering my mouth.

"You know how to find me," she whispered as she broke away and climbed into the car. I stood silently, watching the taillights of her black Jeep vanish from the marina.

When I returned to the houseboat, I noticed that Sydney had headed to the guest room, while Eric was on the pullout in the galley room. I was under no illusions about their relationship. Still, Liz had laid down the law from the very beginning: no copulation in the Smith household for unmarried couples, especially when such activities involved our daughter. It was a rule that included boat houses as well.

Sydney appeared at my stateroom door a little later. "Christine is perfect for you. Not that you need it, but she has the official Sydney Smith stamp of approval."

CHAPTER FIFTEEN

"I can promise you, Dan, that I do not want your money. That is not part of the deal. I will make nothing from this arrangement." I listened intently to the digital recording of the Dallas meeting Liz had sent me from the FBI. It was five in the morning as I adjusted the headset on my iPad and sat on the top deck with a tall cup of fresh coffee. Sydney and Eric were still sleeping and probably would be for a couple of hours.

"What did that prison do to you, son? This isn't the Greg Smith I knew. You're the Engineer. You had no boundaries when it came to making a deal. You were ferocious."

"If prison taught me one thing, it's that I don't want to go back, and I needed to make some changes. The truth is that I've lived my whole life thinking that power and greed are the ingredients for a life well lived. So have you. But there's more. Something that guys like you and me lost somewhere along the line."

"Don't bring that sappy liberal bullshit into this office, Greg. I give piles of cash to charities. You're the one who ensured that I am perceived as generous in the public eye. I fund hospitals, disease research centers, and summer camps for poor kids. There's even a building named after me at my alma mater that cost me millions. Rockwood Holdings and Dan Johnson are solid corporate citizens throughout this state."

Of course, his critics would argue that most of it was a front for his shady political activities.

"Dan, let me get to why I'm here." I told him that I was living quietly and anonymously in Tennessee, assisting my best friend, who also happened to be my brother-in-law, in his efforts to expand the city's men's shelter. Dan listened expressionlessly as I outlined the essential facts, starting with an overview of Kelsey, an up-and-coming town outside of fast-growing Nashville, and how new residents and visitors were flocking to this idyllic community. With this progress, however, the number of homeless people had risen, and the need for a viable and modern shelter—and a program to get these men drug- and alcohol-free and back into the workforce—had reached a critical stage. Then I told him what he already knew: Rockwood was interested in buying the abandoned mill property and developing a world-class resort, but only if the neighborhood was free of its current blight, including plans to expand the Kelsey Rescue Mission.

When I finished my presentation, Dan stood and walked to the large window looking out on central Dallas below. Without turning to face me, he asked if I knew his history with Kelsey and why he bought the mill.

"I do know why, Dan. There's a chapter in your son's book devoted to your grandfather and his family roots in Kelsey."

"Daniel Webster Johnson. Such a proud name, isn't it?" he said, turning back to me. "He worked at the mill his entire life at an hourly wage that would be low by today's standards. But it was enough for him and my grandmother to raise three fine children, including my dad. We would visit them every summer in Kelsey."

Listening to the recording, I felt his genuine sentiment toward his grandfather. I recalled watching his watery eyes, witnessing an emotion I had never seen in him before. I doubted many people had.

"Andrew's book talks about him being generous with his time and money, especially to those less fortunate than him," I said.

The recording continued. "During the Depression, people would knock on his front door every night, asking for something to eat or a quarter to buy bread. He would share whatever he had, often inviting whole families for dinner. He made a row of cots in his garage for temporary shelter. He even made a private outdoor shower with warm water for those who needed to bathe. He believed he was one of the lucky ones with a job and a home."

"Why do you want to buy the mill? Surely you have bigger projects around the world than messing around in a small American city."

I knew the answer, but I needed him to say it. I had always believed that a deeper probe into this man's core would reveal a heart. When I was on one of my soul-searching journeys in the days following my conviction and my private escort to Club Fed in West Virginia, I'd discovered the tiniest flame of humanity still flickering within me. I sensed Dan and I were on parallel courses. There was still something good left for him to do, just as there was for me.

"I want to preserve my grandfather's legacy. His generation—the greatest, as we all have come to believe—was more than courageous generals and smart presidents. The little people like Papa sacrificed everything for their communities and families. Like thousands of others, that man toiled day and night at that mill for forty years. They deserve our remembrance."

"Then let's do something better than build luxury suites and five-star restaurants for millionaires. You own plenty of those. How about we create a complex with a job-training center targeted at smart, diligent adults who need a second chance to prove themselves? I'm talking about the homeless, ex-cons, and those with addictions. You know, people similar to those who came uninvited to your grandparents' house for dinner or slept in their garage."

"Go on. I'm listening."

True to his brand, Dan maintained his stoic tone. I had seen him do it in meetings a hundred times, taking in every word while the room awaited his first reaction, which was often his final verdict.

"I trust my gut reaction more than all the data or algorithms in the world," he once told me.

"There is an untapped resource in this country made up of those the world has given up on. They live under bridges and sleep in alleys. While some without homes make it to shelters, it's only a temporary fix, as good as they are. The real culprits are poverty, alcoholism, and drug addiction.

"Yes, they should have made other choices with their lives. However, the social and economic market is unforgiving after a person makes the first wrong choice. I've met these men. I know their names and have heard their stories, Dan. Most are diligent, well-meaning guys. Hell, at least half of them are conservatives. They might even vote for your candidates." I kept seeing those faces in the morning breakfast line as I talked. "These are good men. Men I have come to know and respect."

"Homeless conservative voters. That's a good one, Greg." Dan's veneer had finally broken. His laughter proved he was taking this all in. "Remind me to call my friends at the RNC and suggest a whole new voter group to target."

"Students at this center could pick from any one of several trade skills that would make them employable or qualify them for college, where they could pursue a real career," I continued. "Yes, you will pay dearly for something like this, but once we demonstrate success, it could be a model for the nation."

"Well, you're still good at spending my money." He was half kidding, but I got the message. Good for him. God knew I had spent gobs of it over the past decade. "Sounds to me like you're turning into a goddamn lefty, Greg." His chuckle rumbled through the recording.

"I haven't gotten to the best part," I said, ignoring his teasing. "I see a whole neighborhood of affordable, subsidized apartments and townhouses where individuals and families can live safely and inexpensively while training for a job or attending college classrooms. Again, your costs would be staggering, but I also know that some members of Congress would support federal funding for a public–private partnership like this. I even have a name: the Daniel Webster Johnson Center for Hope and Opportunity."

If this didn't get him hooked, nothing would.

"If I did this, would we be even?"

It was a quiet question. He possessed the same degree of culpability as me, but I was the one who wore tan khakis with the number FCI8976 on them. Other than his fantastic wife, Joanne, and maybe his kids, no one had ever been more loyal to Dan Johnson, the seventh wealthiest person in the nation, than me.

"Even," I said just as quietly.

I turned off the recording, relieved that I had said nothing to incriminate myself to law enforcement. Neither had he, for that matter, although I was sure some would want an explanation of what he meant by "even." I wondered why they had him tapped and "zapped" with a long-range listening device that could capture in-office conversations. He certainly wouldn't share it with me if he were up to more shenanigans. Thank God.

By the time Sydney and Eric were up and around, I had begun breakfast: pancakes, eggs, and bacon, my regular offering. Still clad in our pajamas, we sat at the round patio table on the bow of the houseboat. My neighbors next door, Cheryl and Susie, were doing the same. I briefly introduced them to the kids.

My iPhone rang. It was Liz.

"Hello, Elizabeth," I answered with the speaker on. "I'm holding your daughter prisoner on my ship and have decided not to let her go."

"Hey, dysfunctional family," Liz replied. "How's it going down there in country-music land? Tom and Jane called me this morning and said they had a wonderful time last night."

"Hi, Mom. Are you still at the hunger conference in Africa?"

"Yep, but I'm getting ready to fly home today. I'll call you tomorrow, but I need a few minutes with your dad." On that cue, I picked up the phone and walked inside, shutting the glass doors behind me.

"You sound serious. What's up, Liz?"

"Have you listened to the recording?" She was in her business mode.

"I did. Just a little while ago. Why?"

"First, I want you to know how proud I am of you. I think you're onto something. I agree that this could be a national model for second-chance homeless people."

"Thank you. Of course, the devil is in the details, as they say. It's just a concept, for now."

"Greg, let me change the subject. I'm on my way to the airport and have to be quick. Do you know a man named Max Weber?"

"I have never met him, but he's quite the mover and shaker in Kelsey—the typical 'big fish in a small pond' type if you ask me. He's the number one adversary for Tom and the Mission."

"Well, get this. Weber is the target of the FBI investigation, not Johnson," Liz stated matter-of-factly. "They have a pile of evidence that Weber is running a huge banking and credit card scam targeted at senior citizens with clever scare schemes that result in them giving up their social security numbers, email addresses, and the like. The operations side of it is offshore, so it's hard to nab them, but the brains of the effort is a Kelsey company called Green Enterprises."

Appropriately named, I mused silently. Weber's pond was bigger than I imagined.

"The Green Technologies address is the same as his real estate company," she continued, "but on a lower floor. Their only interest in Johnson is the possibility that he's involved in it too."

"Dan Johnson would never dive into that stuff," I responded. "Playing hardball politics to get his way, yes. But cheating little old ladies? There's no chance of that."

"Weber is another one to stay away from, Greg. I've heard that he is a ruthless operator beneath the cover of a local civic leader. I know I keep telling you to avoid people, but I couldn't bear you getting into trouble again. Nor could Sydney."

"I'll try." I hadn't told her about the campaign yet. *Is a lie of omission still a sin?* I wondered.

"Great. Got to go. Love to Syd."

"Take care, Liz. Thanks."

CHAPTER SIXTEEN

Sydney and Eric left for their nine-hour drive back to Morgantown. We struggled through our farewell, reminding each other that we would reunite at her graduation ceremony in four weeks.

"I had a wonderful time. So did Eric. Thank you," she offered as tears filled her eyes. "I love you."

I held her for a full minute before letting her go. Our bond was battle-tested and unbreakable, just as it should be. I had to live forever knowing that I had hugely embarrassed her with my illegal hijinks, but I also knew she had forgiven me.

The Coffee Roaster was only a fifteen-minute walk from the marina, just over the bridge and down three city blocks. I arrived five minutes before my eight o'clock appointment, but it looked like Carl Noland had the same idea. He already had a booth by the window with hot coffee in front of him.

I saw immediately why he'd chosen television—or, rather, why TV chose him. With his athletic build, boyish face, and perfectly combed blond hair, he looked right out of Central Casting. I wondered what Christine didn't see in him, except that he must have been what she said he was.

"Hi, Greg. Carl Noland. A pleasure to meet you."

An overly friendly reporter is a danger sign. I preferred a gruff-talking curmudgeon any day of the week. At least they are transparent about their intentions, which is hopefully to be fair and judicious. A gregarious guy showing me his happy face, knowing that tomorrow he could stick it to me with a half-true news story, was one sort of reporter that I hated. I had a lengthy list.

"Good to meet you," I said, aiming for somewhere between polite and aloof. I didn't want to be rude, but I wanted to be clear that this was an intrusion. I did not consider myself a newsmaker, nor did I want to be. "I don't have much time, Carl, so we should get right to the point. Why am I here? If you want to do a story on me, go ahead. I can't stop you, but I have nothing interesting to tell you."

I was making an unfavorable impression, but at least he knew I wasn't a patsy. Most ex-cons aren't.

"How well do you know Max Weber?" I could tell Carl had no problem getting to the point too, but I didn't see this coming. Combined with Liz's call yesterday, Mr. Weber had certainly and suddenly entered my orbit.

"I have never met him, although I know he's leading the effort to stop the Rescue Mission from expanding. Should I get to know him?"

"He knows you; at least, he knows who you are and that, for some reason, you're involved with the Mission. I must admit that I'm a bit curious too."

I laughed. "You mean, what is a recently released felon doing in a nice place like Kelsey?"

"Yeah, something like that," Carl said with a smile. He wasn't taking notes or recording our discussion, so it didn't feel like an official interview. I got the impression that he knew parts of several stories but had not yet put the whole picture together.

I opted for the truth. "Tom Garrity has been my best friend since grade school in Buffalo," I began. "I'm married to his sister. When I got out of prison, I was looking for a place to retreat where I could be invisible. The rest is what you see. Two days a week volunteering in the kitchen at the Mission and the remainder of my time spent repairing a twenty-year-old houseboat to live on."

As I spoke, he showed no eye or facial movement. He just

listened, then asked, "So why get involved in a local political issue if you want to stay hidden and burn your service hours? Getting involved in a hot issue like this seems like it would be the last thing on your mind."

"I have come to love these men. They are well intended and have good hearts. The Mission gives them hope for a second bite of the apple someday, and I'd like to help in any way I can. Besides, Tom is a hard guy to say no to. Tell me more about Max Weber and why he cares about me."

Nolan explained that Weber ran the town, detailing how every key appointment from the police chief to building inspectors and other positions in between required his approval. "He chairs the local Republican Party, so every candidate—judges, city council people, state reps, and the like—must also have his blessing. It's a model built on the old Tammany Hall patronage system in New York City. He then uses his connections to bolster his real estate and construction business, leaving only the crumbs to his competitors.

"As Kelsey has grown from a sleepy mill town to a wealthy alternative to Nashville and Memphis, Weber has become wealthier and wealthier," Nolan concluded.

"And where do I enter the picture?" We had gone beyond the borders of the reporter–interviewee format, locked in a conversation where both of us were now trying to figure out the puzzle. The server came by and refilled our coffee cups. "By the way, may I ask that we go off the record from now on?"

"Background only, Greg. Again, if I ever interview you for a story, I will tell you up front."

"Deal."

"Ah, a deal with the famous 'dealmaker' himself. I am truly honored," he said with a chuckle. I was beginning to like this guy despite knowing the truth about his high school years. "Max Weber sees you as a threat. Part of being a city boss is working twenty-four seven to minimize, if not eliminate, competition. No one can compete with the boss man's acumen when gaining and holding power. Then, out of nowhere, Weber sees a guy who played in the major leagues and paid millions of dollars to advise all kinds of national and international political icons, and it unnerves him. And if you beat him in this campaign, he would be humiliated."

As much as I was intent on running from my past and forging a more humble life, it felt good to have my ego stroked by an admirer, which Carl Nolan seemed to be. Reporters love rubbing elbows with guys who have pushed the system to its limits and beyond.

"So, Weber knows who I am and that I'm helping the Mission with their campaign. Why are you telling me?"

"Max wants me to expose how the Mission is relying on advice and leadership from a cheating political scoundrel. He intends to discredit the Mission by using you as the foil." *This could be an interesting angle*, I thought. "But to be honest, Greg, I resent the hell out of guys like Weber who use reporters to advance their dishonest agendas. Besides, I believe in what the Mission is doing. My brother lived there for nine months a couple of years ago, and it helped turn his life around."

"What do you know of Green Technologies?" I asked.

"It's one of Weber's companies. They have an office on the third floor of the Weber building. It assists companies and local governments, including the City of Kelsey, in collecting overdue debts. Still, I'm not privy to the details. Why do you ask?"

I wasn't about to reveal my conversation with Liz or her discussions with the FBI, but I thought it might be useful to feed on Carl's apparent dislike of Weber. "You did not hear this from me, and I can never be a source. Do we agree?"

"Agreed."

"I have it from a credible source that the FBI is watching Green Technologies as the possible control center for a huge credit card and bank fraud operation. From what I hear, their modus operandi is to call senior citizens with a host of concerns, like turning off their water or heat or canceling their cable television. They pry their credit card, social security, and bank numbers from these elderly people and then drain their accounts."

"I've never been to their office, but wouldn't that require a lot of telephone operators?"

"Only the business part is conducted from the Kelsey office. The calls from other countries make it difficult for them to stop. This office is like the queen in a beehive. Kill the queen, kill the hive."

"Who is leading the investigation? The FBI or Tennessee attorney general?"

"Those are good guesses," I replied. "I'm not sure."

We left it at that for the time being, shaking hands and agreeing to stay connected. As he headed down the city sidewalk away from me, I called out, "Hey, Carl, I forgot to ask: How did you get my telephone number?"

"Max Weber gave it to me. He says he got it from a mutual friend of yours."

• • •

My drive to Kelsey was the perfect way to work off my anger. *Why would Dan give my telephone number to Max Weber? Did he tell Weber he couldn't purchase the mill property as long as I was around?*

It made sense. What better way to remove me as his problem than to get Weber to drive me out of town with a revelation that would embarrass the Mission? Dan gives Weber my number, instructing him to give it to a reporter; it's an old gimmick that I taught him. What goes around comes around. Dan would then pay his debt to me with a million-dollar transfer to my Cayman account.

An hour later, I pulled into the back lot of the Mission and proceeded to the conference room, which was slowly transforming into a campaign headquarters, not unlike the dozens of campaign operations I had known in the past. Christine was clearly in command, quietly working with Mark Stone amid the noise and chaos generated by the ambassador committee members, film crew, and a barber on his once-a-month volunteer schedule.

"Good morning," Christine greeted me perkily. She seemed to be having fun with this, her even temperament a perfect fit for the campaign manager role. "How was your meeting with Carl?"

"I liked him. We had a good chat, and I don't think he plans to do a story on me, which is all I can ask for. Who knows, maybe we can be friends. He is favorable to our side of this, but for now, his value is that Weber considers him to be friendly to their side."

Christine wore a faded pair of skinny jeans, a worn gray Yale Divinity sweatshirt, and new blue Nikes, all below a wrinkled Atlanta Braves baseball hat with a ponytail out the back. I loved her casual look and thought she wore it well. Of course, by now, I loved everything about her.

"It's like a three-ring circus, but as soon as we get the haircuts done, I can start moving people either out or to the back of the room so you can interview them," she said.

"Sounds good. Let's get everyone's attention and go from there."

A sharp whistle abruptly pierced the room, coming from Christine's mouth and stopping a dozen conversations. "Okay, all. Thank you for being here this morning. Greg, it's all yours." My "Brad" moniker had been officially dropped in this company.

"That's quite a whistle, Counselor." I got a laugh from everyone in attendance but saw by her red face that I had embarrassed her. "Gentleman, each interview will take about a half hour, and there are ten of you. We'll do five of you today and five on Thursday. Christine has the schedule. The only ones in the room during an interview, besides the camera crew and me, will be the interviewee, Mark, and Christine. So, when you arrive, wait outside the room until you're called. Any questions?"

"Uh, do we have to get a haircut?" It was Robbie Pool, whom I knew only as the van driver, one of the positions in the Mission with the most responsibility. With blond hair that hung to the middle of his back, ashy white skin, and a wrinkled shirt left unbuttoned down his chest, he looked like an aging rock star.

"No. But you do need to have it washed if that's okay. Also, I hope you will allow the barber to either trim your beard or give you a shave. Thanks, Robbie, for your question."

If we were going to win the hearts of women voters, we needed them to see our guys as their sons and brothers. I had a hunch that the key target group in the campaign was Independent women, who were less inclined to toe the line of either party and showed compassion toward others when deciding how to vote. "Remember, people vote more with their hearts than their heads," I added.

"Meanwhile, fellas," Mark Stone said, "if you are not scheduled today, you can return to your class or job assignment. Make sure you pick up a schedule from Ms. Culpepper. Sammy, I will need you back here at two o'clock to discuss the website with Brad and Christine before they leave. The first one is Jimmy Keefer." Mark was solid and articulate—a genuine leader. The men knew this about him too.

As soon as the room cleared, Jimmy sat in his chair opposite the camera, and I took mine across from him so we could look directly at one another. When Ernie turned on the lights, it resembled an on-location set of a news network. Christine's expression showed me that she was both impressed and surprised by the high production level. Some things from my past weren't about to change, including my insistence on professionalism and quality. The camera, lighting, and audio gear had been shipped in by Power Lens, a rental company in Atlanta I had worked with before my imprisonment. "Back in business, bad boy? Nice to hear from you," Derek, the owner, had said when I called. I gave Derek my new credit card information, and the shipment arrived the next day via UPS.

Because I wanted another camera angle when we edited the footage into thirty-second commercials for TV and longer for the internet, I needed a second camera operator and hopefully one who could also manage the audio. Luckily, Doug Pollard, who once again proved he knew everyone in town, introduced me to Boyd Masterson, a retired engineer and self-taught videographer who volunteered at Doug's church to do online audio and video recordings of Sunday services. When I called Boyd, he eagerly agreed. My crew was now set, with me as the director and Ernie and Boyd doing camera and sound. Our fee was unlimited free meals.

"Speeding," said Ernie, the term used for a camera that had begun recording.

"So, Jimmy, tell me your story. How did you end up residing at the Kelsey Rescue Mission? And please, talk directly into the camera."

CHAPTER SEVENTEEN

We wrapped up our fifth and final interview a little past five o'clock with my new friend Zeke, whose full name was Lorenzo Esposito. I wasn't sure if Zeke got his nickname from his parents or if it had been assigned to him by the Mission residents. I didn't ask. I just loved the name, and I loved him.

I knew sixty-something guys who were living proof of the adage "Sixty is the new forty"; he wasn't one of them. Partly due to a mild stroke that had slowed his gate to a notch above a shuffle, he looked like an older man. His spirit, however, had not been doused, evidenced by his quick smile and a good word for everyone he met, and the stroke did not result in slurred speech. Zeke loved to talk—except, as I learned, when there was a camera present.

"I'm a little nervous. I've never talked to a camera before. Are you sure you want me to do this? We have big talkers around here who would do better than me."

Of course, with some coaching, he turned out to be the best interview of the day. Not because he was a slick orator, which he was not. But he was genuine. Everything with Zeke came from the heart. He knew no other way, camera or no camera.

My first question—"How did you get here?"—was straightforward and brief, a plus when trying to create a thirty- or sixty-second testimonial: "My wife had cancer, and I was her caretaker. Eventually, I had to put her in a care-assisted home, but to pay for it, I had to mortgage my house. It ended up draining my savings. By the time she passed, I had only an old car and a monthly social security check that wasn't enough to pay rent and eat. Everything we had was gone. I was a widower. I was alone and homeless. So, I came here and found people who needed help more than I did, guys I could help get through *their* tough times. I found friends and a community."

Feeling a little teary, I said, "I love it, Zeke, but I need you to say one more thing." I gave him the line "Thank you, Kelsey, for giving me the chance to have a life." He nailed it.

"That's a wrap," I announced. "Nicely done, Zee-O. Great shoot," I said to the crew in the same breath. "We'll be back here Thursday to interview the next group. I appreciate your hard work."

Christine tapped me on the shoulder. "I'm going to slip out and get dinner started. I'll see you around six thirty?"

"I'll be there," I said, smiling like a teenage boy. I can't wait to taste Christine's famous spaghetti and meatballs. "I brought a bottle of the red wine you liked on the boat." I should have surprised her with it, but in my excitement, my mouth worked in front of my brain.

"Sounds delicious. By the way, Cody is having an overnight with his grandparents."

If I wasn't nervous before, I certainly was now. Was this an invitation to something more than simply sharing dinner? Serious romance was in the air, and I didn't want to blow it by being too coy or bold.

I used Tom's private bathroom adjacent to his office to brush my teeth, splash on my favorite cologne, and change into the clean clothes I had brought to the Mission that day. I figured there would not be time to drive to Nashville and return to Kelsey after our filming sessions.

"You clean up well," Tom greeted me as I entered his office. He was at his large desk, his face buried in an oversize computer monitor. "Are you nervous?"

At that moment, he wasn't a pastor or a shelter director. He was just Tom asking his best friend if he was okay.

"Maybe I'm even a little scared. I haven't felt this way about someone since I first asked Liz to go bowling. How old were we?"

"You were sixteen, and she was two years younger. I remember feeling hurt because of not being invited. And she was my sister, for God's sake. Talk about being scared. I thought I was losing you and her at the same time."

"But here we are, still together."

"Yeah, now you're trying to steal my lawyer," he chuckled. "Don't you ever quit?"

• • •

I decided to walk to Christine's townhouse from the Mission. It was a warm evening, and the ten-minute stroll would be an excellent way to calm my nerves. *It's just dinner*, I kept telling myself. *It's just dinner*. But it wasn't "just" dinner.

As I approached the steps leading up to her brownstone, a paper bag clasped around the red wine in my hand, I was giddy. I wondered if she felt the same.

She opened the door, and we exchanged a brief friendly hug as I handed over the wine. Although Christine was dressed casually, she looked classy. Call it casual radiance. She had ditched the Braves hat from earlier, replacing it with a red bandanna that created a small bun atop her head, and wore a royal-blue summer dress that reached her knees and braided white flip-flops. The top two buttons of her dress were open, creating a slight side view of her breast when she bent down. I noticed she was not wearing a bra, although I tried unsuccessfully to look away.

"The house looks beautiful," I observed. It was easy to guess that nothing in her house was accidental. The simple elegance of limited beige furniture adorned with colorful pillows against the bright-white walls and unvarnished wooden floors would be perfect for a trendy decorating magazine. It reinforced my belief that everything she touched somehow turned to perfection.

"I'm glad you said that because Cody doesn't want to live here anymore after seeing your houseboat. So, thanks for that," she teased. "Let me open that wine."

I followed her into the kitchen, which was upgraded with stainless steel and Corian, and sat on one of the two barstools at the counter separating the kitchen from the eating area. "Every house has a history. Tell me about this one."

"I bought it for practically nothing when Cory and I moved here from Washington. Although Monroe Street had begun to gentrify, this was a dump. I have since heard from my police friends that it was once a crack house. We completely gutted the interior and added the patio deck in the back. It's a brand-new house with a hundred-year-old exterior. The whole street is like that."

She was busy demonstrating her multitasking skills as she cooked the spaghetti sauce, tossed the salad, and warmed the bread while conversing. The apron she had thrown on was blue to match her dress, with a bright-yellow sun that said, "Welcome to my Sunny Life." It was perfect for her.

We remained at the counter for dinner, which created a relaxed, less formal feel. I complimented her on the spaghetti sauce, and we discussed other trivial topics. I also briefed her on my meeting with Dan Johnson and the concept of a Center for Opportunity and Hope. However, she seemed far more excited to tell me that she had grown all the ingredients for the sauce in the "urban garden" out in her tiny backyard.

"Your plan sounds pretty dreamy. Is it possible to create or even afford something like that? Does Mr. Johnson have that kind of money?"

"As I see it, the center would be set up as a nonprofit foundation, with Johnson putting up the seed funding to establish it. Public and private grants would then sustain it over time. But yes, he has that kind of money. He's the seventh-richest person on the planet. I know from inside reports he's angry with me for holding him hostage for it, but in the end, it's just a control thing. He'll thank me when he gets a Nobel for his humanitarian efforts."

I explained his family history and personal interest in Kelsey to her.

"Aha, the picture is a little clearer. He wants his grandfather remembered. He can't be all bad."

I thought, *Even Mafia bosses love their grandfathers* but didn't say it. I wasn't yet confident Christine would appreciate my sarcastic humor.

Following a pause in the conversation that had been nonstop since I arrived, Christine asked, "Greg, we are obviously both interested in something more than just a business relationship. Do you mind if we talk about it?"

Through our dozens of walks and talks, whether strolling home from the Mission or sneaking out to her local corner pub, I had learned that blunt honesty was the only path she knew.

"I would like that, Christine, but you go first." I smiled as I said it, and she returned one of her own.

"Okay, let's pretend I'm interviewing you as 'possible boyfriend material,'" she said with air quotes. "First question, why should I trust a guy who committed a federal crime, ratted out his friends, and spent time in a federal prison?"

"You shouldn't." My reply was immediate and confident.

"Oh, this could be a truly short interview, Mr. Smith. I'm not sure you have the right qualifications for the job." I could tell from her animated face and wide eyes that she was playfully goading me, yet it was plain that trust was an essential issue for her.

"Well, at least not until you're convinced that the new and improved Greg Smith isn't like the old one. My advice is to have patience, and when you no longer need to ask that question, you will have answered it for yourself."

"Fair enough," she offered. "I'll give you a B."

As I poured the final drops of wine into her glass and then

mine, she strolled across the kitchen and reached for an upper shelf populated with other red and white bottles. Handing me the bottle and the opener, she said, "Can you do the honors?" Was she trying to get me to spend the night? The Tennessee Highway Patrol were vigilant when it came to driving intoxicated.

"Are you ready for question two of the boyfriend interview?"

"Ready."

"Two-part question," she announced, holding up two fingers. "How can you comfortably retire in your late forties, and was your money earned legally?"

"Ahh, you're impressed by my twenty-year-old houseboat and fifteen-year-old pickup," I mocked, but I considered her question. If I were in her position, I would also want to know the answer. We hadn't discussed the details of my crime, so she only knew what the media had reported, which was sketchy at best.

"I made my initial money charging huge fees and advertising commissions for multimillion-dollar political campaigns. Much of this came from managing Dan Johnson's political activities, mostly by setting up political action committees and getting paid to run them. However, the obscene amount of money came from charging corporations, imposing advocacy groups, and foreign governments for lobbying fees, including charging them even more to arrange meetings with influential government officials. I mostly stuck to Big Pharma, big oil, and foreign governments. You can question the ethics of a system that would allow for such arrangements, but all of it is legal, so long as proper reporting procedures are followed.

"Of course, none of this includes the fifty grand worth of Apple stock my grandfather left me in 2000 in his will. For sentimental reasons, I decided never to touch it. My sentimentality has proven to be the best investment decision ever made."

"How about the fraud and conspiracy, all the stuff that sent the other guys to long prison sentences? What happened to that money?"

"Good question, Counselor. I didn't take any of that money. I was the setup guy but did not benefit directly from it. It was an important factor in my lighter sentence."

"Okay, here's my last question—and it's big. Are you still in love with Liz?"

Her inquiry wasn't a surprise. Liz and I were tied together by a thousand overlapping knots despite being separated for years.

"Tom told me to ask you that one," she confessed.

I should have known. Tom had asked me that question a few times since I had been in Kelsey.

"I'm not sure that Liz or I have a convenient, briefly worded description of what we are," I began without hesitation, "but I can truthfully tell you that 'in love' is not in the equation."

I could have left it at that, but I thought Christine deserved to know more. This was, after all, an official boyfriend interview. I also figured it would help me to understand my relationship with Liz if I said it aloud.

"Liz and I have a lifelong bond that started as children and will never disappear. I can't imagine her not being a key person in my life, and I'm sure she feels the same way. If there is ever to be another husband or wife for either of us, that person will have to accept our friendship, knowing it is respectful and supportive but not spousal."

As I answered Christine's question, she gently placed her hand on top of mine. Without thinking, I linked my little finger to hers, suddenly overwhelmed by her warm, simple touch. When I finished, we held each other's gaze.

"Do you have any questions for me?" she asked softly.

"Just one. Are you thinking of sleeping with me tonight?"

She silently leaned forward from sitting, placing her puffed lips on my mouth. I believe it was the longest kiss of my life.

"Perhaps," she said as she pulled back, her face inches from mine. Christine stood and led me up the stairs to her bedroom, still holding my hand. I was unable to resist and did not want to even try. I decided there was no good reason to tell her that Liz was the only woman I had ever been intimate with.

CHAPTER EIGHTEEN

It was the best sleep I'd had in years. The fully undressed woman nestled in my arms might have had something to do with it, and I didn't want to let her go, even when she mumbled that it was seven o'clock and she was late getting up for work.

"I have a meeting at eight with a woman charged with kidnapping the kids she birthed," Christine informed me. "We're taking on the case partly to show how parental rights laws in this state are desperate for reform."

"I want to be like you when I grow up. Always fighting for the noble cause," I said, still in bed with my eyes half closed. By now, she had donned a yellow satin bathrobe and was standing over me. I wanted her to take it off but sensed that she had begun her day, and any effort made to deter her with a sexual advance would be selfish on my part.

"Maybe you can walk me to my office on the way to the Mission. I'll go make us some coffee," she announced cheerfully as she disappeared out the bedroom door.

I quickly showered and used the new toothbrush she had left on the counter. She had also left a small, sealed envelope. On the outside, it read, PLEASE READ THIS LATER WHEN YOU ARE ALONE. Slipping back into my clothes, I stuffed the envelope in my pocket and walked downstairs, through the well-appointed living room, and into the kitchen. My phone rang. It was Carl Nolan.

"Hey, Carl, what's up?"

"Hi, Greg, sorry to bother you first thing in the morning. Do you have a minute?"

I took two sips of coffee and saw Christine finishing her avocado toast. "I have two minutes, and then I have to head out."

"I have a source that told me your old pal Dan Johnson is coming to town to announce his initial plans for the mill property. I don't know much more, but I thought you'd like to know. I also wanted to ask if you might help me get an on-camera interview with Tom Garrity about his thoughts on the campaign."

"I appreciate knowing about Dan coming. Thanks. In terms of the campaign, Christine Culpepper is the campaign spokesperson. I would suggest calling her directly at the law firm or the Mission and setting up an appointment. I'm sure she'd be happy to make arrangements with Tom."

"Christine Culpepper. Was she Christine Pollard before she was married?"

"The one and only," I said like I had personal pride in promoting her.

"We went to high school together. Small world." He paused. "Oh, I also wanted to tell you that we commissioned a public opinion poll on your referendum." I wasn't happy he referred to it as "my" referendum, but I was far more interested in getting legitimate polling results than worrying about language. In my previous life, detailed polling data was my ultimate guide, and I was frustrated that I had no such information in this campaign. "We plan to make the results public sometime next week."

"Come on, Carl, you're not going to tease me like that, are you? At least give me something."

"The bottom line is that you're behind by ten points, so you have some work cut out. If the election were held today, you'd get thirty-three percent to the anti-Mission side's forty-three percent. Twenty-four percent are undecided and waiting for more information."

"That's very helpful, Carl. Thank you. It means we'll win."

"That's bold. How can you be so sure?"

"The undecided vote will break our way by a wide margin. If undecided voters aren't yet concerned or, worse, frightened by the prospect of more homeless men wandering the streets, they at least have an open mind. That makes them likely to vote yes on the referendum."

On our way out the door to begin our walk, I told Christine that her old boyfriend would be calling to discuss the campaign. "He is not my old boyfriend," she protested lightly. "Did he say that?"

"Just kidding. He only said that you were classmates."

When we arrived at her office, she hugged me around the neck. "I don't want you to go anywhere. Can you stay here and amuse me while I work?"

"Like a pet?"

"Not exactly a pet. How about an obedient boyfriend?"

"Boyfriend? Hmm. I must have passed the test."

"We'll just leave it at 'You don't suck,'" she teased.

• • •

I ducked into the Mission briefly to check on Sammy, who I knew was working on the campaign website.

"Hey, Brad," he greeted me in his usual monotone. "Good timing. I have something to show you." Sammy marched me through the various pages, starting with the home page and proceeding to subpages with names like "Issues," "The Need Has Never Been Greater," "Be a Donor," and "We Need Volunteers." His layout and graphics impressed me, but I thought it was a little light on pictures and videos.

"You get the pics, and I'll put them in," he responded.

"I like where this is going, Sammy. Nicely done. When will we be ready for a public launch?"

"Give me three days, then three days after that, to make everyone's edits. I'd say we will be ready for prime time in a week. That means you need to get me at least the first few videos by the end of this week."

"I better get out of your hair and let you work. I'll also ask Cooper if he can get you as many photos of the Mission as possible. Remember that we'll need a release statement from each of them. I'll write one up and have it to you Thursday."

I walked briskly down the hallway toward the front desk, intending to make a sharp left and head to the parking lot in the back of the building.

"Mr. Brad, you had a package delivered this morning." It was Charlie, the front desk coordinator.

"Thanks, Charlie. My first mail."

"Well, not exactly mail. A private courier delivered it."

Typically, my curiosity would have forced me to open it immediately, but I had other things on my mind. I climbed into my battered truck with its rifle rack and a "Trump for President" sticker left over from 2016 and headed out. The Walmart on North King Street was my destination. When I arrived, I figured that half of Tennessee must have had the same idea. It was packed, and I ended up parking at least a football field away from the entrance. I headed straight for the electronics department to purchase a cheap temporary smartphone with a short lifespan. I'd learned in prison that these so-called "burner phones" were commonly used by those who wanted to hide any record of calling in or out. I paid cash so there would be no credit card bill for my purchase.

My next stop was the UPS store about a block away, where I completed the form to send the phone in a box with guaranteed delivery to Dan Johnson in Dallas. The instructions on the outside read: FOR DAN'S EYES ONLY. URGENT. Inside I included a handwritten note:

> Dan—Take this phone and go somewhere private (a park, a downtown tavern in a back table, or even a busy intersection. not your car, home, or office), and call me at the number

below at precisely 2:00 pm today. It is urgent that you do not mention this to anyone.—Thanks, Greg.

The number I left was the Mission's landline. It would mean an extra day at the Mission this week, but I needed to do this right. I also knew Dan would cooperate. He'd be pissed when he received it, but he knew I wouldn't put him through gymnastics like this for anything frivolous.

∙ ∙ ∙

"Hello, everyone, and welcome to tonight's *Evening News*. I'm Robin Charles. Capitol Hill was rocked today by a Department of Justice report alleging the most massive election fraud scheme in the history of our nation, one that may have affected the results in three pivotal states. Earlier today, FBI agents searched the Virginia home and Washington office of Greg Smith, a Washington lawyer and political adviser to dozens of Republican elected officials, including the president. According to the DOJ document, FBI officials believe Smith coordinated the elaborate plan. It will be interesting to see whether Smith, known in Washington circles as the ultimate dealmaker, has a deal to get himself out of this one. More on this story as it unfolds."

I had seen the broadcast a hundred times since that first night at my home in Great Falls, Virginia. This clip, however, delivered on a thumb drive earlier today at the Mission, had a twist. When the anchorwoman disappeared from view, a male voice came on over the blank screen. He sounded like he was gargling as he talked. "I hope you enjoyed the little trip down memory lane. Don't bother giving it to the police or the FBI. The best forensic expert in the department won't find its origin. I know you like deals, Mr. Smith. So, here's our deal. Leave Tennessee within ten days, and you will not hear from us again. I can guarantee you won't like the alternative."

I stared at the screen, waiting for the "or else" part, but it never came. The one clue I had—the demand to leave the state—suggested the threat came from someone local. Was it Max Weber? He knew who I was, and according to Carl Nolan, he was threatened by my involvement in the campaign. Plus, Weber most likely knew about my relationship with Dan and that I was trying to steer him in a different direction. Johnson could have even told Weber he was forced to back out because of me. Or Weber and Johnson could be in this together, which I doubted but hoped to flush out with Dan as soon as possible.

Sitting on the boat's bow porch, sipping on Maker's Mark beneath a dark sky framed by city lights, I wondered how I'd gone from peeling carrots at a homeless shelter to being threatened by a local thug who controlled an entire city and a former elected official from Illinois. Was I simply a magnet for trouble, plagued forever by my sins of the past?

Maybe going somewhere else would be best for me. In prison, I often thought of retreating to my island home, Vita Felice, and working as a bartender at a beach bar, which right now seemed to fit my original motive of fading into the background and creating a quiet life. But something lived within me that screamed, "Oh yeah, Mr. Weber? Come and get me, you piece of shit who robs harmless old ladies. Same to you, motherfucking Lamar Goodman. You have both met your match. I will defeat you."

My macho meanderings were interrupted by a vibration from the front pocket of my jeans.

"Hey, Counselor, I was just thinking about you." It was true, as I had been considering whom I could speak to about my ominous thumb drive delivery. I was wavering between Christine and the FBI.

"Greg, are you watching the news?" Her question held a frightening tone.

"No."

"Turn it on, now. There's been a shooting in Kelsey. It's one of our guys from the Mission. Jimmy Keefer is dead."

The television came on in time to see Carl Nolan holding a microphone and standing in the middle of First Street in downtown Kelsey with at least four, and possibly more, police cars blinking red and blue emergency lights on both sides and to the rear of him. It was pure chaos as the ambulance quickly left the scene with a siren that momentarily drowned out Nolan's audio. Yellow tape surrounded the crime scene as uniformed police officers huddled in what appeared to be deep discussions away from Nolan and several camera crews from other local stations.

"What we are being told is that a young Black man identified as Jimmy Keefer was engaged in a standoff with two Kelsey police officers. These two officers, not yet named, then called in another patrol car with two additional officers, also unnamed. When Keefer refused numerous demands to put down his weapon and get on his knees, instead choosing to approach the officers, at least one of them opened fire and shot the suspect. The shooting occurred at around ten thirty, which is after local restaurants and shops would have closed."

"Where are you now, Christine?" Anxiety rose in my throat, knowing that she lived only blocks from the crime scene.

"I'm at the police station, waiting for Tom to arrive. My neighbor's daughter came over to be with Cody. We are trying to reach Jimmy's family but haven't been able to yet. But here's what the media doesn't know. The four officers—all White, by the way—pumped eighteen bullets into him in less than five seconds."

Looking back at the television, I saw that Nolan was about to interview Chief Art Drake. "Just a second, Christine. Let me hear what the chief says."

"We take matters like this very seriously," the chief declared. "All four officers have been placed on administrative leave pending further investigation. However, at this time, we have every reason to believe that our men responded appropriately, as they are trained to do in a life-threatening situation. All of them were wearing body cams, so we'll review them before taking further action."

I turned down the volume and returned to Christine, who remained on the line. "What's your next move?" I asked.

"Tom and I will meet with the chief and then with Jimmy's family. His mother and two sisters live in Memphis. We want them to know that we are willing to act as an extension of their family here in Kelsey, but there's only so much we can legally do. Tom is planning a press conference for tomorrow morning at ten o'clock. I'm sure he would love to have you help him get ready for it. How early can you be here?"

"I can come right now if that would be helpful. Otherwise, I can be in at dawn, which I planned to do anyway."

"The crack of dawn is great. Get some sleep but keep your phone nearby in case we need your advice. I have a feeling this could explode."

She was right to be concerned. Although police violence is not expected to happen in a smaller city like Kelsey, it does.

"The most important thing at this point is to remain calm and not fall into the trap that it's wrong to be angry," I offered. "People have a right to be mad. I will be very interested to learn what Jimmy Keefer did to deserve eighteen bullets."

"Don't be surprised if I use that line on a reporter," she answered. "Thanks! I'll see you tomorrow."

As I peeled off my jeans to get ready for bed, the envelope Christine had left for me fell out of my back pocket. In the day's business, I had forgotten about it. I carefully tore back the flap and pulled out a two-sided card, the front boasting a small watercolor image of her home and her name in the upper left corner. I figured she used them for thank-you notes.

> *My beautiful Greg. Oh my, that sounds possessive. Well, I won't apologize. Last night, you were all mine. I felt your heart and looked into your eyes. I have never felt such passion. But can I allow my emotions to rule my head? Can I leap forward with a man I have known for such a short time? Or trust a man with such a (shall we say) complicated history?*

My mother would question my prudence, for sure. What I know is this. I love you for who you are now. So, yes, you passed the boyfriend test. LOL, With flying colors. I can't wait to see what our future brings.

CHAPTER NINETEEN

News about Jimmy's death spread quickly, beginning with the kitchen crew, where Jimmy was a full-time team member and loved by all of us. By the time I walked in at 6:30, Tom was already there, comforting Jimmy's six coworkers, an equal mix of Black and White homeless men assigned to the kitchen. They were an angry brood.

"There is no doubt Jimmy had a drinking problem, but threatening cops in the middle of the street, no way." Mike was uncharacteristically animated, waving his arms as tears streamed down his face and talking several octaves higher than usual. "There is something not right about this, Pastor Tom. Jimmy would never hurt someone. He was a total 'turn the other cheek' guy."

Tom responded calmly. "Believe me, I'm trying to get some answers. I've been up all night. I demanded to see the body cam videos, but so far, the police have them locked up, or so they say." Tom spotted me at the door. "Ahh, Mr. Smith, just the man I need to see. Do you have a second?"

"I need to get these eggs scrambled and the bacon in the oven."

"No, you go ahead with the pastor," Mike said. "We can get this done today. I never thought I'd say this, but today we need lawyers more than cooks and servers."

It felt like the time in the ninth grade when I'd been plucked out of class by the principal for a "special assignment." I remember the other kids calling me "nerd" and "geek" as I picked up my backpack and sauntered out of the room. The assignment turned out to be helping the principal with a speech he was giving at the board of education meeting the following week. I learned at an early age the value of using words and phrases as both offensive and defensive weapons. This was why I knew what was next. Tom needed me to help him with his remarks to the press so that he could weave just the right balance between pain and outrage.

When we arrived at the conference room—now a nascent campaign headquarters with signs, desks, and posters—Christine was at the table sipping on a caramel latte she had picked up at Starbucks on her way in. I knew it was caramel because it was her daily habit. She slid the other two specialty coffees over to Tom and me. "Let me guess," I said. "Caramel lattes."

"With whole milk," she added. "Enjoy."

I had reread her letter at least ten times this morning and now found it difficult to focus. Thankfully, Tom took the lead. "Okay, Christine, what do we know besides Jimmy being taken from us?"

He wasn't wasting time this morning. First the kitchen staff, followed by a briefing from his lawyer, and then thinking of his talking points for the media. I could see his brain whizzing around at high speed.

"Fact number one is that all four officers pulled their guns and slammed Jimmy with a total of eighteen bullets in less than five seconds. Fact number two: Jimmy was not carrying a firearm. However, he pulled out his Swiss Army knife and waved it around. According to the chief, he was also intoxicated and had just left Oscar's Tavern on Second Street." She paused for a few seconds. "And fact number three is that Chief Drake's press conference starts in one minute," she said, picking up the remote and turning it to Channel Four just as the chief came to the microphone.

"At approximately ten o'clock last night, two of our officers on a routine cruise downtown noticed an individual who appeared to be intoxicated walking in the middle of the street, which was vacant at the time. When they asked him to walk on the sidewalk, the suspect shouted obscenities and refused to move."

Behind Drake stood eight uniformed senior members of the police force with grim expressions. The chief continued, "One of the officers then radioed a request for backup on his handheld device, resulting in a second squad car with two additional officers arriving within minutes. When the suspect began walking toward the officers, they could see that he was waving what appeared to be and was later confirmed as a knife, continuing to weave as he walked while also using foul language. At this point, the first officer moved toward the individual to attempt to restrain him physically. Immediately following, the man lunged toward the officer with his knife. The officer took a step back, drew his gun, and fired several rounds into the man's lower body. The other officers, who had already drawn their weapons, also fired at the suspect in defense of their fellow officer."

As the camera pulled back, it plainly showed the mayor and Max Weber standing slightly out of the frame of the camera angle. But they weren't listening to the chief's presentation. Instead, they were engaged in a heated discussion, each gesticulating and talking loudly in what appeared to be an argument. "The deceased has been identified as James Allan Keefer, currently a resident at the Kelsey Rescue Mission," the chief continued. "Our thoughts and prayers are with Mr. Keefer's family. Now, if any of you have questions, I will try to answer them as best I can."

"How many bullets were fired?" It was Carl Nolan, often the most aggressive of the local reporters.

"To our knowledge, there were eighteen rounds, but that has not yet been confirmed."

"That sounds like a lot of bullets for a drunk man carrying a knife, Chief Drake. Why so many? Wouldn't one round in the leg have been enough?" The question came from Angie Toomey, a local reporter from the *Kelsey Daily*. A frequent critic of police practices, mostly surrounding the unfair treatment of minorities, the newspaper was one of the few things in Kelsey that Weber didn't control.

"Angie, I'm not going to dignify that with a response. Our officers who protect you and the other citizens of this city every single day also must protect themselves. Don't start making it political like they do up north in those big cities, or this press conference is over."

"Then allow me to rephrase my question," Angie said, undaunted. "How will you explain to Jimmy Keefer's family that it took killing their son with eighteen bullets to stop him from bringing harm to an experienced police officer with a knife?"

He ignored her question, choosing instead to end the press conference. He immediately joined Max Weber and the mayor, who plainly had not worked out their differences. I wished I knew what they were debating.

Even through the TV, I felt the stir of an unsettled audience, primarily reporters and those privileged enough to get inside the courthouse, who seemed put off by the chief's arrogance in defending why it took a pile of ammo to stop a drunken homeless man who swore a lot. Drake's hot temper was legendary, as were his close ties to the Kelsey elite, evidenced by Weber's presence despite the party leader holding no position or title with the city.

Tom flipped off the television. "My press conference is in one hour. Let's get to work. I hope I do better than the chief."

"A ham sandwich would do better than the chief," I said. "I think you've got this."

Christine, who had exited the room fifteen minutes before to take a telephone call, reentered with her hands together to signal a "T" for a time-out.

"I don't think you all know what is brewing outside, but you might want to take a look," she announced in her usual matter-of-fact manner. "The parking lot and the street behind us are full of people and getting more crowded."

When we ran down the hall to peek out the double glass doors in the back, we could see that Christine had underestimated the size of the crowd, which had swollen to what I guessed was over 500. A chant of "Justice for Jimmy" was being repeated over and over. Five television trucks were lined up on either side of the parking lot, each with reporters working the crowd for interviews.

"Greg, can we talk for a minute in my office?" Tom asked. I followed him into his private lair. "What do we do with this? That's an angry mob out there."

"You are going out there and doing what you have always done. You speak directly from the heart. Get this crowd on your side. Be as mad as they are—but assure them that justice will prevail."

That's all I needed to tell him. Tom immediately took charge, emerging from his office with new determination.

"Cooper, get a few guys and set up that small raised platform outside the doors. Then grab Ernie and tell him to hook up the speaker and microphone. I need this done in thirty minutes. Let's go," he shouted to everyone in earshot. "Christine, do you mind calling your dad and asking him to get as many pastors and reverends as possible to the Mission to stand behind me? Make sure we have a balance of Black and White clergy. Thanks!"

By the time the stage had been set up, the crowd had grown to the second street beyond the parking lot. As the podium was brought in, the dozen or so TV and radio crews scrambled to attach their microphones to achieve a quality audio feed. Eight pastors, including five Black ministers, lined up behind Tom in an impressive demonstration of unity.

"May I have your attention, everyone," Tom asked the crowd. "May I have your attention?" The din of several hundred conversations waned, replaced by an uncanny silence. "For those of you I haven't had the pleasure of meeting, my name is Tom Garrity. I'm the senior pastor and director of the Kelsey Rescue Mission, where Jimmy Keefer lived and where he was loved by all of us. We will miss him terribly.

"I spoke to Jimmy's mother about an hour ago. She and her daughter, Jimmy's younger sister, are driving to Kelsey as we speak. They come with the same question we are all asking: Why? Why did such a warm, funny, and generous young man get gunned down? We deserve answers, and I promise we will not rest until we get them."

The cheering was deafening as it swept through the mixed-race audience. Tom spoke of Jimmy with the emotion of a parent. The police had killed one of his guys for no apparent reason, and he was as angry and focused as I had ever seen him. "Justice for Jimmy" chants again arose, with Tom finally joining them.

"I want to bring Pastor Timothy Gains to the podium. Pastor Tim heads up the First Brethren Church of Kelsey, where Jimmy was a member. Tim is also the president of the Kelsey NAACP and has some important news."

Gains approached the podium, embracing Tom with a big hug before taking the microphone. "My brothers and sisters, this is a time for prayer and remembering our friend, Jimmy. It is also a time for peaceful protest. Police violence against our community must end now. The world will be watching what we do here in Kelsey. Let's ensure they see people of all colors, religions, and ages coming together as one undivided community in our quest for justice."

Pastor Gains hit just the right chord with this seemingly combustible crowd, which for now had been defused.

"Instead of allowing the darkness of our hearts to lead us, let us ask God Almighty to pull us through this tragic moment." He paused as the applause grew louder—a promising sign and much preferred over the riots other cities had experienced in times such as this. "I received a call from the Reverend Richard Clayton shortly before walking down here to the Rescue Mission to ask if he could speak at Jimmy's funeral this Saturday."

The eighty-three-year-old Clayton was one of the last living members of Dr. Martin Luther King's inner circle and easily one of the most respected Black leaders in the nation. I turned to Christine and shouted above the crowd, "With Clayton coming to Kelsey, this whole thing has just gone national."

Just then, we both spotted Charlie at the glass doors, waving with one hand while holding the other up to his ear, indicating a telephone call for Christine or me. We left our position next to the stage and reentered the building, where Charlie was talking so fast that we couldn't understand him. Something about the news was all we heard.

"Slow down, Charlie," Christine soothed him as she took his hand. "Who is on the phone?"

Charlie took a deep breath. "NBC in New York wants to speak with Pastor Tom. They want to interview him on national TV."

"Thank you, Charlie. Let me take it," Christine said firmly as she took the receiver from him. "Hello, this is Christine Culpepper. I'm the lawyer for the Kelsey Rescue Mission. Pastor Garrity is currently speaking to the rally outside. Should I have him call you back, or is there something I can do for you?" She listened for several seconds before replying, "Yes, we can schedule the pastor for an interview at two o'clock at the Mission. Did I hear correctly that you are sending a Nashville news team?"

She nodded along to the voice on the other end of the phone.

"Okay, we'll see Carl Nolan and his crew in front of the Mission at about one. Thank you."

Nolan would get the interview he'd asked me to arrange after all. Then I remembered my telephone date with Dan Johnson at two o'clock.

Christine and I spent most of the next two hours with Tom, helping him prepare for the sit-down interview with Nolan. The fact that it would be recorded and then broadcast on national television tonight was irrelevant to Tom. "I'm going to say the same things regardless of who I'm speaking to, so the size of the audience doesn't matter."

The press conference had been scratched in favor of his speech at the impromptu rally, followed by a flurry of questions from press members. Tragic circumstances had placed my old buddy in a bright spotlight, and I was impressed by how he managed it.

As scheduled, the television crew arrived at one o'clock to set up on the front lawn. Christine and Carl agreed that the interview would take place there, framed by the outdoor signage for the Mission, which would appear over Tom's left shoulder. From my perch in Tom's office, peering through the blinds, it seemed that Christine and Carl were having a friendly reunion. Two childhood classmates, each playing essential roles in an emerging national news story.

I continued to watch as Tom joined them and took a seat on the stool next to Carl. A makeup person worked on Tom's face while adding some powder to Carl's. A few spectators remained from the rally but were kept behind the fence, ironically by Kelsey Police officers assigned to the Mission's safety, at least for today.

Tom's office phone buzzed with Charlie's voice, interrupting my joy at watching Tom preparing to step out as a national spokesman for people without homes. "Mr. Smith, you have a call on line one."

CHAPTER TWENTY

"Hello, Greg Smith here. Is this Dan?"

"You know damn well who it is. What I want to know is why you have me calling you from a shopping mall parking lot on a cheap-ass Mickey Mouse phone?"

I could tell he was pissed or at least flummoxed. But I was right: Dan Johnson knew me well enough to go along with it.

"Is there anyone who can hear you? Not even your driver should be in earshot."

"He's twenty feet away in the car. I'm the only idiot wearing a suit and tie on a summer day in Dallas. Seriously, Greg, let's get to the point."

"The FBI is watching and listening to you, including your office and telephones. That may include your car or your home, I don't know." I delivered the bad news flatly and factually. Johnson preferred it that way. His silence was a sure sign he was listening.

"Where did you get this intriguing information?" he finally responded, this time in his "quiet" voice, indicating that I might know something.

"You know I can't tell you that, Dan, but if you thought about it for five seconds, you'd figure it out. So, here's the good news. The feds aren't after you directly. It's Max Weber they want. They think they have enough on the guy to make sure his golden years will be spent walking circles with his fellow inmates in a courtyard once a day." I took a few minutes to regale my former client on what I knew about Weber's alleged credit card scam.

"Max fucking Weber. You have to be kidding me. He's too stupid to be a good criminal."

I considered how miserably stupid I had been to be caught in a "low-risk" scheme to steal an election.

"It seems he's smart enough to get you to buy the mill property and have you fly here next week to sign the papers and announce the renovation publicly." My sarcasm didn't sit well with the Rockwood CEO, who hated, above all else, being disrespected, especially by someone he considered an underling.

"Wait just a minute, you little pug. I'm not coming to Kelsey to do anything public with Max Weber. He's full of shit."

I didn't entirely understand the insult. I was a cute little lapdog, maybe? "You might want to know the feds have you on tape referring to me as an 'arrogant little prick.' Is that the same thing as a pug?"

"Holy shit, you've heard my conversations from my private office. Someone's head could roll for that."

"And you will prove that how?" Johnson and I were now locked into what I would call at least a heated argument, and I needed to find a way out—a détente. "Look, Dan, we've come too far to let this happen to us. Can we take a deep breath and push the reset button? As my friend, I called to inform you that you must be careful. Have your phones and office debugged. Tighten up your security. Do what you want. But for God's sake, stay away from Weber."

"Good advice, as always, Greg. I'm sorry. I still have that bad temper. You remember?" The reset button had been pushed, and I was thankful. "Look, I was coming to Kelsey to tour the mill property with a team of engineers and architects. I have purchased it outright with no restrictions on what I put there. Weber and his investors have my money, and I have a pile of old, rat-infested buildings."

"Do you plan to meet with Weber?" He'd already told me he wasn't, but I had to be assured.

"Fuck Max Weber. He's a two-bit local political boss. I've dealt with creeps like that before. So have you. And now you tell me he has this other problem. Hell, I might ask the FBI how I can help, but I have nothing to give them. This is the only business I've done with him, and I hardly think buying a piece of land no one else wants is illegal."

"Dan, do me a favor. When you're here, let me take you to the Rescue Mission. I want you to meet Pastor Tom and some of the men. It will change your perspective."

"That's a deal, Greg. Thanks. But I think I'll let things die down a bit. You tell me when it's a good time to come. Thanks for the heads-up. And yes, for the record, sometimes you can be an arrogant prick." Oddly enough, I wasn't offended by his sentiment.

I hung up and looked out the window to check on the interview, which was in full swing. Carl and Tom were seated on stools next to each other before a cadre of cameras and lights, while Christine was off to the side with a clipboard in her hands, taking notes.

My conversation with Dan made it clear that news of Jimmy's shooting hadn't yet gone national. Otherwise he would have brought it up. Tonight's *Evening News* telecast would change that, as would Reverend Clayton's visit on Saturday. His PR machine would ensure it, just as Tom's interview would help put a national spotlight on the need to take the homelessness crisis in America more seriously. I kept thinking about the eighteen bullets fired into Jimmy's thin body and wondering how any sane person could see that as self-defense. A tragedy of enormous dimensions had occurred three blocks from where I was now sitting. I had no doubt the police chief—like all Kelsey officials, a Weber loyalist—was already preparing some cosmetic justification.

I recalled being in their shoes when a client of mine, the governor of Illinois, had to explain why he waited three days to call out the National Guard during a riot in Chicago. It is never easy having to explain why you waited to do the wrong thing.

The ring on my cell signaled a text from Christine. ALL IS WELL. TOM IS DOING GREAT. ARE YOU OKAY?

I WOULD PREFER LYING ON A CARIBBEAN BEACH WITH YOU AT MY SIDE AND A COLD RUM RUNNER IN MY HAND, I shot back.

WHEN DOES THE PRIVATE JET LEAVE? I'M READY. LOL.

I looked out the window again and saw her smiling while she read my text. She pointed to my window with her left hand while touching her heart with her phone hand. I "hearted" her back but wondered why she would take a chance on a relationship with a guy like me, a proven cheater and lawbreaker. I'm sure she had never so much as received a speeding ticket.

I crept out of the office and headed to the cafeteria for lunch. The line was gone, but five minutes remained before the serving window would be shut. I got a tray of fried chicken and mashed potatoes—the ultimate comfort meal—and sat across from Mark and four other Black residents. The room's mood was noticeably mournful and vacant of the usual din of coinciding conversations.

"Hey, Mr. Brad," said Jonah, Jimmy's best friend and meal buddy on most days, once Jimmy finished in the kitchen.

"Hey, Jonah, how are you doing?"

"I'm angry. I want to hurt those cops who killed my best friend. They deserve prison, or worse, for what they did." Jonah, who was typically friendly and outgoing, barely looked up from the tray before him. His grief was too overpowering, and his need for revenge was too deep.

"What those cops did to Jimmy will not be swept under the rug," I assured him. "I'm confident about that, Jonah. Pastor Tom will not let the Kelsey old boy club brush this off."

I was spinning. What did I know about consoling a young Black guy whose best friend had been shot down and killed?

"Here's the thing," Jonah continued, finally looking at me. "Jimmy was one of the good guys. Sure, he drank too much. Lots of good people drink too much. But he never hurt anyone. He was a mama's boy. Am I right?" He glanced around at a table of heads nodding in assent. "And that knife he had? He used it for fishing. He had been out at the river all day trying to catch a few basses like he always did on his day off from the kitchen."

The cafeteria had emptied, leaving only my table occupied when Christine and Tom walked in. "Is it over?" I asked. "How did it go?"

"Pastor Tom was a superstar, as usual," replied Christine. "He did a wonderful job."

Tom sat next to Jonah and put both arms around him, resulting in Jonah collapsing his head into Tom's chest. His initial weeping turned into wails and convulsions. Tom didn't let him let go, choosing instead to hold him tighter.

"You're going to get through this, son. We all will." Tom spoke softly, barely above a whisper. "We need to make Jimmy's loss mean something to our city and the world, and that can't happen by taking up arms and fighting back with violence. They want us to do that. Please don't fall for it. And that goes for all of you."

I remembered an incident in high school when Tom and I were eating our sack lunches in the cafeteria, minding our business, when we saw a commotion across the large room. It turned out to be two fellow seniors taunting a smaller, younger boy for being gay, calling him out with degrading names that were common for the time: "Hey, faggot, if you like boys so much, why don't you give my friend a kiss?" The boy started to cry as students gathered to spur on the duo. Tom surged to his feet, and I followed him through the crowd.

Tom had no way of knowing whether the boy was gay, and it wouldn't have influenced his decision anyway. He gripped the arm of the louder bully and bent it behind his back. His 200-pound wrestling physique made the brief struggle a foregone conclusion.

"You make one move or say one word, and I assure you this arm will break," my friend said calmly. Looking at the bully's partner, he said, "I will come after you and break both arms. The only way out of this is to apologize to this young man, saying the words, 'I am sorry and won't do it again.'"

The other students went silent as the one in Tom's grip repeated the words.

"Louder, punk. I want to hear you, and you too, you little shit-wad," he said to the second violator. Both hoodlums babbled at once, "I'm sorry and won't do it again." I honestly think one of them peed their pants. Tom let go, shoved the bully to the floor, looked at the younger boy, and said, "Come on, dude, you're eating lunch with us," at which point the lad grabbed his tray and followed us back across the now-silent cafeteria to our table.

From that day until we graduated three months later, Randy Pittman, a freshman, ate lunch with us. Years later, a handsome young man introduced himself to Liz and me after she spoke at a campaign rally in Buffalo. He said his name was Randy.

"Ms. Smith, you have my vote, but I came tonight because I hoped you might tell your brother that I'm all grown up and will graduate from medical school at Columbia next year. I think he would be happy to know that I did okay."

The afternoon went by quickly, with no word from the police despite Tom's hourly requests to see the body cameras and gain insight into what had occurred the night before. By now, the city was swarming with news trucks and reporters from throughout the state and region, many clamoring to speak with Tom, who had assigned the competent Christine Culpepper to conduct countless interviews about Jimmy's tragic death. I saw the exhaustion on her face as she went from one standing discussion to another. All interviews took place outside due to Tom's strict order that the men inside be left alone. Kelsey was now central to the nation's latest police shooting, and the Kelsey Rescue Mission was the eye of the hurricane.

In the middle of the dinner hour, Tom took to the microphone.

"Listen up, guys. May I have your attention?"

Mission residents knew that when Pastor Tom asked for attention, he didn't intend to ask twice. The room hushed.

"I just want you to know that God is with you tonight. He will not abandon us in this challenging time. We all loved Jimmy, just as I love every one of you. We don't have all the facts yet, but from what I know, there can be no good reason why Jimmy's life was taken from us. This incident will challenge your faith. It will cause some of you to question the existence of God. I get that. But I implore you to talk to each other and those of us here, like Cooper and me, and the counselors volunteering their time, if you need to let off some steam. This is not the time to take the law into your own hands. Justice will prevail. I can promise you that."

Immediately following dinner, Christine, Tom, and I joined the residents, packed like canned sardines into the TV room to watch NBC's report.

"Good evening, and welcome to the *Evening News*. I'm Robin Charles. Heading our report is the tragic news of a police shooting in Kelsey, Tennessee, outside of Nashville, resulting in the death of Jimmy Keefer, a homeless man residing at the Kelsey Rescue Mission. According to Kelsey Police Chief Art Drake, Keefer threatened the lives of four officers with a pocketknife, resulting in all four officers riddling the victim with eighteen rounds in four seconds. Although there were no witnesses to the incident, all four officers wore mandatory body cameras. However, the footage has not been released publicly.

"Meanwhile, several thousand Kelsey citizens gathered at the Kelsey Rescue Mission to protest what they believe is another example of unnecessary police violence. Carl Nolan, from our affiliate in Nashville, sat down today with Pastor Tom Garrity, who heads up the Mission. Here's part of that interview. The entire interview can be viewed online and will be rebroadcast tonight at eleven."

The room was silent, and each eyeball focused on their tough but beloved leader as he fielded various questions from the experienced interviewer. Although Tom had a national audience, he spoke directly to the hearts of those in the room, many of whom were wiping their tears as the interview progressed. Finally, the interview ended with a series of questions, not from Carl Nolan but from Tom.

"When did we decide that it was acceptable for the richest nation in the history of the world to tolerate more than a million of our fellow citizens living without a home? How often do you need to drive by a family living on the street and ignore that those kids might be helping their parents dive into a garbage bin for dinner tonight? How do you say to a homeless veteran, 'Thank you for your service' without feeling shame? And when did we start approving police executions of innocent homeless men?"

"Pastor Tom Garrity, thank you for your time and thoughts on this most important issue. I'm Carl Nolan from the Kelsey Rescue Mission in Kelsey, Tennessee."

CHAPTER TWENTY-ONE

"Dad, are you okay? I'm here with Mom, and we're worried about you and Uncle Tom. We watched him on the news tonight."

"I'm fine, honey. Thanks for calling. I'm on the freeway, about halfway to the marina from Kelsey."

"Happy you're okay. Here's Mom."

"Hey, Mr. Smith. How involved are you in all of this?"

"I would say up to my keister, but that would be a lie. More like my eyeballs at this point. Do we have some bad apples at the Mission? Do some of them have a soiled history? Yes. But the vast majority of these guys have good hearts. They need a little respect and a chance to prove themselves." I knew I was singing to the choir. No one in Congress has championed homelessness and poverty issues more than Elizabeth Garrity Smith.

Still, I thought I knew what was coming next: a "Liz lecture" about staying out of anything controversial. Think about your daughter and going back to prison, she was going to say. But I was wrong.

"Good for you, Greg. I am proud of what you and Tom are doing down there. Do not let them get away with this." I chose not to tell her I had been threatened to leave the state. Nor did I mention that I was paying Joey Martino for twenty-four-hour "security" at the marina. Come to think of it, I hadn't told her about the warden telling me to watch my back.

"Liz, I think they executed the kid in cold blood, which is why they haven't released the body-cam footage. They killed an innocent homeless guy for public drunkenness."

"My, aren't we the crusaders for the betterment of mankind."

I knew Liz was teasing, but she correctly read me, as usual. In my previous life, my every move was calculated. I didn't have time for silly things like compassion and empathy. But all of this—homeless men, Jimmy's death, Tom, and Christine—had stirred something. Kelsey was changing me.

Liz went on, "Listen, this is inside poop, but I've decided not to run for reelection. It's been a good eighteen years, but I want another adventure. I think I can do more good outside of Congress than within. There's just one thing I want to do before walking out of here: pass the American Houselessness Act, or the 'Aha' Act, as we like to call it. I also want to include federal funding for your center in Kelsey, but I'll need private investors for at least half of it."

Pulling into the marina parking lot, I observed our new security guard making his hourly rounds. His presence made me feel a little safer. Regardless, I had no intention of leaving the state.

"That's great news, Liz. What can I do to help?" *Why did I offer that?* No one offered to help Liz unless they wanted a significant task assigned to them. But she got me a "Get Out of Jail Free" card, so I owed her.

"Well, I'm happy you asked. Can you be up here in DC next Wednesday to meet with my staff? I chair the Special Committee on Homelessness and would like you to brief my staff on your concept for the center. We're getting ready to debate a bill that deals with several items to get people into homes and jobs. The center isn't included in the bill yet, but I think I could sell it."

"Would it be a private meeting?" I asked. "I'm trying to stay out of the public eye." Between the campaign and now the shooting, though, I might have been failing.

"It would be private. It's not a hearing. Just a half dozen or so policy wonks who are writing the bill, with box lunches brought in from catering. I'd like them to hear your thoughts. In the evening, I hope you will go with Sydney and me to Rob's thirty-fifth birthday party. His wife, Laurie, has rented the 1789 Restaurant."

Rob Kearse, the White House chief of staff, was an old friend, and she knew I wouldn't decline. Fourteen years ago, Liz and I hired Rob for his first political job to manage Liz's reelection campaign. He was twenty-one and hadn't graduated from the University of Buffalo yet. Republicans were coming after her with a Tea Party candidate, and she was on everyone's list as a casualty of the leftward drift of her party. When she won by a mere 175 votes, the closest House race in the country that year, he became her new chief of staff, and I got dubbed Rob Kearse's "mentor." While I was in prison, he called me weekly to check in and update me on the "real news."

"Will your girlfriend be jealous that the Smith family is reunited?" I asked.

"Susan will be fine with it. She knows and respects that we're unbreakable. I could ask that about your girlfriend too, you know. But I have way too much class for that." As much as Liz tried to sound harsh, she started to laugh.

"You're an ass, Liz. You know that, don't you?" We were both laughing now. "Besides, I only auditioned for the boyfriend role last week and haven't heard her final verdict."

"Sydney told me she likes Christine a lot, but I suspect you already know that." *Jesus, she even knows her name. Are there no secrets with this woman?* "I hope she likes naughty boys. Anyway, it was great talking to you. I'll see you next week."

Still a naughty boy. As much as I aimed to shed my reputation, I supposed some things were embedded. My mom always said, "We are known by our behavior, not our thoughts." My life had been spent stretching boundaries. I couldn't be Tom. He was goodness personified, like his sister. And here came Christine into my life. The three of them were in a moral league of their own. *Why in the hell would they want to hang out with me?* I wondered.

As I climbed out of the truck, I heard footsteps crossing the gravel parking lot behind me. "Are you Mr. Smith?" The deep male voice turned out to belong to the uniformed security guard, visible thanks to the streetlamp lighting up the parking area.

"I am, and you would be our new security guard?"

"Yes sir, I'm Brady Gaul. This is my first night. I'll be trading off with three other guards from the firm, but we are all retired cops, so you're in pretty good hands."

He had no way of knowing that cops were not high on my list of reassuring company at present, but we shook hands anyway. "Nice to meet you, Brady. I'm Greg Smith."

"We had a little incident tonight that you should know about. I saw two guys climbing over the rail to board your houseboat around nine o'clock. I didn't think you would be climbing over your gate, so I approached them and asked which one was Greg. When I put my flashlight on their faces, I assumed neither was you because both were wearing ski masks. They immediately ran to the back of the boat, jumped onto the dock, and ran off. I tried to keep up with them, but they were too fast."

"Did you report it to the police?"

"No. I waited to ask you what you want me to do."

That was a wise decision, I thought. Although alarmed by his report, I didn't need the attention a squad of cops would bring. I was pretty sure I could defend myself if they came back. I immediately thought about Lamar Goodman but was more alarmed that he might now have an accomplice.

I would call the security company tomorrow and arrange to have cameras installed. "But I did find this," the guard continued as he handed me a credit card with the name Joel Palmer. "I think he was using the credit card to unlock your sliding door, and he dropped it when he saw my flashlight."

"Thank you, Officer Gaul. I appreciate how you handled it. Say, do you know this guy?" Once a cop, always a cop.

"Everyone in law enforcement knows Joel Palmer. He heads security for Max Weber. Joel and I worked together for a long time here in Nashville. He was one of the dirtiest cops I ever knew. It looks like he hasn't changed much."

"Again, I appreciate everything. It's good knowing you're here. Do you mind if I have the card?" I wasn't sure why, but I thought it might be helpful.

"Sure, he dropped it on your property, so I guess it's yours. Are you sure you don't want me to write a report?"

"Go ahead and write the report, but please keep it internal for now. I want to have a record of it in case it turns into something. The attorney in me is showing," I laughed nervously, wondering if Goodman had a connection to Weber. Could they be working in tandem against a common enemy: me? Knowing that I had to live looking over both shoulders was disconcerting, reinforcing my original intention of simply disappearing somewhere. *Would Christine go for St. Lucia?*

I climbed aboard the boat and used my key to unlock the same glass door Mr. Palmer had submitted his credit card to. *Why would Max Weber instruct his goons to break into my boat?* I recalled the fear I felt when I was picked up at my home in a van and taken to prison, and the time I lost five-year-old Sydney for five minutes in the crowd at Disney World. Compared to those events, this was a picnic. Nonetheless, it unnerved me. I had to figure out how to deal with Weber in the short term. But I would be patient. I was pretty sure, given his current Green Technologies problem, I just needed to sit back and watch him unravel.

The phone ringing interrupted my thoughts, and I reached for it immediately. It was a very agitated Tom. "Greg, I've seen the tapes of Jimmy's shooting. I was right from the start. It was an execution. They killed the kid in cold blood. I can't believe what they did. He swung a fishing knife at them from ten feet away, and they fired. Every one of them." Tom was yelling into the phone. I had never heard him this angry. "It's just awful."

"Where are you now?" I asked calmly.

"At the Mission. Christine is here too. And Mark just walked in. Here, I'll put you on speaker."

"Hi, Greg, it's Christine. We have a thumb drive from the body cameras. It was dropped off at the front desk in an envelope by a Mission resident. An unidentified cop apparently instructed him to do so. How they got it, we don't know, but we have it, and Tom is right. It is beyond anything you or anyone would ever want to see. And he left a note, saying, 'This is going up on social media tonight at midnight. Be prepared.'"

"Holy shit, the city could erupt when this thing goes online," I replied, again trying to keep my cool. "I suggest we try and get ahead of this if we can. Tom, call the mayor. Get him out of bed if you have to. Tell him you've seen the recording and that by tomorrow morning, the city police need to be on high alert. Also, remind him to call the governor for support from state National Guard units. You should call as many pastors as you can tonight, asking them to get the word out to their people and call for peaceful, not violent, protests." I was rattling orders like a battlefield general. "Please download that tape and send me a link immediately. I will give this to Liz so she can work at the federal level for support. Our first responsibility is to ensure this doesn't become a full-blown riot."

After a moment of silence, I added, "Christine, can you sit down and write from your heart about what you are feeling right now about the city you love? The place you grew up in and the home that we all share. Convey a sense of community that this is our time to be united, not torn apart by the actions of a few bad cops. Speak for Jimmy, as if he were calling us from the grave to come together and be one. We can deal with injustice, politics, and everything else another day, but at the moment, our most important goal is to stay calm and be unified. The minute that shooting goes up on social media, post it on the Mission's social media pages."

"I can do that," said Christine, reflectively, as if she were already writing the words in her head. "I think I'll also call Carl Nolan and Angie Toomey and send them links to the recording."

"Great idea, Christine. And, Mark, get the ambassadors downstairs ASAP and let them know what's happening. They need to be deputized as peacekeepers. We'll rely on them to let the other guys know that they will be under the watchful eye of the citizens and the media, and they must be on their best behavior. They are the victims here, just as much as Jimmy, and the temptation to go out and cause trouble will be too much for some of them to resist. Ask them if we can video-record some of their statements for social media tomorrow. I'll be there in an hour. I think we're in for a very late night."

Working with Christine as a close partner had become seamless, with each of us anticipating the other's next moves. Our chemistry was upbeat. Despite my self-loathing and shame, she behaved as if my past didn't matter. Not having her in my life was quickly becoming unimaginable.

CHAPTER TWENTY-TWO

The Mission was eerily quiet when I arrived. Curfew had passed an hour ago at nine o'clock, and most of the men had retired to their beds. Only a few were in the cafeteria, chatting in small groups and sipping on the tar they called coffee that was available twenty-four hours a day. During the hour-long drive, I'd made the best of my time, first briefing Liz, who said she would send the recording to the White House and the FBI. She once again urged me to use caution about being out front with the situation and was relieved when I reassured her that my role was totally behind the scenes.

I did not tell her about the break-in attempt on my houseboat, saving that for another day. Right now, it had not reached the top of my concerns.

After parking, I headed directly to the campaign office, walking past the reception desk and down the hall. Christine and Tom were talking in the hallway outside the closed door. "Thanks for coming down," Tom greeted me. "I needed my best friend tonight."

"No worries, buddy. I want to be here for you. What's the latest?"

"We have everything in motion," Christine replied. "The mayor, governor, and all the pastors have all been called, and Mark did a great job giving the ambassadors an update. I also finished writing my post calling for calm and reason. I'm ready to put it up as soon as the video goes up." She was mentally sharp despite the late hour, but she had to be exhausted.

Tom answered his cell. "Hello, this is Pastor Tom. Oh, hello, Carl."

It was Nolan. I had sent him the link to the video and figured he was taking me up on my suggestion that he call either Tom or Christine for more information.

"Say, Carl, do you mind if I put you on speaker? I have Christine and Greg here with me."

We walked into the empty campaign room, taking seats around the conference table, now shoved against the wall and being used for workstations.

"Hello, all," Carl said. "Thanks for the link, Greg. It's pretty gruesome. I just talked with the police chief, who is unhappy with this getting out. He thinks it was smuggled by one of the police support staff, maybe a secretary, although he isn't saying exactly who he suspects."

"Who did is hardly the issue," I volunteered.

"Exactly right, Greg," Carl responded. "But it does suggest where the chief's focus is on this. He's far more interested in catching the guy who ratted on them. As far as I can see, he has done little to prepare for possible demonstrations tomorrow. We're running this as the lead news story tonight at eleven, with clips from the video. We are not saying who gave us the video. Pastor Tom, I'm interested in any comment you might want to provide before we air the footage."

"I can only say, Carl, that we are thankful the truth about this horrific tragedy has come out. We hope justice will be done, and we ask the citizens of Kelsey to keep their protests peaceful. Jimmy Keefer would have wanted it that way. We are coordinating with the city's faith community to keep our city in their prayers."

"The chief told me that if the Mission could control its residents better, things like this would be less likely to happen. How do you respond?"

"I think the chief needs to control his people better." Tom's delivery was dry, flat, and bitingly sarcastic. "Jimmy Keefer was shot down in cold blood. The chief should arrest them, not make excuses for trigger-happy cops." Bam. No one cut through the bull better than Tom Garrity.

"Thanks, Pastor Tom. Will you be available for an interview tomorrow?"

"I'm not planning to go anywhere. Thanks, Carl." He ended the call. "Well, guys, we've done all we can for the night. I'm going home and getting a few hours of sleep. Something tells me tomorrow will be very long. Thanks again, Greg, for coming down. Do you need a place to sleep tonight? I'm sure Jane wouldn't mind if you used the guest room."

"He's crashing at my house," Christine swiftly volunteered, but by the looks of her red cheeks, she probably wished she hadn't. "He is welcome to come home with me and save himself the drive to Nashville."

"Well then, I'll see you both back here for breakfast." Tom knew I would consider Christine's house the better offer, although there would be questions. I was sure of that.

A little later, Christine and I sat at her kitchen counter, each with a large glass of cabernet sauvignon. It tasted expensive. According to the babysitter, Cody had been in bed since eight.

When Christine turned on the eleven o'clock news, a grim-faced Claude Mosely, Channel Four's beloved longtime anchorman, appeared alone on the screen, looking dapper as always in his suit, light gray to match his neatly trimmed graying hair.

"Let me warn you that our lead story tonight is troubling. Channel Four has obtained the body-camera videos that show in gruesome detail last week's shooting in Kelsey of a homeless man, Jimmy Keefer, by four Kelsey police officers. The following is about one minute of the footage that leads up to the actual shooting."

We watched in horror what we had already seen, this time with the understanding that thousands of other people were watching too. The entire video would soon go on social media, where millions would see it by tomorrow morning.

Following the videos, the anchorman reappeared. "It should be noted that the police did not officially release the body-cam footage. Someone took it from within the department without the permission of Chief Art Drake. In a telephone interview shortly before airtime this evening, the chief told our reporter, Carl Nolan, that he would 'turn over tables and chairs in the department,' and I quote, 'to find and arrest the one who smuggled the video footage.' He also warned the Kelsey Rescue Mission to get better control of their men, referencing that Jimmy Keefer was a resident at the Mission. In an interview, also by telephone, with Pastor Tom Garrity, who heads up the Kelsey Rescue Mission, he said it is the Kelsey Police chief who, and I quote, 'needs to control his people better.' Let's bring Carl Nolan into the discussion."

The camera pulled back to reveal Carl had joined Claude at the anchor desk. "Carl, can you give us the latest on this taut situation?"

"Claude, I have talked to the governor's office and am told that he has ordered the National Guard to be on high alert. Their concern is that as the video of Jimmy Keefer being shot by the police officers spreads, it could lead to massive protests tomorrow. Both the mayor and the governor are urging people not to overreact and to allow our system of justice to play out. Although the four police officers are on administrative leave, this will surely amp up the call for their arrest. We can only wait and see what tomorrow brings in Kelsey."

"Let's get some sleep," Christine said as she turned off the TV. "You can have the guest room. Cody's here, and I'm not ready to answer uncomfortable questions about where you are sleeping when he wakes up. But I will accept a kiss goodnight if you're willing." I took her in my arms, and our lips gently touched. "Thanks for understanding," she said softly as she turned toward her room. "Good night."

It was still dark when I awoke in the morning with Christine seated on my bed, stroking my hair, now nearing shoulder length. I noticed that she was fully dressed and ready for the day.

"Hey, unofficial boyfriend. Good morning. You need to rise and shine and get ready to head down to the Mission. You have kitchen duty today, you know."

Nothing like youthful energy, I reckoned. Maybe a girlfriend who wasn't fourteen years younger would have been more my speed. The only problem was that I had already fallen in love with everything about her and doubted I could put the toothpaste back in the tube.

"How can you be up so early?" I managed to mumble.

"I wanted to check social media. The video got over a million hits in the first four hours. It's gone viral, just as we suspected. The national cable and network morning shows are already promoting it as their lead. By the way, I'm keeping Cody out of school today. My mother will pick him up in ten minutes. You can come out of hiding after they leave. Your shower is right across the hall, so it should be easy to keep yourself busy."

"Sounds good," I replied, thinking that I hadn't snuck around like this since I used to crawl through Liz's window in high school and later up the back stairs at her college sorority house.

Christine drove us the few blocks to the Mission. Along the way, we noticed that Tennessee Avenue, Kelsey's main street, had been blocked off by police barricades; no traffic allowed. A small crowd, mostly African Americans, had assembled outside the police department, shouting organized slogans. Jimmy was one of their own. Many of them might not know that Jimmy was one of ours too.

He was a member of a growing multiethnic population with no home and little hope until he came to the Mission and slowly became a viable part of a caring community. My growth wasn't that dissimilar from Jimmy's. Although my privileged finances would forever keep me from being technically "homeless," when I was released from Morgantown, I was nonetheless estranged from practically everything resembling a home—until I came here and started peeling carrots and potatoes twice a week and looking into the faces of strangers who came to call me "bro."

Without self-awareness to hold me back, I began to quietly hum the final chorus adapted from the Victor Hugo opus *Les Misérables*, when Jean Valjean, having been given a second chance in life "to become an honest man," sings with Fantine and Eponine.

At the end of my little concert to myself, Christine burst out with the final line: "To love another person is to see the face of God." I blinked at her, embarrassed that I had been humming louder than I realized.

"Truly one of my very favorites," she said, smiling. "Maybe you're my Jean Valjean?" Pulling into her assigned parking spot in the back of the Mission, she added, "I hope so because I'm ready to go fight the bad guys."

Tom was waiting for us inside the back door. "Hey, guys, we need to talk." We each poured a cup of the worst coffee ever made and sat at a table at the far end of the cafeteria. Christine hadn't stopped for lattes today, perhaps because she was too busy singing a duet with me.

"Hey, Pastor Tom, are you taking my kitchen volunteer away from me again this morning?" Mike yelled good-naturedly across the room.

"He'll be in, just a little late today. We'll dock his pay."

"Again?" I asked loudly so Mike could hear me.

Turning back to Christine and me, Tom drew a severe expression. "The mayor called me at home this morning. He woke me like I did him last night. He told me the chief is unhinged over the footage getting out of the building and that 'heads will roll' when he finds the culprit. But more importantly, the chief told the mayor to stay out of his business, and the only one he's responsible to is Max Weber, the one who put him there."

Now the heated exchange between the two of them made sense.

"So, Weber is calling the shots at city hall and police headquarters," I summarized. *And breaking into houseboats*, I thought, but that was a subject for another time.

"Exactly. But get this. The mayor—who was also put into office by Weber—is ready to break ties with him. He claims the corruption has reached a point where he's willing to come out and estrange himself completely from the party and its boss. So, I invited him to breakfast to talk to the best political strategist I know, Gregory Bradley Smith. He should be here any minute."

If Weber didn't hate me enough already, my advising the mayor on how to break ties with him would surely put him over the edge. Maybe I needed to quadruple security at the marina.

Mayor Frank Simmons arrived five minutes later, his dapper blue suit and red tie standing in sharp contrast to the casual attire of the Mission. "Good morning. Thank you, Pastor Tom, for inviting me down," he said with a proper Southern accent, standing over us with an extended hand. Christine was the first taker. The mayor's towering frame, pasty skin, and slicked-back hair made for an imposing figure, especially if you were seated.

"Nice to see you, Mayor Simmons," she said. "Meet Greg Smith. He is one of our most active volunteers and also happens to be a lawyer and a political consultant. He's offered to help."

"Oh, I know all about Mr. Smith, and I must ask why such a moral man like Pastor Tom and you, Ms. Culpepper, would be in such close cahoots with a man convicted and imprisoned for election fraud, among other notorious crimes."

I had to hand it to him. He got right to the point.

"And I might ask you, Mayor Simmons, how you have been so closely associated with a nefarious character like Max Weber?" Tom was also good at getting to the point.

"Fair enough," Simmons replied. "None of us are without poor judgment in our past. So, Greg, I want to get out of Weber's clutches and do what is right. I guess you and I might share something in common."

"Let me ask you a question, Mayor. Who is the number two guy at the police department, and do you trust him?" I had a plan, but I needed to lead him to it.

"That would be Captain Larry Casey. He is an outstanding

officer passed over for the chief's job because Weber convinced me we needed to bring Drake in from the outside. It was the worst mistake I've made as mayor. I see now that Drake has done nothing but create a culture of aggressive police action against poor people and minorities. It must end."

"Here's my thinking," I began, deciding to take him at face value. As long as actions followed words, I had no reason to doubt his change of heart. "Christine will draft a letter from you terminating Drake, effective immediately. You have the authority to do this, and believe me, Weber is in no position to stop it legally. You will then appoint Casey as the interim chief. Your reasons for firing the chief are insubordination, failure to train officers properly, and anything else Christine can think of. All of this will happen by noon today. Are you with me so far?" I had not intended to be so direct, but I could not stop my trained instinct to plot and plan.

"Yes, I like what I'm hearing."

"At one o'clock, you will get in front of the protestors, which by midday will undoubtedly number in the thousands, to announce that you have fired the police chief and have instructed the city attorney to seek a grand jury indictment of the four officers for murder. Then, you can introduce Casey as the new chief and discuss the need to move forward as a united city and the fact that police violence will not be tolerated on your watch. Not now or ever. You will fire, hire, and inspire in the next four hours. If all goes as I think it will, you will be responsible for quieting a city on the verge of exploding. And that, my friend, is called leadership."

CHAPTER TWENTY-THREE

"Mayor Simmons, why don't you and I head to my office? I can get the termination letter written from there. Greg is late for his scheduled work assignment in the kitchen, and we shouldn't keep him from his duties." Christine took over complete operational control of the plan while reminding me of my real purpose in the Mission: preparing and serving breakfast.

"She's right, Mayor. There are scrambled eggs and pancakes to prepare, and I'm the man to do it. Good luck. You are in good hands," I replied while smiling at Christine.

When I reached the serving window to dish out my finest cuisine, the line was more than double its average size, prompting me to ask Mike if he could prepare a second batch of food.

"Where are these people coming from?" I asked him.

"They're the homeless folks who aren't residents of the Mission, the ones who live out there on the streets and under bridges who are probably scared shitless over all the commotion. They're seeking temporary shelter from all the bullshit going on out there."

We turned on the small TV atop one of the shelves in the kitchen and saw that Kelsey was indeed the morning's lead story on the national news. The on-screen reporter talked about how the body-camera video had gone viral overnight and now numbered over two million views. He also read Christine's tender and well-written post about keeping the city she loved peaceful despite those who wished to divide us further. As tears sprang into my eyes, I realized I hadn't even read it yet.

We could also see in the background of the live report that the crowd around the police station had tripled since we drove by an hour before. The governor then appeared at a press conference from his capitol office, announcing that he had authorized the deployment of the state's National Guard to arrive in Kelsey by noon to begin assisting local police in peacekeeping efforts. A gruff-looking Arthur Drake followed the governor on the telecast with a stern warning to those who would enact any violence or looting, reminding them his police had far more billy clubs and rifles than they did.

If he intended to "maintain" the calm, he was most certainly failing.

As I filled up the trays as quickly as possible, watching the line grow longer by the minute, I heard Tom's booming voice on the in-house sound system and looked across the room, where he held the microphone. Standing next to him was a petite Black woman, probably about fifty years old, dressed in a black dress and matching bonnet that looked like proper funeral attire. Beside her was a pretty young lady in her early twenties.

"Gentlemen and the ladies who are present, listen up. May I please have your attention?" The room quickly went silent. "I want to introduce you to Mrs. Maddy Keefer, Jimmy's mother, and his sister, Mary Keefer. They have driven over from Memphis for Jimmy's funeral this Saturday and wanted to see Jimmy's home in Kelsey and meet his friends."

The entire room broke into applause. In seconds, they all stood, giving Mrs. Keefer an ovation for at least a full minute, maybe longer. Tom handed her the microphone as the cafeteria crowd resumed their seats.

"Thank you, Pastor Tom, and to all of you who loved my son. Jimmy was a good boy. Not perfect, but good in his heart and spirit. And if you knew Jimmy, you also know he wouldn't hurt a soul. I am sad about how he was taken from us, and I am sure you are too. But we must do what Jimmy would do today: not act hatefully or meanly. Jimmy wouldn't want that. Love your enemies. Justice will be done. Thank you." She handed the microphone to Tom, who engulfed her and her daughter simultaneously in a hug.

Again the crowd rose to its feet with applause, many people with faces covered in tears, like mine. When the clapping finally died down, a chorus of "We Shall Overcome" arose from a corner of the cafeteria and soon spread throughout the large room. Black and White, old and young, arms linked, all were singing the anthem of the civil rights movement, made so famous by Dr. Martin Luther King. I had never experienced such a spontaneous outpouring of emotion.

I felt my phone vibrating in my pocket and pulled it out despite the sticky latex gloves I was still wearing from serving food. "Hey, Christine, what's up?"

"Are you cutting an onion?"

I fessed up to feeling a little emotional and told her about Mrs. Keefer.

"Oh my God, do I hear 'We Shall Overcome'? This is amazing, Greg. I'm bummed that I missed it, but we are making great progress over here. The letter is done, and the mayor is walking it over as we speak. He is laser-focused, for sure. He's going to order that a public address system outside of the police station be set up so he can announce it to the crowd, which is huge. I'm working with the town's media person to call every news station and newspaper in Tennessee."

"That sounds great. It's imperative that you aren't anywhere to be seen, Christine. We can't have any public connection between the Mission and the city. This is entirely the mayor's thing."

"I agree. I'm staying put, but a few of the usual suspects have asked me when Tom might be available. I told them to call him on his mobile phone, and he'd be happy to answer questions."

"On another note, Ernie recorded Mrs. Keefer's little speech on his own, so you might think of coming over here and getting that up on social media."

"Nice. Yes, I will do that, but first, ensure it's okay with her. I don't want anything coming back to bite us."

"Listen, Pastor Timothy Gains, the head of the local NAACP, called to ask my thoughts on where to have Jimmy's funeral. I suggested the park. They have that nice pavilion, the seating for concerts and events, and the huge grassy area for folks to sit. Thoughts?"

"That's a great idea. I'm sure you'll have to get a permit from the city, but we have a new inside man for that, don't we?"

The singing had died down by now. As the crowd dispersed, I stepped out to the back.

"I need to tell you something that I haven't shared with anyone yet."

I proceeded to update her on the video I'd received threatening me if I didn't move out of the state within ten days and the attempted break-in of my houseboat the previous night by Weber's private gestapo. I also told her that the security team I had hired for the docks was installing an alarm and remote cameras on the boat tomorrow, which I could monitor from my phone.

"Just as long as you turn them off the first time I spend the night there," she responded in her most flirtatious voice.

"Has anyone ever told you that you are a naughty girl?"

"I don't think so, but I never had a bad boy who would notice." Aha, Liz was right. I would never shake my past. "And just for the record, I'm not being bad. I'm falling in love. There's a big difference, you know."

• • •

Mayor Simmons's announcement was being carried nationally on all cable stations, each with its spin. I picked HMN and was soon joined by Christine, Tom, Mark, and Jimmy's mother and sister. We saw that the city workers had set up a temporary stage and sound system. The cameras panned the crowd, which had reached a multitude of 5,000, maybe more. I saw the faces of several Mission residents, including Jonah Mays, Jimmy's best friend. The network anchors were filling airtime as the cameras stayed on the stage, where the mayor and Captain Casey were both visible.

Simmons stepped to the microphone. "Good afternoon. It's so good to see so many of my fellow citizens who want the same things as I do for our great city. First, we want justice for Jimmy Keefer, who was shot down in cold blood on the very street that houses our government and our police. This is why I have issued an executive order removing the four officers from service and am asking our county prosecuting attorney to send them to the next meeting of the grand jury for indictment for second-degree murder. I intend to make sure that they will be prosecuted to the full extent of the law."

In waves, beginning with those closest to the stage, loud applause filled the air, followed by a chant of "Justice for Jimmy. Justice for Jimmy."

After several minutes, the chanting was finally subdued so Mayor Simmons could be recognized and heard again. "I have also terminated the employment of former Chief of Police Arthur Drake, effective immediately. He has been escorted from the building and will no longer be welcome anywhere at city hall or the police department. Kelsey will not be governed by unelected political bosses and those who report to them, especially those in public safety positions."

The crowd was so loud I doubted Simmons would get in another word. However, after much arm-waving and time-out signs by the mayor, he made himself heard one last time. "I would like to introduce to you an old and trusted friend. A man who has spent his entire career with the Kelsey Police and a man I will now call Chief Larry Casey."

More applause, followed by another chant, this time, "Larry. Larry. Larry." The fact that Larry Casey also happened to be Black sent an important symbolic message. Still, it was his impeccable credentials and reputation that set him apart.

The noisy crowd was at peak volume when Casey took to the microphone.

"Thank you. Thank you." He waved enthusiastically as he tried to calm what could reasonably be described as admirers. "I look out at this amazing crowd and see so many friends. Many of you were my schoolmates here in Kelsey. Many more of you are new. But all of us call Kelsey home. We are one. And now it is time for us to come together. I assure you that I will work to do my part and restore your confidence in your Kelsey Police Department. Thank you."

When the speechmaking ceased, the crowd began to break apart, but the mayor and the chief remained for an impromptu press conference, patiently answering questions and conducting on-camera interviews. "Who are the political bosses you referred to?" "Do you expect a lawsuit from Art Drake?" "How sure are you that you can get an indictment?" "Do you know who leaked the body-camera video?" and many similar inquiries. Carl Nolan asked, "Mayor Simmons, what role did the people at the Rescue Mission play in your decision to take such decisive action today?"

Around the conference table, the press conference was only in the background as we informally discussed other items, such as funding for the expansion campaign. However, Nolan's question about the Mission brought us back to the TV screen.

The mayor responded without missing a beat: "The Rescue Mission's role was invaluable. Pastor Tom and his team both inspired me and advised me."

"In what way did they inspire you?" Nolan followed up.

"To be a leader and to do the right thing." Then, looking directly into the camera, he said, "Pastor Tom, if you and your folks are watching, thank you. And darn it, guys, let's get that expansion referendum passed."

"Was that an endorsement from the mayor?" Tom asked excitedly, then answered his own question. "Yes, we just got an endorsement from Mayor Simmons."

There would be no riot, at least for today. The fuse that seemed so hot only hours ago had been extinguished. The National Guard units assigned to the Kelsey regional airport grounds—a small facility used primarily by private airplane enthusiasts—for easy access to the city were instructed to return home. Chief Casey held a mandatory private meeting with his officers and staff, calling for a new day at the Kelsey Police Department. I pulled Christine aside.

"Is there any way Cody's grandparents might want him for another night?" I asked.

"That has already been arranged, and my bag is in the car," she replied as she pecked me on the lips. "I forgot to tell you I'm spending my first night on a houseboat."

CHAPTER TWENTY-FOUR

"Mayor Simmons' decision to take swift action and fire Chief Art Drake took everyone by surprise, but even more stunning was his accusation that political bosses and not elected officials had been running the city. This is a likely reference to party leader Max Weber, a powerful local businessman now heading up the opposition campaign on the referendum to expand the Kelsey Rescue Mission, a shelter for homeless men. We have been unable to track down Weber for a comment. However, former Chief Drake told me in a telephone interview that he intends to sue the city for what he calls an illegal firing.

"Meanwhile, Mayor Simmons is being given high praise for his demonstration of strong leadership. His actions avoided potential violence in the aftermath of the camera footage being leaked that showed Jimmy Keefer being shot and killed by four Kelsey police officers. One interesting footnote is that Mayor Simmons claims to have gotten his inspiration to act decisively from the Kelsey Rescue Mission. From downtown Kelsey, I'm Carl Nolan, Channel Four News."

I muted the television so it could be seen and not heard and turned my attention back to making breakfast. I had fried the bacon and was now working on my famous creamy scrambled eggs. My not-so-secret technique was adding a quarter cup of half-and-half to the eggs when they started to cook.

The thin wall separating the tiny galley kitchen and the even smaller bathroom made it easy to hear Christine inviting me to join her in the shower until she realized two people would never fit. She was learning quickly that life on a boat is an endless array of small compromises.

When she appeared in the kitchen with her wet hair, wearing only a white towel wrapped around her dark skin that dipped just slightly beneath the tops of her tiny breasts and a smile to melt hearts, my breakfast chores were suddenly secondary. She leaned over, turned off the gas fire under the eggs, and took my hand, leading me back to the bedroom. I offered no protest.

An hour later, after falling back to sleep, we heard banging on the sliding glass window in the helm. As scheduled, the security installation team had arrived at nine. I met them at the door in a T-shirt and a swimsuit I had quickly thrown on. The kitchen was still messy, including half-cooked eggs in the pan that I quickly threw away. Christine entered the room as I was telling the servicemen where I wanted the cameras, this time fully dressed and assembled, and announced she was running late.

"I loved sleeping on the boat," she said as we exchanged a long hug. "The benefits aren't bad either. Call me later."

I watched her walk to the end of the dock and into the parking area, where her black Jeep Cherokee sat next to my truck. How could she possibly love me? It never made sense that she would see me as anything but a money-mongering, power-hungry criminal with questionable ethics.

But then again, I told myself, *let's look at myself from a less self-loathing angle*. I had not lied or misrepresented myself to her. I confessed my guilt, even admitting that I gained an unfair pardon because of my political connections. She knew I was a doting dad and that I was on excellent terms with my ex-wife, and my best friend was Tom Garrity, a true saint. I had been transparent with this amazing, accomplished woman, and she loved me enough to ignore my history.

As she drove away, I realized I hadn't moved since she left the boat. The ringer on my phone interrupted my thoughts. It was Dan Johnson. "Mr. Daniel Johnson, how the heck are you, sir?" I acted happy to hear from him but wasn't sure that was true. It depended on why he was calling, which was often a mystery with Dan.

"Couldn't be better. Say, I watched all that crap in Kelsey the past couple of days. When I heard that mayor speak, I knew it had to be Greg Smith directing the orchestra. It was a brilliant move, my friend."

"What gave me away?" I laughed.

"That stuff about leadership. How many times have I heard you give that sermon to candidates over the years? I knew it was you."

"Well, his remarks probably saved the city a lot of property damage and injuries, so it's all good. Some cities would have burned to the ground over an incident like this. But thanks, Dan, I appreciate your thoughts."

"Let me get down to business. I am totally on board with your concept for the mill property. I'm having one of my architects draw preliminary schemes, including an artist rendition of the new exterior when it's completed."

"That's fantastic, Dan. Thank you."

"Now, there are a few commas and periods we need to work through, but I think we can do that. First, I need to form a new team on the ground. I am not using Max Weber or any of his companies. All he'd do is rip me off anyway. So, if you don't mind, Greg, please think of someone you might know. I'll bring in all the engineering and architectural folks from the outside. They're all on my payroll, so I might as well keep them busy."

"I'm with you. How far along are you on the artist's rendition? I'm asking because I'm going to Washington next week to present this idea to Liz's congressional staff. It would be great to show them something."

"It's done. I'll send you a link today. But you bring up my second condition. I'm willing to spend a lot of money to build the center, but to do it right and sustain it, I need the federal government to work out a private–public partnership with me."

"I will have more news on that later next week. Thanks, Dan."

I immediately called Liz and got her voicemail.

"Hey, Liz, call me when you get a minute. I talked to Dan Johnson. He wants to build the center in Kelsey. He's totally behind it but wants a federal government buy-in. Exciting news."

Liz texted back, HEY THERE, I'M IN A HEARING. I WILL CALL WHEN WE'RE DONE.

Just as I pushed the disconnect button, Liz called. I was out on the front porch, away from the busy three-person security team that was still drilling holes and hanging up cameras.

"Hello, Congresswoman Smith. How are you today?"

"Ooh, so formal. I guess you've had some interesting days down there, Smith. How does it feel to fight a good battle, for once?"

"Truthfully, it feels nice. I gave the mayor essentially the same leadership speech I gave you in our first campaign."

"Ahh, I like it when you say 'our' campaign. It was, you know." She was in one of her softer moods, her authentic self. The kick-ass, take-no-prisoners Liz was largely an act, albeit one she performed to perfection. "So why did you call? It wasn't for a walk down memory lane, was it?"

"No, not at all." I briefed her on the thumb drive and the attempted break-in, finishing with my call to the local FBI office, which she listened to attentively without comment.

"Well, you are handling everything perfectly, from what I can tell. And I assume you're staying away from the public eye as much as possible."

I assured her that I was, which wasn't a massive effort since my work had always been backstage. It occurred to me that Liz had been "mothering" me my entire life.

"The most important reason I called," I continued, "was to tell you that Dan Johnson wants to fund the learning and career center for the homeless." I informed her about his desire for an investment deal and naming rights after his grandfather. "I might even have an artist's rendition of what he sees as the grand vision by the time I come up next week."

"That's awesome, Greg, and I'm glad you brought that up. Most importantly, keep in mind that my committee staff is, for the most part, full of card-carrying lefties who are suspicious of you and all Republicans. They are in this for the cause. I know they'll love your presentation, but don't be surprised if the cold shoulders come out before the warm handshakes. I also want to mention that the contemporary word for 'homeless' is 'houseless.'"

"Sounds a little 'woke' to me," I said disparagingly, my conservative roots exposed.

"Oh my God, woke rules Capitol Hill these days. Even I have a problem with it sometimes. At the end of the day, I'm a dockworker's daughter from the First Ward, but it is what it is, and it ain't worth fighting. The cause is more important than the language."

"Duly noted on the houseless thing, but old habits die the hardest." It did make sense. Even my guys at the Mission had a home if home was defined as meals with plenty to eat and a sense of belonging to a community. They didn't have a house. Still, "homeless" would be challenging to discard from my vocabulary.

"Hey, before I let you go, would you mind if I arranged a meeting with our lawyer and accountant to discuss where you and I want to go with the marriage? It might be time."

"I agree it's time. I think Christine might be the one, and at some point, we will have to deal with it. Go ahead and set it up. I'm staying for a couple of days."

"Is my boy falling in love? That is so nice. I'm happy for you. But it does make me just a little jealous."

"We'll always be family. You know that." I meant it, knowing my life would be awful without her. "And Christine knows it, too. She's quite an admirer of yours."

"By the way, I insist you stay at the house when you're here. Your closet still has enough clothes to fill a men's store, and I had your

Mustang yanked out of the garage and fully serviced and cleaned. It hasn't been driven in over three years."

When our call ended, the camera security team was finished and waiting on the top deck to show me how everything worked. There would be four cameras outside and one in the helm area. Each was controlled by an app we downloaded onto my phone. With one click, I could arm or disarm it and play back video clips with sound whenever I wanted. A message buzzer would alert me to intruders.

• • •

The following day, after seeing Christine off to work, my first task was to call the deputy director of the Nashville FBI office, Bryce Lundgren. Agent Lundgren had been assigned as my local contact. While I was not required to report to him, my discussion with the FBI director and Liz convinced me that establishing a relationship would be in my best interest, safety-wise. I had not met him personally, but we had chatted on the telephone a few times and exchanged texts.

"Hey, Greg. What's up? I've meant to see your new digs, but I've been so darn busy."

"You're welcome anytime," I offered. "The beer is always cold on *The Sydney*."

"That sounds good. How can I help you today?"

"Listen, Bryce, five days ago, I received a thumb drive with a disguised voice that said he knew who I was and that I had ten days to leave Tennessee or something bad would happen. At the time, I suspected it might be Max Weber, who, for some reason, is threatened by my involvement in the voter referendum to expand the Kelsey Rescue Mission. It was a local reporter by the name of Carl Nolan who told me Weber has it in for me."

"Carl is a good man. We go to the same church, and our wives are friends."

How small is the Nashville–Kelsey world?

"The story gets a little stranger. Two nights ago, our security guard at the marina scared off two guys trying to break into my houseboat. He didn't get a facial ID, but one of them dropped a credit card, which our guard thinks he was using to unlock the sliding door that serves as the main entrance into the boat's interior. The name Joel Palmer is on the credit card."

"He's Weber's security guy," Bryce said. "We know him well."

"That's what the marina guard said. He also told me he had a bad reputation. They worked together on the Nashville police force a few years back."

"I need three things," Bryce said without hesitating. "The card, the name and contact information of the security guard, and the thumb drive with the recording. Then, if you don't mind, I want to send a guy over to dust for prints on your door. Palmer's prints are filed like all cops and former cops. It would also be helpful if you'd come by and give us a recorded statement, repeating what you told me. Can you do all of that by COB today?"

"Sure can. No problem."

"Greg, there's another important matter I've been authorized to discuss with you. Do you have a few extra minutes?" Bryce turned even more serious than usual.

"Of course. Am I in trouble?"

"No, not with us anyway. But you might want to watch out for Lamar Goodman. The judge who ordered a new trial for Goodman also gave him the freedom to roam. We have a sighting of him here in the area."

"I'm one step ahead of the FBI on this one. Lamar stayed at the Mission for a few nights." I filled him in on my brief encounter with him, the shovel incident, and the subsequent text messages. I told him I didn't see his face in the warehouse.

"Jesus, Greg, you need to tell us shit like this when it happens. We have instructions from as high as you can get to keep you safe." I knew he meant the White House, but I was happy he didn't say it.

"You're right. I fucked up. I didn't want it to become a big deal and decided to handle Goodman myself," I said, still trying to get used to the idea that the FBI was on my side.

"Just take every precaution you can think of. Anyway, I'll see you around three o'clock at the bureau office."

CHAPTER TWENTY-FIVE

"How about you grab Cody, pack an overnight bag, and return to the boat? You two can have the guest room, and I'll order a large pizza for the three of us." It was four o'clock, and I had just finished my meeting with Bryce. I called as I strolled along the river toward the bridge leading to the marina side.

"Oh my, two nights in a row as a sailor. I don't know if I can handle that," Christine teased. "Can I sit at the captain's table?"

"I am sure that can be arranged."

"I just need to be back in Kelsey at seven tomorrow morning. I promised the mayor I would coordinate the funeral in the park tomorrow. That also includes helping Tom write his introduction of Reverend Clayton, who is giving Jimmy's eulogy. It seems early to wake Cody up and haul him off the boat."

"I can keep Cody with me. We can have some guy time, you know—do some kayaking and swimming. And when you're done working, I can bring him home."

"That sounds like a great plan. You are about to make a little boy very happy."

I reflected on how my life had changed in the past few months, especially since meeting Christine. I could never have predicted the surprises that had come my way since arriving in Kelsey. The last thing I expected was to fall in love. Nor did I expect to be hunted down and receive threats against my life.

When I arrived at the marina, a band up at the patio bar was playing a pretty good rendition of "Margaritaville" to a small crowd of patrons scattered at various tables. With two hours to kill, I found an empty stool at the outside bar, where Joey was busy serving half-priced drinks for happy hour. "Mr. Smith, I knew if I lived long enough, you'd show up at my bar and have a drink. We have a great new IPA. The first one is on the house."

"You're on, Joey. Thanks."

From behind me, I heard a friendly greeting. "And I'll buy your second one?"

I turned to see Carl Nolan.

"Hey, Carl, what are you doing here?" I could use a bar buddy until Christine arrived. "Aren't you on the air tonight?"

"I recorded everything earlier, and I'm covering the funeral in Kelsey tomorrow, so I have the evening off. Besides, my little brother is in the band, and I try to catch them when possible. He told me they were playing at the marina tonight, and I said why not? Maybe I'll run into Greg."

"Well, here I am. What's the latest?"

"Max Weber's hatred of you is intense. He not only blames you for the mayor's sudden surge of 'balls,' as he put it, but now he claims that you convinced Dan Johnson not to do business with him anymore and that his services for managing the mill property project will no longer be needed. He intends to sue you personally for interfering with his business."

Carl had confirmed what I already suspected to be true.

"You see that security guard down there? He's part of a three-man rotation, twenty-four seven, to patrol this one pier, the one with the houseboats where I live. Max Weber is the reason I hired them. Yes, I am very aware of his anger, and I fully briefed a team of FBI agents on the situation this afternoon." I went off the record with Carl, filling him in on the video threat and the break-in.

"Have you heard anything about the Green Technologies investigation?" Nolan asked.

"No, I was hoping you might have learned something."

He ordered a second round of IPAs in tall sixteen-ounce glasses.

"I asked my FBI contact about it," I added. "All he said was that stuff is above his pay grade."

"The only thing I have been able to uncover—and I'm reading between the lines, so my intel is sketchy—is that there is indeed an investigation into Weber's operation. I also heard the feds were prepared to raid Green Technologies this week, but with the mayor's announcement about corruption at city hall, they think they might have even more on Weber, so they've delayed it. The fact that he's now threatening you could add to his list of violations."

"So, how frustrating is it to have all of this information and not be able to report on it?" I could see he wanted to blast Weber out of the water but didn't have enough to go public yet.

"Truthfully, it's beyond frustrating. Reporters live for this kind of thing." I remembered the media's abject glee when they were going after me. "But I'm an old-school journalist, not a 'gotcha' reporter like the cable news charlatans. Patience is usually a virtue when it comes to covering a story. It will happen, and right now, I have an open line of communication with all sides of this."

"Tell me, Carl, are you playing with me, or are we chasing the same thing, like partners? How do I know you're not telling Weber stuff about me?"

"Because the real story I want to tell is how a bad guy became a good guy, and if I break your trust for me now, I won't get to tell that story. I happen to like you, and your life story is interesting. You should write a book."

"That'll be the day," I said. Carl didn't know the shame and embarrassment I felt for what I had done. My conviction and imprisonment only added to it. The Washington political community, where I was once a prince, treated me more like a pariah than a colleague. Realizing they were never real friends was a harsh lesson. Although I had come to accept my fate, choosing to cherish my few friends—people like Rob Kearse—instead of dwelling on the past was helpful.

It was now after five o'clock and time to start thinking about heading down to the boat. Christine and Cody would be here soon. I ordered two pizzas to go and two more beers for Carl and me. He asked if Christine and I were dating. His inquiry didn't feel like an intrusion, just a casual inquiry.

"We are together, yes. She and her son will be here in about a half hour, which is why I'm getting two pizzas."

"I tried to date her in high school but was too conceited for a self-assured girl like Christine. She would have none of me," he laughed as he recalled the memory. "Christine Pollard was our class's prettiest, peppiest, and smartest girl. Did she tell you that she was the prom queen and valedictorian?"

"No, she hasn't mentioned either, but I'm not surprised that you or any other boys would have wanted to date her. Thanks for the—what do you call it—intel." I paid for the beers and pizza with cash and headed out. "Thanks for stopping by, Carl. I enjoyed it. All off the record, right?"

"You got it. Stay in touch."

I walked down the bar's steps to the parking lot to head toward the houseboat dock and spotted a plain white Ford sedan parked near the security tent that Joey had put up for the guard on duty. In front of the car, which featured a blue-and-white federal license plate, Brady was talking to two guys I assumed belonged to the vehicle.

"Ah, Mr. Smith, these two gentlemen are from the FBI and want to talk to you."

"What's up, guys?" I was as friendly as possible, considering it was Friday night and my girlfriend was due any moment, not to mention that I had already downed three IPAs.

"We were sent over to dust for fingerprints, Mr. Smith. Is it okay if we do that now? We're just doing the glass door, so it will only take about fifteen minutes."

"Absolutely. Follow me. Thanks, Brady."

The men went to work, dusting with a black powder and then covering the discovered prints with a white rubber "lifter." They took a photograph of the prints. It was evident that this wasn't their first trip to the rodeo.

"How many people have used this door since its last cleaning?" one of them asked.

"Not counting me, I would say Joe Palmer and whoever was helping him."

"It's good news that there are so few. That will make it easier to identify the intruders. That's all we need for now, Mr. Smith. Have a nice evening."

I watched the two G-men head up the dock, moving slightly to one side to let Christine and Cody go by them the opposite way.

"Do not run on this dock, Cody Culpepper. Walking only."

"Aw, Mom, he's excited. Give him a break," I shouted down from the top deck.

"He needs no encouragement from you, Captain," she laughed, "but yes, I rarely see him so excited about something."

"Hey, Mr. Greg. Permission to come aboard?"

As kids went, I decided he was one of the cutest ones I had ever met.

"Permission granted, but make sure that your mom is okay first. Only gentlemen are allowed on board."

"Come on, Mom. I'll help you," he said, taking her small bag of personal items.

It was a classic summer evening, hovering in the high seventies with low humidity and a light breeze. The lights of Nashville towered above us on one side of the Cumberland River while the band on the patio sang "Sweet Caroline." Indeed, good times had never seemed so good. So, so good.

After I showed the duo to their room, Christine had a chance to change from business to casual attire—a gray tee with YALE emblazoned on the front, cut-off jean shorts, and orange flip-flops—we met on the top deck, where I had pulled out both pizzas, a root beer for Cody, and two bottles of Coors Light for Christine and me. I had changed into my typical boat togs, consisting of baggy blue swim trunks, a white Yankees tee, and no shoes.

I told her about my day, including the security devices that would only be activated when I was gone, my FBI meeting, and my chance encounter with Carl Nolan.

"And what did Mr. Nolan have to say?" she inquired.

"Well, for starters, I learned that a certain Christine Pollard was her class's prom queen and valedictorian."

"Oh my God, he told you that?"

"He also confessed that he had a serious crush on you but that he was a teenage dick in those days, and you blew him off."

"Well, he has that right," she said, laughing. "But he's turned into an okay guy, it seems."

"How does tomorrow look? Is everything ready for Jimmy's funeral?"

"I think so. Tom selected eight of the men as pallbearers. The new chief had security in order and a stage set up for the speakers. And the First Baptist Church choir will be singing. I don't know if you have heard them, but they rock. I swear, they could win *America's Got Talent* if they had the chance."

"Channel Four is televising the entire thing so I can watch from here. Have you met the Reverend Richard Clayton yet?"

"Oh yes. Prince Richard, we've been calling him behind his back. You would think the Second Coming had occurred. But he will bring national attention to the Mission and our cause and honor Jimmy's life in a way no other could, so I'm happy he's here."

"Pepperoni pizza is my favorite food, Mr. Greg. Thank you for getting it."

I could tell Cody was a little fed up with adult business talk.

"You are so welcome. Thank you for bringing your mom to visit."

Of course, the lad had no idea she was also here last night.

"Do you love my mom, Mr. Greg? You don't have to answer, but if you married her, I would get to live on the boat too." He reminded me of my precocious Sydney, who would have asked the same question at nine.

"Cody, that was rude. You don't ask questions like that. Now, you apologize."

"No, it's okay. Cody has a right to know my feelings about his mother. Your mom is the best person I've ever met, and I love her." She reached over and put her hand gently on mine. I looked into her watery green eyes, and she mouthed silently, "I love you, too."

"But, Cody, getting married is very serious, and right now, I'm still working on being the best boyfriend to your mom that I can be."

At that moment, no other thing or person mattered except Christine and the two of us—three, counting Cody—being together. Everything that had gone wrong in my world, mainly brought on by my greed and need for conquest, had vanished. I was absorbed by her hopeful expression and the joyful reverence that seemed always to surround her.

She plopped on my lap and threw her arms around my neck. "Well, I love you too, Mr. Greg, and I have no intention of stopping." Cody got up and made it a three-person hug.

As we finished our pizza, I looked up toward the patio deck, where the band continued to play. It was a much larger gathering than earlier, although Carl had departed. But in the same barstool he had occupied—carrying on what appeared to be casual bar talk—was another man who looked eerily familiar. I grabbed my binoculars from the wooden box under the captain's chair, aiming them in his direction. The close-up image confirmed my worst suspicion. Lamar Goodman knew where I lived.

CHAPTER TWENTY-SIX

We continued to lie on the double chaise on the top deck, gazing up at the stars in silence. Knowing that Lamar Goodman was fifty yards away had me in knots, as hard as I tried not to let it bother me. The ringtone on my phone broke the silence.

"Hey. Dad, what's up with you lately? Mom told me, 'Your father has gone from arranging meetings between the defense minister of Turkey and the Senate Foreign Relations chairman to making sure cities in Tennessee don't blow up in a riot.'"

"Mom has it all wrong. I am only an observer."

"That's a lie," Christine intervened. "He had everything to do with it. That's what your father does. He sits backstage and directs the actors. You should have heard the little talk he gave to the mayor."

"Did he do the leadership speech?" Sydney asked dramatically. "He gave that one to me in the eighth grade when I ran for class president."

"And did you win?" Christine asked.

"Of course she won. She's Sydney Smith," I interrupted. "Anyway, you're welcome to join us anytime. Did you know I'm coming to DC for a few days this Wednesday?"

"Can't wait to see you, Pops. The Mustang is all ready for you."

Christine said she would miss me this week when I ended the call. "And what's the story on the Mustang? Aren't you a man of interest and intrigue," she added with a raised eyebrow.

I briefed her on the purpose of the trip, emphasizing the meeting with Liz's staff and the birthday party for the president's chief of staff, at which I intended to lobby for a presidential visit to Kelsey. "And the Mustang is my pride and joy—a fully restored sixty-five with a convertible top and only fifty thousand miles on the odometer. And is it ever pretty! Baby blue with white interior."

"Ooh, a classic," she responded.

"It hasn't been touched since Sydney and I took it out for a cruise along Skyline Drive to take in the fall foliage the day before the prison van picked me up."

"So, what's up with you and Liz? Are you married, separated, or divorced? No offense, but I think we've reached the point where I deserve to know."

"Oh, that's also on the agenda when I'm in Washington. We're meeting with our attorney, accountant, and financial adviser. The divorce papers are final and waiting to be signed. I told her about you, and she's very happy for us. There's someone in her life, too."

"Oh, that's nice. Anyone famous?"

"As a matter of fact, she is famous. Susan Hutton."

Christine stared at me. "*The* Susan Hutton? Wow. I love her." Then she went expressionless, her blank, soft eyes staring at me. I wondered if this was how we all appear when experiencing an "aha" moment, when something previously unknown suddenly manifests—that second when your brain succumbs to "Okay, I get it now."

Before heading downstairs for bed, I took one last look through the binoculars. Both Carl and Lamar had left. Telling Christine I had to retrieve something from my truck, I walked to the guard station and showed Brady a picture of Goodman on my phone. "Make sure this man is never allowed on the docks," I instructed. "And if you see him here, call me immediately."

It was time for Christine to know about Goodman.

• • •

When Cody walked sleepily into the kitchen the following day just short of nine o'clock, his mother was long gone back to Kelsey. Clad in his black Batman pajamas and curly brown-blond hair pointing in every direction, he remained the cutest little guy I had ever seen.

"First Mate Cody Culpepper, this is your captain speaking, and I say today the task is for us to have a fun day on the water."

"Just the guys," he replied. "No girls allowed." I'd told him about "our day" last night. He was thrilled, which made me feel even more a part of Christine's life.

"Let's sit you up at the counter and get some pancakes and orange juice while I clean up a little. Your toothbrush is in the bathroom. Then we'll get the kayaks out and go for a long paddle. Are you up for it?"

I wanted to be back by two o'clock to watch the funeral coverage on TV, but I had set the recording button just in case we weren't back in time. I would have preferred to be with Christine, Tom, and the guys, but we all agreed that, once again, my public presence could be a distraction, which would not be good for our effort or my mental health.

At first, I was a little rusty with Cody, but in a short time, my kid skills returned. If you talk to them like they have a brain, they'll show you they have one. At nine years old, almost ten, Cody could carry on a far more interesting conversation than most adults I knew. And he asked great questions. "Mr. Greg, will we paddle upriver on the way back?" This allowed me to tell him that Brady, the security guard, would be picking us up at Triangle Park and driving us back. "Triangle Water Park," Cody shouted excitedly. "Are we going on the giant water slides?"

"Only if you're brave enough," I teased.

The river float, followed by going down every slide at Triangle Water Park, was a blast for both of us. We finished by having their famous chili dogs and fries and were exhausted when Brady arrived in his company security truck. Cody's need for a steady adult male figure in his life was palpable; it was a role I was prepared—and excited—to fill.

On the short ride back to the marina, I realized it had been seven months since I arrived in Kelsey. Had I changed? Would returning to the intoxicating environment of Washington for the first time in three years, back to the scene of the crime, reignite a flame for past conquests? I looked at Cody, who was slurping out the last of his strawberry milkshake. *Please, God, let this be real*, I prayed silently.

We restacked the kayaks in the shared storage shack near the houseboat and headed up for showers. By two o'clock, we were both on the couch and ready to watch the funeral service for Jimmy Keefer, which was being called a "celebration of life."

"There's Mom," Cody pointed out excitedly. Carl's handsome mug was a close-up on the screen, but Christine was visible behind him on the stage, ensuring everyone was in their proper chairs.

We watched her exit the stage as Carl informed the TV audience that the service would begin. The crowd, consisting of people of all demographics, filled every inch of the large park. Many were seated on the grass with folding chairs or on blankets. Others stood. Each was quieted by the opening chords of the First Baptist Choir marching down the roped-off center aisle, singing a beautiful acapella rendition of a hymn inspired by the Twenty-Third Psalm.

> The Lord is my shepherd; I shall not want.
> He maketh me to lie down in green pastures: he leadeth me beside the still waters.
> He restoreth my soul: he leadeth me in the paths of righteousness for his name's sake.

When the all-Black, mixed-gender choir arrived at their seating area beneath the large stage, the congregation went silent, turning to watch the ten members of Pastor Tom's ambassador committee march quietly down the same path as the choir had taken. They carried the casket containing Jimmy Keefer's body. Led by Mark Stone pushing Jarred Mackey, who used a wheelchair and had lost a leg as a member of an elite Army unit in Afghanistan, the remaining eight each had a grip on the casket rail. The casket was placed securely on the raised metal stand before the stage, Tom's signal to approach the podium.

I watched my old friend—clad in a simple black suit, black tie, and white shirt—bend down and present Jimmy's mother, dressed in a traditional black funeral dress and veil, a bouquet of yellow tulips, followed by a warm hug. By the precision and beauty of the service, it occurred to me that Christine had likely relied more on her experience as a pastor than any of her legal or other organizational skills, which were many. I was sure there were thousands of tear-filled eyes, including mine. Meanwhile, Cody had fallen asleep at the other end of the couch.

"Good afternoon, my brothers and sisters. I'm Pastor Tom Garrity, director of the Kelsey Rescue Mission." Tom's deep, booming voice had earned it the nickname "the voice of God." Not him. Just his voice. "To you, Mrs. Keefer and Mary, we mourn with you today as we say goodbye to your son and brother and our friend, Jimmy. We are blessed that you are with us, as our Lord is with you. To the First Baptist Choir, all I can say is wow. As always, you brought it today. We look forward to hearing more from you later in the service."

It wasn't Tom's job to deliver a message. He was merely setting the table for the Reverend Richard Clayton, the out-of-town celebrity preacher who had made it his ministry to speak at high-profile funerals around the country, always flying in his private jet. I would have preferred to hear Tom do the eulogy. He knew Jimmy and loved him dearly. But when four White police officers shoot a Black man, it is understandably going to draw national attention, including movement leaders like Clayton.

"To the pallbearers," Tom continued, "each of you members of the best rescue mission in America, I am so proud of you guys and all of the men from the Mission who are here, which I think is everyone." Then, looking out at a crowd that easily numbered in the thousands, he said, "And finally, to all of you, thank you for being here today to support Jimmy, his family, and his community."

Somewhere in the world, there might have been a better person than Tom Garrity, but I didn't know of any. He continued for a minute or two, ensuring he introduced everyone on the stage, including the new chief of police, Larry Casey, and Mayor Frank Simmons. Then he finished, "As the eyes turned toward Kelsey this week to witness the tragic shooting of Jimmy Keefer, the nation also witnessed something extraordinary about the unified spirit that binds our community and its people. It is a spirit that says, 'When one goes down, we all go down, and when one rises, we all rise.' That is the way we roll. I call it the Kelsey Way. And that leads me to the Reverend Richard Clayton.

"Reverend, you have traveled here to help us heal and see with your eyes that radical love can conquer ultimate evil. We are honored by your presence today and your message of unity and peace in our beloved city." Then, looking at the crowd: "My fellow citizens of Kelsey, it is my distinct honor to present the Reverend Richard Clayton to you."

It was brilliant. In front of thousands of people, a live TV audience, and millions more watching online and later tonight on the broadcast news, Tom had told Reverend Clayton that he was expected to address Kelsey's better angels and not exploit political confrontation as was often his practice. We only wanted to say goodbye to a loved one. The reverend got the message.

When he reached the podium, Clayton embraced Tom with both arms. He was replete in black robes and a gold vestment around his neck. "Please stay here for a minute," the reverend said to Tom.

Then, looking out to the assembled, he said, "Thank you, Pastor Tom, for your warm introduction. You are a hero for the work you do. Mayor Simmons, Chief Casey, and Pastor Culpepper, can you join us by the podium for a minute?"

Simmons and Casey both looked surprised by Clayton's invitation to join him, probably because they were. Richard Clayton continued with the four—Tom, the mayor, the chief, and Christine—standing side by side.

"To my brothers and sisters of Kelsey, this is what strong, compassionate, and principled leaders do. They lead. In the tragic events of this past week that took the life of Jimmy Keefer, these individuals said, 'Not in my city, not now, not ever again.' You should be proud to have such fine people at the helm, and America, if you're watching, I pray you will choose more men and women just like them. From this day forward, when people hear 'the Kelsey Way,' be proud that you know where it came from."

Those who were seated stood. The ovation was thunderous. Clayton was good. Very good. He found a way to follow Tom's lead while sending an important political message. Kelsey, Tennessee, a small Southern city, had joined an elite group of towns nationwide where civil and social justice were synonymous with their names.

CHAPTER TWENTY-SEVEN

The end of the funeral service was my signal to get ready to head back to Kelsey, starting with showers and a clean change of clothes for Cody and me.

"Hey, little man, I think it's time we head home, and I can't take you back looking like a river rat."

We would pick up Christine at five and then head to her parents' house for dinner, where Tom and Jane had also been invited. I was excited to get a firsthand report of the day from everyone.

"I want to stay on the boat," Cody said as he woke from his two-hour snooze on the couch, rubbing both eyes. It had been a splendid day for both of us.

"You'll be back. But right now, I'm under strict orders to have you home. Do you want me to cross your mother?" I teased.

"Not a good idea," he answered solemnly.

Once I had Cody in the shower and the clothes his mother had sent laid out in the bedroom, I checked my email on the laptop perched on the small desk in the helm area. I immediately noticed an email from Dan Johnson. SUBJECT: ARTIST'S RENDITION. He asked me to let him know what I thought.

Navigating quickly to his download, I stared in stunned silence at four full-color drawings, the first being the gated entrance to the Daniel Webster Johnson Center for Hope and Opportunity. It was beautiful. The other three drawings were of one of the classroom buildings, a landscaped outdoor courtyard with tables and umbrellas, and a row of apartments that I assumed would be located at the back of the property. Equally compelling was that the original mill buildings remained in place, suggesting that Johnson had decided to renovate and preserve the historical structures instead of razing the buildings and erecting new ones. It would be a massive do-over, but the idea of marrying the past with the present was poetic and profound.

I quickly printed out the pictures, intending to share them with everyone at dinner tonight, but not before I responded to Dan: You are the man! The drawings are amazing. Thank you. I then forwarded the drawings to Liz with a brief message: Check it out.

An hour later, we were met on the steps of Christine's brownstone home by a smiling mother and girlfriend who was happy to "see her boys."

"Mom, Mom, we had the best day ever," an overly excited Cody shouted from the car. "We went kayaking and then went to the water park. We took the biggest slide thrice, ate burgers, and had strawberry milkshakes."

He rushed up to the door, where mother and son embraced. "I'm so happy for you, Cody. Did you say thank you to Mr. Greg?"

"Thanks, Greg. I had a blast." I hadn't had a chance to tell her that I told him it was okay to drop the "Mr." title, but she didn't seem to mind.

"So, it's 'Greg' now," she mused, regarding me with a mischievous smile. "Well, are you ready to head over to Papa and Nan's? We're running just a little late, and we have a lot to talk about."

Christine spelled out directions that led us to the outskirts of town and into a well-groomed, upscale neighborhood thick with tall elms, firs, and oaks that hid most of the houses from the street. After two right turns and one left, she announced, "This is it, home sweet home, where I was born and raised."

It wasn't as large as some of the other houses, but it was elegant just the same, set back from the street with a manicured lawn leading up to a front porch with white rockers.

"Not a bad neighborhood to grow up in," I teased. "You didn't tell me you were a spoiled rich kid."

"Guilty on both counts," she confessed. "My parents have reaped the rewards of having successful lives. As you know, Dad owns the largest funeral home in Kelsey, but you may not know that Mom is a pediatrician. I've been told that when they first moved here—before I was born—their interracial marriage was an issue, but that was before she delivered nearly all the babies born here in the past thirty years. She's now an icon," she laughed.

"So, your mom births them, and your dad buries them?"

"Gregory Bradley Smith," she said sarcastically, "if you were the first to come up with that joke, I might laugh."

I spotted Doug and Cindy Pollard in the porch rocking chairs, sipping from their wineglasses, joined by teetotalers Tom and Jane drinking what I imagined to be lemonade. As we headed up the front walk, it was immediately apparent where Christine got her beauty. Darker in complexion than her daughter, Cindy Pollard, whom I assumed to be around sixty, would rival most forty-somethings on the youth-and-beauty scale.

"Greg, it is nice to meet you finally," Cindy said as she firmly shook my hand. "You are all my daughter and grandson talk about." Her warm, dignified demeanor was fetching, and I couldn't help being drawn in by her Southern accent, which Christine must have shed during her years at Yale and Washington.

"Mother, please don't give him a big head."

Tom informed us all that my big head had been left somewhere at a prison in West Virginia. *Thanks, Tom*, I thought. Doug brought out wine for Christine and me and proposed a toast.

"Here's to Christine for organizing such a wonderful celebration of life for Jimmy Keefer," he began, "and here's to Pastor Tom for keeping Reverend Clayton, shall we say, focused today. It was masterful."

"How did you get the job of organizing a funeral service?" her mother asked. "It doesn't sound like something a lawyer would do."

"It isn't, Mom. It's something a pastor would do. Unlike you, the mayor remembered that I had a prior vocation."

Although Christine had not mentioned it to me, I sensed that mother and daughter might have unresolved issues.

When Christine's phone rang, she glanced at the caller's name and decided to take it, retreating to the driveway connecting the front porch. I was on my own. *Start talking*, I told myself. *Charm them. Please do something to convince them that you are worthy of being involved with their fully grown, mature, and super-wise daughter, who has been making good decisions for a long time.*

Christine returned five minutes later with an anguished expression. "It was Angie Toomey from the *Daily*. They're running a front-page story on Greg's involvement in the Mission's campaign in tomorrow's Sunday edition. Max Weber accused the Mission of hiring an ex-con to manage their expansion campaign. She wants a comment from Tom or Greg and has a deadline in one hour."

My first visit to Christine's parents had now gone from not very good to teetering on the edge.

"I think I need to take this one," Tom responded immediately. "Call her back and put her on. Do you mind, Cindy? I apologize for the rudeness of the media, who think it's okay to call on Saturday evenings."

After reconnecting with Angie, Christine handed the phone to Tom. My first impulse was for me to take the call, but Tom was right. We needed to keep this as much as possible about the Mission and not me. He put her on speakerphone and conducted the interview in the same rocking chair he had been sitting in before her call.

"Hello, Pastor Tom, I am sorry to bother you on a Saturday, but Max Weber is accusing the Mission of hiring Greg Smith to run your campaign. Is this the same Greg Smith who was sent to prison for fixing campaigns in three states, and if so, why would you bring in someone of such ill repute?"

Ouch. "Ill repute" sounded worse than "notorious felon." Cindy took her grandson inside the house so he couldn't hear us. Or, perhaps, so she couldn't hear us. *Good move, Nan. Cody still thinks I'm a good guy.*

"Angie, Greg Smith has volunteered in our kitchen for seven months. He came here after his release because he's my best friend. And yes, he has also helped with the campaign, but only as a volunteer."

"Given Mr. Smith's reputation for dirty tricks, is this a sign that we might see rough campaigning in the next few weeks?"

"Angie, you know me, and you know the Mission. That isn't going to happen. Greg is here to heal as well as help. The Mission is all about turning lives around. The men at the Mission have rescued Greg Smith just as much as he has helped rescue them. Max Weber might want to think about joining us. If anyone needs to reset his priorities, it would be him. Now, if you don't mind, I'm going to get back to my wife and friends and enjoy my dinner. Good night, Angie."

It occurred to me that Tom was spot-on. I had indeed been rescued by a bunch of men who wore old hoodies and discarded jeans that didn't fit. I finally realized it was part of Tom's plan.

Despite Angie's interruption, my fright over being outed in the newspaper tomorrow, and wanting to win over Christine's parents, I had a wonderful evening on the back patio that overlooked the Pollards' large swimming pool. Doug grilled steaks and shrimp, which we eagerly consumed around a large table, swapping stories until after eleven.

"So, tell me, Tom and Greg," Cindy asked at one point, "how did the two of you first meet?"

"Our mothers introduced us in the maternity ward at Buffalo Hospital," I answered. "We were born the same day."

"But there was only one doctor, so my mom had to wait until he was born. I spent the next eighteen years of my life letting him go first," Tom added to everyone's laughter.

"That gives a whole new depth to the term 'lifelong friends,'" Doug observed.

It then struck me that I had forgotten to bring in Dan Johnson's drawings. "Can you all excuse me for a minute?" I asked as I pushed my chair from the table. "There is something I want you all to see."

By the time I returned, the group had finally gathered in the kitchen for the strawberry shortcake Cindy had prepared for dessert.

"As you all know, Rockwood Industries wants to remake the mill into a center of training and education for the homeless if Congress will match Dan's funding. Something I am working on, by the way. In any event, Dan sent me these artists' renditions of what the center might look like."

Each member of the dinner party looked at the four drawings, passing them around the high table with six stools.

"This is remarkable," Doug offered. "It could be a model for the entire nation."

I basked for a minute in the approbation of this generous, kind man who had found time in the midst of building a respected business to develop the Kelsey Rescue Mission, all while shunning the spotlight for his good deeds.

"I love these, Greg. What a beautiful vision," Christine said with teary eyes. She might have resembled her mother in appearance, but she was Daddy's girl. She saw life with her emotion-filled heart. I told them about my upcoming trip to Washington and my meeting with the committee staff overseeing the American Houselessness Act.

"Good luck with that," Doug said as he shook my hand.

• • •

Christine was brewing our morning coffee when I walked into the kitchen and saw the Sunday newspaper on the kitchen counter, showing two full-color pictures. On the left was me dressed in an orange jumpsuit with handcuffs at the Washington federal courthouse, being led away by bailiffs after my sentencing. The picture on the right showed me looking straight into the camera from the other side of the serving window. I liked the second one better, showing my long hair, scruffy beard, and Yankee hat. The headline read: PRESIDENT'S FORMER HIT MAN AND EX-CON NOW RUNNING KELSEY RESCUE MISSION CAMPAIGN.

Other than the insinuation of being paid, the article began with the facts:

> Max Weber, Kelsey businessman and chairman of the city's Republican Committee, has accused the Kelsey Rescue Mission of hiring a convicted felon to manage its local referendum campaign to expand the Mission. His name is Greg Smith, a former presidential adviser and confidant of several members of Congress, including his estranged wife, Congresswoman Elizabeth Smith (D-NY).

It ended with Max's heartfelt concern about the welfare of the Mission: "I just don't understand why our respected Rescue Mission would want to get mixed up with a convicted criminal who has made it his business to cheat the system. It doesn't speak well for the Mission's reputation."

In between was an overview of my career and an explanation of why I had moved to the area. It did not, however, talk about my desire to shrink from public view and live a quieter life. No, this was a "hit" piece designed to tarnish the Mission by using me—a commonly used political tactic that reporters almost always cover and the public eagerly consumes. I had deployed it many times in campaigns over the years, never caring whose family members I might hurt or whose reputations I would ruin. I decided to resign as a volunteer carrot peeler and campaign adviser immediately.

"I just want you to know that orange is not your color." Christine delivered her fashion statement with both arms around my neck and her lips a half inch from mine. "But those handcuffs have given me a few ideas," she said in a mock alluring voice.

"Are you two kissing again?" Cody asked, standing at the kitchen entrance in his pajamas and squinting up at us.

"Yes, Cody dear, which is what people do when they are in love," Christine replied as we broke apart, discreetly removing the newspaper from her son's sight.

My phone buzzed with a message from Carl Nolan: WTF, GREG. WE AGREED THAT I WOULD GET AN EXCLUSIVE ON YOUR BACKSTORY LATER. I FEEL A LITTLE BETRAYED. I'M NOT HAPPY.

Impulsively, I stepped back to the guest room and called him. "Carl, I didn't initiate this story, and Angie never spoke with me, nor did I withdraw from my promise to talk to you first. Your anger is a little misplaced."

"You have a point, but now that you're outed, will you sit for an interview and tell your side of this whole thing?"

I thought for a few seconds, remembering my commitment to stay out of the public storm and seeing it as an opportunity to clear the air. "I will do that, Carl. When and where?"

CHAPTER TWENTY-EIGHT

"Your so-called resignation is not accepted, Greg. I'm sorry, but you are stuck with me and what we're doing here." Tom was adamant, and I knew his Irish temper too well to cross him when he got worked up like this. "You of all people should know that a few knockdowns along the way are no reason to quit."

We were in his office getting ready to face a dozen TV and newspaper reporters in the cafeteria, where they had gathered on this bright Monday morning to follow up on the *Kelsey Daily*'s Sunday article.

As we stepped up to the podium together, Tom took to the microphone. "Good morning," he began with a broad smile and a bundle of typical Tom Garrity energy. "Before we take any questions, I would like to formally introduce you to the guy on my right, whom you may have seen around here lately, mostly cooking and serving breakfast a couple of times a week. This is Greg Smith, my best friend, whom I love like a brother. Or, more accurately, a brother-in-law because he also married my sister.

"When Greg was released from prison this past March, I invited him to Kelsey to get involved with the Mission and prepare for his next phase. This is what we do here. We help turn people's lives around; in this way, Greg is no different than the guys we serve daily. Greg has pointed his life in a new direction, and I could not be prouder of him."

I looked at the cameras around the room, knowing it was highly likely that my old DC crowd—friends and enemies alike—would catch some of this on the news. What would they think about Greg Smith, the hard-ass political "dealmaker," now working in a shelter for "houseless" men? Would they think the so-called lion of warfare politics had turned into a pussy cat, a defender of losers?

"Okay, any questions?" Tom ended his prefatory remarks and threw me to the wolves.

"Mr. Smith, Max Weber says you are running the referendum campaign. Is that true?"

"No. I put forth my ideas, and they take or leave them."

"Are you trying to influence Dan Johnson and Rockwood Industries not to develop the old mill into a high-end resort?"

"Dan Johnson makes his own decisions."

"Did you advise the mayor to fire Chief Drake and replace him with Larry Casey?"

"Yes. And I would do it again." I should have added that the mayor asked for my advice, but I knew it wouldn't matter to this group of bloodthirsty hounds.

"One of the residents here at the Mission informs me that you are way more hands-on in the campaign than you suggest. Do you care to elaborate?"

The question came from Angie Toomey herself. I harkened back to the picture on yesterday's front page of me smiling in the serving window and remembered that Ernie Sanchez had taken that picture two days ago. He even asked me to smile.

"I think I've already answered that question, Angie. I want to ask you why you wrote an article with one aim: to diminish the Mission's reputation. My follow-up question is this: Are you paying Mission residents to take pictures of me, or are they doing it out of civic duty?" I could see Ernie behind one of the cameras, recording the entire event.

"I think you called a press conference to answer questions, not ask them," came her curt reply. "For an old pro at this game, Mr. Smith, I'm surprised you would launch an attack on the media like that."

"My attack, as you say, is directed only at reporters with an agenda. Think about it. I'm here as a volunteer, trying to help good men reclaim their lives. I advised a mayor to fire a corrupt police chief and save this city from the unrest that has engulfed so many other cities in the aftermath of police violence. I asked for none of this. I wanted to move on from my past and begin a new, peaceful life. What part of that is so difficult to understand?"

At that moment, Ernie walked out from behind the camera. "Mr. Smith, I'm sorry. Mrs. Toomey gave me fifty dollars to take that picture of you. I didn't know it was going to be used like this. Please forgive me." The news cameras all turned toward Ernie. "Mr. Smith is just trying to do the right thing for all of us."

Tom leaned over into the microphone. "Thank you, Ernie, for your confession. We will discuss our house rules on anonymity later," he responded as the room erupted into laughter. "Meanwhile, are there any other questions?"

"Just one," Carl Nolan asked. "I am receiving a report at this minute from my station that the FBI has just raided Green Technologies and arrested its owner and your accuser, Max Weber, on charges related to a massive credit card and personal banking scandal that has defrauded senior citizens of millions of dollars. Do you have any comment?"

The room was instantly abuzz with dozens of simultaneous discussions about the stunning news. Nolan and I had known it was coming but didn't know when until now.

"Well, Carl, if anyone knows anything about being caught by the FBI for a crime, it would be me, and I can tell you from my experience that Mr. Weber is in for a very rough and shameful ride."

I did not mention that the FBI office in Nashville called the day before to inform me that Weber's security head, Joel Palmer, had left fingerprints all over my boat.

• • •

I met with Christine and Mark about our budget. We were already past Labor Day, the traditional start of the November general election, and we wanted to be on the air as soon as possible. Ernie had now privately apologized three times to me, each instance receiving my sincere exoneration. Angie Toomey knew that fifty bucks was a lot of money for an unemployed homeless shelter resident and played to his weakness. "Let's just get our work done, Ernie. It's no big deal," I finally told him.

I would never trust Angie again, nor would Christine or Tom. By favoring Weber, she had played to the wrong side of history.

Mark reported that we had $300,000 in the bank, and we needed every penny to compete against our opponent's TV ad blitz. Liz had done a great job motivating the national houseless advocacy community to send us large donations, while Doug worked in the local community for smaller gifts. As I scanned the list of donors, I noticed that Diane Swanson, wife of Judge Swanson, had contributed $10,000 in her name. I'm sure the judge would be unhappy with his wife's decision. Of course, all of it would be reported publicly next Tuesday, a mere six weeks from Election Day.

Charlie from the front desk knocked quietly on the office door and stuck his head in. "Mr. Brad, there is a Dan Johnson on line two. Would you like to take the call?"

"Yes, Charlie, thank you."

I had never not taken a Dan Johnson call.

"Dan, how are you?"

"I'm watching the afternoon news on cable and seeing a swarm of FBI agents carrying computers and boxes of files from Weber's building. They also took him out in handcuffs, the son of a bitch. I hope he gets life. Say, I'm calling to ask if the Wednesday after Election Day would be a good time for me to come your way and meet with my pre-building team at the mill. Let's wait for my trip until we know what Congress does."

"Only if you keep your promise to have lunch here at the Mission and let Tom show you his plans for the expansion."

"I look forward to it, amigo. And remember, you promised to help me build a management team in Kelsey to work with the construction folks and manage the project. We'd train whoever we hire, but we're looking for someone who has been in the real business world and can make sound decisions independently, especially when he can't get hold of me."

I instinctively knew he had just offered me the job; it was his style to have me ask for it first. But that wasn't going to happen. I didn't want the job, and no amount of money would change my mind.

"I have the perfect man for you, Dan. I will arrange for you to meet him when you're here. You can judge for yourself."

"That sounds good, Greg. I appreciate it. Whomever you pick will be fine with me. Good luck in Washington. If you see my son, the congressman, tell him he still has parents in Texas, and his mother misses him."

I hung up the phone and looked at Mark and Christine, who, although pretending not to listen, had been glued to every word of the call. "Mark, what are your plans about staying here at the Mission?"

"It's interesting that you ask. I told Tom yesterday that I'm here until after the campaign. If possible, I want to get a job and rent a small place somewhere in the area. Why do you ask?"

"I want you to head up the management team in Kelsey for the Rockwood Industries project at the mill. It would easily be a two-hundred-fifty-thousand-dollar gig, and when it's done, you'd be first in line to be the CEO to administer the center. It will be set up as a nonprofit foundation, cocreated by Dan Johnson and the feds, but regardless, it will need someone to be at the top, and I can't think of anyone better."

"Oh my God, Mark, what a great opportunity for you," Christine exclaimed. "Greg, you are a genius to think of him."

I thought Mark Stone was going to cry. Given all this man had come through, including the shame of committing a serious crime, three years in prison, and losing everything in his life, to be given a second chance was overwhelming. Dignified as always, he looked directly at me with wide eyes. "You are either the craziest, smartest, or most caring man I have ever met," he stated. "Thank you."

"How about this?" I continued, knowing that he would accept Dan's position. "How about you make it a rule that the team you hire will include as many residents of the Mission as possible?"

"I love that," Mark replied excitedly. "I can think of several guys I could train to do a very professional job."

I told them we could talk more about this later. It was four o'clock and time for me to head home. Mark hugged me before leaving. "Thanks again, Greg."

With the room to ourselves, I told Christine I'd call her after the news tonight. "Say, would you like to have dinner at Anthony's tomorrow night?"

"Ooh, is Mr. Greg asking me on a real date? Absolutely. I'll get Doris to watch Cody. Maybe you could bring an overnight bag tomorrow," she said as she kissed me goodbye.

As soon as I was in my truck, I returned Carl's call.

"Hey, Greg, thanks for getting back to me."

"Sure, no problem, Carl. When do you want to do the interview?"

"What I would like to do is have my camera crew take some B-roll footage of you at the Mission—working in the kitchen, meeting with Tom, eating with the residents, etcetera—and then sit down in the campaign office for a talk that would focus on your transformation from political bad boy to champion of the homeless. We want to run it as an extended special insert on the nightly news. Can we do that tomorrow morning?"

"Tomorrow works. I'll be in the kitchen cooking breakfast at six. See you then."

"Sounds good, Greg. Thanks."

CHAPTER TWENTY-NINE

"Are you watching?" I had Christine on the speakerphone as I poured a glass of pinot grigio that had chilled overnight in the refrigerator. To complete my triple balancing act, I was also watching the six o'clock news.

"It's surreal. Seeing Max Weber being arrested and taken away in handcuffs is truly unbelievable. Did I ever tell you I was best friends with his daughter, Kelly? My dad and Max were pretty close too. Max even hosted a few golf tournaments to raise money for the soup kitchen in the early days."

"Nothing surprises me about Kelsey anymore. It seems everyone knows everyone. What happened to your friendship with Kelly?" The clip of Weber being put into the car was now on the TV.

"When I was elected prom queen, Kelly came in second place. Kelly was fine with it, even happy that I won. But Kelly's mother was so angry that she declared we couldn't be friends. I cried for a week when she told me, and my parents cut all ties with them, which was awkward because they lived across the street. They still do."

"Hold that thought. Let's listen to Carl," I said.

"Max Weber, chairman of the Kelsey Republican Party and influential businessman, was arrested by FBI agents this morning on multiple charges. The feds also confiscated dozens of computers, servers, and files from one of Weber's companies, Green

Technologies, a financial collections and billing company that serves mostly small businesses. According to authorities, however, that was merely a front. In a press conference immediately after the arrest, US Attorney for Tennessee's Middle District Alex Boykin explained that they had enough evidence to prove that Weber was running one of the largest credit card and bank fraud scams in the country, an operation that has stolen millions of dollars, much of it then laundered through a political action committee run by Weber and funneled to politicians and office holders.

"Just one day ago, Weber charged the Kelsey Rescue Mission with hiring ex-convict Greg Smith as their campaign manager in the upcoming referendum to allow the Mission to double its size. Max Weber will now have bigger things to concern himself with than preventing the Mission from expanding. For Channel Four News, I'm Carl Nolan."

"Did you hear that an interim party chairman has already been named?" Christine asked.

"You know I don't follow all that town gossip, so I give up. Who is the new chairman.?"

"Art Drake."

"Great, they replaced one knucklehead with another one. That's hilarious." I laughed as I said it, but Christine reminded me that despite the mayor's commitment to clean up corruption, Drake still had a loyal following among city employees and police. She was right. Drake's new position as the party leader in a city run on an old-fashioned patronage model was no laughing matter.

"Listen, Greg, you need to be careful. The Weber folks already blame you for their misfortune in Kelsey. Now you've had his police chief fired, and his security head was caught breaking into your houseboat. And if I had to guess, a jail cell won't keep Weber from calling the shots. He still controls the family checkbook."

I wondered if Christine and Liz had been talking because they sure sounded alike.

"I promise to be careful, but there is something else you need to know."

Christine remained silent throughout my recap of my meeting with the FBI. I walked her through every detail, including the agency's suspicion that Lamar Goodman could be seeking a confrontation.

"Your and Cody's safety is my most important concern," I concluded.

"Then keep us safe," she replied without hesitation. "I trust you to do that."

• • •

When I arrived at the Mission the next morning, the Channel Four media team was already setting up lights and cameras in the kitchen area, much to the annoyance of Mike, who was busy preparing the morning meal.

"I'm sorry about this," I told him. "I promise to get them out of here as quickly as possible."

Carl interrupted, asking if I could take over the stove from Mike, who was flipping pancakes. After about two minutes, he asked if I could go through my typical routine and let them follow me with the camera. I obliged him by slipping on my bright-red apron, collecting boxes of chicken and salad ingredients from the walk-in that would be cooked for lunch, and retrieving the serving utensils for serving breakfast, which would begin in fifteen minutes. The line had already grown to about twenty, each patiently awaiting their first meal of the day.

Once we started serving, Carl directed the two cameras to get shots of me dishing up the food, one from outside the window and the other from behind me, to show the faces of the men, some of whom could not resist the temptation to tease me a bit.

"Hey, Mr. Brad, are you a movie star?"

"Look, everyone, it's our pretty boy. Smile for the cameras, Mr. Brad."

It was embarrassing and the last thing I wanted to do, but Carl had been good to our cause and me, and I couldn't tell him no. When we finally sat for the interview in the cafeteria, breakfast had ended, and the residents had disappeared to their work assignments or morning classes, depending on their schedule.

"Speeding," Carl's camera operator announced.

After a few introductory remarks and what I considered warm-up questions, Carl dug in. "Greg, I think I'm most interested in your transformation, going from a national policy and political adviser and dealmaker with heads of foreign governments, all for extraordinary fees, to federal prison, and now serving as a volunteer at the Kelsey Rescue Mission. That's quite a journey. How did you end up here in Kelsey?"

"Two-plus years in prison was a humbling experience. It made me rethink my priorities. When I got out, I headed here because of my relationship with Tom Garrity, and the next thing I knew, I was a kitchen volunteer at the Mission. But something very important happened during my time in Kelsey, especially at the Mission. I grew to love these guys and realized there could be a fine line between having it all and having very little. I identified with them and wanted to help."

"Is being an advocate for the homeless your new cause, as it has been for Pastor Tom and your estranged wife, Congresswoman Elizabeth Smith?"

I had expected the question but not the mention of Liz, which threw me off.

"I would say that's a fair assessment, and having role models like Tom and Liz isn't such a bad thing. So, yes, count me on the side of people experiencing homelessness. I want to be on the opportunity end of the equation, asking not how we put more people in a shelter but how we get them out to start a new life, one with economic stability and free of drug- and alcohol-addiction issues."

Carl glanced at the clipboard on his lap and then back at me, seated directly across from him. "What do you want to say to the voters of Kelsey who are concerned that doubling the size of the homeless shelter could lead to urban decay and crime?"

"I would say that you need to get to know us a little better. We are pretty good neighbors. Sure, we have folks with addiction problems and a few who are facing mental illness challenges, but whose family doesn't encounter roadblocks like these? I think most of us want our loved ones who have had some bad luck to have a second chance."

"You knew Jimmy Keefer personally. How did his death affect you?"

Another question I didn't expect. Carl was very good at this job. He asked pertinent questions, but always with a sense of curiosity, never hostility. "Jimmy was one of my favorite guys. We worked together in the kitchen, and I got to know him well. He liked to talk more than he enjoyed working hard, but he talked about things that mattered, like how he missed his mama and sister and how someday he wanted to buy them a house to live in. His death had a huge impact on me. It moved me from what in the past would have been a story on the news in a faraway town to 'Hey, this stuff really occurs.' But mostly, thinking about Jimmy's murder just makes me sad. And angry."

"You call it a murder. Why?"

"Because that's exactly what it was. Being homeless should never be a reason to get gunned down by police."

"Greg Smith, political adviser to presidents, senators, and kings, now a volunteer at the Kelsey Rescue Mission. I look forward to your book," he said with a broad smile. "Thank you for your time."

"Thank you, Carl."

"Cut," Carl shouted. "That is a wrap."

"Are we even?" I asked. "No more interviews?"

He knew I was poking fun at him. "Nope, you still owe me a beer."

"Anytime." I meant it. I liked Carl.

"Say, Greg, one more thing. The station is doing another poll in the aftermath of the shooting and now Weber's arrest. We start the poll tomorrow. It should take about three days, so we'll have the data next week. I'll be sure to get a comment from Christine or Tom."

"What does your gut tell you about the referendum?" I had learned that while relying on gut feelings in politics with any degree of confidence was foolish, they were sometimes legitimate.

"You're still behind, but not as much as before. People are seeing the Rescue Mission in a more favorable light, and there is a greater awareness that the local controlling party is corrupt. The trend is in your favor, but you're not there yet. Anyway, that's my two cents."

・・・

"By any chance, did you call ahead for this table?"

It was the only one near the front oval window, with a view of Queen Street, the well-lit and trendy epicenter of Kelsey's nightlife. Anthony's, the only Italian cuisine restaurant on the block, was surrounded by several other eateries and taverns, each with its specialty.

"Oh, you didn't hear the news? I passed the boyfriend test and assumed additional responsibilities."

"Your interview with Carl was amazing, Greg. I mean it. You were warm, reflective, and bold, all at the same time. Home run."

Christine and I had watched it together at her house before walking down to Anthony's. This after she had spent all day in her office without a visit to the Mission, a rarity.

"Thank you. I missed you today."

"Well, I had an interesting meeting that I wanted to tell you about. The mayor called and asked if he could drop over to discuss something, which he did at around noon, bringing two lunch bags of Chinese food. It ended up being a two-hour luncheon meeting. Meetings with elected officials are part of my pro bono work because they bring goodwill to the firm."

"Don't keep me hanging. What did he want?"

"Like most people at city hall, the in-house lawyer for the city, Brandon Lowe, is a party loyalist who was put there by Max Weber. The mayor wants the four officers who shot Jimmy to be prosecuted, but Lowe is telling him they are protected under the 'line of duty' provisions and doesn't think the city can fire them, much less prosecute them. The bottom line is that the mayor wants a lawyer he can trust."

Our waiter emptied our bottle of chianti into our glasses while two members of his serving team brought us the chef's special of osso buco that she had made from scratch, including the handmade pasta. The candle between us gave the table a romantic glow. I should have steered the conversation away from office and business talk, but between Christine and me, I was pretty sure that would be fruitless.

"Did you make any decisions?" I asked, confident that whatever Christine decided would be sound and in Kelsey's best interest.

"Yep, I told him to fire Lowe and hire a new attorney."

"Good advice. Did he bite?"

"He did more than bite. By the end of the day, Lowe had been canned, and Ted Copper—remember him? the young guy from my firm whom you met at our first meeting?—was hired to replace him. It's a win-win for the firm and a huge victory for the mayor."

"You don't mess around, do you, Counselor? I'm impressed." I meant it.

Christine reached across the table and took my hand in hers. "I need to tell you something, Mr. Smith. I will miss you for the next three days, and I'll think of you every minute you're away. I don't mean to preach, but I know returning to your former haunts could be challenging. It might conjure up the old Greg, and you would have to fight it every step of the way. You'll need to be strong."

"Sound advice, as usual. Thank you. I would be lying if I told you I wasn't a little nervous about it. But I'll have Sydney there to remind me that being a dad she can be proud of is the most important thing to me."

"And you'll have Liz, and that's okay with me, Greg. She's your best friend. Lean on her." She paused. "And then get your butt home to me because I'm getting pretty used to having you around."

CHAPTER THIRTY

For people who spend much of their working life flying, there is something comforting about returning to your home airport. Its familiar environs signify the end of an arduous journey, of days filled with constant motion. Business meetings, hotel check-ins and check-outs, taxis and car rentals, cocktails and dinners with people you hardly know, or sometimes explaining to your kid over the phone that you can't be at the big soccer match. When you leave the airport, you do it in your vehicle, one you choose for yourself and not a car temporarily assigned to you by a computer. You drive to your neighborhood, your street, and, finally, your house—the one with your dog, your children, and your spouse or partner, all showering you with love and welcoming you back like a conquering hero.

My home airport back in the day was Reagan National Airport, located just across the Potomac River from Washington, DC, in Arlington, Virginia. I was stirred with memories as I gazed out my window at the short approach, getting ready to land there for the first time in four years. Below me sprawled a breathtaking view of the National Mall, starting at the Lincoln Memorial and continuing to the Capitol, with the Washington Monument in the center. Off on the wings were the White House and Jefferson Memorial.

DC. This had once been my sandbox, but no more. Today, I was merely a visitor, a regular citizen with a chance to introduce what some would say was a great idea to help the poor and houseless. Others would call it a horrible waste of taxpayer money.

Upon disembarking, I headed straight toward the exit, passing the other gates at a good clip. Then, seemingly out of the air, came a voice I would know anywhere. My favorite kid. "Dad, over here." And she appeared. Eric trailed along behind her.

"Sydney, I didn't know you were meeting me." I hugged her so tightly that I might have collapsed one of her lungs. She wore a Yankees jersey, hat, white shorts, and dark-blue Nikes.

"It was Mom's idea. I brought you the Mustang," she said, handing me the keys. "It's in parking lot B, space 312. Eric and I are going to the Nats' game. They're not playing our team, but I'm telling folks who I'm for anyway." It was a Smith family requirement to be a Yankees fan. "Mom also called down to the guardhouse at Rayburn to allow you to park there, so you're all set. Oh my God, I have missed you so much."

A second hug, only this time it was my lungs in jeopardy.

"One other thing: I thought you should see this." She handed me today's *Washington Post* with a below-the-fold headline that read, FORMER WASHINGTON BAD BOY NOW A CHAMPION FOR THE HOMELESS. Next to it was a current picture of me, long hair and all. "Don't worry, it makes you look good. Besides, having a dad who's a 'bad boy' automatically qualifies his daughter as a badass." I hugged her again and shook hands with Eric, who had remained silent during our brief family reunion.

"Will I see you tonight?" I asked as they turned away.

"Yes, we'll take an Uber back home, get ready, and meet you at the party at eight tonight. Remember, lot B, space 312."

Home airports were very comforting indeed.

The Mustang looked and drove great. I'd purchased it twenty years before and restored it to its original showroom condition over the next five years. I couldn't have been in a better mood driving over the Fourteenth Street bridge from the airport and into the city, top down and the stereo blazing. When I reached the garage entrance of the Rayburn House Office Building, the guard greeted me.

"Good morning, Mr. Smith. I've been expecting you," he said. "The congresswoman called me personally to ensure you had a guest space. Pull right over to the side, and I'll take it from there. By the way, nice article on you in the paper today."

Twenty-nine years ago, I arrived at the congressional doorstep for the first time to do a three-month college internship and became a student of the institution's history, processes, and traditions. I learned the local language. And I made friends, one of them being Walt Kanish, the chief of staff to my first boss, my hometown congressman Charles Tomes. Eight years later, I would help defeat Kanish with a young, progressive candidate named Elizabeth Smith.

Kanish took a liking to me early on, patiently teaching me the ropes and the rules of this pulsating yet insular world. Following my internship, Walt hired me full-time as a congressional aide. In time, he taught me how to thrive, primarily in its shadows, in what came to be my constant pursuit of influence amid Rayburn's wide corridors and marble pillars. I was Anakin Skywalker to his Obi-Wan Kenobi. Except for my mail-carrier father, Walt Kanish was the most ethical man I had ever known. As I grew professionally, Walt tried his best to influence my career choices, only giving up on me when my slide to the "dark side" of politics for profit and power was complete.

In my first month in prison, Walt surprised me at FCI Morgantown. I hadn't seen or talked with him in over twenty years. Walt had turned sixty-five and decided to retire from the Hill, where he had worked for forty years, serving five different members of Congress, including one senator. Liz was also visiting that day, for the first time since my incarceration.

Before the day was over, Liz had convinced Walt to delay retirement to be her new chief of staff for the Select Committee on Homelessness, a newly created entity in the House, which the Speaker asked her to chair.

As fate had it, Walter and I would do one last thing together. The elevator took me to the lobby, where I cleared security and took another elevator to Liz's office. The receptionist ushered me immediately to her private office.

"You made it," Liz said excitedly as she stood and embraced me. "Of course, you know Walt." Walt and I exchanged a bro hug. "I'd like you to meet the best houseless policy team in Washington," Liz continued.

There were two men and two women, none older than thirty, each dressed in what I would call traditional Capitol Hill attire—a certain conservative, buttoned-down look, heavy on the navy blue and gray.

"This is Greg Smith, new to our cause but not to the wicked ways of Washington," Liz said, smiling. I shook each hand, sensing from them a mixture of professional politeness and serious apprehension, with a slightly heavier dose of the latter. A copy of today's *Washington Post* with my picture lay open on the conference table. I was guessing they had all read it.

Liz's office had not changed an iota. At one end, where the staff team sat, was a small worktable, balanced at the other by a large oak desk and a high-back black leather chair. There were two framed pictures on her desk. One was the same as before: a professional family portrait of the two of us with nine-year-old Sydney. The new one was of Susan Hutton interviewing Liz on her news program. *Safe choice*, I thought, *making it look like her only interest in Susan is professional.*

"Greg, we are all eager to hear about your concept. However, I must warn you that we are presently one vote shy of winning this committee. All of the Republicans are against it for financial reasons. We expected that. But three Democrats who represent conservative-leaning districts are holding out. Our strategy is to proceed with the hearings and hope the testimony will persuade any doubters. If not, I will postpone the vote to keep it alive."

I thanked Liz and launched into the history of the mill property and our efforts in Kelsey to convert it into a model center to assist homeless people in learning new work skills and reentering the workforce. I told them about Dan Johnson and his historical connection to the city and, most importantly, his desire to partner with the government in its funding. It occurred to me that ten days ago, they would have never heard of Kelsey, Tennessee, but now, with Jimmy's death, the "Kelsey Way," as it had been dubbed in the national media, was familiar to everyone. The tragedy had become a rallying cry for houseless advocates who saw Jimmy's murder as symbolic of those they compassionately sought to protect.

"I brought an artist's conception of the center—four images—that may provide a clearer picture of what Dan Johnson has in mind."

I laid the drawings on the table for the group to pass around.

One of the staffers, Meghan Larson, looked up after viewing all four renditions.

"These are beautiful. And I love the whole idea of learning centers and second chances. But if I am to be honest, how can we trust people like you and Dan Johnson?" Glancing at Liz, she said, "I'm sorry, Congresswoman. I hope I didn't speak out of turn."

Liz smiled. "It's okay, Meghan. Greg can handle himself. And so you know, Greg, Meghan was the policy director for one of the congressmen who was defeated in your Illinois scheme. Your involvement in our side of an important issue may seem confusing and a little personal to her."

"Meghan, I understand if you despise me. Hell, most days, I despise myself for what I did. But this is a chance for all of us to put our parties and our pasts behind us and do the right thing," I answered. "I don't always like the way the Left pushes the whole woke thing down my throat or thinks I'm evil because I don't want to drive an electric car or thinks that open borders are a good idea. But not being given a chance at a productive life and being denied the dignity of a roof over one's head is something we can unite on.

"I went to prison for my mistakes. You can look beyond that or not. That's your choice. As for Dan Johnson, yes, he's an SOB capitalist, but I can tell you that he is genuinely trying to do something good in his life. Feel fortunate that he's chosen the very issue you care most about."

When I finished, Meghan probably didn't like me any better, but her liberal lips were sealed, at least for now.

"I say we do the numbers and write this into the legislation," said Gavin, one of the young men at the table. "I can get to work on it ASAP. And for what it's worth, I agree with what Meghan said, but I also think you're right, Greg. We have a chance to pass this now. It might not be here for us next year."

"Okay, let's all get to work. We have a hearing in three weeks," Liz commanded. "Greg, thank you for bringing this to us. You and I will be late for our lunch appointment if we don't hurry."

On our way down the elevator and back out to the lobby, Liz never stopped talking, mostly about how she loved the drawings and what this center would represent.

"We could even create an office complex and invite some houseless advocacy organizations to locate their headquarters there. It could become the nerve center for research and policy development for the houseless nationwide."

"Sounds like an interesting idea," I responded. "But we shouldn't get ahead of ourselves just yet."

"Greg, I'm just so thrilled that you and I are working on the same side together. We haven't done that since I was first elected," she laughed. "It's cool."

One of Liz's junior staffers had gone downstairs ahead of us to fetch her car, agreeing to meet us in the circular driveway outside of Rayburn. In the elevator down to the ground level, a congressman I did not recognize turned to Liz with a cold stare.

"I guess if it's your spouse, it's okay to harbor criminals in the Capitol. You have a lot of nerve, Elizabeth."

Liz looked straight ahead for a few seconds. I could tell she was trying with all her will to ignore her colleague's rudeness. However, as the elevator stopped, she couldn't help herself.

"And I guess it's okay for you to chase every intern skirt on the Hill, using your power to get them on your couch. Maybe you're the one who needs a couple of years in a federal prison." We marched out of the elevator and left him standing speechless.

Once we were securely buckled in, her aide drove us to La Chaumiere, a French restaurant in Georgetown, where we would meet our legal and finance team.

"I am sorry I have made you endure that sort of thing," I said about halfway to Georgetown.

"You know what, Greg, you should be sorry. I won't lie. You made it hard on all of us who love you. Weirdly, I'm glad you got to witness it today because that sort of thing happens more often than you think. I'm proud of you for working to change, but please forgive us if we don't fully trust you yet." She grabbed my hand and held it tightly.

Liz had wisely reserved a private room upstairs so we wouldn't have to whisper confidential information to one another. "Mr. Smith returns to Washington," said our attorney, Ed Peyton, in a deep voice. "How are you, my friend?" he added as he shook my hand and drew me in for an awkward shoulder hug.

"I'm good, Ed. And you? It's nice to be back." It sounded like a good thing to say, but I didn't mean it. I did not belong here anymore. Once, it was only the summer humidity that felt oppressive. Now it was the political air. And because of today's paper, I felt watched by everyone.

"Hey, great puff piece on you in the paper today. Is it all true?"

"I think they pretty much caught my sweet side," I answered teasingly, puckering my lips. I hadn't even read the damn thing, I realized.

Liz burst out laughing. "We've been waiting on that for a long time."

The team was complete in minutes when Gary Lipton, our finance consultant, and Kathleen Sutton, the CPA, arrived simultaneously. We ordered our meals and a bottle of the house sauvignon blanc to share.

Ed immediately took charge. "Liz needs to be back on the floor to vote at one thirty, so we must get right down to business," he began in a lower voice than was his habit. "Welcome to the friendliest divorce in history. And because we all love both of you, we are grateful you have made this easy for us."

The word "divorce" sounded so blunt. Couldn't he have thought of a gentler way to say it? Perhaps "forgo future intimate bonds" or "suspend current treaty."

"Given their unique friendship, they have agreed to one lawyer, me, and equal access to all assets, which I will visit in a minute. Sydney is an adult, so there is no custody issue. However, she will have an irrevocable fund established to collect only the gains and interest until she is thirty-five, which will be hers. Gary, you will manage her fund and set up a regular payment plan. It should be a healthy allowance for her living expenses. I should add that all funding for her graduate degree or degrees has already been set aside."

As lunch was being served, Ed took a short breath, commented on how good the food looked, and continued. "Liz and Greg also agree to take possession of 'their stuff,' regardless of when it was purchased, so Greg, yes, you get to keep the Mustang."

"Okay, the meeting is over," I quipped. "That's all I care about." I wiped my hand across my forehead with a "whew."

"They will also split the three properties they own, with Liz taking full possession of the house in Great Falls, Virginia, and the condo in Buffalo. Greg will get the bungalow in St. Lucia. Both are mortgage-free."

"Oh yes, the bungalow," offered Kathy. "The one with five bedrooms and an infinity pool that looks over the ocean. That bungalow?" It was good for us to laugh, I decided. It kept Liz and me from breaking down and crying over the grimness of the topic.

"But I get it four weeks a year," Liz said.

"Yep, it's written into the agreement, Liz. However, should Greg sell the property, that provision does not travel to any new home he might purchase."

"She can stay in my house anytime," I offered.

"Finally, Gary and Kathleen, this is where we'll need your input in the upcoming weeks: The Smiths are not separating all their holdings, investments, or cash. Instead, they are forming a legal partnership in which equal funds can be withdrawn monthly. The remaining is to be managed by Gary for growth. By the way, we will continue to abide by Liz's strict rules about companies they invest in, following environmental, social, and governance best practices guidelines. I have all this documented and ready for each to sign." Ed handed out thick notebooks to the others.

I turned to Liz sitting next to me at the round table and only then realized that she'd had her hand clasped firmly over mine throughout Ed's entire spiel.

"Are you good?" she asked softly.

CHAPTER THIRTY-ONE

When we arrived at Rob's birthday party, it was in full swing, complete with a small jazz trio and a hundred of Washington's most beautiful people. One gander around the room told me that an invitation likely meant you were considered by Laurie Kearse, Rob's wife and party hostess, to be part of Washington's elite political class, with members of both parties well represented.

Of course, we were here because Liz was not only a prominent member of Congress but also Laurie's closest gal pal in Washington. Once upon a time, Rob and I were inseparable. The Kearses were our constant Friday- and Saturday-night friends, often gathering around our pool with a patio fire or playing cards at the kitchen table.

When Laurie saw us come through the door, she beelined to greet us. "Oh my God, it's true. I saw your picture in the paper today with the hair and facial stubble, and I thought, *Who is this gorgeous man?*" She moved into my arms for a giant hug, which I needed to overcome my insecurity about being at a Washington social gathering for the first time as an ex-con. While the din of the affair didn't stop when I entered, there was a palpable movement of eyeballs in my direction. "And, Sydney, you look fantastic. Beautiful as always."

"Thanks, Aunt Laurie. Susan took me shopping last week, where she buys all of her stuff for television. It's my 'newsgirl' look," she giggled. Good for Sydney. She was embracing both Susan and Christine. *Aren't we just the hippest family in town?* I laughed under my breath.

I felt a tap on my shoulder and turned to find Rob's smiling face. "Dude, you look tan, healthy, and strong. What is your secret?"

"Good living, man. That's all I can say." I didn't mention living on a houseboat with my shirt off half the time or a morning biking routine that was now up to fifteen miles a day.

After serving as Liz's chief of staff for four years, Rob Kearse went to work with me running a winning Senate campaign, resulting in him being selected as the newly elected senator's chief of staff. Four years later, when his senator was elected president, Rob moved to the White House as deputy chief of staff, where he found himself in the right place at the right time, despite his young age, to move up to the top spot upon the sudden death of the president's first chief of staff.

In politics, like life itself, timing can mean everything. At each step of his career, I lobbied hard for Rob's advancement. Of course, these days, my endorsement would work in reverse. I was reminded tonight how everything could be lost instantly, the same observation I often experienced at the Mission when watching the men.

"Hey, let's break out of here for a few minutes to the bar so we can talk," Rob urged. "Laurie, I'll be right back. Come get me if I stay in the bar longer than I should."

Rob got to business after we ordered double Maker's Mark on the rocks. "Listen, Greg, the president has followed everything you're doing in Kelsey. The referendum campaign, the volunteering in the kitchen, and especially the keeping of the peace after the shooting, which, by the way, he's been briefed by the FBI that you orchestrated the whole thing. He's now super intrigued by this center for the homeless you want to build and wants to help."

"Wait a minute, who told him about that?"

"Come on, Greg. Are you a little rusty? It was frigging Dan Johnson who told him. Billionaires always get their calls returned by presidents. I only confirmed it when he asked."

"You're right. I should have known Dan couldn't keep this under wraps." I wondered who else he had told.

"But wait, my friend, here's the huge news. The president is all in on Liz's homeless bill and wants to put the full weight of the White House behind it. He even wants you to bring a group of your residents at the Mission to the White House to stand with him when he announces his support. Could you make that happen?"

"Jesus, Rob, that would be fantastic. But it would be insanity for him, politically. Wouldn't he take a huge hit for going against his party and supporting this bill, not to mention inviting a bunch of homeless 'losers' to the White House?"

"Probably, but here's the funny thing. He doesn't care. He has two years left before he and the First Lady retire to their cabin in Maine and he's done with politics forever. And he wants to go out having done something bipartisan. I know it sounds trite by this point, but the president is truly sick and tired of the polarization; he has a do-gooder bucket list of things he wants to do before he leaves, and this is one of them."

I'd always wondered why more presidents didn't follow that course—a lame-duck strategy that said, "Screw this, I'm going to fix a problem or two before I go, and to hell with the politics."

"Then, yes, I will bring our ambassadors committee, ten men who have agreed to be on their best behavior and represent the Mission's good intentions."

"Great, get me their names so the Secret Service can vet their backgrounds. I want you and Tom Garrity with them. I'll have a speechwriter contact you for background information so she can prepare the president's remarks. Regarding dates, we will have to time it with Liz's committee hearing date. I'm thinking it's three to four weeks from now."

We both looked up as Laurie approached from across the bar area, tapping her wrist to signify that Rob's time was up. "I know you two would prefer an evening alone somewhere, but your private campfire is over. Rob, it would be best if you mingled a bit. I also want you to thank everyone for coming."

When we were back in the party area, I headed toward Liz and Sydney, each with white wine in hand and talking with Dan's son, Andrew Johnson, and his wife, Julia. "The Honorable Andrew Johnson, I presume, and his even more honorable wife, Julia," I greeted cheerfully.

"Ah, my wayward campaign consultant, fresh from his battles to protect the houseless and prevent Southern cities from erupting into violence," Andrew responded as I exchanged brief one-armed hugs with both. "I loved your comeback article in the paper today."

"Say, Andrew, I come with a special message from a certain Dallas, Texas, citizen who made me promise to deliver it personally if I ran into you."

"Let me guess. The citizen you speak of said, 'Tell my son the congressman that he still has parents and that his mother misses him.' He gives the same instructions to everyone who comes here." Of course, everyone had a good laugh. "Greg, what you are trying to do with a center named after my grandfather is awesome. Thank you."

"Does that mean Liz can count on your support for the homeless bill?"

"I'm not a member of her committee, so I'm off the hook. However, if it gets to the floor for a full vote of the House, I have promised to speak on behalf of the bill and try to get a few moderate Republicans to come over. It means a lot to my dad, who has been a different person lately. I can't quite explain it. It's like he has a heart all of a sudden."

I looked over at Liz, who winked at me. Andrew had no clue I had left his father off my tattletale list four years ago partly to save Andrew's career.

• • •

I decided to drive back to Tennessee the next day. My business was done, and Sydney was leaving with Eric for a week before they started back to school after Labor Day. Sydney had opted for the University of Buffalo, while Eric would complete law school in Morgantown. It would be interesting to see how their relationship progressed with a five-hour drive in between.

My reason for driving and not flying was to reunite my Mustang with its rightful owner. I intended to rent a storage unit less than a mile from the marina and park it there.

"I didn't get a chance to ask you last night about your talk with Rob," Liz said as we sipped our coffee and shared a toasted bagel that morning before I left. We sat in the nook just off the kitchen that overlooked the gardens and the pool where we had sat together and talked on thousands of mornings gone by. "I know what he asked, but he wanted to tell you himself. There is one part he did not include," she continued. "I want your guys from the Mission to testify before my committee after they visit the White House."

"You want them to sit at that table before your houseless committee and answer questions? Whoa. That could be a little—no, a lot—intimidating, don't you think?"

"It depends. I'll arrange it so that Tom or Christine and maybe just one of the residents answer the questions. The rest of them would be there to be introduced."

"You mean, as props," I said.

"Kind of," she answered truthfully, "but come on, Greg, this is Washington. We use whatever angle we can, especially on a close vote like this."

"Let's do it," I said. "Say, before I take off this morning, I want you to know that I plan to ask Christine to marry me after the divorce is final. I hope you'll be okay with it."

I talked further about my love for Christine and how I thought we were right for each other and saw Liz's eyes tearing up as she stared at me in either shock or disapproval, neither of which I expected.

"You know, Smith, I have practiced hearing those words from you ever since I told you that I was gay. What's that been—seven years ago? I knew it would happen someday. Now look at me. I told myself that it would be okay for you to love someone else and that you deserve to have someone else. And that's true. I do feel those things. But I will always love you, Googie. You will always be my comrade in arms, that voice in my head, and I would do anything for you."

She was now openly crying as I cradled her head to my chest.

"She had better be good to you, or she will have one angry hen to contend with." Liz must have meant it. She hadn't called me Googie in years, the name she gave me before she could speak complete sentences.

"You know, my sweet Lizzy, I don't deserve you. I have let you down in so many ways."

She lifted her head and looked me in the eye. "Look, I told you we all have trust issues for what you did. But here's the truth. You committed a crime and paid your debt. You need to move on. Never let anyone tell you you're not good enough. I know your heart. And I think Christine does, too."

One more long embrace, and I was out the front door with a nine-hour drive ahead of me, a straight shot consisting of three interstates and two exits. Taking a final look at the beautiful home we had built together almost twenty years ago, I headed down the long driveway. Liz and I had finally crossed the inevitable Rubicon, walking the bridge together and learning to reinvent our relationship, as we had done many times since our early childhood.

With the Mustang top down and the sun out, it was a beautiful drive as I passed by Shenandoah Mountain and the stark greenery of the Virginia countryside. I felt good about my short trip back to my old haunt. The homeless committee staff had responded favorably—if not to me, at least to the concept I had presented—and my discussion with Rob at the party was mind-blowing. I wondered what the ambassadors would think when I told them they would meet the president at the White House.

Unfortunately, however, my good day would soon unravel.

The trouble began shortly after I left Virginia and entered Tennessee, somewhere on the outskirts of Bristol. It was just shy of two in the afternoon. The tank was nearly empty, as was my stomach, so the billboard that read, JERRY'S EAT 'N FILL, NEXT EXIT seemed perfect for my two vital needs. Once I got the tank full of the supreme grade, I parked and entered the café. I was wavering between having two chili dogs or one giant cheeseburger. Of course, either choice would include large french fries. I was led by a young, pretty hostess whose peppiness reminded me of Sydney to a four-person booth against the window that looked directly at my Mustang, which was what I was staring at when two muscular men, both about my age, plopped down at my table, the larger one beside me on the outside of the bench and the other directly across. I had seen them moments before, getting out of an old Chevy van. I noticed that the van driver remained in the vehicle.

"Excuse me, gentlemen, but I'm eating alone this afternoon," I said, sensing this was not the Bristol welcome committee. The one across from me, whom I had seen before but couldn't immediately place, made it a point to slide a pistol out of his carrying bag and put it on his lap. I tried to slip out but pushed against an estimated quarter ton of human body weight. The mountain man wasn't letting me out.

"Don't try anything, or a bullet from this silenced gun will be fired right at your dick, which wouldn't be good for you or Ms. Culpepper." The first guy was the mouth of the operation. "We told you to leave Tennessee or there would be consequences. When you caught that plane yesterday morning, we thought you had taken our advice, but here you are again, back in our state. So, welcome to your consequences."

And then I knew that Clean-Cut had a real name. It was Joel Palmer, Weber's security guard. The bad cop who had now gone corporate. He looked just like the picture the FBI showed me.

"We'll take a short walk outside and get in that van. We have a little trip planned for you, Mr. Smith."

"Listen, Palmer, you're already in deep shit. The FBI has your fingerprints all over my boat, and if you're still taking orders from Weber, who will spend the rest of his life in prison, you're an idiot. Unless, that is, you plan to join him, which you will do if anything happens to me today."

"Get up, asshole." Which I did. Besides the hostess and an elderly lady cook, the café was empty. The fight I wanted wasn't in here but out in the open, where I figured I stood a better chance to win or run. As we shuffled out of the café with Joel directly behind me, I mouthed a silent "Help me" to the hostess. I also got a clear look through the window at the driver, who had gotten out of the van and opened the sliding door on the side. Two steps later, Mountain Man opened the glass and metal door to lead me out. While Palmer held it, I used my body weight to slam against the door, surprising Palmer and knocking the gun from his hand.

The weapon fell to the floor. I saw and heard the hostess yelling something about a fight into the phone and assumed she was talking to the police. Still on my feet but being wrestled down by Palmer, I kicked the gun across the floor toward the hostess. Mountain Man lunged for it while Palmer proceeded to beat the crap out of me with his fists, but the hostess got to the weapon first.

It was during Palmer's third punch to my jaw that I heard the deafening shot that saved my life. Palmer screamed and rolled off me, writhing in pain and holding his leg, a bullet from a nine-millimeter Luger lodged securely in his left femur. I opened my eyes to see the hostess standing with the gun, now pointed directly at Mountain Man.

"One move and you will get the same. Or maybe I'll aim for a different body part."

We all turned toward the dirt parking lot as the van peeled away, pursued by a dust cloud. The hostess then turned to me. "Can you walk?"

"My jaw and ribs hurt like hell," I said.

"Grandma," she yelled, "it's okay to come out. I need you." A tiny woman wearing a cook's apron appeared near the register. She was at least eighty. "Get some towels and make sure this dickhead doesn't bleed to death. I don't need a second-degree murder charge on my hands." Then, pointing to me, the hostess told her grandmother, "When you get that done, this nice man needs to be cleaned up. He might have a broken nose. Please take care of him. Can you do that for me?"

Grandma must have been a combat nurse, I thought as she tightened a tourniquet on Palmer, then tended to my nose and several cuts. Unfortunately, she couldn't do anything for my ribs. I slowly got up, with Palmer still holding his leg and Mountain Man being lorded over by the hostess, whom I had come to admire as a very savvy and decisive young lady.

CHAPTER THIRTY-TWO

The Tennessee state police descended upon the Eat 'n Fill within minutes. I watched from the booth where I was receiving tender loving care from Grandma as four cars with two troopers in each one screeched to a stop in the parking lot and sprinted to the front door of the café. An ambulance with siren blazing was on their heels. I had never been on a crime show set, but this had to be how it looked to the director once he yelled, "Action."

"These two tried to take that one at gunpoint," the hostess explained to the lead trooper. "I got the gun, shot this one in the leg, and held this one until you got here."

"Get him in the ambulance," the trooper barked at one of his subordinates, pointing to Palmer. "Go with him and question him on the way there. I will question these two here," he said, pointing to Mountain Man and me. "Someone is getting arrested today. We have to figure out who the good and bad guys are because I'm not sure right now."

At that point, Mountain Man started bawling like a baby. "I didn't want to do it," he sobbed. "Mr. Weber ordered it. I'll tell you everything."

Oh boy, I thought, *this is good*. Instinctively, I was once again weighing the political advantage of the situation. Weber, who was out on a million-dollar bail for robbing senior citizens of their life savings, would now be charged with attempted murder, or at least kidnapping. The men at the Rescue Mission would look like angels in comparison.

"Shut the fuck up, Earl," Palmer screamed from the stretcher as the EMTs carried him outside to the ambulance. "Don't say a word." But Mountain Man had already testified to Weber's role in this near-tragic plot and would be hard-pressed to retract it.

A second team of EMTs, who had arrived only minutes after the first team, then decided that my head and ribs hurt too much to let me go, so they took me to the hospital too. They grabbed my mobile phone and backpack from the Mustang at my request, and we went in the ambulance. I saw five urgent messages from Christine.

I sent her a text back. HAD A LITTLE ACCIDENT. GOING TO A HOSPITAL IN BRISTOL. SORRY. It was all I could say before the Demerol took hold. I was out.

• • •

I opened my eyes and looked up toward the ceiling. Glancing sideways at the medical monitors told me that I was in a hospital room. My vision was slightly blurred, but I saw a nurse leaning over me, asking how I felt. "My ribs hurt," I said groggily.

"We kept you overnight," she replied. "We also kept you asleep to make sure your brain didn't swell, which it didn't, so it appears you dodged a serious brain injury. You do have a few visitors who have been here for several hours. The doctor said it was okay for them to visit. Is that all right with you?"

The door to my room opened, and Christine entered first, running to my bedside and hugging me around the neck, followed by Tom, Sydney, and Liz. They formed a circle around the bed. Liz was the first to speak. "Okay, Smith, I told you to be careful. When are you going to listen?" Even her sarcasm was comforting.

"Dad, are you okay? We were so worried." I could tell that Sydney had been crying.

Looking at Liz, I said, "I'm so happy you got to meet Christine."

"I love her. She's my new best friend."

Somehow, I knew they would become pals. But meeting in the hospital room where I was the patient was something I didn't see coming.

They all started to chatter at once, giving me a worse headache than Palmer had. But I was happy to talk. I was alive, and that was all anyone—including me—cared about for the moment. In the next half hour, I heard how Christine received my text, followed by a call to the only hospital in Bristol. But because Christine wasn't "family," they wouldn't give her any information. She called Tom, who then called Liz and Sydney, and everyone jumped in a vehicle and headed to Bristol. I was told they all slept in the waiting room.

A woman in a white coat entered the room, and the voices went quiet.

"Mr. Smith, I'm Dr. Stubblefield. You have no concussion or broken bones. However, several of your ribs are badly bruised. I will let you out of here today, but only if you don't drive."

"Dibs on the Mustang," Tom yelped to everyone's laughter.

Dr. Stubblefield proceeded, "I'm going to give you some strong stuff for the ribs and ask that you remain at home, mostly lying or sitting, for the next week. Your pain medication will keep you pretty drowsy for a few days. Is there someone who can look after you?"

"That will be me," offered Christine. "And it won't be on the houseboat."

"Great, I am referring you to a neurologist in Nashville, an old friend whom I want you to see next week for a follow-up. Unfortunately, there isn't much we can do for the ribs except let them heal."

A new face appeared at the door as I received my instructions. It was the hostess, whom I waved over. "I don't even know your name," I confessed.

"I'm Angel," she said softly, a far cry from the pistol-wielding field general of yesterday.

"Family, this is the young lady who saved my life. Thank you, Angel. You are a brave young woman."

She held my hand for a full minute, telling me to care for myself and reminding me how blessed I was to have such a caring family. And then she was gone.

By the time I was released, it was noon. Liz and Sydney had already left to ensure Liz didn't miss any more votes than necessary. Sydney wanted to stay and come home with me, but when I reminded her that Mom hadn't driven in seven years, she quickly realized that Liz alone on a highway for five hours wasn't a good idea. Christine helped me into her Jeep, and Tom gleefully took the keys to the Mustang.

As Christine and I admired Tennessee's rolling green hills and pastureland passing by at seventy miles per hour, we took advantage of the time to get caught up. "What do two lawyers do on a three-hour car ride together?" Christine asked. "They 'de-brief.' Get it?"

"Oh, you want to compete for corny jokes? What did the judge say to her husband when she wanted a divorce? 'You're dis-missed.'"

"That was bad, Greg. Speaking of divorce, how did all that go with Liz?"

"It went well. She gets the house in Virginia. I got the one in St. Lucia. We each keep all our stuff and receive a monthly check from the trust that we will co-own under the management of our accountant and attorney. It should be final by Christmas."

"I just love her, Greg. I hope she will always be in our lives."

"What did the two of you talk about all last night? It couldn't have been all about me."

"I learned that a certain Greg Smith arranged for a group of residents from the Mission to visit the White House and testify in front of a congressional committee. Oh, and get this, I learned that this same Greg Smith promised that I would be with them the entire time and would be the spokesperson at the committee hearing. How much do you know about this Greg Smith character? It sounds to me like he's a dealmaker."

"Very funny."

Just then, the soft music on the radio was interrupted by a news break. "Heading this hour's news is a report from Kelsey, Tennessee, where Max Weber, a powerful local businessman and the city's longtime Republican leader, was re-arrested on new charges one day after making bail. Weber is now facing charges of attempted kidnapping with intent to harm.

"The new charges against Weber are in addition to allegedly running a nationwide credit card and bank account scheme targeted at seniors. They stem from an incident yesterday in Bristol, Tennessee, in which two men, both employed by Weber, attacked former presidential adviser Greg Smith at gunpoint and violently beat him. One of the attackers, identified as Merle Denver, confessed to Tennessee state troopers at the scene that it was Weber who, in Denver's words, 'ordered the hit.' Police are now searching for the van driver, who left before the police arrived. They have asked anyone with information about a brown 2008 Chevrolet van with Illinois license plates to call their nearest police station."

"It was Lamar Goodman," I screeched so loudly that Christine jumped in her seat. "It was Lamar fucking Goodman. I saw him."

I quickly punched the number for Bryce Lundgren, my FBI contact in Nashville. I was relieved that he picked up on the first ring.

"Greg, are you okay? I'm following this whole story with the reports we're getting, but right now, it's in the hands of the state troopers."

"Bryce, listen to me. The driver of the van was Lamar Goodman. I saw him before I got the shit beat out of me and the pain meds took over. I saw him plain as day."

We drove a few more miles with the radio turned low in the background before Christine started laughing. "So much for you staying out of the limelight. You're probably on the front page of every newspaper in Tennessee. I can't believe your new buddy Carl Nolan hasn't called you yet."

I looked at my phone. "Carl left six voicemails this morning. I haven't called him back yet."

"See? It was only a matter of time. How do you feel about appearing on TV with your face covered in bandages?"

"There is no way I am going on TV looking like this. Aren't you the campaign spokesperson?"

Just then, my phone rang. It was Dan Johnson. "Hello, this is Greg."

"Greg, CNN is running a breaking story that Weber tried to have you killed. Is that true?"

"As true as the summer heat in Dallas," I answered, "but thanks to a very brave café hostess named Angel, I'm okay. Sore head and ribs, and a few scratches. I'm on my way back to Kelsey now with Christine." I looked over at Christine, who smiled back.

Once Dan was satisfied that I was fine, I briefed him on my meeting with the congressional staff, explaining that they were all in. I also told him what Andrew had said about having his support and a handful of Republicans to make it bipartisan once the bill went to the entire House.

"That sounds encouraging. Are we still on for the week after the election?" he asked.

"Still on. Nothing has changed. Christine will reply with the details, but we look forward to a great day."

"Okay, that will be November 9. I'll fly the company jet directly into the Kelsey Regional Airport. I can be there by ten o'clock. Can you send a driver? My senior architect and engineer will be with me, so a large vehicle would be nice."

I now had the phone on speaker so Christine could also hear.

"I also want to meet with whoever you've selected to manage this operation for me."

Listening to Dan bark out a plan of action, expecting me to carry it forward, I felt like a previous chapter of my life had been reopened.

"That works on our side, Dan. Thanks."

I immediately called the mayor.

"Hey, Greg," he answered. "Are you okay? We're all very worried about you."

"I'm fine and on my way home, Mayor. Thanks. Say, Dan Johnson called to tell me he's coming to Kelsey the week after Election Day to announce that he is going forward with his plans to renovate the mill. Can you hold a joint ten o'clock press conference and briefly welcome the audience? It's going to be a public event." The drugs were making me groggy, and I wondered if my speech was slurred.

"I'm in, Greg. No worries. Hey, do you have another second?"

My ribs hurt, and my head ached, and I just wanted to take a nap. "Sure, what's up?"

"I was told privately that the county prosecutor is leaning against sending the four Kelsey police officers to the grand jury for indictment. She thinks that active-duty police are protected under state law for taking 'appropriate' measures to defend themselves."

"But they weren't threatened, Frank. That's what she needs to remember. Can't you do anything at the city level? Letting those guys go free will unleash a public backlash that will undo everything you've done to keep the peace. Besides, it's just wrong."

"You're right, but I'm limited, Greg. The county and the state have jurisdictional authority in matters like this. Remember, the prosecutor is an elected position. I can't fire her like I did the police chief."

"But the chief could fire the officers," Christine offered as she kept her eyes straight on the road ahead. "He would be on firm legal ground to say they acted recklessly and did not follow prescribed protocol, as they had been trained to do."

"I agree with Christine," I opined. "Would Larry fire the officers? It could open the city up to a wrongful termination suit, but ultimately, the city would prevail."

"I will have the town's attorney write up four termination letters," the mayor responded. "Thanks, guys. It was good to hear from you. Get well, Greg."

I called Liz. "Hey, how are you?" she answered on one ring. I could tell by the hip-hop music in the background that she was still in the car with Sydney. It was the only music that would keep Sydney awake after being up all night.

"The pain pills are great," I lied. I explained to her that the local prosecutor had cold feet about indicting the officers who killed Jimmy. "If this town erupts, it could jeopardize the referendum and the center, not to mention our newfound reputation as a city that works through difficult situations instead of rioting over them. A personal call from the attorney general to the prosecutor urging her to proceed with an indictment would be persuasive."

"So, let me guess." I was no longer hearing the music, meaning she had turned it off and was taking my call seriously. "You want me to call Gerald and get him to call the prosecutor? That's a big ask, Greg."

Gerald Sheffield and Liz were elected to Congress for the first time the same year. They had side-by-side offices in the Longworth House Office Building for four years before he was elected to the United States Senate from New York, thanks partly to Liz serving as his campaign chairperson. Our families had become dear friends and neighbors in Great Falls, Virginia, where Sydney and their daughter, Laurie, had grown up as best friends.

"I would call him myself, but he can't chance making deals with ex-cons."

"Okay, email me the pertinent points and the prosecutor's contact information. I'll call Gerald this evening. By the way, I'm so glad you're taking it easy," she added sarcastically.

CHAPTER THIRTY-THREE

"As late as yesterday afternoon, there were rumors that County Prosecutor Eileen Davis would not be sending the four officers responsible for Jimmy Keefer's shooting to the grand jury for indictment. Sources explained that Davis thought they would be protected from indictment because they were merely responding to a life-threatening incident while on duty. But what a difference a day can make.

"Prosecutor Davis today announced that she has reversed her earlier considerations and will indeed seek grand jury indictment for each of the men for second-degree murder. Insiders tell us that Davis changed her mind after receiving a late-night telephone call from an unnamed high-level government official. Meanwhile, Chief of Police Larry Casey today fired the four officers, sending each of them a letter saying their actions violated internal protocol, leading to an unnecessary death.

"His action has been praised by Timothy Gains, president of the Kelsey NAACP, and others, including Pastor Tom Garrity, who heads the Kelsey Rescue Mission, where Jimmy Keefer resided at the time of his death. While we don't know if any of these matters impact the upcoming referendum to allow expansion of the Mission, today's edition of the *Kelsey Daily* has released poll results representing a significant shift from a plurality of voters being against Mission expansion to a majority being for it. For Channel Four News, I'm Carl Nolan."

There was a point in every campaign I'd managed or guided, whether for a candidate or a referendum, weeks ahead of Election Day, when I knew we would win or lose. The worst feeling was the gnawing sense of a pending defeat. It was devastating to still have to go through the motions, ensuring the right things were said and supporters kept their enthusiasm. On the other side of the emotional spectrum was the euphoria of everything going our way. I called it the victory vibe. I could feel it in my gut, like a tide moving in our favor, and I knew we would win.

After watching Carl's report and with exactly four weeks to Election Day, that was the feeling I had about the referendum campaign that would allow the Kelsey Rescue Mission to expand. We were going to win. I knew it.

"Have you seen the paper today?" Tom greeted me as I entered the Mission on Tuesday morning. "Their poll has us winning by double digits."

I wasn't scheduled to work in the kitchen this morning but had walked over from Christine's house, where I was still in temporary residence, convalescing from my café mugging. Tom had scheduled a conference call with Liz, who was expected to call at seven to update us on the committee hearing date and the White House visit.

"I only heard we were winning, but not by that much. That's great news," I answered as I followed him into this office and plopped down in one of the two chairs on the other side of his desk. "Let me see it." He handed me the paper. The poll showed that the events in Kelsey over the past several weeks had brought considerable change to how voters viewed the issue of homelessness in general and adding on to the Mission specifically. By 53 to 40 percent, voters intended to vote for expansion. In polling two months ago, the numbers were virtually the opposite.

According to the poll, the factors most important in the turnaround of voter sentiment were the Jimmy Keefer shooting and the downfall of Max Weber, the leading opponent to the Mission. Voters also liked the upbeat television commercials that featured residents of the Mission telling their stories and intensely disliked the other side's commercials of the gloom and doom that would occur if the Mission expanded.

"Sorry, guys, for running a little late. I had to wait for my dad to get to the house to watch Cory." Christine hurriedly entered the office, followed by Mark.

"We were going over the poll in today's paper," Tom declared.

His office phone promptly rang, and he put it on speaker.

"Hello, all." The congresswoman was friendly and upbeat, as always—unless she was angry, of course.

"Hey, sis, it's Tom, Greg, Christine, and Mark Stone. Mark is a resident here and will be named by Dan Johnson when he comes to Kelsey as the new CEO of the Johnson Foundation, who will oversee the new center."

"Nice to meet you, Mark. Sorry for sounding like I'm in a hurry, but I have a roll call vote in ten minutes. The committee has set the hearing dates for the American Houseless Act for the ninth, tenth, and eleventh of October," Liz began. "I have your people slated to be the final witnesses before we vote on the eleventh, after lunch at one thirty. I spoke with Rob at the White House, and they have your group scheduled for ten thirty that morning."

Tom was the first to respond. "Liz, I love what you're trying to do, and you know I will always trust your instinct, but I must confess that I'm at least a little worried. This is a foreign stratosphere for a group of homeless folks. Remember that most of our population suffers from drug and alcohol addiction, mental health challenges, and poverty. Some from all three. I don't want to throw them to the wolves." He was defaulting to his role as the sheep herder, protecting his flock.

"Mark, let me ask you a question." Liz was clever. Instead of directly answering her brother's concerns, she would get the homeless guy on the call to answer for her. "Can you get me five, six, or seven residents, including yourself, who could handle the pressure of a congressional hearing and White House visit? Remember that Tom and Christine will answer most of the questions and be with you at the witness table."

Mark didn't hesitate. "Yes, Congresswoman Smith. I can do that." He told her about the ambassadors committee, which he had headed since the beginning of the year.

"Good. Make sure we have racial balance and a range of ages. It would also be good to have a veteran, preferably one who served in combat. Greg, are you okay with putting them through one of your executive training classes on correct language and protocol? Maybe you could give them the leadership speech."

The whole room groaned. "Not the leadership speech. Please not that," Tom choked through his laughter.

"Okay, scratch the speech, but you have the best public presentation coach in the business right there. Use him. By the way, Greg, how are your ribs?"

"I'm fine, Liz. I'll have the group 'DC-ready' by October 11."

"Big brother, are you okay with everything?"

"I'm as good as I'll ever be, I guess. Let's do this."

Back when Tom was an all-state wrestler in high school, he always scanned the stands for Liz when he took to the mat. She was his security blanket and still the one he looked to for confidence, along with Jesus.

"See you all soon. Bye-bye." Liz ended the call and left us momentarily staring at one another, wondering where to go.

"The first thing we need to do is pick the team," offered Christine.

I spoke up first. "Of course, I would recommend Mike from the kitchen. And I'd add Jarred Mackey to it. He is strong, speaks well, and he's a vet who lost one of his legs for our country."

Tom went next. "I like Billy Coble. Yes, we need to watch him like a hawk—an honor bar in a hotel room would probably send him to the edge—but he's smart, college-educated, and could field questions if needed."

"I like the young man who was Jimmy's best friend," Christine suggested. "What's his name?"

"Jonah Mays," Mark answered. "He's a great choice. If asked about Jimmy's death, Jonah would bring an emotional element."

Over the next half hour, several others were identified and agreed upon, including Raymond "Bugsy" Stephens. Bugsy, nicknamed at birth by his older brother because he looked like a bug, had arrived at the Mission three months ago. He was recently released after serving five years at the US Penitentiary in Allenwood, Pennsylvania, for selling cocaine. We became instant friends, being correctional institute alums and all. He liked to joke that I was in "pussy prison." "That's what we called those Club Fed jails. I heard you guys had a spa where you could get massages," he told me.

"That's not true," I informed him. "But we could have extra bacon for breakfast if we asked nicely."

He was one of the guys I was helping with résumés, although he didn't need me.

Tom also added my buddy Zeke to the group and a couple of others, bringing the total to seven. We had a nine-person contingent with Christine, Tom, and Cooper, the assistant director. "How about you, Greg?" Christine asked. "Won't you be going?"

"I'll be with you, but in the background. I could be a media distraction, and we want the attention to be on the new center, the Mission, and the cause of homelessness. Liz brought this up, and I have to agree with her."

After the meeting broke up, I told Christine that I needed to get back "home" to my houseboat. I hadn't been there since I left for Washington, and it was probably a little dusty.

"Are you okay driving and crawling up and down all those ladders? I'm worried about your ribs."

"I'm still sore, and this bandage on my face needs to be replaced twice daily, but I'm okay. Would you like to come with me? I'm taking the day off tomorrow and spending it outdoors. We could have some lunch up at the patio bar."

"You're on. I have to ask Mom and Dad to take Cody."

I popped into Tom's office to retrieve the keys to my Mustang over his objection. "You're taking my car from me? After all that I do for you?"

"Sorry, pal, you can have the shirt off my back, but you can't have my Mustang."

I told him I was finally going home and taking his lawyer with me. "Call us tomorrow if you need anything," I told him.

I arrived at Christine's to pick her up at noon, having first stopped by the Taco House to pick up a couple of burritos for lunch. "We can eat these on the way. I was starving."

"Wow, my first ride in Greg's chariot. I am honored."

With the top down and lunch to go, we headed off, talking and laughing like teenagers. Christine had wisely and stylishly wrapped her head in a bright-red scarf that matched her lipstick, as I had warned her this would be a "wind in our hair" trip. The distance from Kelsey to the marina in Nashville was a blessing, a time for us to decompress and not be required to think about homeless men, wayward cops, and sleazy politicians. Once on the highway, I inserted a Kenny Chesney CD, and we sang to the lyrics, her in tune and me not so much.

"I've been meaning to ask you if your parents have come around on me yet?" I turned down the radio when the song ended and shouted to be heard above the wind.

"Dad is fine with it. He's like, 'Whatever makes you happy.' He's also had ample time with you, and Tom strongly influences him. But Mom? Let's say we have work to do. She isn't convinced people can change, but more importantly, she's afraid we haven't been together long enough to be making forever plans."

"She has some good points, I guess. Are we making long-term plans?"

"I think two things. One, my mother doesn't run my life. And two, I love you. Oh, and here's a third thing. Every day together is one day longer than yesterday. In my life, one day at a time is long term. Besides, every woman knows a boyfriend is way better than a husband." The last part came with a massive hug around my neck.

As we pulled into the marina, it felt like I had been away for weeks, not days. I spotted my refurbished houseboat in a row of others, each different in size and design but unanimously tethered to the same dock. I felt its pull, calling me to spend a few days in the hot sun and gleaming river with a beautiful woman to whom I was also tethered.

CHAPTER THIRTY-FOUR

The next day on the houseboat was supposed to be the last rest either of us would have for a while. I spent the morning hours hosing and scrubbing the decks, including the bird poop, while Christine pitched in by cleaning the windows, inside and out. After completing our chores, we headed to the marina café for cheeseburgers and fries, which were washed down with a cold IPA. We eventually fell asleep on the top deck on our two cushioned chaises. It was the lazy day both of us needed.

It didn't last long.

Our afternoon slumber was interrupted by Bryce Lundgren yelling from the deck below. "Greg, are you up there? It's Bryce. I need to speak with you. It's urgent."

Suddenly awake, I hastened to the boat's edge to look down. "Bryce. What's up? Is anything wrong?"

"Do you mind if I come up?"

My FBI liaison nimbly climbed the ladder to the sundeck. By the time he appeared, Christine had hurriedly put a T-shirt on to cover her bikini top. After brief introductions, Bryce apologized for the intrusion and got down to business. He appeared troubled.

"Lamar Goodman has abducted Sydney and taken her hostage. He is demanding a two-million-dollar ransom. We tried calling you, but there was no answer. The congresswoman has also been notified."

Lamar had struck where he knew it would hurt the most—my daughter.

"Fuck, the one time in how long I decide to spend a little time without my phone. I left it downstairs. What else do we know, Bryce? Is she okay?" I demanded.

Christine retrieved my phone from the kitchen and handed it to me. A dozen messages from the FBI office, Liz, and one "unknown caller." Instinctively, I pushed the voicemail to replay the latter. "Hello, Greg. I did want to kill you, but I thought of something that would hurt more than your death. Here, someone wants to say hello to you."

"Hi, Daddy. Here I am." Sydney paused nervously. "At Camp Granada," she continued. I could tell she was frightened out of her wits.

Lamar said calmly but sternly, "I've sent you a text saying where to wire the money. You have until midnight. Or I will ruin your family, just like you ruined mine." Then silence.

"Can't you ping his phone and get his location?" I asked Bryce.

"We're trying, Greg. He has the phone heavily encrypted."

"I know where they are," I said. "She sent me a signal."

"When did she do that?" Christine asked.

"We sent her to a girls' camp each summer from fourth grade on: Camp Lucille. In her first year, she would call every night for two weeks and beg to come home, and we would sing the Camp Granada song and laugh."

"Are you saying they're at a girls' camp?" Bryce asked.

"I doubt they're at the camp, but I guarantee they're near it. I know my daughter."

Bryce was immediately on his phone to the FBI office in DC, repeating what I'd said. "Sydney's father is certain she's been taken to a location near her old camp. He sounds pretty convincing. I would suggest getting a team down there and doing a full-court search."

Kidnapping was always taken seriously by law enforcement, but abducting or injuring a member of a congressperson's family was an even higher level of criminality. Finding Sydney would be a high priority, but not as high as it was for me.

"I'm going to Virginia," I told Christine.

"And doing what?" she asked.

"Finding Lamar Goodman and getting my daughter back."

∴

Two hours later, Christine, Bryce, and I landed in the tiny town of Morris, Virginia, on the edge of Shenandoah National Park in an FBI helicopter. The landing pad was a hotel parking lot that had been cleared of all vehicles except for those belonging to several law enforcement agencies. Getting cleared to make the trip on the FBI aircraft required a call from Liz to the FBI director, who immediately contacted Nashville with his approval. Several dozen agents were already on the ground, prepared to do a massive search, all predicated on a subtle message provided by Sydney. Why else would she have said, "Here I am at Camp Granada"? Morris was a fifteen-minute drive to Camp Lucille.

We were quickly escorted to a waiting black Chevrolet Tahoe and whisked to the Morris Police station, about seven blocks away. The tiny station was overwhelmed with the presence of FBI agents, who had taken it over as their temporary command post. To my surprise, one-page identity sheets featuring pictures of Lamar Goodman, Sydney, and the van he had been driving were posted in stores, offices, and service stations throughout the town. Agents also went door-to-door, asking residents if they had seen the individuals or the van. To keep Goodman from knowing about the search and for Sydney's safety, the decision was made to keep this out of the media for as long as possible.

The agent in charge—whom I remembered from four years before as a member of the team who searched my home—approached me as soon as we entered the building. "Mr. Smith, I'm Agent Brock. We are searching every corner of the town and have sent local law enforcement officials to check the campgrounds. We will do everything possible to find your daughter and bring her to safety."

"It's good to be on the same team this time, Agent Brock," I said seriously. I shook his hand just as my phone buzzed with the same "unknown caller" banner as in previous calls. "Hold on. This might be Goodman." I cleared my throat. "Hello."

"I haven't seen any funds added to my bank account, and the day is half over. I assume you want your daughter back safely." He spoke with a matter-of-fact tone, neither threatening nor agitated, which greatly unnerved me. Agent Brock made a hand motion for silence.

"That is all being set up now, Lamar," I pleaded. "It's not like we have two million dollars in a checking account. It will be ready at the end of the day. Let me talk to Sydney."

"Hey, Dad. I'm okay," Sydney said hesitantly on the speakerphone. She wasn't okay. I heard the trembling in her voice. She was brave, for sure. But scared.

"Has he hurt you?"

"No." She paused, then meekly sputtered, "I'm still your Little Bo Peep," sounding more fearful.

Was she sending me another message? As a little girl, "Little Bo Peep" was her favorite nursery rhyme. "Have you eaten anything, honey?" Sydney's hypoglycemia required a regular meal and snack routine to keep her sugar levels up. Long periods without eating could cause dizziness and fainting.

"Yes. We stopped at a convenience store and loaded up on snacks and drinks." This was another possible clue that Goodman wouldn't pick up on because he had no clue we were close to him.

"Okay, I have some work to do to ensure we can transfer money to him. Just do as he says, and we'll get you out. I love you."

I hung up and immediately turned to Agent Brock and Christine. "The nursery rhyme was a clue, but I'm unsure what she was saying."

"Could she be telling you they are on a sheep ranch?" Christine offered.

"That has to be it," I responded. I was excited. "Christine, you are brilliant."

A heavyset man in police blues walked through the front door.

"Hello, Chief. Anything?" asked Agent Brock, who had rank over the chief.

"Nothing yet," answered the chief in a slow Southern drawl.

"Let me ask you something," Agent Brock said, "are there any convenience stores in town?"

"We have two, one at the main intersection across the street and the other at the interstate exit to town."

"Great, can you send your fellas to both stores and show the employees the flier? Also, ask them if they have surveillance cameras hooked up." The chief grabbed his microphone and passed on the agent's instructions to all personnel, ending with "This is urgent."

Agent Brock continued. "Do you know of any sheep ranch around here, Chief?"

"There are at least a half dozen good-sized ones and a horde of smaller ones. Most of them are north of town and near the foothills. The sheep business is big around here."

Twenty minutes later, a young officer marched into the station with his phone in the air. "Hey, everyone, you will want to see this. I have a video of them at the Go-Go Store earlier today." The officer had recorded the store's digital monitor as it played back, making it a recording of another recording. Nonetheless, it showed the aging Ford van, tan in color, to be the same one I saw at the café. It also clearly showed Lamar Goodman putting gas in the tank. Another video showed him making purchases of potato chips and candy bars at the checkout counter.

"Okay, team captains and pilots, gather around," instructed Agent Brock. "Let's get into the air. I want all six choppers and their surveillance personnel up immediately. As we speak, the coordinates of the larger sheep operations are being uploaded on your scanners. We are looking for a tan-colored Chevy van, approximately fifteen years old. The chief will give directions to those in agency vehicles and assign a local officer to each of you for directions. We are going door-to-door to every sheep ranch in the area."

A young woman officer entered the room and whispered in the chief's ear, who in turn whispered to Agent Brock. "One of the farms is known as the Goodman Ranch," he announced. "It could be a coincidence, but let's zero in on that first."

Within five minutes, the station had cleared, and the troops headed back to the hotel parking lot, where the helicopters, vehicles, and more than twenty agents remained gathered. Although the proceedings hadn't hit the airwaves yet, the citizens of Morris were paying attention as they began to appear on the streets and in their front yards to watch the commotion.

Christine and I stayed at the station with Agent Brock, who directed the search from the conference room. We listened to his call to the FBI office in Chicago: "This is Agent David Brock out of the Richmond, Virginia, office. We are currently in a search for an Illinois man, Lamar Goodman, in a possible kidnap-for-ransom situation."

"Good old Lamar, one of Chicago's finest," came the sarcastic reply. "What do you need?"

"Would you happen to know if he has relatives by the same name in Virginia?"

"Let me run a check on him. I'm putting you on hold."

After about five minutes, the Chicago agent came back on the line. "Agent Brock, you're in luck. Yes, his dad's parents live in Morris, Virginia. It looks like they're sheep ranchers."

Agent Brock quickly thanked his Chicago colleague, hung up, and went to the door. "Chief, I need those coordinates and the address of the Goodman Ranch. And I needed it five minutes ago." Through the window that separated the inner office of the police station and the conference room, I saw the chief and the policewoman huddled over the computer monitor. The same precision I had seen nearly four years ago when the FBI raided my home was on display, only this time in my favor.

"The Goodman Ranch is out on McGill Road," the chief declared. "Here's the coordinates. The address is 5026. I suggest you get this to your teams, and I'll take you out in my SUV. It won't take more than fifteen minutes."

"Let's do it," barked Agent Brock. "Come on, you two," he said to Christine and me. "Let's go get Sydney."

With full siren blazing, we peeled out of the station garage below the building and were soon racing at a hundred miles an hour. When we reached the outskirts of town, the agent headed north on a two-lane country road that turned to gravel about five minutes later. He maintained his speed as the helicopters flying above us came into focus, each hovering above the scenic property. Behind the white wooden fences, hundreds of sheep could be seen grazing on the tall green grass. It looked like a framed oil painting against the brilliant afternoon sunshine and blue skies. We saw a farmhouse in the distance. Ranch workers were scattered throughout the property, oblivious to what was happening inside the owner's house.

"We have the house in sight, with a tan van parked in front," a voice from one of the choppers above said. "We're going down."

"Roger that," Agent Brock responded into the mic pinned to the front of his jacket. "We're one minute away." As we pulled into the half-circle driveway, I realized this had become real. My daughter was inside that house, being held captive.

"I doubt that he's armed," I told Agent Brock. "I know him. He's not a killer."

"You might be right, Mr. Smith, but at this point, it is protocol that we assume he is armed and dangerous."

"I want to go in," I demanded. "I can talk him down."

"We can't let you do that. We've only let you come this far because we trust you. We don't need you playing hero."

"Listen to him, Greg. Please." Christine squeezed my elbow. I could see the pleading in her eyes. She knew my brain was spinning in a hundred directions, and she also knew what I was about to do.

As soon as the car stopped behind the van, amid the loud noise of the helicopters landing on the expansive front lawn, I bolted from the rear passenger door and sprinted toward the house. Three agents—Brock from the front seat and two from the helicopters—yelled for me to stop. Despite their loud commands and my aching ribs, I sprinted up the front steps onto the wide porch, bursting through the door with a madman's vengeance.

"Sydney. Where are you? Are you okay?"

"I'm upstairs, Daddy," came her desperate, frightened response.

I flew up the stairs two at a time and found her seated on the floor in the first room I came to. She was tied with rope to a dresser. Dropping to my knees, I wrapped my arms around her, bringing her head to my chest. She was sobbing, forcing me to cry too. Agent Brock was the first agent in the room after me. His speaker crackled, "We have eyes on Goodman running out the back into the pasture. Chopper unit above him at a hundred feet. Vehicles in pursuit. He won't get far."

I untied Sydney and joined Agent Brock, watching out the bedroom window as three SUVs surrounded Goodman and the helicopter touched down. The sheep had long scattered from the chaotic scene. Sydney crawled to the closet door and reached up to unlock it, revealing a large walk-in with garments lining the walls. Sitting on two chairs with tape over their mouths were Lamar's grandparents, who appeared to be in their eighties. "Are you both okay?" she asked as they peeled the tape.

"Yes, we're okay," the grandfather replied.

"Please don't hurt him," the grandmother pleaded. "He's confused right now, but he's not a bad boy."

I watched from a distance as Goodman fell to his knees with his hands in the air. Agents immediately pulled his arms behind him and put cuffs on his wrists. This once proud, determined man with whom I had shared countless hours guiding his career from a Chicago alderman to the state senate and finally to secretary of state would spend the remainder of his life behind bars. Our plan to land him someday in the governor's mansion was a faded memory. As a candidate, Lamar was the complete package—handsome in a Don Draper way, very charming one-on-one and before an audience. Only average on the intellect chart, he had always accepted the direction of the Chicago political bosses without question. Just as he was now doing by following Max Weber's orders.

When the agents brought him through the back sliding door, we came face-to-face in the house parlor: two felons who had lost their moral compass. Although I had felt remorse for my role in his downfall, I now felt only contempt. Swinging for the fences with a shovel aimed for my head and now his latest stunt of kidnapping my daughter had erased any ounce of goodwill I might have had for him.

"I would have never hurt your daughter," he said quietly. "But you knew that, didn't you?"

I stared into his dark eyes.

"Fuck you, Lamar."

CHAPTER THIRTY-FIVE

With Weber and Goodman securely locked away, I felt safe for the first time since arriving in Kelsey. A swinging shovel, the grief of Jimmy's death, a houseboat break-in, an attack at a roadside café, and now Sydney's kidnapping were hardly the reception I expected when I moved here. The others I testified against would serve their time and also get out. But they didn't have the nerve to come after me or my family.

It was after midnight when Christine and I returned to Kelsey—along with Agent Lundgren, who had stayed with us the entire day—on the same FBI helicopter that had taken us to Virginia ten hours earlier. Sydney was being flown back to Fairfax, Virginia, to a hospital near her home, where she was to remain overnight for rest and observation. Liz had landed in Morris shortly after Goodman's capture and accompanied our shaken but strong daughter home.

"I was sure you'd get the Camp Granada clue," she had told me as I watched her strap herself into the helicopter seat, "but the nursery rhyme? I had my doubts."

"That was Christine's doing," I answered. "She figured that one out."

"I have an idea," offered Liz. "The next time we all get together, let's not do it at a hospital or crime scene."

Everyone laughed, including the agents. I wasn't yet used to being their friend.

The following day, I wanted to focus only on the campaign, where the signs of an active race were everywhere. There were posters on fences, buildings, and windows in whatever direction you looked. A CITY WITH A MISSION: VOTE YES ON MEASURE 1, read one of our Kelly-green-and-white signs. SAVE OUR CITY. VOTE NO ON MEASURE 1, read the one next to it. Meanwhile, on TV and radio, the thirty-second commercials from both sides played one after the other. The clutter of ads on the internet was equally ubiquitous. Even with Max Weber in prison, someone in the opposing camp still had access to his deep checking account. I suspected it was Art Drake, who was now heading the anti-Mission campaign. Our funding matched their contributions dollar for dollar, largely thanks to Liz's effectiveness in convincing the national homeless organizations that Kelsey was a test case for how far any community could go to limit shelters and rescue missions' growth and size. "This is a 'must-win' for the entire movement," she told them.

The anti-expansion campaign ran mostly negative commercials intended to create fear. One ad superimposed a silhouette of men as shadows against downtown walls, streets, and bridges, with an eerie male narrator that concluded, "Don't let downtown Kelsey be a place you can't take your family to at night. Save our city. Vote no on Measure One." This attempt to demonize the residents of the Rescue Mission was upsetting to Tom, who knew that not one crime had been committed by a Mission resident in the three years he had been there.

"It's their only play," I told him. "They are on the desperate side of a losing referendum and the wrong side of history, and they know it." As a practitioner of negative campaign tactics, I was not proud to admit I was an expert. There were few political boundaries not protected by the Constitution's provision for free speech, including distorted facts and lies.

"Look, you've been around here long enough to know that there are many guys in here with urgent mental health care needs," Tom proclaimed in anger. "There are others with drug and alcohol addictions. But guess who is making sure they get the medical care they need? Who's making sure they're off the drugs and teaching them there's a better way? We are! My guys aren't committing any crimes, and for them to run commercials like that is a lie."

"Well, my friend, that is a topic for another time. We must start getting 'your guys' ready for a field trip to our nation's capital."

Tom grabbed my elbow as we walked down the hall to the campaign room. "Are you up for all of this after what happened yesterday? I would understand if you wanted to leave this whole thing behind."

Christine had kept Tom in the loop by phone throughout the day. We both considered it a miracle that it had been kept away from the media, at least so far.

I wished he knew how much this place and these men had done to restore my spirit and give me purpose. "Nope, this is where I belong," I replied. It was more than an honor. It was atonement. Although I had asked God to forgive me for all the bad things I had done, I suspected He had not yet made it through my extensive list of wrongdoings. These men—and the ones who would come after them—were my focus.

When we entered, Ernie gave the group a sneak preview of our new TV commercial. We had been introducing a different one on the local airwaves and the internet once per week for the past month.

"Hi, I'm Mike Hart, manager of the kitchen you see behind me. But this is no ordinary kitchen. It's located here at the Kelsey Rescue Mission, and we serve over three hundred hot, balanced meals a day to people who no longer have a home of their own. Men like me. Thanks to the Mission, I'm getting back on my feet and turning my life around in a new, positive direction. But the work of the Mission—and my new life—would not have been possible without your help. That's why we need your vote on Election Day. Please vote yes on Measure One."

"Whoa, Michael. You look like a movie star," I proclaimed as his face blushed red. "Maybe you can play yourself when we make this a movie." Although I was teasing, Mike's soft, warm delivery made him appear believable, if not loveable.

"Listen up, men, here's the deal." Tom wasted no time getting everyone's attention, using his deep voice and large frame to his advantage as he often did. "In case you haven't heard, we're all flying to Washington, DC, next Tuesday, the tenth. We will stay overnight in a hotel. The next morning, we'll meet the president at the White House. Later that afternoon, we will go to Capitol Hill, where we will testify in front of a congressional committee supporting the American Houselessness Act. I picked each of you guys as the representatives of this Mission because you're smart, and I trust you. I know you'll make us proud. Any questions?"

The men who were hearing this for the first time were in shock. Expressions ranged from looking like they'd just won the Powerball lottery to appearing as if they had been sentenced to the electric chair. Tom was the kind of pastor who would often explain that Jesus loved you without telling you first who Jesus was. The process was never as important to him as the results.

"Pastor Tom," I said, "perhaps we should explain why we want them to go to Washington."

"Good idea, Greg. Why don't you go ahead?"

I patiently explained that Congress was considering passing a law to assist homeless people in affording better opportunities to restart their lives. The legislation would include over a hundred billion dollars to incentivize communities to build affordable housing while providing rental assistance and down payments for first-time homebuyers. In addition, it would offer tuition funding for low-income students of all ages to attend training schools and colleges. I added that there were also special provisions for military veterans and a considerable increase in mental health funding.

"If passed and signed into law, it would be the most sweeping measure in our nation's history to address the needs of the homeless," I proclaimed. "And by the way, the proposed law includes massive new funding in matching grants for a new national center for the homeless that will be built across the street from here at the old mill."

"I don't get it," Billy Coble blurted out when I finished. "Why would they want us to testify?"

Christine jumped at the chance to respond. "Because the committee chairperson overseeing this legislation is a remarkable congresswoman named Elizabeth Smith, who has been championing the cause of the homeless for nearly twenty years. Unlike many politicians in Washington, Liz Smith cares and wants this to get done." Christine wasn't kidding when she told me she was a "fan" of Liz.

"Caring for the homeless runs in her family," Tom added quietly. "Liz Smith is my younger sister."

Mike Hart had the next question. "No offense, Pastor Tom, but isn't your sister kind of using us as pawns, as in 'Oh, look at those poor losers. We need to help them.'"

"That's where you're not thinking the right way, and by the way, no offense taken, Mike," Tom began. "She wants her fellow members of Congress to see homeless individuals as real people and learn from those representing a broad cross section of the homeless community—real people with real dreams who have experienced a few setbacks but can still contribute to their families and society."

"What about the White House visit? I didn't even vote for the guy." Leave it to Zeke, our beloved house Sicilian, to use a little levity to break the tension. "Are you sure he'll let me in?"

"Let you in? Look at me. I'm an ex-con," Bugsy added to more laughter.

Mark raised his hand. "If I might jump in here, Greg, I want to say something to my fellow Mission residents. Look, men, no one in this building grew up dreaming of living in a shelter for homeless men. But thank God there are people like Liz Smith and Pastor Tom, and others like Christine and Greg, who believe that we can make it out of here and still live a good life with a little luck and hard work."

The men listened to Mark in a way they didn't listen to the rest of us, for obvious reasons.

"It is not by accident that you are in this meeting today. You were chosen, just like Jesus chose his disciples. They also went forward without knowing what would happen because they had faith. Now it's your job to live up to the confidence Pastor Tom has in you and have a little faith."

He had inspired not only the residents but me as well.

"Okay, guys," announced Tom, again taking the lead. "I appreciate that you have all agreed to be part of this. Mark will be handling the scheduling, reservations, and everything logistical. You need a current ID. If you don't have one, please check with Cooper. He can ensure you do. Also, I want everyone to look sharp. A sports coat and tie would be great, but an open shirt is okay. You can get whatever you need at the thrift store. Thank you, gentlemen."

After the meeting, I stayed with Mark and Christine.

"That went well," offered Christine. "They're a little nervous, but I think they'll be okay."

Although I believed in Liz's strategy of showing her colleagues that homeless folks were nonetheless real human beings, I remained nervous, even frightful, about putting these guys through the ordeal of the national spotlight, a make-believe world they were ill-equipped to comprehend. But something else was missing. I could see it in their faces.

"Maybe they just lack the certainty that government or any institution does anything worthwhile when it comes to them."

"That would make us much like the average citizen," joked Mark.

"For the rest of this week, I want serious movies and documentaries like *Selma* in the theater room. We can even show some schmaltzy ones like *The American President*. I want them to be inspired by the idea that we all have a voice and can change things with our voices."

"This is hard for them," Christine commented. "When they walked through those front doors and said, 'Here I am, I'm hungry and tired, and I have no other place to go,' they felt shame and humiliation. Now you're asking them to go before our nation's leaders and the public and be noticed for their mistakes and failures. That's a lot." As usual, Christine got right to the heart of the matter. We were asking a lot.

Mark then looked me in the eye. "I've been meaning to ask you, Greg, what keeps you going so strong? Why are you so devoted to our cause?"

It was a good question and one I might have expected from my new dear friend Mark Stone. After thinking for a few seconds, I finally replied. "The Rescue Mission isn't just for the homeless. Did you ever stop to consider that I'm being rescued too?"

CHAPTER THIRTY-SIX

By the time we began gathering in the parking lot after breakfast to start our trip to Nashville International Airport and from there to Washington, DC, it was 9:30. According to Cooper, who had drawn the short straw of serving as trip coordinator, we were right on time. There were eleven in our entourage, including seven Mission residents, Christine, Tom, Cooper, and me. It was a low-key group, not unlike a small team of business associates traveling to make a pitch for a new sale or product. Most of us engaged in small talk unrelated to the trip.

In the days leading up to the journey, the men had been briefed for hours on the protocol of congressional hearings and had rehearsed their answers to possible questions many times. This was reinforced by viewing videos of dozens of hearings from the past, easily found online. None of this changed the reality that they were stepping into an intimidating and unforgiving world unknown to any of them. Capitol Hill and the White House, the epicenter of national politics, could be daunting.

"Are they ready?" Tom asked me quietly as we watched them step into the two vans that would carry us to the airport.

"I think they are. They were great on their final run-through last night, and Mark did a fine job making sure they were dressed appropriately and either shaved or trimmed their beards." Mark had become a valuable partner to both Christine and me, performing tasks without seeking attention for his deeds. In the narcissistic world from which I had come, not seeking credit was almost a foreign concept.

Once aboard the plane, I was pleased to have been assigned a seat next to Tom, giving us a chance to chat on the way. "Well, did you ever see this coming?" he laughed. "The Buffalo boys teaming up to change history?"

"It has been quite a ride, my friend." I was reminded that when I was released from prison, I'd only intended to stay a day, head to my beach-paradise house, and retire to a life of rum runners and margaritas.

"It seems this experience has changed you," Tom averred with a serious tone.

"If you mean religiously or spiritually, I'm not sure. Maybe a little," I said truthfully. "I'll never be a Tom Garrity or a Christine Culpepper when it comes to the God thing, but I believe we are here for a purpose greater than just serving ourselves. I never fully understood that until now."

"I haven't asked you in a long time, but what's in Greg Smith's future?"

Sitting in the row ahead of us, Christine popped her head over the top of the seat. "Sorry for eavesdropping, but I wouldn't mind hearing the answer to that question," she teased with her amazing smile.

"We haven't had time to plan it, but whatever it is, it will be with this nosy lady in the aisle seat of row four."

"Is that a marriage proposal, Mr. Smith?" Christine teased before ducking back into her seat.

I gave Tom the briefing on tomorrow's hearings, reminding him that Christine was well prepared to take the lead. She would introduce the group and read her remarks to the committee supporting the proposed legislation. Each committee member would be given a chance to ask questions, which she would either answer or refer to Tom for a response. Liz had two of her Democrats out sick this week and two others from conservative states openly opposed to the legislation, so she needed one Republican to come over.

It was unusual to hold a hearing in which one didn't know the outcome, but Liz figured that if she lost this one, she could turn it into a campaign issue the following year and raise the public profile of its importance.

"I hope we have an impact," Tom replied after listening to me ramble on for ten minutes straight. "Of course, I know how much this means to her. She sees it as her congressional swan song. Come to think about it, I'm going to miss bragging that my sister is a congresswoman."

"Some folks are talking about her as a future presidential candidate," I informed him.

"Wow, wouldn't that make Dad proud? But don't count on it. I don't think she wants the personal scrutiny a national campaign would bring. Besides, she's tired. I think she wants to work in her garden and live a private life—like the path you've taken," he said with a huge laugh that drew a few glances our way. "By the way, how's that serene life working out for you?"

"Don't ask."

Somewhere over southern West Virginia, about halfway through the hour and forty-five-minute flight, I received a text from Mayor Simmons. WE ARE RECEIVING WORD THAT THE GRAND JURY HAS INDICTED MAX WEBER ON MULTIPLE CORRUPTION CHARGES AND ATTEMPTED KIDNAPPING WITH A FIREARM. HIS ARRAIGNMENT DATE HAS NOT BEEN SET. I'M WORKING ON A STATEMENT.

He included a link to today's electronic version of the *Kelsey Daily* with the headline WEBER INDICTED ON CORRUPTION CHARGES AND KIDNAPPING. Then, below the Weber story, was a smaller headline: THREE KELSEY POLICEMEN TO FACE MURDER CHARGES.

I gave my phone first to Christine and then to Tom, who had nodded off in the window seat. "Tom, wake up. You need to see this." He read the text messages and the news links and put his hands over his face in dismay. Christine crawled into the empty middle seat between us, making our three-way conversation much easier.

"Busy day for the grand jury," sighed Christine. She then looked at her phone. "Oh my, the word is out. My phone is blowing up with calls from reporters. What should our response be to all of this?"

I knew what it felt like to be charged with a serious, high-profile crime, one that I knew I had committed. By now, Max Weber was suffering. He had humiliated his wife and three grown children and besmirched the name of his beloved parents. He was also an open target in the media. For the remainder of his life, it was likely that Max Weber's grandchildren would only see him in a prison jumpsuit.

Tom said, "I'm going to tell them this is a sad day for the people of Kelsey, but we believe our justice system is fair and will ultimately prevail. Our hearts go out to the Weber family."

"Perfect," I responded. This was another indication that Tom—and the entire Mission team—didn't need me anymore. They were doing fine on their own.

"Why aren't there four officers being indicted?" I asked.

"It's in the article," said Tom, who had returned to reading the links while Christine talked. "Ballistics tests show that the fourth officer—a rookie cop named Randy Browning—didn't fire his gun. It also says that Officer Browning was the one who smuggled the body-cam video out of the station and gave it to us."

• • •

Going to the White House is a big deal, regardless of your position in life. People with the privilege of working for a president arrive every morning with a sense of awe and respect, the same feeling that cabinet secretaries and senators have when going there for meetings. Its brilliantly kept grounds, crowned by the historic building itself, instill a sense of reverence, regardless of its current occupant. Wherever you walk, the ghosts of Lincoln, the Roosevelts, JFK, Ronald Reagan, and many more walk beside you.

It wasn't any different for the seven Mission residents who

entered the presidential mansion on a beautiful October morning to begin the process of being escorted to the West Wing to meet the president, except for the fact that each of them woke up yesterday morning in a homeless shelter in Tennessee.

"This is not a place I ever thought I'd be," Mike said quietly as he walked beside me. "Everything is so perfect."

"It's unbelievable," added Bugsy. "I hate to repeat myself, but I still can't believe they let me in."

Our amiable guide—Pamela, according to her name tag—offered us a history of each room we entered as our heads tilted collectively up and down and back and forth. Although I had been to dozens of meetings and receptions in the White House, this was my first time experiencing the public tour, which included the Blue Room, Red Room, and Green Room; the State Dining Room; the China Room; and a view of the White House Rose Garden.

When the tour ended, we were led outside and around to the front entrance of the West Wing, home to, among other things, the Oval Office and Cabinet Room and some of the senior staff to the president. Most presidential staff members were next door to the White House in the Old Executive Office Building.

"Good morning, everyone," greeted Janet Cordova, the receptionist, as we entered the lobby area. "Welcome to the West Wing. I will lead you to the reception room, where the president will meet you in just a few minutes. You can help yourself to our famous freshly baked White House donuts, coffee, and juice while you wait." She paused for a few seconds before looking in my direction. "Greg, it's nice to see you again. I know the president is looking forward to seeing you."

If there had been any doubt in the minds of my men or girlfriend that once upon a time, I had lived another life in an alternative world, that notion had now been dispelled.

"You know the president, as in personally know him?" Billy asked. "Dude, who are you?"

I only winked at him as we continued down the hallway.

"Ooh-wee." Jonah smiled teasingly. "Mr. Greg is a big shot at the White House. Hey, Christine, did you know your boyfriend was someone *im-por-tant*?"

Christine rolled her eyes.

We entered the reception area adjoining the media room. Some of the guys checked out the paintings of former presidents while others headed to the coffee and donuts. A minute later, the president entered, accompanied by Rob Kearse. Both went directly to me. The president shook my hand and brought me in for a half hug. Rob did the same.

"Greg, we want to meet your friends," the president said.

I led him around to each person in our group. "Mr. President, I would like you to meet Mike Hart, who runs our kitchen, and this is Billy Coble, a Maryland grad."

"Always good to meet a fellow Terp," laughed the president. When he met Jarred Mackey, he thanked him for his service and asked what he thought of the care he was receiving at the Veterans Administration. He exchanged words in Italian with Zeke and asked Bugsy if he was working on turning his life around. As always, the president, the ultimate people person, had been well briefed.

The men stood in line as the leader of the free world was introduced to them one by one, each receiving the same warmth and sincerity. It had been said that while you might disagree with the president's politics or decisions, you rarely disliked him.

When finished, he thanked them as a group for coming. "I want you all to know how much it means to me that you would come all this way to spend time with us this morning. In a few minutes, we are going through that door to announce my support for the American Houselessness Act to the media, and I want you beside me when I do it. And yes, you are being used as props, but it's for a good cause, so I doubly appreciate your help. My support includes funding for the Center for Hope and Opportunity, where I understand that Mr. Mark Stone will serve as the inaugural director. Good luck, Mark. This is important work you will be doing."

As the president, looking distinguished with his dark-blue suit, tan skin, and white hair, emerged into the glare of the television lights, he was followed by the seven residents of the Kelsey Rescue Mission. I imagined fifty of their fellow residents gathered in chairs and couches to watch C-SPAN in the television lounge back at the Rescue Mission, cheering when these ambassadors came into the frame. After all, the president of the United States of America had treated their brothers and friends—homeless men—with respect and dignity.

"Good morning," the president began as his audience of a hundred or so reporters listened. "I am thrilled to have seven Kelsey Rescue Mission members and the Mission's director, Pastor Thomas Garrity, with me today."

Staying with our policy of keeping me out of the public eye, I did not go onstage with the president. Christine remained with me as we watched on the monitor in the reception room.

"Surely, you have heard of Kelsey, Tennessee," the president continued, "the city that just a few weeks ago so profoundly demonstrated to the nation that major issues can be resolved instead of fought out on the street. A city where a tragedy such as the murder of Jimmy Keefer, a resident of the Rescue Mission, is one felt by all citizens and not just a few. And now a city that, instead of ignoring people experiencing homelessness, has become a national symbol for finding solutions to what I believe is an American embarrassment. Solutions, not politics. It is what has been called the 'Kelsey Way,' and for the two years I have left in this job, I will work to see that it becomes the American way as well. I look forward to reaching across the aisle and working closely with Congresswoman Elizabeth Smith and other leaders to ensure the American Houselessness Act is passed."

He paused, turned back, and looked at each Mission resident along the row where they stood. "Thank you, gentlemen, for coming to the White House today. I am honored. And be assured, I will be there with you to open the new Center for Hope and Opportunity.

"Now, are there any questions?"

CHAPTER THIRTY-SEVEN

Capitol Hill is a beehive of human activity. To the first-time visitor, it is a confusing scene of constant movement in every direction, each "bee" flying to and from a different queen. Even the most secure outsider feels out of place. Although the public is welcome to visit, few of the inhabitants will go out of their way to make you feel welcome. It's not that they are unfriendly people. It is merely part of the unspoken mystique that what they do is ultra-important and not to be delved into with the common folk who wouldn't understand their culture even if it were explained with illustrations. It is a self-absorbed class of Americans, and when here, as a mere commoner you are likely to be a fish out of water, as the saying goes.

The Hill is where urgent people do urgent things, well, urgently. To pass laws in the name of saving, restoring, creating, or stopping something, all of which we average folks are obliged to obey. These laws relate to our economy, environment, defense, health, and more. And while those involved will claim they don't want to waste public money, they will fight to pay for things they believe in, whether they are liberals or conservatives, Democrats or Republicans.

Of course, this chaos is not limited to the 535 men and women elected by voters back home and sent here—the ones who carry the title "Honorable." Although the elected ones are the ultimate target of this commotion, Hill occupants also comprise thousands of congressional staffers, policy experts, lobbyists, and government officials, both domestic and foreign, engaged in the most competitive exercise known to humankind: American democracy. It is messy, chaotic, and intense. And oh my God, did I love it.

Observing the quiet expressions worn by the Mission residents as our hired minibus navigated from the White House up Pennsylvania Avenue and then crossed over toward the Rayburn House Office Building, I decided they seemed excited, like a high school classroom on their first field trip to the Capitol. But they were apprehensive as well.

"Tell me something, Greg. Are you sure we're not in over our heads?" Mike asked from behind me with a nervous laugh.

"You guys will be great," I replied. "Trust me."

"We trust you. It's ourselves we doubt."

Who wouldn't be intimidated testifying at a congressional hearing? Talk about ganging up on someone. And yes, I wondered if we were throwing them into a situation for which they were unprepared. It had been my one nagging doubt about this exercise from the beginning.

To calm their nerves, I stood when we were almost at our destination and spoke to the group, telling them that Walt Kanish would be meeting us. I explained that Walt was my first boss and mentor when I came here to work during college. More importantly, I told them they were in good hands and that he and Congresswoman Smith, who would chair the hearing, wanted them to be comfortable and be seen positively.

"They are on your side," I emphasized. Knowing this about Walt and Liz was comforting. I didn't share the not-so-small detail that there were those on the committee who didn't want my friends to succeed.

We arrived at the Rayburn Building's circular driveway a few minutes later. Walt had joined the security guards in front of the building to greet us as we deboarded.

"Walt, thank you so much for meeting us. Let me introduce you to my team."

After he met Tom and Christine, I presented the seven residents, telling them that Walt was in charge of the hearings. It was unusual for a person of Walt's stature to also serve as the official greeter. Still, in an early-morning telephone discussion, he had agreed to do whatever it took to keep the residents from collapsing under the pressure.

"Treat them like you want them here and they're important," I told him. "That would go a long way with this group. When Tom or I tell them that, they think we're just blowing smoke up their asses."

Walt rose to the occasion. "Thank you all for coming," he greeted us as we stood in a semicircle. "Follow me through security and then up to the committee room. We still have time to go over any questions you have."

I walked with the men, who surrounded me in a loose ring as I took over the role of tour guide to get them thinking about something other than facing a hearing.

"This is one of the three buildings where the members of the House of Representatives and their staffs are located. It's named after Samuel Rayburn, the Speaker of the House in the fifties. House committee staff and meeting rooms are also here, as well as in the other two House office buildings, the Longworth and the Cannon," I explained. "The Rayburn is the newest of the three and generally reserved for the most senior members. They meet as a body across the street in the Capitol, but it is here, in the 'corridors of power,'" I said with air quotes, "that the real work of the House takes place."

"Is this where you worked, Mr. Greg?" Billy asked innocently.

"Let's just say I spent a lot of time here during my career," I answered, withholding that I operated in whatever venue best served the peevish and profitable interests of my clients and myself, this being only one of the locales.

Christine and Tom walked about fifteen yards in front of us with Walt, chatting the whole way up the wide hallway to the committee room. When we entered, an instant sense of wonder swept over the group. All heads pointed upward as they took in the ornate decor, dominated by a polished mahogany ceiling and a matching dais of leather swivel chairs and microphones at each station.

"Up there is where the committee members will sit," Walt said as he pointed to the dais. "Chairwoman Smith will sit in the middle and conduct the meeting. The committee members will take turns asking questions, mostly directed at Christine and Tom. Back here is the gallery, where members of the media and the public will gather."

He led them to a long table in front of the gallery with numerous chairs facing the committee. "This is where you will sit. Your nameplates have already been put on the table. How about if everyone takes their assigned seat?"

Walt began to pace back and forth in front of them like a college professor. "Committees are an essential part of how Congress works. Every member of Congress serves on at least one committee, usually several. Before a vote on a bill in the chamber of the full House can occur, it must first be passed in a committee. In the committee, members often want to hear from experts, usually from both sides of the issue they are considering."

Walt explained how Democrats sat on one side and Republicans on the other and how every committee member received equal time to ask questions or make statements regardless of party affiliation.

"Mr. Kanish." Billy raised his hand. "Will they be asking me questions? Because sometimes I say things folks don't want to hear."

Walt joined us in a burst of laughter.

"Amen to that," said Tom.

"We have asked that the committee members direct their questions to Pastor Tom and Christine, and should those two wish to ask any of you to help answer something, that will be up to their best judgment."

Following the briefing, we were led into a holding room behind the chairperson's seat, where sack lunches of turkey sandwiches, potato chips, and a slice of apple pie had been brought in from the downstairs cafeteria. We hadn't eaten since early that morning at the hotel, and one thing I had learned in the past few months was that the men of the Kelsey Rescue Mission did not like to miss a meal.

An hour later, the men were escorted back into the committee room. This time, however, the committee chairs were mostly filled with members, and the gallery was at capacity. It was a full house, made more intimidating with cameras, lights, and reporters. I stayed back in the holding room, where I would watch the proceedings on the monitor, again staying out of the spotlight. "Good luck, guys," I said. "You'll be fine. Let Christine do as much of the talking as possible." I felt like a head coach sending my team on the field for the conference championship.

The last one through the door was Tom, who bear-hugged me before going out to face the music. "You've done well, my friend. You've done well."

I flashed back to arriving at his house in Kelsey after my release from prison and how he had dragged me to the Mission the next day. I thought about how he told me they needed help in the kitchen and the serving window—and how he kept adding tasks along the way, including my involvement in the referendum campaign, which began only as a legal matter. Suddenly, I knew what he had done. Tom Garrity had placed me in my own individualized rehab program. And he did it the same way he always did it: by pointing a person in the right direction and giving him the tools to figure it out. My falling in love with his attorney was a surprise, but the rest was vintage Garrity, and I fell for it. *Thank God*, I thought.

At the appointed time, Congresswoman Elizabeth Smith entered the room and sat in the chairperson's chair on the top row in the middle of the dais. "It appears we have a quorum present, so let us begin."

Liz was clear and concise, delivering her opening with her familiar smile and grace.

"Good afternoon, everyone. Welcome to our final hearing of the week on the American Houselessness Act, House Bill Number 397. Today, our guests are seven residents from the Kelsey Rescue Mission in Kelsey, Tennessee. We welcome each of you," she said warmly. "With them is Pastor Tom Garrity, the director of the Mission, and Christine Culpepper, the Mission's legal counsel. In the spirit of full disclosure, Pastor Tom is my big brother, so all of you on the other side, please show some respect," she said as chuckles rumbled around the room.

Turning back to the table, she addressed her guests. "I know that you visited with the president earlier today, and I understand he has embraced the Kelsey Way as the American way, just as he has embraced this legislation. With that in mind, we look forward to learning more about your stories."

From the look of the jam-packed gallery, far more interest in this bill had been generated than I ever imagined. This was no doubt fueled by the national attention Jimmy's death had received and the way the mayor had deftly defused a ticking bomb in the city. The president crossing the partisan aisle and endorsing the legislation likely also contributed to an uptick in public attention. Still, Liz told me the night before that she wasn't sure about the vote. "It will be close," she had said. "The fiscal hawks on the committee aren't likely to budge. But it will pass if we can get the bill to the floor. And if it passes the Senate, where I think it will survive the filibuster, we know the president will sign it."

Liz continued with her opening remarks for a minute longer before giving the ranking member, Mickey Hamilton—the leader of the minority party on the committee—the same opportunity to address the committee and the visitors.

"After meeting you, Pastor Garrity, I now see that helping those in need must be the Garrity family business. I'm sure you and the honorable chairwoman must have had a wonderful mother and father to have instilled such high-minded values in their children." It was clear where he was going with this, which was straight to the almighty dollar. "But as urgent as the need might be, the funds are just not there for such a massive spending bill. For those sitting on this side, changing our minds would take something huge."

It would take a phone call or text from Dan Johnson, Hamilton's largest donor in the past three elections. I had already sent Dan a text and received a one-word response. DONE. The next thing I saw was Hamilton looking at his phone and then motioning a member of his staff to his committee desk.

It was then Christine's turn. Speaking from a prepared text, she thanked the committee and its leadership. "This is a historic day," she began. "Instead of these men tending to their tasks at the Mission, or worse, being outside on the curb or camping below an overpass, they are here with you, inside our most hallowed democratic institution, the United States House of Representatives. They aim to ask Congress to invest in them and the millions of other Americans without a home. They ask for your help for a second chance and an opportunity to build a productive life. Not because they deserve it or because you owe it to them but because our nation will be stronger with them as a part of it than with them sitting on the sidelines."

As Christine spoke, Congressman Stewart Hager, a Republican from Indiana, rose indiscreetly from his seat and padded down the steps of the dais to the long table where the Kelsey delegation was seated. When he arrived, he knelt and embraced Jarred Mackey, seated in his wheelchair. With tears running down his face, Jarred returned the congressman's warm hug, which lasted for a full minute.

By now, the scene had utterly distracted the 200 people in the gallery and Christine. She appeared uncertain whether to continue speaking.

"Excuse me," interrupted the chairwoman. "Excuse me. Can the gentleman from Indiana please return to his seat and explain why he decided to take a walk while a committee guest provided such an important perspective?"

Hager strolled back to his seat and immediately pulled his microphone toward him. "Madam Chairwoman, I sincerely apologize for interrupting the proceedings. And to you, Ms.

Culpepper, I also apologize. I hope you will forgive me for being swept away by my emotions."

The congressman paused, taking a napkin from his coat pocket and wiping his teary eyes. A few seconds went by before he composed himself enough to speak. I had known Stewart Hager for a long time. When he was first elected ten years ago, I was his campaign media consultant and strategist. Not once had I seen this seriously conservative former Marine officer show emotion of any kind. He was a tough guy, rugged through and through.

"Madam Chairwoman, if it would please the committee, I would happily explain."

"The gentleman may proceed," Liz responded.

"Fourteen years ago, this man, Jarred Mackey, saved my life and the lives of five other Marines by falling on a grenade in a surprise attack by enemy forces in Afghanistan. It is where he lost his leg." The entire room was hushed, listening intently. "I lost touch with Sergeant Mackey, but every voter in my Indiana district knows his story. That's because I tell it in practically every speech I make. It is a story of honor, courage, and duty. So, when I looked down at the table and saw him, knowing that he was homeless, my heart broke. Jarred Mackey is an American hero, and I would not be sitting here if it weren't for his courage and bravery. He gave me a second chance."

I knew what was coming next. The entire room knew it. Stewart Hager, a recognized leader of the conservative wing of Congress and known champion of armed service veterans, was about to disrupt the predictable pattern of Capitol Hill.

"Madam Chairwoman," he announced, looking up at Liz, "you have my vote on this legislation, one hundred percent, and I urge the members on my side of the aisle to do the same. A vote for the American Houselessness Act is for our veterans and those who have earned a second chance."

The response was sudden and intense as the room surged to its feet as one and applauded. The committee members stood and clapped, first on Liz's side and then on Stewart's. The congressman pointed to Jarred and then put his hand on his heart. You did not need to be a professional lip reader to interpret, "Love you, bro."

The bill passed unanimously, all but ensuring its passage by the full House.

CHAPTER THIRTY-EIGHT

Dan Johnson's private Boeing 757 touched down at the Kelsey Regional Airport at precisely ten o'clock, exactly one week after Election Day. The customized jet was just as I remembered it: a deep maroon color with the Rockwood Technologies logo emblazoned on both sides. As it landed, I was reminded of the many times I'd flown on this luxurious liner as it carried Dan and me on various pursuits. With its soft gray leather seats, private office, and bedroom, it was an experience beyond anything the average traveler would ever experience. The jet was Dan's ultimate ego statement—a rightful reward for his enormous success.

Three weeks had gone by since the Washington trip. As expected, the journey to the White House received widespread public attention, and the Kelsey Way, thanks to the president, was now part of the national dialogue. The American Houselessness Act passed the House with bipartisan support and was expected to do the same in the Senate. Tennessee Senator Ben Patson, invited to today's festivities, was the sixtieth vote to break a threatened filibuster. When Dan and Tom got through with him, he didn't dare oppose the bill. Of course, the best news was that after the indictments against the disgraced Max Weber, Kelsey voters overwhelmingly approved the referendum to allow the Rescue Mission to expand.

Now it was Dan Johnson's turn to take the spotlight, a place he loved to occupy. Christine, Mark, and I waited on the tarmac as Dan, followed by who I assumed to be his architect and chief engineer, disembarked through the open door and descended the stairway pushed against the aircraft.

"Greg Smith, it is great to see you. You look like you've healed up a bit," he greeted cheerfully as we shook hands. Although the cuts on my face had largely disappeared, my ribs would take weeks to reach the point where I was entirely mobile. I still had a slight limp. I had decided not to tell him about the kidnapping. It would come out soon enough when Goodman went before a grand jury.

"Meet the best architect and engineer money can buy," he laughed. He said their names, but I didn't catch them in the busyness of the moment. "And this must be the lovely Christine Culpepper, whom I have heard so much about—from Greg. It is very nice to meet you. Let me know if you need an airplane for your honeymoon," he said gregariously with a sweeping arm gesture toward his pride and joy. "It's all yours."

"Thank you, Mr. Johnson," she replied politely, looking surprised, perhaps that I had told Dan about her. "But Greg hasn't told me anything about a wedding. Is there something you need to tell me?"

"Ms. Culpepper, I know when a man is in love."

As we walked toward the small terminal building, I introduced Dan to Mark Stone, informing him—not asking—that Mark would be his new guy in Kelsey, serving as the CEO of the new Daniel Webster Johnson Foundation, the center's governing body.

"I read over your résumé, Mark. Very impressive," Dan stated. "I also did a background check and know all about your criminal record and conviction."

He certainly had the right to bring it up.

"Forgive me if I sound like a jerk," Dan continued, "but how can I believe you wouldn't steal from the foundation—funded with my money and the taxpayers' money—if you had the chance?"

Fortunately, I had anticipated and rehearsed this question with Mark.

"Because you're giving me a second chance, and I'm not foolish enough to blow it," Mark answered without hesitation, sounding more like a Boy Scout than a candidate for a CEO position.

"Then, upon Greg's word, you have the job. I'll need you in Dallas next week for a few days to get things started. I plan to introduce you today during the press conference. Are you ready?" I'd had Mark wear his best business suit, a dark gray, with a white shirt and red tie, the quintessential corporate look.

"I am ready, sir, and cannot thank you enough."

"Then let's get this launched," Dan announced as we climbed into the Mission's van, a decade-old, nine-passenger vehicle used chiefly to transport residents to medical appointments. Dan said nothing about riding in a vehicle that reeked of male body order. For the next two hours, he knew that he was in my hands, and other than the jet ensconced at the airport, I wanted him to be seen as a regular guy, the Rolex around his wrist notwithstanding.

On the way to the mill, the site of the event and the press conference, Christine briefed Dan and his associates. "We are handing these out to the reporters," she said, showing them a folder with inserts, including the artist's rendering of the center. "Pastor Tom Garrity, the director of the Kelsey Rescue Mission, will be the emcee. He will mention dignitaries in attendance, including Mayor Simmons and Senator Patson. The mayor will give a short welcome. Pastor Tom will then introduce you. After your remarks, I hope you will take questions from reporters. Afterward, we'll walk the property and head across the street to the Kelsey Rescue Mission for lunch."

Dan looked up from the itinerary. "This looks great, Christine. Thank you for your hard work. Greg tells me you are an attorney. Now that I've broken ties with Weber's company, I need an ace real estate and business lawyer. Would you be interested?"

"Thank you, Dan, but real estate isn't my area. However, my firm has a team of real estate specialists. I will be happy to introduce you to my managing partner, Jerome Williams, who will be at the event today."

Dan turned to Mark. "Ultimately, picking your team down here will be your job, so forgive me if I seem a little aggressive. It's just my nature."

"A little aggressive?" I blurted out, laughing. "There's the understatement of the year." The architect and engineer also joined in the laughter, although somewhat nervously.

By then, we were pulling up to the front of the mill, where several TV trucks and at least a hundred people had already gathered. An official welcoming committee headed by Tom and Jane stood by the gate. Doug and Cindy Pollard and Mayor Simmons joined them. We had just received word that the senator was en route and would arrive any minute.

Christine was the first out of the van, followed by Dan. She proceeded to introduce the billionaire to each of them. When she got to her mother and father, she said, "And these are my parents, Doug and Cindy Pollard."

Dan gently interrupted her, taking her mother's hand into his.

"Hello, Cindy, you look great," Dan said softly.

"You don't look too bad yourself, Danny," she replied. "It's been a long time."

Two parts of this exchange floored me. The first was that Dan Johnson and Cindy Pollard, Christine's mother, had known each other long ago. But the other, even more impressive aspect was that I had never heard anyone dare call this giant of American industry and political clout "Danny." He hated that name.

"Holy sheets, Mother, you two know each other?"

"Our grandfathers worked side by side at the mill and were best friends, honey. When Danny came here to visit during the summer months, he played with my brothers and me almost every day. That would have been in the mid-sixties. And let me tell you something about my old friend Danny Johnson. Danny refused to swim in the city pool on the hottest, most sweltering days. Do you know why? Because if Black kids weren't allowed to swim there, he wouldn't swim there either."

"I just remember those Sunday suppers," Dan added, quickly changing the subject. "Every Sunday, rain or shine, our two families would meet after church for a huge meal. And your mama would always invite a low-income family to join us. That woman . . ." he trailed off, shaking his head. "Who didn't love Mrs. Washington? Well, listen, let's get caught up later. Your daughter has me booked today, and I think I'm already behind. It's good to see you." He paused and added, "Dr. Pollard."

The warehouse team at the Mission had hauled over a hundred chairs to the mill and arranged them into neat rows in front of a collapsible stage brought in from city hall, courtesy of the mayor. The audience, however, had unexpectedly swelled to over 300, leaving more people standing than sitting.

"Friends, if I may have your attention. Please, if I may have your attention."

In a few seconds, the crowd's buzz died down, and all gave their eyes and ears to Pastor Tom, standing behind the podium in a dark-blue suit and neat striped tie that I was sure Jane had helped select that morning. The welcoming committee members and Dan sat behind him on the stage. Christine, Mark, and I stood with the architect off to the side of the stage.

Tom, an experienced emcee, ensured that those expected to be recognized were acknowledged. The list included the pastors, members of the Mission's board of directors, city council members, and Senator Patson, arguably the most important person at the event—except for Dan—due to his vote for final passage for federal funding of the center.

Following the mayor's brief welcome, Tom was again at the podium.

"This is a great day for Kelsey," Tom began in his booming bass voice after thanking everyone for attending. "Thanks to the generosity of Dan Johnson and Congress, the Kelsey Mill property will finally be revitalized. But as you will soon learn, this isn't your average urban renewal. It is a statement that a million homeless people in our wealthy nation are one million too many. It also says that everyone deserves a second chance at achieving a good life. It is my pleasure to welcome Dan Johnson to Kelsey."

Dan shook hands with Tom as he approached the podium to polite applause. As always, Dan looked great. He could easily be mistaken for a Hollywood star at six foot four and athletically trim, with neatly combed gray hair and a tailored, royal-blue suit. He flashed his white teeth to the audience in a broad smile.

"Thank you, Pastor Tom, for your kind introduction and for the work you do here. And to you, Mayor Simmons, for your leadership and compassion in turning one of this city's worst moments into its finest hour."

Dan delivered his speech with eloquence and warmth. His heartfelt connection to the city was genuine, especially when he shared stories about his grandfather and his grandfather's best friend, a Black man named Cody Washington.

"Cody and Granddad worked side by side at this mill for thirty years. They and their families were inseparable; they always had room for someone else in their homes and at their tables. I believe this spirit of giving that these two men established so long ago lives on at the Kelsey Rescue Mission and throughout the city, and it is the one I hope will guide the Daniel Webster Johnson Center for Hope and Opportunity.

"The men and women coming to this center will get here the old-fashioned way. They will earn it with hard work and commitment. When completed, the center will house two hundred residents at a time, competitively selected from shelters throughout the country, each enrolled in a two-year career-training or academic program. We hope to have our first class enter this great new center in just two years. I am excited, and I hope you are as well. I thank you, the citizens of Kelsey, for setting such an amazing example for other cities to follow. Before I go, I am proud to introduce our new CEO for the Johnson Foundation, the organization that will oversee the restoration project, Mr. Mark Stone. Mark, please wave your hand, wherever you are. Again, thank you, everyone, for coming today."

As the crowd dispersed, Christine guided Dan to a roped-off area near the stage, where several reporters were gathered to ask him questions. For someone who had never been a media coordinator, she was getting quite good at it. Meanwhile, I slipped out to pick up Cody from school for an early release because Christine had promised him he could be included in the tour. Like most Kelsey residents, Cody had only seen the mill property from the street and never up close. Doug and Cindy told Christine they would take him home after lunch.

"Hey, little dude, are you ready for the tour?" It was only a ten-minute walk to the school, a path we would now repeat on returning to the mill. My ribs were still sore, and every step was killing me.

"I can't wait," he said excitedly. "After that, Grandpa is taking me to the recreation center to swim in the indoor pool." *If he only knew how times have changed*, I thought.

The tour was led by Dr. Caleb Dane, a retired history professor from nearby Vanderbilt University who lived in Kelsey. Dane had done extensive research on the Kelsey Mill. He was the author of *A Factory City No More*, a definitive book that looked back on the city's origins and evolution into a wealthy rural outlier of Nashville. He took us deep into the property, pointing out where various machines were located and the functions of each area of the mill during its heyday. Although in his mid-eighties, Dr. Dane was spry and alert and quite capable of answering questions, mostly from architects and engineers, along with a few from the reporters, who also tagged along.

When the hour-long walk-through was over, Christine thanked everyone for coming. "Our time has ended, and we must move on with Mr. Johnson's schedule. Thank you all for your interest," she announced energetically. I admired her poise through what had been a stressful morning. "Come on, Cody, hold Mommy's hand," she instructed.

"And who might this young man be?" asked Dan as he looked down on the nine-year-old.

"Mr. Johnson, this is my son. He's nine years old. Can you say hello to Mr. Johnson?" It wasn't a question. Christine was a stickler when it came to teaching the lad good manners.

Cody reached out to shake hands with Dan, who politely returned the gesture. "What is your name, young man?"

"My name is Cody Washington Culpepper," he said clearly.

"That is a wonderful name. It's nice to meet you, Cody Washington." He looked over and winked at Christine and Cindy, trying to hide the tears in his eyes without success.

CHAPTER THIRTY-NINE

"Are you excited to be back?" I asked Christine as the plane approached Nashville International Airport the following spring.

It had been six months since Christine, Cody, and I left for St. Lucia, although several extended visits by her parents and then Sydney and one shorter stay from Tom and Jane kept us close to our families. Christine and Cody settled into a home-school routine, completed by noon every day, leaving our afternoons and evenings free for such pursuits as sailing, collecting sea glass, and beach fires.

I took it upon myself to continue my self-education by fixing and restoring things around the house and property, something I had learned I had a knack for with my houseboat. Whether it was laying a new tile floor, painting the entire interior and exterior of the house, installing a water and heat pump, or redesigning the landscaping, I was proud of the work I was doing with my hands, with a heavy assist from online videos. All my acquired skills mattered, especially when I put the house on the market and had a perfect offer in less than a week. Christine and I agreed that it was time to come home, and the island getaway was a luxury we didn't need.

Of course, we followed the local news while we were gone. Max Weber and his security chief, the one who assaulted me in the café, had both been convicted and sent to federal prison, each with twenty-year sentences. At sixty-nine, Weber would likely spend the remainder of his life there. Three of the four police officers accused of killing Jimmy Keefer were convicted of murder—life, with no parole. The prosecutors benefited greatly from the testimony of Randy Browning, the rookie cop who did not fire his gun and then turned state witness. He testified that Drake took orders directly from Weber, including instructions to target Mission residents.

Following several delays, Lamar Goodman's trial for kidnapping was just beginning. Most court watchers predicted a speedy conviction and a lengthy prison sentence.

"Yes and no," Christine answered me thoughtfully now. "I have left and come back before, and each time, I felt this is where I belong. But I loved being away with just us and don't want anyone or anything to interfere with what we have." She buried her head in my chest. "Promise me that will never happen."

I had finally worked up the courage to ask Christine to marry me, popping the question on bent knee during a barefoot sunset walk on the beach. Cody sat on my leg. "I know you're way too good for me," I told her, "but would you marry me anyway?"

"Are you in on this, Cody?" she said with her quick, self-effacing laugh.

"Guilty as charged, Mom. It was a guy thing."

"My amazing boys. Of course, I will marry you."

I just happened to have a bottle of champagne, two glasses, and a soda for Cody in my backpack so we could celebrate. I had come full circle. My second chance in life would include a second family.

It was about to be a hectic time, which would be weird after growing accustomed to Caribbean time, a familiar way to describe the slower pace of island life. Christine and I would have exactly four weeks to plan our wedding, which we decided would be held at the Rescue Mission with Tom officiating. Sydney would be her maid of honor, while Cody would stand up for me. The residents and a few dozen of Christine's local friends and relatives would be invited. On my side, in addition to Sydney, only Liz and Susan and my parents from Buffalo would be attending. I hadn't seen Mom and Dad since before my arrest four years ago when Pop disowned me for embarrassing the family. According to Sydney, he was now over it and desired a reconciliation. He was seventy-eight and had recently been diagnosed with lung cancer. It looked like saying hello and goodbye to the best man I ever knew would happen at the same time.

Meanwhile, Christine was preparing for a new career in academia. While in St. Lucia, the dean of the highly respected Vanderbilt School of Divinity called and invited her to join his faculty to teach a class called Ethics and Society. She described it as her "dream job," an opportunity to combine her past professions and her activism for the homeless. Her class would meet on Tuesdays and Thursdays, giving her ample time to continue working part-time in the law firm as their pro bono specialist, including managing the legal needs of the Rescue Mission.

This left us to decide where we would live. "I think it's best to live in my house," Christine had opined, "and for us to keep the houseboat for weekend getaways." It was an easy agreement on my part, and as it turned out, it was equally easy to figure out my next career move.

"I'm going to be a handyman," I declared to Christine on our last night in St. Lucia. "I already have a truck. I'll need new tools and a few customers to get started. Folks need someone they can call to repair their washers and dryers, fix a lock on their back gate, or paint a bedroom. I'll rent a storage shed to keep all my stuff in so it won't mess up your garage. And I want to return to the kitchen at the Mission, cooking and serving breakfast on Tuesday and Thursday mornings."

Tom and Jane had left the Mustang at the airport the night before, texting me with its location. We were traveling only with carry-ons, having shipped several boxes of clothing and personal items home. The April day was warm enough for the car's top to come down. Cody and I were thrilled. Christine perhaps not so much. I reached into the glove compartment and pulled out a blue scarf to wrap around her coiffed hair.

Our first stop was the Mission, where we sat in momentary disbelief over the progress that had been made. The exterior of the second floor was completed, including the windows, giving it a much larger presence. Once inside, we heard the construction upstairs, reminding us that it wasn't entirely done.

"Hey, Mr. Greg. Hi, Ms. Culpepper," greeted front-desk Charlie, who was not at the front but at the back, cleaning the glass door. "Welcome home."

"Thank you, Charlie. It's nice to be back. How's the back feeling these days?" I asked.

"Strong as an ox." He was lying, but that was okay. Playing injured was in itself a sign of strength, I thought.

I saw Mike strutting across the cafeteria floor. "Stop that man," I yelled. "He's up to no good." When Mike stopped and saw that it was me, he headed my way.

"Hey, bro," he said as he hugged me. "I have missed you."

"I've missed you too. And don't worry, I'm starting back tomorrow morning. Is my spot still open?"

"Greg, come and look at this. You won't believe it." Christine was looking out the front of the building toward the old mill. She was right. It was almost surreal. Instead of urban ruin littered with falling bricks, split pavement, and blowing debris, there were clean, flat surfaces. The building that had been left was in the process of restoration while new buildings were being framed. Giant cranes and stacks of drywall dotted the area, in addition to what seemed like a hundred or more workers. Just off the left of the front gate was a white mobile home with a significant ROCKWOOD TECHNOLOGIES painted on the side.

I took Cody's hand and looked at Christine. "Let's go. We have someone to say hello to."

I hadn't spoken with Mark Stone since we left. Like I told the mayor and anyone who wanted to listen, including Dan Johnson, my consulting days were over. They were all on their own. To their credit, they had respected my desire to move on. The only ones exempt were Liz and Tom, my childhood chums.

I opened the door of the metal structure, now converted to a field office, and met the surprised stares of Jarred and Billy, each typing at their desks. Through the opening of the work area, I spotted Mark in his office, currently whispering on the telephone.

"Mr. Greg. Christine. Wow, what a surprise." Both Billy and Jarred moved in our direction for a warm handshake. When Mark came out, dressed smartly as always, in a blue golf shirt and gray slacks today, he looked like a corporate manager.

"Where did you recruit this good-looking staff?" Christine asked playfully.

"At that job-training center across the street," he laughed. "The one they call the Rescue Mission."

"You look great, Mark. I'm proud of you," I said.

"Greg, none of this would have happened without you, for any of us. Always remember that. We owe you more than we could repay."

I looked at Christine, who was wiping away a tear.

"All I did, Mark, was remind you who you are. You all did the rest."

∙ ∙ ∙

Thursday morning at five hit me hard. It had been a long time since I'd gotten up so early.

The "welcome home" dinner at Tom and Jane's the night before ran way longer than anyone anticipated, with Christine's parents, along with Sydney, Liz, and Susan, who flew in from Washington, joining us. At the end of dinner, Tom offered a toast with wineglasses raised.

"Here's to my best friend, who came to Kelsey, Tennessee, and was involuntarily rescued," he began. "And here's my choice for Kelsey Citizen of the Year: To Christine. Welcome home, guys. And you too, Cody."

I had been welcomed home so many times that I was starting to believe it was true. Maybe this was home after all. Kesley was a bridge from an old life to a new one. I just needed to cross it. And by crossing it, I arrived at an unfamiliar place. It was called Happiness. I prayed—this time for real—that I would never look back.

I looked beside me at my beautiful Christine, now slumbering gently beneath the covers with her head on my pillow as she stretched diagonally across the bed on her side. I watched as her small breasts beneath her satin nightgown rose and fell with every long breath. She had become the never-ending love song in my head, a tune of such rich and delicious joy that life without her had become inconceivable. We had been virtually inseparable during our six months away, and I struggled with the idea of being six blocks away from her this morning.

After a warm shower and leisurely walk to the Mission, I finally found my way to the kitchen and my familiar spot at the serving window. I looked left and right along the line of twenty men who had arrived a little early. It had been more than a year since I first saw their faces and began to know them as people—some temporarily displaced, others with mental health or addiction issues, but real people, with hearts and dreams. Ones I had encountered and befriended in the course of regaining my freedom, not only from the prison that held me for two years but from the self-serving life that had engulfed me. They rescued me, and I would be eternally grateful.

They were the best men I had ever known.

THE END

ACKNOWLEDGMENTS

In writing my first published novel, I learned there is no better therapy for fearing rejection than letting someone read your manuscript. When Debbie Welch (spouse, love of my life, best friend, etc.) read my first novel, she earned her stripes as a critic by throwing it in the trash, saying it was terrible. Write another one, she suggested. She had tons of credibility, therefore, when she said after reading this novel, "I love it." So thank you, Deb, for your honesty and for coming up with the title, *Kelsey's Crossing*. In every way that counts in life, you are my amazing partner.

Thanks also to Greg Fields, my friend since sixth grade and a best-selling novelist, for being my chief encourager. He told me for years that I was a good writer. I still don't believe him, but I am thankful, nonetheless. This book would not have been written without his gentle nudging.

I also wish to thank my beta readers. These are the ones the author goes to and says, "Hey, I wrote a novel. Would you like to read it?" My beta group consisted of an engineer, a couple of teachers, a judge, a therapist (mine), a marketing executive, a banker, and a hairstylist. Thank you, Kelly Chuma, Barbara Reynolds, Joanne Wadsworth, Emily Keefer, Christine Glover, Laura Sutton, Mary Kearse, Jennifer Mason, and Aida Yodites, for your feedback and critiques, even the blunt ones that kept me up for weeks.

I especially want to thank the men of the homeless shelter, where it has been a privilege to volunteer. You guys were my inspiration.

Although the story is fictional, there are real guys behind every character. They are among the hundreds of thousands of children, women, and men without a place to live. It is an American tragedy. As a nation, we must do better.

I am grateful to John Koehler and the team at Koehler Publishing, especially my editor, Hannah Woodlan. It is an honor to be part of your publishing family. But mostly, I am thankful for you—the ones who purchased, borrowed, or checked out *Kelsey's Crossing* and read it. Thank you for giving this first-time author a chance.

www.ingramcontent.com/pod-product-compliance
Lightning Source LLC
LaVergne TN
LVHW091715070526
838199LV00050B/2415